Trail of the Gods

Trail of the Gods

Book Four
The Morcyth Saga

Brian S. Pratt

Trail of the Gods
Book Four of The Morcyth Saga
Copyright 2007,2008 by Brian S. Pratt

Books written by Brian S. Pratt can be obtained
either through the author's official website:
www.briansprattbooks.com
or through any online book retailer.

ISBN-10: 1438269277
EAN-13: 9781438269276

The Morcyth Saga

The Unsuspecting Mage
Fires of Prophecy
Warrior Priest of Dmon-Li
Trail of the Gods
The Star of Morcyth
Shades of the Past
The Mists of Sorrow*
*(Conclusion of The Morcyth Saga)

The Broken Key

#1- Shepherd's Quest
#2-Hunter of the Horde
#3-Quest's End

Qyaendri Adventure

Ring of the Or'tux

For my grandparents who took me places and gave me the joy of travel, and of seeing new sights. The yearly treks to Alberta, Canada where I worked on my uncle's farm are some of my fondest memories of my childhood.
Thank you both.

Chapter   One

Easy, not too much now.

He stares across the small room to the focal point of his attention. Slowly, only a minuscule amount at a time, he lets the magic flow. As the magic reaches the object, it activates the latent spells embedded within. He begins feeling a subtle drawing of power as the object absorbs magic from him, and his excitement starts to mount.

A smile begins to break out on his face, he can feel how it draws the magic from its surroundings as well as himself, into itself. A subtle red glow grows within its center as it gradually holds more and more magic.

Bang!

The crystal explodes sending shards all over the room. James holds up his arms in an attempt to protect his face but several of the flying shards still find their mark in his cheek. Once the danger has passed, he lowers his arms which now have many small dots welling blood from where the shards have struck.

"Damn!" he curses as he looks back at what remains of the crystal. The floor around the small table upon which it had sat is strewn with a thin layer of shattered crystal from earlier experiments.

Walking back over to the table, he picks up a large shard, the shard he first acquired in the swamp. The shard which had given him the idea that they may in some way be able to absorb and store magical energy. *How'd they do it?* Shaking his head, he brings the shard over to his workbench and settles down on the stool. Rolling the shard between his fingers absentmindedly, he thinks about what happened.

Every time, they explode! Why? Can they only hold so much power before they blow? If so, then how much?

A knock at the door brings him out of his reverie. "Yes?" he calls out.

Ezra's voice can be heard from the other side, "Lunch is ready, sir." Her grasp of the language has improved, especially since she is now completely immersed in it. She still has an accent and he hopes she never grows out of it, he enjoys listening to the way she speaks.

"Be right there," he hollers back.

Still, he wishes she would stop calling him sir. When he first came to live at Hern's old place, he asked Roland and Ezra to come work for him to help take care of the place. He figured he would be gone most of the time or just not have the time or inclination to do it himself. Also, it seemed like a nice thing to do. They agreed and from that point on, she had called him sir.

He spoke to Roland about it, but Roland just shrugged and told him that it was just her way. Roland has no problem calling him James, and to little Arkie, he's Uncle James.

Before leaving his workshop, he picks the shards out of his arm and face. Sighing, he gets up and walks out of his workshop. It's set a ways from the main house since he doesn't want to put anyone but himself in jeopardy with his experiments.

Off to the side, he sees where the workmen are busy with the construction of another house. That one will be the one he'll live in and where his guests will stay. Hern's old house will be Roland and his family's, as long as they're here. Several other buildings are sprouting up as well; a stable that will be large enough to hold over a dozen horses and another barn seeing as how Hern's old one must have been built a century before and is in poor repair.

It had taken him the better part of a week to recover from the fight at the pass. During his recovery, he arranged to take possession of Hern's old place. He mentioned to Corbin how he would like to have a place around Trendle in which to live. The next day, the mayor showed up personally to give him the deed to Hern's place.

The mayor had refused payment, saying how it's ample reward for what he did for them. At first he was highly flattered that the mayor had troubled himself to come all the way out here to give it to him personally. That is until he realized it had been just an excuse to get away from his wife and spend time with his old drinking buddies.

In the course of one conversation or another since acquiring it, he referred to Hern's old place as 'The Ranch' and the name stuck.

Coming through the back door into the kitchen, he sees the others have already taken their seats at the table. Illan and the rest of Miller's old band are there as well. For some reason, they've attached themselves to James, sort of become his bodyguards. His own private secret service as he's begun to think of them. All that is but Hinney. Ever since his friend Keril died back at the pass, he's been melancholy. One day, he mentioned having family in a little town in the northern part of Madoc and left the following day to spend some time with them.

"James!" Tersa cries out when she sees the blood welling on his face and arms. Getting up from the table, she takes a towel off the counter and dips it in a bucket of water. Coming over to him, she quickly dabs the blood off, as well as picking out several more pieces of crystal out of his cheek.

"Another mishap?" Jiron asks from where he sits at the table.

"Yeah," he replies. Taking the towel from Tersa, he says, "Thank you."

"You're welcome," she replies as she moves back to take her seat.

Moving around the table, he comes to his seat at the head. No one has yet begun to eat, Ezra won't allow it. He's the master of the house and no one better begin until either he's there, or they know he's not coming. Woe to the man who crosses her. Some around the table had learned the hard way the first couple of days they were together. After eating scraps outside after the meal was over for a day, they soon did as she said.

Since taking over the household, she's changed from the sweet nice woman they had traveled with to a stricter disciplinarian. James doesn't care. As long as she maintains order, he'll back her. Besides, she's not so strict with the 'master of the house'.

Once he's seated, they wait for him to help himself first. Another of Ezra's rules, since he's providing, he better be the first one to eat. Taking a bowl of tubers, potatoes really, he places two on his plate. As soon as the first one hits, everyone else begins grabbing the nearest source of food and filling their plates.

"I just can't seem to make it work," he announces to all.

"We know it can," Miko says from James' left. "That large shard we saw over the pool did, so I'm sure you'll be able to figure it out." James had thought that once the Fire was no longer in his possession that he might revert back to his former self. But that wasn't the case. It seems the changes wrought while the Fire had been in his possession are going to be permanent, which saddens him. No one should ever be robbed of his youth like that.

His skill at arms has remained as well, though nothing like it had been while the Fire had taken control. He practices with Illan and the rest, and they say he's one of the best swordsmen they've ever crossed blades with.

It wasn't long after he recovered that the Fire had gone into hiding. He purchased a small iron chest and had Miko place the Fire within. Now, only James knows exactly where it's hidden. He snuck out one night with the chest and buried it.

After swallowing a piece of the tuber, he asks Jiron, "How soon will Delia be back? I used the last of the crystals." Delia, with the funds the ten gems Jiron acquired back in the underground complex, had bought a couple wagons and begun the life of a trader.

Having had a taste of it during their sojourn through the Empire, she decided that's what she wants to do now that they're back. Unable to gainsay her, he handed over the gems. The pit fighters had all agreed to hire on with her as caravan guards, once Jiron had finished talking with them about it.

"Should be any day," he replies. "She had to go all the way to Cardri to get your money from Thelonius."

"I know," he says. He gave her a letter from Alexander, the money lender here in Trendle, for his brother asking him to relinquish James' money. Only way he could've done it without the letter was to go all the way there himself. And Delia was more than happy to do it, for a small fee of course.

Alexander had been more than happy to advance him some money to set up The Ranch and to begin construction. Which brings him to his next problem, he needs to somehow generate a steady flow of income for The Ranch. All these mouths to feed, not to mention any and all supplies he's going to need, will cost many golds. Plus he understands there's a property tax due to the town at the beginning of the year. How is he going to afford all this?

One thing at a time. He needs to get the crystals to hold magic. Where the Fire lies now is not going to be good enough forever and for what he has planned, he needs the crystals to secure the Fire forever.

Tasting the fried chicken, he turns to Ezra and says, "Perfect, as always." She beams as the others at the table offer their appreciation as well. James has realized that she needs him to make some comment about every meal to her. It was during the second dinner she had fixed that he failed to say whether it was good or not. The next day, she was more subdued and he could see that she was troubled by something. He asked Roland what was wrong and he said that she felt he didn't like her cooking. Of course, he immediately went to her and told her he did, which improved her mood immensely.

"It's just that she's insecure and wants to please," Roland told him. "After a while, she'll know you like it and it won't matter if you say anything. Just try to make some comment during every meal, no matter how small, for the next week or so."

He had no problem with that, she really was a great cook.

Outside, a rooster crows from the makeshift coop they threw together out back. Ezra now has dozens of hens and two roosters she has to keep separated or they'll fight each other. Fresh eggs in the morning and fried chicken once a week is reward enough for putting up with them.

"What do you plan to do now?" Illan asks.

"I still have the crystal I originally found," he replies. "I'll probably just study it until Delia shows up with more, though I don't want to risk it. There may be something about it that I'm not seeing, which makes it different than the others."

"Could be," he says. "By the way, I'm going to take the boys out and do some hunting in the forest. See if we can't lay in some supplies."

"Not a bad idea," agrees James.

The sound of a rider approaching the house can be heard before they finish their meal. Illan gestures for Yern to go and see who it is.

From the front room, they hear him call out, "It's Shorty."

James gets up and heads for the front door. As he enters the front room he asks, "Is he by himself?"

Yern turns from the window and nods, "Just him."

Opening the front door, he steps out just as Shorty pulls to a stop. "Anything wrong?" he asks him, worried.

Shaking his head, he pulls a sack filled almost to capacity off his horse and hands it to James. He can see Jiron and Tersa standing in the doorway behind him. "Everything's fine," he assures them. "We picked up a shipment back in Bearn that had to be in Wurt first thing in the morning, so she sent me here to drop off your stuff."

James opens the sack and finds it stuffed with crystals, the common ones he's been working with. Smiling, he says, "Tell her thank you."

"Will do that," he says as he pulls out a letter. "This is from Thelonius back in Cardri."

Taking the letter, he asks, "Would you like to stay for lunch? We have plenty."

"No, she told me to get back fast before they moved much further down the road," he tells him. Pulling himself back up on his horse, he turns to leave.

"You tell her to stop by when she passes through next time," he says to Shorty.

"I'll do that," he replies. "Goodbye, James."

"Bye Shorty," he says. "And thanks again."

Giving him a brief wave, he kicks his horse into a gallop and races back down the road to rejoin the caravan.

As he turns back to the house, he sees Jiron and Tersa standing there. Holding up the sack, he says, "At least she dropped these off before she headed north."

"She wouldn't forget about you," Jiron assures him.

"No," adds Tersa. "She knows how important those are to you."

Coming back to the dining room, he takes his seat and pulls out some of the crystals and sets them beside his plate. While he finishes his meal, he closely examines them. As far as he can tell, they're exactly the same as the one he took from the underground complex. It has to be with how he's doing it. It has to!

Once he's through eating, he gets up from the table and takes his plate and cup into the kitchen where he sets them on the counter. He knows it annoys Ezra that he does it, the master should not have to clear his own dinnerware. But he just can't leave it there, his mom and then his grandma had ingrained that in him too well.

He returns to the dining room and puts the crystals back in the sack. Illan and the others are beginning to leave for the hunt, "We're going to take Miko with us."

"Good idea," agrees James. "He's pretty good with that crossbow of his."

"So he keeps telling us," Illan replies with a grin.

Miko stands up, all six foot two. He's quite the man physically, but inside, he's still a boy. Giving James a grin, he goes to his room to retrieve his crossbow and bolts.

"Be back by dark," Illan tells him as he leads the others out through the front room. Miko quickly joins them before they get too far away from the house. James watches him as he walks with the others. They've really taken a liking to him, sort of taken him under their wing so to speak. Their initial wariness back at Lythylla has long since worn off.

Ezra and Tersa are busy in the kitchen and dining room, getting everything cleared off and cleaned up. Roland grabs an axe and heads out to lay in some firewood. Though fall is still well over a month away, he needs to get busy so they'll have plenty when it does arrive. James tells them that he'll be going into town for a few hours to see Alexander.

Taking his sack of crystals out to his workshop, he sits them down by his workbench. Then he heads over to the old barn where his horse is currently stabled and prepares him for the ride into town.

A smile comes over him as he remembers that time with Corbin when he first mounted a horse. He's come a long ways since then.

When his horse is ready, he leads him out of the barn and then mounts. Riding out to the so-called road that passes by the end of his lane, he passes where the workmen are hard at work on the new buildings. They wave to him as he rides by.

Townsmen from Trendle, they're happy to have this work. Seems there are many who are barely able to make it around here and those that got this job are sure thankful. The buildings are going up fast, they should be done before fall gets here. At least that's the general consensus.

As he rides into town, the people on the street pause as they call out a greeting or wave to him as he goes by. Ever since that situation at the estate in the forest, he's become some sort of celebrity around here. He waves back cheerfully, taking it all in stride.

He pulls up in front of Alexander's shop and ties his horse to the post outside. Going in, he finds the same guards as had been there the last time. One of them opens the door to the back and tells Alexander he's here.

James moves to the window in the wall and Alexander's head appears just as he gets there. "Ah, James," he says. "I take it you've heard back from my brother?"

Pulling the letter out, he hands it over to him.

Taking but a moment, Alexander opens the letter and reads the contents. "Seems you still have quite a sum here," he says. "Do you wish to have the same type of account you had last time?"

"Yes, that would be fine," he replies. "Could I have a hundred golds of that broken into smaller coinage?"

"Not a problem," he says. "Just give me a moment and I'll be right back."

"Okay," replies James as Alexander ducks back inside. He waits there only a couple minutes before he reappears at the window with two bulging sacks of coins.

He sets the sacks of coins down on the window's counter along with several papers. "Here," he says. "I just need your signature on these and we're all set. After taking out what I've already loaned you and the hundred you're taking with you, you still have three hundred and ten golds left."

Nodding, James takes the offered quill and signs where he's told to. Once done, Alexander takes the papers and says, "You're all set. In the sacks there, I put 60 gold coins and 397 silver and 600 copper. That almost wiped me out of what smaller coins I had."

"Sorry," James says.

"Don't worry about it," he assures him. "I still have plenty."

"Thank you," he says to him as he bends down to pick up the heavy sacks. The guard takes one and escorts him back out to his horse. Alexander says, "Come again if I can help you with anything further."

"I will," he replies as he exits the shop. Securing the sacks behind his saddle takes some doing but with the guard's help, he manages.

He tells the guard thanks for his help and then mounts. So as not to over tax his horse, he takes it slow all the way back, the sacks of coins jingling behind him.

Once back at The Ranch, he goes to the main house and removes the sacks from his horse and takes them into his bedroom where Hern's old money chest sits. It's barely large enough to accommodate the coins but he manages to get the lid closed and the lock secured. Hern had only had two silvers and a handful of coppers in it when he found it.

He's going to have to have Delia acquire him some writing materials so he'll be able to keep a ledger of his spending. It would also be nice to be able to keep notes about his experiments with the crystals.

Sighing, he knows he should go back out to his workshop and try to figure this out. As he passes through to the back door, he finds Ezra there in the kitchen baking bread for the evening meal. The aroma smells good.

Arkie is sitting in a highchair he bought for him. He's got a piece of bread in one hand that he's happily gnawing on. His cup is resting on its side on the floor, the milk within it spreading in a pool.

He gives Ezra a nod and pats Arkie on the head as he leaves through the back door. The sound of wood being chopped reaches him from over where Roland is splitting them into the proper size. He can see he's already accumulated quite a pile since he left for town.

Tersa is out in the garden they planted when they first arrived. He can see many shoots coming up out of the ground. He was worried that planting so late in the season wouldn't yield much, but he left it to their judgment. Ever since pulling the new shoots out of his aunt's garden when he thought he was successfully weeding it, he's known he has no clue about gardening.

Back in his workshop, he reaches into the sack of crystals and pulls out several, setting them in front of him on the workbench. *C'mon guys, what am I doing wrong?*

He thinks about the last time. What he's been trying to do is create a spell in which the crystal will draw and store power from the world around it. Taking only minute quantities from each individual living thing within its radius at a time, they would store it within themselves. They would also use the stored power to keep the 'leeching' spell active, always maintaining the maximum amount. Sort of like a continuously recharging battery, a magic battery you could say.

But the problem he's been encountering is that at some point, it explodes. That's what he has to figure out, a way to keep it intact. There has to be a way to have it 'charge' to a certain point and then stop.

Perhaps along with a spell that leeches magic from its environment, there should be one that checks for internal integrity. One which ensures the crystal never reaches the point where it shatters by shutting down the other spell which is drawing in the power. Then allowing it to resume drawing in power once the amount of stored power has dropped below the maximum capacity.

Might work, he thinks as he carries the largest of the crystals over to the table where the previous experiments have been. Brushing aside the shattered remnants of earlier experiments, he sets the crystal down and then moves back to a safer distance.

After a moment's contemplation to work out the spell needed, he concentrates on the crystal and slowly lets out the power. This time when he's completed the spell, he holds his breath as once more, it begins to glow red with the power being drawn from him. When the crystal has begun to glow a deep crimson color, he senses a gradual diminution in the power being leeched from him until it all but disappears.

Using his magic, he examines the crystal down to the micro level. A smile breaks across his face as he realizes that it's working. It's still drawing power, but it's such a slight amount that he can barely feel it."

"Excuse me," a voice says as a hand taps him on the shoulder.

Abruptly breaking his concentration, he inadvertently sends a wave of energy toward the crystal, causing it to shatter into a hundred tiny fragments. His head begins hurting and he feels almost as if he's about ready to pass out.

Turning on the intruder, he comes to a stop when he sees it's a stranger standing there. Something in his eyes must've given the man pause, for he takes three quick steps backward and backs out the door

"What!" James yells at the man as he follows him outside.

Jiron must've heard him all the way from the house and he sticks his head out of a window to see what's going on. When he sees James standing there in anger in front of a stranger, he quickly rushes to his side.

"Uh," the man stammers, his voice failing him. Clearing his throat, he glances backward as he hears Jiron coming and then turns his attention back to James. "Are you James, the wizard?"

"What?" James asks him again, not exactly understanding what he just said.

"You okay?" Jiron asks as he arrives, one hand on a knife hilt.

Indicating the man, he replies, "This idiot interrupted me, almost got me killed."

Taking the man's arm, Jiron says, "You better leave."

Wrenching his arm out of Jiron's grasp he says, "But I need your help! And I'm willing to pay!" He glances from one to the other and back again as they take in what he said.

To Jiron, James says, "Take him to the house, I'll be there in a few minutes."

The man says, "Thank you," as Jiron leads him over to the house.

He returns back inside to the shattered crystal, angry that it was destroyed. But at least he's on the right track, it didn't explode until that idiot disturbed him. *It had been working!*

Chapter Two

He finds Jiron and the stranger sitting in the front room, Ezra having already given the man a small bite to eat and something to drink.

"...only hope he can help me," the man says. When he sees James enter the room he quickly comes to his feet, almost causing the cup holding his ale to tip over.

Jiron catches James' eye and rolls his eyes as he gives a sidelong nod at their guest.

"Thank you for taking the time to listen to my dilemma," the man says to him.

"I am very busy," replies James, as he sits down in one of the chairs. "Say what you came here to say."

Sitting back down, the man begins, "I shall be brief then." Glancing to Jiron, he continues, "I was telling your friend here somewhat of my problem and am hoping you might be of a mind to help me."

James glances to Jiron and then asks, "What sort of problem?" Jiron gives him a brief, amused smile.

"Well, it's like this," he explains. "I own a small business in Osgrin." When James doesn't respond to the name, he adds, "It's a town just a little south of here."

"Oh," says James.

"Anyway, I'm a dye merchant," he continues when no further comment is forthcoming. "And recently a competitor has set up another shop close to mine."

"And?" prompts James.

"And, he's hurting my business," says the man. "He's selling his dyes far cheaper than I'm able to. How, I don't know. If something isn't done, he'll ruin me!"

"And you want me to do what?" he asks.

"Why, cast a spell on him or something that will make his dyes be of lesser quality," he explains. "Exactly what, I'd leave to your judgment."

Where Jiron is amused, James is anything but. "Let me get this straight," he says, coming to his feet. "You want me to ruin a man's business because he's cutting into your profits?"

"Yes," replies the man in all sincerity. "I'd pay you for your troubles."

Eyes smoldering, he says to Jiron, "Get this fool from my sight!"

"You better go," Jiron says as he brings the man to his feet.

"But," the man says as Jiron begins to lead him to the door, "I'll give you a hundred gold!"

"Get out!" yells James. The frustration he had felt before when this idiot disturbed his experiments blossoms into full fledged anger. "I'll not take a million for such a deed. How dare you even ask me!"

Struggling against Jiron as he's being pulled from the house, he cries out, "But you're a mage! You're supposed to do things like this!"

Ezra pokes her head in from the kitchen to see what's going on.

Roland appears at the door, axe in hand. James glances at him and says, "Assist Jiron in getting this man off my property." To the man he adds, "Don't you ever come back here again!"

Setting his axe on the floor, Roland takes one arm while Jiron takes the other and they drag the dye merchant out of the house. James watches from the window as they take him to the end of the lane.

"He doesn't understand," he hears Ezra say from behind him.

Turning around, he sees her framed in the doorway to the kitchen, "Understand what?"

"You," she says. "You are not like other mages we hear about. You are kind and considerate, no one expects that from one such as you."

His anger slowly subsides until he's simply frustrated. "I suppose," he says.

"All our lives, the stories we hear of those with the power are ones of terror and pain," she explains. "People just can't believe that a mage, wizard, or whatever can be anything but bad."

Sighing, he nods his head, "I know. Whenever anyone has found out I'm a mage, their first reaction is usually one of fear or trepidation. Only by getting to know me do their opinions change."

"That is true," she agrees. "Sorry to have intruded, but I thought you should know."

"Thank you, Ezra," he says. "I do appreciate it."

She then returns to the kitchen to resume whatever it was she had been doing.

Turning back to the window, he sees Jiron and Roland returning, the dye merchant stands at the end of the lane for a moment. It almost seems like the man still hasn't grasped the idea James isn't going to be helping him. Jiron turns around and yells something at him. When the man still doesn't leave, he draws one of his knives and advances on him.

Seeing the drawn knife, he finally gets the idea and starts running down the road toward town.

Jiron replaces his knife and catches up with Roland as they walk back to the house. James moves to the doorway as they walk up, "He wouldn't leave?"

Shaking his head, Jiron says, "That guy simply would not listen. It wouldn't sink in that no amount of money could sway you." Cracking a grin, he adds, "So I finally had to chase him off."

Returning the grin, James says, "Yeah, I saw that."

"The problem is," explains Roland, "is that word about you is getting around. People are talking I'm afraid."

"Oh?" he asks. "And just what are they saying?"

"Mainly that you're a mage and that you've helped some people out," answers Roland.

"Great, notoriety," sighs James. "That's just what I wanted." Glancing at Jiron, he continues, "Would you mind going into town tonight and find out just what they're saying? I'd like to know."

"Sure," he says. "I can take a couple of the guys and down a few at the Squawking Goose." Then he smiles and a short laugh escapes him.

"What?" James asks.

"Did you ever hear why the place is called the Squawking Goose?" he asks.

He sees Roland start to grin as he shakes his head and says, "No."

"Well, it's rumored that the owner's wife never shuts up, and, well that's it," he replies.

"He named it after his wife?" James asks incredulously. "Doesn't she get mad?"

"This is the funny part," says Roland. "The wife doesn't know, she thinks it's because they serve goose a lot. But she does talk more than most."

All three start to laugh. Roland grabs his axe from where he'd set it down and heads back to the wood pile. They can hear his laughter as he walks away.

"Going back to the crystals?" Jiron asks.

"I think so," he replies. "I might have had it, if it wasn't for that pest."

"I'll keep an eye out and make sure you're not disturbed again," he assures him.

"I'd appreciate that," James says. He turns to go through the house and out the kitchen door as Jiron exits through the front door. Giving Ezra and Arkie a quick nod, he leaves the house and makes for his workshop.

Once inside, he closes the door and relishes the peace and quiet of it. Before resuming his tests, he sits at the workbench and tries to calm himself and to get his mind to stop churning about the interruption.

Picking up another of the crystals that lay on his workbench, he rolls it between his fingers absentmindedly as he recalls the spell he used the last time. When he thinks he's remembered it exactly and his mind is better able to focus, he takes the crystal and places it on the table after clearing a spot for it among the shattered remains of his previous experiments.

He moves back to where he was before and then concentrates only briefly before letting the magic flow. This time he lets it go quickly and braces himself for the crystal to shatter, but it remains intact.

The leeching of magic from him begins and the reddish glow can be seen growing within it as it holds more power. When it darkens to a deep crimson, he backs a few more steps away nervously, just in case. But, as before, the crystal reaches a certain point and the leeching diminishes until it's almost imperceptible.

He watches it for several minutes, giving it time to explode if it was going to and then starts toward the table where he picks up the crystal. The deep crimson color isn't a light, it's simply a part of the crystal. The leeching of power suddenly stops altogether. *Must've reached its limit so it shut down.*

Satisfied, he sets the crystal down on the workbench. He picks up another of the crystals and takes it over to the test table to see if he can duplicate the results. Setting it down, he moves away from it and casts the spell again.

This time, the leeching of power is much less. *Odd,* he thinks to himself. *I would've thought it would be the same.*

He watches the crystal and the reddish glow begins to form within, just as the previous one. As it reaches the deep crimson color, it begins subsiding again as if it's losing power.

The leeching abruptly stops and he watches as the red glow within the crystal begins pulsating from light to dark. Gradually, almost imperceptible, he starts feeling a vibration in the air.

Taking a few steps back from the crystal, he looks around the room for the source of the vibration. Suddenly, his eyes fall upon the first crystal that's lying on his workbench. It too is going from light to dark and back again. *They're leeching each other!*

The vibration in the air begins to get worse and he can see the two crystals begin to vibrate where they sit. Casting out his magic, he tries to stop each of the crystal's active spells. But instead, his magic is sucked into them, each taking half and almost seems to be fighting for what the other had taken.

Cutting off his magic, he looks to the crystals and now both are a deep crimson after having taken more of his magic. The vibration increases and a high pitched tone can be heard.

Realizing he may not have much time, he dives for the door and hits the ground outside just as both crystals explode at the same time. The resultant explosion is by far the worse yet of any failed experiment and actually cracks one of the walls of his workshop.

As he gets up off the ground, he sees the girls coming out of the kitchen door and Jiron and Roland running around the side of the house. Roland has his axe ready and Jiron's knives are out as he looks for attackers.

James holds up his hands and says, "It's okay, I'm alright."

"What happened?" Tersa asks as she comes to his side.

"Just another experiment that didn't go quite the way I planned," he explains.

Replacing his knives, Jiron says, "You need to be more careful."

"I know, but there's no one to teach me about this stuff," he tells them. "I try to be, but magic isn't exactly the easiest thing to work with."

"Probably why there're darn few mages in the world," Roland adds.

Nodding his head, James replies, "Most likely."

"Are you sure you're okay?" Ezra asks. When she gets an affirmative from him, she says, "Alright then, just don't do it again." Then she turns and with Tersa in tow, returns to the house.

"Let's see what happened," Jiron says as he moves toward the workshop.

The interior of the workshop is a shambles. His desk now has a large hole in it and the test table has completely disintegrated, shards and pieces of wood coat every surface of the workshop. The other crystals that had been lying on the workbench are gone, most likely are part of the crystal shards scattered all over. He checks the sack of crystals on the floor and finds them unscathed, much to his relief.

"Man, what a mess," exclaims Roland as he enters the ruined workshop. Shaking his head, he picks up a broom in a corner and begins to sweep up the debris.

"Here," Jiron says to James as he takes one end of the ruined workbench, "let's take this out."

Taking the other side, James lifts it up and they carry it out where they set it down along the side of the building. When they come back in, Roland pauses in his sweeping and says to James, "You go on in the house while I clean this up. You look like you could use a rest."

Suddenly feeling how tired he really is, he replies, "Thanks, I think I'll do just that."

"We'll get this place cleaned up and you can start again tomorrow," Jiron assures him.

"Alright," he says and then leaves them to finish cleaning up the mess. Returning to the house, he's greeted by Ezra in the kitchen with a cup of ale. Taking it, he says, "Thank you." He then moves on out to the front room where he sits in a chair by the window and stares out while he sips his ale.

The spells had taken more out of him than he realized, must've been concentrating too much on the effects of the spells and less on the effects they were having on him. He sits back and relaxes as he thinks of what went wrong.

When the second one began to leech from its surroundings, of course it would take magic from the other one. Then when the first began to drop in power, it started leeching from the second, and so forth.

The strain of them working against each other must've been what caused them to begin vibrating and ultimately explode. Going to have to find a way around that.

He must've dozed off for a while, for when he comes awake, it's near dusk and he sees Illan coming back with the hunters. They have several large game animals and Miko seems very happy with himself. Getting out of the chair, he opens the door and goes outside.

"James!" hollers Miko exuberantly when he sees him come out. Rushing over, he says, "I got the biggest one!"

Uther comes up behind him and claps him on the shoulder. "He sure did," he affirms. "Put us all to shame." Giving James a grin and a wink, he returns to the others who are taking the animals around back where they'll begin getting them ready for the fire.

"You better go with them," James tells Miko. "If you killed it, you better help butcher it."

"You're right!" he says as he turns and rushes to follow them.

James grins at the exuberance of his friend. He's sure come along way since James first found him on the streets of Bearn. The changes the Fire had wrought doesn't seem to bother him the way it does James. Guess most boys wish to grow up quickly.

He walks around the house to the workshop and again sees the ruined workbench sitting outside. When he goes inside, he's amazed at just how well they have already cleaned up most of the mess. They even brought in another workbench for him, though not nearly as nice as the other one had been.

His sack of crystals rests on the floor beside the new desk. Going over to it, he reaches inside and pulls one out. Holding it up, he peers within it, not really looking for anything.

From the door, he hears Jiron says, "Haven't you had enough for one day?"

Turning to him, James gives him a sheepish grin and shrugs. "I hadn't planned on doing anything more tonight," he replies. "Just came to see how the workshop turned out." Glancing around, he continues, "You guys did a good job, thanks."

"Not a problem," he says. "Just try not to make it a habit."

"I won't," assures James. "Promise."

"Tersa said that dinner's almost ready," he tells him. The aroma from the house makes his stomach cramp and growl.

"Then let's go. I'm starved." Leading the way, they go into the kitchen and find that dinner is about ready to be served. The table is set and many of the dishes are already upon the table. They don't take their seats, instead they move on into the front room to wait until all is ready. One of Ezra's rules is no one sits down until everything is on the table. Miko had tried in the beginning and was thumped in the head with one of her spoons.

When the meal is finally ready, everyone comes to the table except Miko, Illan and Uther. They're still out getting the animals ready for the smokehouse. One of the dishes on the table is boiled tubers, one of Ezra's favorites. One of these days, James plans to suggest mashed tubers and gravy. He hasn't seen anything like that since coming here, seems too simple an idea to not have been tried.

Midway through dinner, he clears his throat and once has everyone's attention, makes a couple of announcements. "First of all, I'd like to let you all know that I finally got the letter of account from Thelonius in Cardri today. I went to Alexander's and cashed it in so will be able to start paying you all." He gets a round of applause at that.

"Now, before you all get excited, let me explain a few things. First of all, Roland will be in charge of the money seeing as he'll be here when I'm gone and is going to be my administrator as well. If you should need extra money for equipment or supplies, see him. I'm going to sit down with him later to figure out exactly how much each will receive a week. After dinner, I'm going to give each of you two silvers and then we'll go from there." He sees several heads nodding agreement to what he's saying.

"Now, another thing. Today, a man walked in here and disturbed me while I was in the middle of an experiment and it almost killed me. I want you all to keep alert for any strangers approaching the property and turn them away, gently and nicely if possible. If they seem to have a good reason to see me, and I mean it had better be a good reason, then take them to the house and have them wait while you get me."

"What would constitute a good reason?" Jorry asks.

"Imminent death, perhaps," suggest James. "I don't know, just not for their own selfish reasons." He then goes into the reason the man had come here seeking his help and what happened. When he's done, he asks, "Do you understand now?"

Nodding, Jorry replies, "I think so."

"Good," he says. "I really don't want a repeat of earlier today." He takes another bite and then continues, "Also, I understand there are rumors circulating about me. Jiron is going to go into town after dinner and try to find out just what is being said and by whom. If any of you wish to go with him, I'm sure he wouldn't mind."

Jiron nods his head indicating he would welcome any and all who want to come with him.

"Be subtle, don't ask any questions," he explains to them. "Just sit back and enjoy the evening, but keep your ears open. Oh yes, and don't get drunk or cause any problems, please."

At that, several of them grin and one even chuckles.

"I mean it," insists James. "I don't want to go down tomorrow and pull your sorry butts out of jail."

"Alright, James," Yern says. "We'll be on our best behavior."

Once dinner is over, James goes into his room and returns with the promised silver pieces. He hands one sack of coins to Ezra saying it's for the household expenses.

With money in hand, Jiron and the others going with him leave for town. Roland stays at the Ranch, as well as those assisting Illan and Miko with the carcasses.

By the time James goes to bed, Miko and Illan are still out there slicing and preparing the meat for smoking. He can smell the meat that has already been placed within the smokehouse.

The next morning when he wakes up, the sound of a wagon leaving can be heard. He quickly gets out of bed and looks out the window, only to find farmer Hunst heading back to the road with his load of milk jugs. A local farmer, he sells milk and butter to the various people living in the area.

He gets dressed and takes out his shaving kit and mirror, something he acquired shortly after coming to The Ranch. The dull knife he uses to shave the stubble off has been magically imbued with the ability to only cut hair. You could run the edge along your wrist without the fear of opening a vein, yet run it along your jaw line and the stubble comes off easily.

Breakfast is the only time when he isn't required to be at the table before anyone else gets to eat. Others rise much earlier than he does and that wouldn't be a very practical rule. He scoops a cup of soap out of a large barrel sitting in the corner of his room and then grabs a set of clean clothes.

Leaving his room, he goes through the kitchen where Ezra hands him a towel before he exits out the back door. A little ways past his workshop is a good sized stream where he had a deep pool dug adjacent to it, allowing the water to flow in and out. His bathing pool, at least during the summer that is. He's not about to use it when there's snow on the ground.

Removing his dirty clothes, he steps into the cool water and then sits on the sandy bottom. It's just a couple feet deep and only comes to his mid chest when he sits in it. Using the soap liberally, he gets all the dirt and grime of the day before off as well as thoroughly washing his hair. All that he needs now is a toothbrush and he'd be set but he hasn't been able to locate one yet, not to mention a suitable toothpaste. He figures he'll have to make one himself, but hasn't had the time yet.

Once he's clean, he rests in the water and just enjoys the sensation of being surrounded by it. Everyone here thinks him slightly crazy to want a bath every day, except Miko who tends to join him more often than not. Most of the others wouldn't bathe at all if he hadn't made it a requirement.

Everyone has to bathe at least once a week, more if they're exceptionally stinky. He's going to have good hygiene on his place.

When he finally brings himself to leave the pool, he dries himself on the towel Ezra had given him and then dons the clean clothes. Back at the house, he drops the towel and the dirty clothes in a basket for Ezra to wash later on.

She already has a plate of eggs and tubers ready for him upon his return. Jiron is there as well as Jorry, both looking as if they had too much fun the night before. Between bites, he asks, "You guys okay?"

"Just a little hung over is all," admits Jiron.

"We didn't get into trouble though," offers Jorry.

"Did you hear anything?" he asks them.

"Not too much," says Jiron. "They might've known we are with you so didn't gossip as they might of otherwise. But the general opinion of the people there is that you're okay."

"That's it?" he asks. "Just okay?"

"Well, it's better than being called evil or demon spawned," jokes Jorry. "At least they accept you and aren't afraid of you."

"That's something, at least," agrees James. He sees them exchange glances and asks, "What?"

"Well, one traveler who was passing through asked if you were possessed by a demon," Jorry explains.

"Why did he ask that?" he asks.

"Seems someone fitting your description is said to have been possessed by a demon a while back," replies Jiron. "In some town called Willimet, there's a woman who's claiming that you were."

"Oh my god!" exclaims James. "That's absurd."

"You know this woman?" asks Jorry incredulously.

"In a way," he admits. "Here's what happened…" He relates to them the events as actually transpired back in Willimet. When he gets to the part where he and Miko are forced to leave the angry crowd, Jiron can't stop himself as he starts laughing.

"You needn't worry though," Jorry says, a grin on his face as well. "The people around here don't take any stock in it. They just dismiss it as idle gossip."

"That's good news," James says, breathing a sigh of relief.

"But it makes for a good story," Jiron adds. "I expect it to spread fast."

"Can't be helped I suppose." Changing the subject, he says, "I plan on going into town today. Need to see the blacksmith."

"What for?" Jorry asks.

"Want a special chest made," he replies, not expanding any further on why.

"Like some company?" Jiron asks him.

"Yes, I would," he says. "Plan on leaving right after breakfast."

Finishing his last bite, Jiron says, "Well then, I'll just go get the horses ready while you finish eating."

"Thanks," James says.

Jiron gets up and leaves the kitchen through the back door. James finishes eating quickly and then goes to his room where he fills one of his belt pouches with thirty gold coins. Then he returns to the kitchen and leaves through the back door. Making his way over to his workshop, he searches through his sack of crystals for five of the largest, all roughly the same size. Once he has them in another of his pouches, he leaves the workshop and heads over to the barn.

Outside the workshop, he can smell the meat being smoked in the smokehouse. Glancing over to it, he sees Miko and Illan sitting in a couple of chairs, talking. Looks like Illan is instructing him in the finer points of smoking meat.

As he approaches the barn, Jiron comes out with the horses. They mount and are quickly on their way. Uther's standing guard at the end of the lane leading to The Ranch where it meets the road into town.

"What're you doing?" Jiron asks him.

"Making sure no one approaches the house," he replies. "After hearing what you said at dinner last night, Illan set up a schedule for watches out here."

"Seen anyone?" James asks.

Shaking his head, he says, "Not a soul."

"Be back in a couple hours," he tells him.

Uther just gives him a nod as they turn on the road and head into town.

Chapter   Three

They find the blacksmith overseeing an apprentice who's working on some nails, his hammer ringing with every blow. His other apprentice greets them as they ride up and asks them to wait a few moments while he tells his master that they're here.

When the apprentice has finished the nails, the blacksmith comes over to where they're waiting. "What can I help you gentlemen with?" he asks.

"My name's James and I wish to have a small iron box built to specific dimensions," he says as he holds out his hand.

Taking the hand, the blacksmith gives it a shake then replies, "Kraegan, nice to meet you. What sort of box did you have in mind?"

Using his hands to show the dimensions, James gives him a rough idea what he wants. "Also, I need the inside to be padded to prevent the contents from coming to harm," he explains. "On each of the four sides, as well as the top, I need to have a crystal embedded within it."

"Hmmm," he says as he considers the request. "The box and inner lining I can do with no problem. The crystals now, that's another matter. I know someone who can do it and can get with him to do that part once I'm done with the box."

"That would be fine," James assures him.

"For what you're asking, I'd have to charge seventy five golds for everything," Kraegan says.

Sighing, he knew it would come to this. He begins the haggling process and eventually works him down to fifty three. "I have forty golds on me," he tells the blacksmith. "I can give you the rest upon delivery of the box."

"Agreed," the smith says as he leads him over to a table where they count out the coins. Once the count is agreed upon, he asks, "Do you have the crystals with you?"

James removes the five crystals from his pouch. "Now, there can be no flaw in the crystals," he insists. "And they must be centered in each of the sides as well as the top."

"I understand," the smith tells him. "Don't worry, we'll take care of it for you."

"Thank you," he replies. "If you can get it done by the end of the week, I'll throw in another ten golds."

"Doubt it," says the smith, "but we'll see what we can do." The smith takes the golds and the crystals into the building adjacent to the forge area.

"Back home?" asks Jiron.

"Yeah, I've got a lot of work to do before the chest is done," he tells him.

As they're riding back and after they've left town, Jiron asks, "Is it for the Fire?"

Nodding, James replies, "Yes, and I'd appreciate you not saying anything about this to anyone."

"No problem there," he assures him.

They see four people standing at the end of the lane to The Ranch, three women and a man. Uther, Illan and Jorry are standing there barring their way.

"He's not here," they can hear Illan's voice telling the people.

At the sound of his approach, they all turn toward him. He can see relief evident upon Illan's face at seeing him returning.

"Is that him?" a lady with a red hat asks the man she's with.

"I think so," the man replies.

The other two ladies both back up a step, their eyes never leaving him.

"What's going on?" James asks as he comes to the group.

Everyone starts talking at once, finally Illan's voice roars over everyone else's. "Enough!" he shouts and everyone stops talking. Turning to James, he says, "They've come to see you, but they wouldn't say why."

The lady with the red hat steps forward though she's obviously nervous about approaching him. He sees her and asks, "Yes?"

"We were told you could help us," she replies.

"Who told you that?" he asks incredulously.

"I don't rightly remember his name," she tells him. "You see, I need a charm for my daughter here," she says as she brings forward a comely looking girl of about fourteen. "You see, she's infatuated with the butcher's son but he has his eye on another."

"Despite what someone may have told you," he says to her, "I don't do charms or anything else like that." When he sees the disappointment on her face, he softens his voice and says, "I'm sorry."

The girl seems almost on the verge of tears, he dismounts and comes to her. "You shouldn't need a charm to ensnare a man's heart, your beauty should be able to get you anyone you desire," he says. "Where I come from, the girls don't rely on magic, but on their own charms and abilities. There's a saying where I come from, 'The way to a man's heart is through his stomach'. Maybe you should try to impress him with your charm and cooking abilities. Find out what he likes to do and tell him how well he does it, how impressive he is, that sort of thing. You'd be surprised how much you can turn his head with the simplest things."

"Do you think so?" she asks, hope springing to her eyes.

"Never know until you try," he tells her. "Besides, if this boy is blind enough to not want one such as you, then he's probably not worth your time anyway."

She gives him a shy smile and says, "Thank you."

"You're welcome," he replies and then gets back up on his horse. To the mother, he says, "A good day to you ma'am."

As he goes by Illan, he leans over and whispers, "Keep them out."

Illan gives him a brief nod.

Turning to Jiron he says, "Let's get back. Still lots to do."

"You got that right," he tells him.

He glances back to the end of the lane after riding a dozen yards and he sees that Illan has moved them along. The man and the ladies are walking back toward town. *This could get irritating. No wonder all the stories of mages and wizards always have them living in far away and inhospitable places. Probably move there just to get away from this sort of thing.*

Before reaching the house, Sean the master builder comes over from the construction site and waves him down. Slowing down, he says to Jiron, "You go on ahead and I'll be up shortly."

"Alright," he says as he continues on while James stops and talks with the builder.

"Sir, if you have a moment?" Sean asks. He's the one who's overseeing the entire construction project.

"Sure," he says as he gets down from his horse. Holding the reins in his hand, he follows him over to where the house is being constructed.

"The cistern you wanted us to put in on the second floor is going to need more support than we had originally anticipated," he says.

James ties his horse to a wagon parked nearby loaded with lumber and other building supplies while he follows Sean within the skeletal construction.

He shows him where the additional support beams are going to need to be placed. "I'm afraid it will shorten your reception area by a foot, but I don't think we have a choice," he says.

"Very well," he tells him. "If we need to sacrifice a foot, so be it."

"It won't be completely wasted, however," he explains. Bringing him closer, he shows where the pipes are being set to allow the water to flow from the cistern above to a smaller tank below. "We can reroute the pipes to run within the new support area, so will save some room there."

"Good thinking," James says, agreeing to the idea.

"Never seen anyone do this before," he tells him.

"Well, the idea is to have water in the house without having to go outside to fetch it," James says. He had to explain this several times before Sean was able to understand the rationale behind it when he first started the construction project. He wanted at least partially running water, and a way to heat it for baths in the winter time.

"Other than that, we're running right on schedule," he says. "We should be able to finish the main house by fall and the rest before Solstice."

"Excellent," comments James. "You're doing a great job."

"Thank you sir," Sean replies.

James leaves him to his work as he goes back and retrieves his horse. The barn not being too far, he decides to just walk him over to it. Jiron has already taken care of his horse and has gone to the house by the time James enters the barn. His is the first stall, being master of the house definitely has its perks. Of course in the winter time, he may want the last stall to be as far from the cold as possible.

The sound of Roland splitting more firewood can be heard while he removes the saddle and tack. A quick brushing and his horse is set. Leaving the barn, he checks in with Ezra and finds lunch still an hour away so he heads over to his workshop.

The ruined workbench has been removed, probably chopped into kindling. Not good for much else now anyway. Inside he takes out another of the crystals and sets it on the workbench before him. The spell he applied last time had worked beautifully, as long as there isn't another crystal in close proximity.

Maybe I could incorporate a 'signature' of some kind within each of the crystals that would prohibit another from leeching from it. If so, that would solve the problem.

He finally comes up with an idea. When the crystal feels a drain on it, it will send a signal to the source. Each crystal will be set up to recognize that signal and when they receive that signal from a source of power they're attempting to leech from, they'll stop.

When he has it set in his head exactly what he wants to do, he releases the magic. The crystal on the workbench before him begins to leech from him. He again sees the now familiar red glow that will eventually deepen into a crimson color.

Allowing the crystal to leech power from him for a minute, he then sends the signature signal to tell it that it shouldn't leech from him. And sure enough, he feels the leeching abruptly stop. The glow within the crystal stops growing and remains constant. Without the primary source from him, there's not very much else close at hand to draw from.

One of the many flies in the area lands on the crystal and James watches in wonder as it seems to shrink in on itself and then stops moving. Reaching his fingers to it, he discovers it has died. All its magic has been sucked from it.

Maybe magic isn't just magic, but the world's life force? And when a living thing loses all of it, he dies? May have to keep that in mind.

He reaches down and pulls out another of the crystals out of the sack. Flicking the dead fly off the one sitting on the workbench, he picks it up and then heads outside. Moving away from the buildings, he enters the forest and walks further into it another dozen yards or so before stopping.

For his next experiment, he doesn't want to be too close to anyone or anything. He sets the crystal that's already glowing on a stump and then walks over to a fallen log several feet away and sets down the other crystal.

Backing away to a safe distance, he casts the same set of spells on the new crystal as he had on the previous one. When he's done with the spells, he watches as the second crystal begins to glow. At the first feeling of it leeching from him, he sends the signal telling it not to leech from him and in a moment, it stops.

He watches the two crystals for several minutes, until neither seem to be behaving erratically as the two earlier had just before they exploded. *It worked!* Grinning to himself, he turns to leave the forest. He'll come back tomorrow to see what's happened, he needs to find out the effects of leaving them active for a prolonged time.

Back at the house he finds lunch almost ready so he washes up and goes into the front room to relax until it's ready.

Illan comes in through the front door and sees him sitting in his favorite spot by the window. "I've left Uther and Jorry out by the road," he tells him. "We may have to have a permanent presence there to keep people away."

"More showed up?" he asks him.

"You could say that," he says. "A bunch of kids who heard you were here wanted to come and 'see' the mage. Like it or not, you're attracting a lot of people."

"Maybe we could sell souvenirs," he says, jokingly.

"Souvenirs?" he asks.

"It's something people can buy to remember coming here," he explains. "Maybe we could make a shirt that says, 'I came to see the mage but only got this lousy shirt'." He starts laughing at the picture of a farmer wearing it as he leads a team of plow horses.

"Maybe," he says, actually sounding interested.

"No!" James blurts out. "I was just kidding. We start doing something like that and they will flock here from all over. No, we will turn them away nicely, if we can."

"Okay, you're the boss," he says with a smile.

About that time, Ezra calls them in to the dining room for lunch. "Where's Miko?" he asks as they get up to go eat.

"I have him monitoring the smokehouse," Illan replies. "Have to make sure the fire stays constant so the meat smokes evenly and cooks just right."

"I bet he loves that," comments James.

"Actually, he's been very interested in the whole process," Illan tells him.

They sit down to a quick meal of cheese, bread and some meat off the carcasses they've been smoking. James savors the smoky quality to it.

James slices off two pieces of bread and makes himself a sandwich. Everyone else has begun to copy him ever since the first time they saw him do it. They like the idea they can make it anyway they choose from the selections Ezra has prepared.

It being so hot, James has been trying to remember how his grandparents had made homemade ice cream, but hasn't had any luck. He usually showed up about the time to crank the handle. Once he asked his grandparents why they didn't just buy an electric one, they said it never turned out as good.

After lunch, he returns to where he left the crystals and Jiron decides to tag along. When they get there, they find both of the crystals have reached a deep crimson glow. Also, around each is an almost perfect circle of wilted vegetation.

"It's just like back near those skull pyramids," observes Jiron.

"Yes, it is," agrees James. A quick look shows that the degree of withering is greater among the vegetation closest to the crystal. Both crystals seem to have a radius of about four feet. Outside that area, everything looks normal.

"What're they doing?" asks Jiron.

"Rather not say, if you don't mind," counters James. Glancing at Jiron, he can see the confused look on his face. "It's just that, what you don't know can't be tortured out of you."

Nodding, he says, "I understand." Then in a whisper he asks, "The Fire?"

"In a way, but that's about as much as I'll tell you," he says. Each of the crystals has several dead bodies of insects upon and around them. *Gonna have to slow down the rate of leeching so as not to alert anyone who may pass by that something is going on.*

As James turns to go, Jiron asks, "Are you just going to leave them here?"

"I'll check back on them in the morning," he explains. "I want to see to what extent the wilting will increase in that time, if it does at all."

"I see," Jiron says as they work their way back to the main house.

Throughout the rest of the day, James stays in his workshop and fine tunes the spells he's been using on the crystals. Over the course of the afternoon, he's been able to reduce the rate of leeching to only a minimal amount.

During one such experiment, he wonders what would happen to the crystal should the spells be removed from it while it held power. Not willing to risk further damage to his workshop, he takes one of the crystals out into the forest, far from where he'd left the other two earlier.

Setting the crystal down on the ground, he backs away thirty feet and cancels the active spells. Nothing happened, and the glow remained constant. He leaves it where it is and plans on coming back to it sometime in the morning to see whether or not the glow will still be there. See if it loses power over time.

Ezra soon calls them in for dinner and afterward they settle into the front room. Most evenings they spend here, swapping stories, some true others highly suspect. Occasionally one will sing a song but for the most part, they just use it as a chance to wind down after the day and spend time together.

James is usually one of the first to bed, the efforts of the day's experiments often leave him feeling drained and exhausted. The leeching of the crystals takes a lot out of him, at least he's found a way to shut off the leeching so as to preserve his own reservoir of power.

He lies in bed listening to the others who've remained out in the front room. They quiet down for his sake but he'll be glad when the other house is built and he can have his privacy. The last thing he hears before falling asleep is a story Uther is telling about how he and Jorry had taken a job to escort this princess and...

Bwaaak!

A noise from outside wakes him up. At first he doesn't even realize he is awake until he hears the chicken squawk again. *Damn those chickens!* Turning over, he tries to go back asleep.

Bwaaak!

There it goes again. Must be some animal disturbing them again. Knowing he's not going to be able to go back to sleep until he deals with this, he gets up from his bed and throws on some clothes.

Stepping carefully, he opens his door and almost collides with Roland. In a whisper, he asks, "Chickens?"

Roland nods his head, "Yeah. Ezra heard them and woke me up to take care of it. Sorry you were disturbed."

"That's okay," he says. "Let's get this over with."

Moving through the house, they make their way to the back door in the kitchen. Suddenly, James feels the familiar prickling sensation that always coincides with someone doing magic. Grabbing Roland's arm, he quickly stops him. In a barely heard whisper, he says, "Magic is near!"

In the darkness he can hear Roland's intake of breath before he asks, "Are you sure?"

"Very. I'm going to go check it out," he whispers. "Wake up Illan and let him know what's going on and that whoever it is, is probably out back. Whatever you do, don't wake up Miko! Then take Tersa and your family into your room and lock the door. Understand?"

"Yeah," he replies as he goes back the way they'd come.

James moves to the door and looks out the window. Several shadows can be seen moving around out there, primarily near the chicken coop. The fact that someone's doing magic and they're out back by the chicken coop can only mean one thing. *They're here for the Fire!* For that's where he'd hidden it, figuring the chickens would give him some alarm should someone come looking for them, which they did.

A touch on his shoulder causes him to jump. "Sorry," he hears Illan whisper behind him. "What's going on?"

"The Empire's men are out there," he tells them.

"Are they looking for the you-know-what?" he asks.

"I can't imagine they'd be here for any other reason," James replies. "There's a mage with them, I can feel it."

"That could make things interesting," he says. Just then, Jorry, Uther and the rest show up and Illan quickly fills them in on what's going on. When Jiron shows up, he has Uther and Jorry go around one side of the house and Yern and Fifer the other.

Before they leave, James tells them, "We can't afford to let any leave here alive. If possible, take one alive. If not, take 'em out. But don't do anything until you hear the signal."

"What'll that be?" asks Uther.

"You'll know it when you see it," replies James.

"Oh yeah, right," he says.

They keep looking out back at the shadows moving around. James knows it's only a matter of time before they realize exactly where it is and dig it up. To Jiron he whispers, "I could use some of those crystals out in my workshop."

"Don't think I could get them without being seen," he tells him. "Too many out there."

"Hold on a second," Illan says as he moves back into the house. Returning shortly, he hands James three crystals. "Will these do?" he asks.

"Where did you get these?" he asks as he takes them.

"I was curious about why you were interested in them," he explains somewhat guiltily. "So while you were gone today, I grabbed a couple to take a closer look. I was going to put them back in the morning before you got up."

"It's okay," James assures him. "We'll give the others another minute to get into position and then we'll go."

Illan takes out his sword and stands ready.

A minute passes and James says, "Alright, let's go." He quickly casts the magic gathering spell, upon the crystals and slowly opens the door. The draw of the three crystals on him at once is almost overpowering, but he needs them to be charged at least a little for what he has planned.

When it's clear between him and the coop, he throws the crystals toward those standing around the coop. A cry goes up as one of the enemy spots the three glowing crystals flying toward them. James suddenly feels a surge of the prickly sensation as the enemy mage prepares a spell.

When it's cast, the magic of the enemy mage's spell is immediately absorbed by the crystals, all which begin to fluctuate as they leech magic from one another as well as the mage. This time, he did not incorporate the spell to prevent them from drawing on each other. In fact, he's counting on it.

His orb bursts to light overhead, illuminating the entire area. Along with the mage, are another dozen men in black armor who spring to attack.

Jiron and Illan move in front of James as the men rush to attack. A slug flies between them as James takes out one. From behind the charging men, they can see their four friends rushing fast to close with them from behind.

Once they're close, Jiron and Illan move to attack. They maintain a defensive posture as they wait for their friends to join the battle from behind. As yet, their attackers are still unaware that they're even there.

From the coop, James can feel the pulsating of the crystals as each continues to draw power from the others. The enemy mage is quickly having his power sucked from him and has fallen to the ground, all but unconscious. He can see him there in the pulsating glow of the crystals, attempting to crawl away.

When Fifer and the others join the battle, they take out three men quickly before they realize they're among them. Now evenly matched, each attacker faces off with one defender.

With only one man now to contend with, Jiron is able to go on the attack. The enemy before him is no ordinary fighter, he quickly realizes. Every attack he tries, the man blocks and with being heavily armored, he's finding it hard to get an opening for his knife.

The back door suddenly swings open again as Miko rushes out in just his underclothes, sword in hand. He moves to aid Illan with his opponent.

"Miko!" James cries when he sees him rushing to the fight.

Fifer's enemy falls to the ground, his sword stuck between the man's ribs. He reaches down and takes the other man's sword and moves to help Yern who's having a harder time with his.

The crystals are beginning to emit the high pitched tone, similar to the one which had been emitted by the others earlier in the day before they exploded. The mage now lies unmoving, one of the crystals less than a foot from his outstretched hand. In the light of the crystals, it looks as if his skin has been pulled in tight around his skull. His eyes look shrunken and his hands almost skeletal.

"Down!" James yells at the top of his lungs. "Everybody, DOWN!"

Those still engaged with enemies abruptly break off and fling themselves away and to the ground.

Ka-Boom!

A tremendous explosion erupts as the three crystals explode. The shockwave rolls over them and knocks down the remaining enemies who hit the ground, dazed. Those closest to them quickly move to dispatch them before they're able to regain their senses.

Looking to where the chicken coop once had stood, James sees a small crater where the explosion had created a hole over a foot deep and six across. There's no sign of the mage that had been there, several dead chickens can be found lying here and there.

Everyone gets back up, James searches for Miko who's helping Illan up. "Are you okay?" he asks him.

Miko turns and says, "I'm fine."

James looks into his eyes and sees that he is fine. He was afraid that battle might have triggered latent effects from the Fire, but he's glad he had been mistaken.

"Everyone okay?" Illan hollers out as he gets up.

Only a few minor cuts and one on Yern's left arm that'll require stitching. Otherwise, they came off well.

"Is it over?" Roland asks from the doorway to the kitchen.

"Yeah," replies Uther. "Ask Tersa to come and help Yern, he's got a bad cut needing to be sewed."

He turns back to those waiting in the kitchen a moment and then hollers back to Uther, "Bring him inside."

Uther walks with Yern into the house as the others survey the scene.

"Gather the dead," Illan tells Jorry and Fifer. Miko pitches in as well. Walking with James to the hole where the chicken coop once stood, he asks, "Is this where you hid the Fire?"

"Seemed like a good idea at the time," he replies. "I was hoping for the chickens to let us know if someone disturbed them. It worked." They see one of their shovels lying near the hole, the entire top half of the handle gone. Picking it up, he continues, "Guess we'll need a new shovel."

"Not only sightseers, now we have to worry about possible attacks by the Empire," says Illan.

"I figured they would come, eventually," admits James. "I just didn't expect it this soon."

"Are you close to having it ready to be secured away forever?" he asks.

"Getting there," he answers. "Still a couple things I need to work on."

Fifer comes up and asks, "What are we going to do with the bodies?"

"We'll dig a hole out in the forest and dump them in," Illan replies.

"I'm going to go see the mayor tomorrow and let him know what happened," James announces. "I think he has a right to know, maybe he can get word to Ceryn who could keep an eye out as well."

"Good idea," Illan says. To the rest he raises his voice, "Everyone grab a shovel and pick, we've got a hole to dig."

When James starts to head to the barn to grab a shovel to help, Illan stops him and says, "You leave this to us." Then he moves along with the others to get this deed done.

Uther comes out of the house with a lantern and joins them.

James walks back into the kitchen and sees Yern sitting at the table, Tersa finishing securing the bandage on his arm. "You okay?" he asks.

Yern gives him a smile and replies, "Been better, but with this lovely angel's help, I'll survive."

Tersa blushes slightly as she begins clearing away the blood and the soiled rags.

"Who were they?" Roland asks.

"One was a mage, the others soldiers of the Empire," he tells them.

Ezra gets a scared look in her eye and clutches Arkie tighter. "What were they doing here?" she asks.

"The Empire has little love for me, I'm sure," he says.

Roland chuckles a little as he adds, "After what you've said you did, I don't think we can assume they'll just leave you alone. Besides, you're a rouge mage, not under their control and they will most likely see you as their greatest threat."

"Oh I doubt that," James says. "But we should be cautious from this point on." Turning to Ezra he continues, "Tomorrow I'm planning on going into town to talk to the mayor. I'll also see about getting more chickens, the ones we had are dead."

"You leave it to me to get the chickens," she tells him. "I know someone who was saying at the market just the other day how she has too many now that her boys are gone."

"Very well, tell Roland how much you think you'll need," he says. Getting up, he moves over to the window and looks out. He can see the light from the lantern off in the forest where they're digging the grave. Suddenly tired, he says, "I'm going to bed."

"Good night James," Ezra says to him.

"Good night to you all," he replies and then leaves the kitchen.

Getting into bed, he lies there for awhile as he thinks about the attack. *I've got to get the Fire out of here, it's putting innocents in jeopardy. Next time we may not be so fortunate. How long till next time?*

Finally sleep wins out over worry.

Chapter Four

The following morning when James heads into town, Jiron and Miko accompany him. Illan told him that after last night, he shouldn't be out alone. At the end of the lane, he finds Jorry and Yern standing guard to stop anyone from coming onto the property.

They wave at them as they pass by and soon are nearing the outskirts of town. With Jiron on his right and Miko on his left, they move through the outlying buildings of Trendle.

"The streets look a bit more crowded than before," Jiron states.

James had been thinking about the night before and hadn't been paying very much attention. But now that he is, he sees what Jiron means. The crowds are slightly more crowded and there are many faces he's never seen before.

When they begin moving among the people, he can hear hushed conversations and every once in a while catches someone pointing at him out of the corner of his eye. *Irritating*.

Once at the mayor's office, they dismount and leave Miko to watch the horses while James and Jiron go up to see the mayor. "Just be careful," he warns Miko. "As long as the crowds keep their distance, don't do anything."

"Alright," he replies. Miko stands at the ready with his back to the building, one hand resting on the hilt of his sword.

James tries to hide the grin that wants to escape at the sight of Miko being so serious. "Let's go," he says to Jiron who opens the door for him. They quickly move up to the second floor and down the hall to the mayor's office. When they knock on the door, they receive no answer. Jiron opens the door and looks inside. "No one's here," he says.

After closing the door, they retrace their steps back down the hallway. When they come abreast of a door on their right, several people can be heard talking on the other side. James stops and looks to Jiron who only shrugs.

Jiron knocks on the door and the talking abruptly ceases. The door opens and a man peers out who asks, "Yes?"

"We'd like to see the mayor," James tells him.

"Do you have an appointment?" the man asks.

"Well, actually no." he admits. "But this is rather important."

"Then you'll have to come back another time," the man says. "He's in a meeting with the town council."

As the man begins to close the door, James says, "Just tell him James was here to see him."

Before the door closes, it opens back up quickly and the mayor stands there. "You come on in, James," he tells him. To the other guy, he says, "James here never needs an appointment to see me."

"Yes, sir," the man replies.

Within the room, he sees seven other men, Corbin being one of them, sitting around a large table. He gives James a nod as he enters. The mayor takes his seat at the head of the table and the man who answered the door pulls two more chairs over for James and Jiron.

"Gentlemen," the mayor announces, "for those of you who have yet to meet him, this is James." A murmur begins which the mayor quickly silences.

"Now, you know Corbin here," the mayor says. "Next to him is Polin, and then Berill, Monn, Durik, Aarron, Igren. This is the City Council of Trendle."

"Good day to you all," says James. He receives an answering salutation from the council members.

"We were just talking about you," Corbin says.

"Yes," John, the mayor jumps in. "It seems your notoriety had attracted many people to the area."

"I'm sorry about that," apologizes James. "I hadn't planned on that."

"No, don't be sorry young man," Polin says. A man of middle years, dark hair and dressed well, Polin gives off an air of friendliness. "In fact, we were just talking about how we could increase it."

Getting a dark look, James asks, "What for?"

"All these people are going to need a place to rest and food to eat," Monn replies with a grin. Monn being a fat man with slightly stained clothes, James figures him as some kind of innkeeper or possibly someone in the service business.

"There's a profit to be made here," adds Aarron, an older man, all but grey.

"But at my expense!" James exclaims. His outburst takes the council aback.

"You're not having to pay for anything," Berill interjects. A younger man with a slight attitude, he looks at James like he shouldn't have to state the obvious.

Corbin jumps in and says, "I think what James means is that he'll be paying with his privacy. Isn't that right James?"

"Yes, Corbin," he replies. "Exactly. Already I've had people out at my place who are disturbing me. I've even set up guards to keep them off my lands."

"Do you think you should do that?" Durik asks. Another middle aged man, he fits in with what Corbin had said a long time ago about John's drinking buddies. "If word gets around that you turn people away, they may not come."

"Good!" he exclaims. "I don't want them to come, and I certainly don't want to become a tourist attraction just so you all can fatten your purses."

"Now James," the mayor says as he gets to his feet. "There's no need to get upset."

Jiron laughs and everyone's attention is drawn to him. Even James glances to him wondering why he's laughing.

"What's so funny?" asks Igren, a small man with a keen eye that seems to take in everything.

Standing up, Jiron says, "He's not upset, gentlemen. I'd say he's merely annoyed. He's the last person you'd ever want to see 'upset'." He glances around the table, his mood slowly turning serious as he makes eye contact with each councilman before continuing. "While you're here deciding upon the best way to exploit this situation, things are going on that you're not even aware of. Last night, a mage from the Empire with twelve soldiers attacked us and we nearly lost the battle. This is just the first one, you can be sure there will be more."

"The notoriety that you are counting on to draw the people here to put money in your pockets will also draw those of an unsavory nature as well. And I'm not talking just of those from the Empire. With people, come thieves and all that goes with them, think about that."

James stands up and says, "I ask you not to go forth with any plans that will draw people to me. Aside from being irritating, it could very well put them in jeopardy." To Jiron he says, "We've said all that needs to be said, let's go."

As they leave the council chamber, Corbin gets up and follows them out into the hallway, closing the door behind him. "Is everyone okay?" he asks, concern evident on his face.

"Everyone's fine," Jiron replies. "Yern has a nasty cut, nothing else major."

"I'm glad," he says. "Sorry about that in there, I remember how much you like your quiet."

"It just makes me mad," he says. "They're planning on making a profit off of me at my expense. I like Trendle, but it isn't the only town on the map. If it gets too bad, I'll move."

"I know and I'd hate to see that happen," Corbin says. "I'd better get back in before they go and pass a ruling without me."

"Thanks Corbin," he says, holding out his hand.

Taking the hand, Corbin says, "Come out for dinner sometime, Mary and the kids would love to see you again."

"I may, just really busy right now," James tells him.

Corbin opens the door to the council chamber and then goes back inside. James can hear them talking, about what he can't quite make out through the door.

As they move down the hallway and begin descending the stairs, Jiron asks, "Were you serious about moving?"

"Not for a while and only if it gets bad around here," he replies.

Outside, they find Miko still standing by their horses. At their approach, he glances back at them and then turns to face them. "No one's bothered us," he says as he pats his horse.

"That's good news," James says as he mounts. As they ride through the streets, he again hears the whispers and catches people pointing at him. Ears burning slightly from the attention, he kicks his horse into more of a canter and they quickly leave the town behind.

"I think I may not come back here for awhile," he announces once they've ridden a ways out of town.

"Don't blame you," Miko says. "I find it unnerving and it's not even directed at me."

Before reaching the lane to the Ranch, they see three men walking away from Jorry who's still on guard duty there. As they ride past the men, one of them looks like he's about to say something to them. James hurries on past before he has a chance to get it out.

At the lane entrance, Jorry says, "So far, those guys are the only ones to show up today."

"What did they want?" asks James.

"Just asked if you were here," he explains. "When I told them you had gone into town, they turned around and started back."

James looks back and sees the three men paused there in the road, as if they're deciding whether or not to come back now that he's there. Finally, they turn and continue down the road back to town.

"Irritating," he says as he starts down the lane to the main house. Out back he can see where the hole in the ground from the crystals exploding last night has already been filled back in and Sean has begun laying out a new framework for another coop. Jiron rides to the barn while he goes over to talk with him.

"Well master builder," James says as he rides over to him, "got tired of working on the house?"

Grinning, he says, "No, but they've gotten it under control for the moment so I thought I'd put together another coop for you before nightfall. Your cook asked me if I could. You don't mind do you?"

"It's fine," he replies. "Do you have everything you need?"

"All but the chicken wire and I understand one of your men has gone into town to get that."

"Good," he says. He turns his horse toward the barn and soon has him settled in. Around the back of the house, he finds Roland chopping wood. When he sees James approaching, he puts the axe down.

"Ezra has borrowed your builder for the day," he tells him.

"Yeah, I saw that," he replies.

"You don't mind do you?" he asks. When James shakes his head, he continues, "It's just that she's arranged for three dozen chickens to arrive here tomorrow and wanted a place ready for them."

"That's fine," he assures him. "Where did she get that many?"

"From several of the neighboring farms, from what she tells me," he explains.

"I'll be out in the workshop if anyone needs me," he says.

"Okay," says Roland as he picks up his axe again and commences splitting logs into firewood.

Rather than going directly to his workshop, he heads for the crystals that were left out in the forest from the day before. He goes to the one off by itself to see if the glow still remains after being deactivated all night.

When he at last finds it, he can still see the glow within and it looks to be just as strong as it had the day before. It hadn't been exactly full to begin with. Maybe the more power it has, the more it will lose and once it reaches a certain level it doesn't lose anymore? Going to have to see if that theory is sound or not.

Feeling really good about the whole thing, he replaces the crystal back down where it had been. May as well leave it to see how it behaves over the next couple days. Now to the other ones.

He can easily tell where the other two crystals were left. Before he even gets close, he can see where the withered area has grown much greater than it was the day before. Where there were two distinct areas, now there is but one. The two areas surrounding the crystals have grown together and expanded further out.

Everything within a foot of each crystal is completely dead. Both have a deep crimson glow and look to be filled to capacity. Canceling the spells, he bends down and picks them up. They don't feel any different, still hard and feels like their weight hasn't changed. He puts one back in his pocket and the other he takes over to where the first one lies. He sets the crystal down next to it, figuring to come back the next day and compare the two to see if the one with more power will lose it faster.

Going back to the workshop, he takes several crystals out and casts the leeching spells upon them, the ones that will only draw minute quantities at a time so as not to kill the vegetation. He also adds the signature spell to each to make sure they won't leech from each other. Unless there are special circumstances, he'll always incorporate the signature spell.

He prepares four separate crystals and then takes them out to the forest, placing them in different areas. In the morning he'll see what kind of effect they leave on their surroundings. If he's done this right, there should be very little in the way of noticeable withering of the surrounding vegetation.

When he returns from the forest he goes over and helps Sean with the chicken coop. Miko and Fifer are already there helping him. They've finished the initial framework and were starting the roof when he joins them. By the time the evening meal is ready, they've nailed the last of the roosting boxes securely to the walls.

Ezra steps out to call them in for dinner and notices that the new chicken coop is finished. Coming over, she nods her head and says, "Very nice. Yes, very nice indeed. Thank you."

"You're welcome," Sean says to her. Then to James he says, "I better get over there and see how they're doing on the house."

"Shouldn't have messed it up too much," James says with a grin.

"They'd better not have messed it up at all if they expect to go home tonight," he tells him as he heads on over.

Fifer just laughs as he and Miko go and get cleaned up. James follows them and they're soon sitting at the table having their dinner.

James tells everyone about the meeting with the town council and he hears angry muttering from the ones who've been standing out at the road keeping everyone away. "It's bad enough now," Jorry says. "Today alone I had to turn away at least seven people, some took it okay. Others got downright angry at not being able to talk to you."

"What do they want?" he asks.

"Most won't tell me, others are just stupid things," he replies. "One woman wanted you to remove a wart and another is sure that someone has put a curse on him."

"A curse?" asks Illan, amused.

"Yes, a curse," replies Jorry. "He claims that his continued losing at cards is due to a curse. I told him it's probably just that he's no good. He didn't like that and told me so in not very friendly words."

"I'm sorry you guys have to put up with that," he says. "Maybe when the word spreads that I don't see anyone, then they'll go away."

"I hope so," Jorry sighs. "If not, I'd like a shack or something out there we can relax in. Now's not too bad, but in the winter, it could get bad out there."

They eat in silence for a while, each digesting what's been said. Suddenly from outside, they hear the sound of wagons rolling toward the house. Uther gets up and goes out to the front room and shortly his voice can be heard as he says, "Delia's back."

Jiron gets up and hurries out, Tersa right behind.

James finishes another bite and then says to Ezra as he indicates his plate, "I'm not finished yet." Then he gets up and goes out to meet them as well. He finds Delia and Tersa giving each other a hug in welcome. Shorty is getting down from where he'd been driving the wagon and Scar, Potbelly and Stig are dismounting from their horses.

"I told you we'd make it here by dark!" he can hear Potbelly say to Scar.

"Alright, here," Scar says as he hands over several coins.

"How's the trading business?" James asks Delia when he approaches.

"Not as good as I'd hoped," she tells him. "But I'm just starting out and have no contacts. Few will trust me with their loads, but give me time and I'll win them over."

"I'm sure you will," he says. "We've just sat down to dinner. You're welcome to share with us."

"That's okay," she says. "I doubt if Ezra had planned on so many, we'll just eat our own food tonight. Though tomorrow morning we'll take advantage of her cooking before we set out."

"Leaving so soon?" he asks.

"Afraid so," she tells him. "The merchant we dropped the shipment off to in Wurt has commissioned another one to Bearn. And of course it needs to be there yesterday so we haven't any time to dally."

"I understand," he says sympathetically. "The customer comes first."

"At least now that I'm trying to make a name for myself," she says.

"Thanks for sending Shorty with the letter and the crystals," he says.

"You're welcome," she replies. "I knew you were looking for them and there was no need for you to wait because of some impatient merchant."

"I appreciate that," he says. "I know you've got things to do, so come on in once everything gets settled."

"I will," she tells him.

He hears Jiron and Tersa catching up on things with Stig and the others as he walks back to the house. When he enters the kitchen, Ezra looks to him with a slightly strained expression. "Don't worry," he says, "they're not coming to dinner."

"We might have enough," she says as the tension begins to leave her.

Shaking his head, he tells her, "Delia knows you haven't planned for them and doesn't want to drop in at the last minute with so many mouths. She said they'll fix their own but will be looking forward to some of your cooking before they pull out in the morning."

Relief now evident on her face, she nods and says, "They'll not be disappointed."

Next to her, Roland pats her on the hand and says, "I'm sure they won't be."

James sits back down and finishes his meal. Jiron and Tersa never make it back in by the time he's done and Ezra is ready to clear the table. He tells her to go ahead, that they'll not likely be back to finish.

He goes out to the front room and sits in his favorite chair by the window as he watches them finish getting the horses and wagons set for the night. Roland comes in and builds a fire in the fireplace in anticipation of the cool of evening. Even though it gets hot here in the day, after the sun goes down, it tends to get a little bit of a chill in the air.

Outside, he can hear Jiron telling them about the attack last night. Delia has her guards rotate watch around the wagons in case of a similar event tonight. When all is settled in, they break out their rations and have a quick meal while the sun makes its final descent to the horizon. By the time they're done eating, it's dipped below and the stars have begun to appear.

Delia, Jiron and Tersa come over to the house when they're done eating, he notices Jiron is carrying a small box. "Sitting by yourself again?" Delia asks him as she enters through the door.

"It's peaceful," he tells her with a grin. Nodding his head to Jiron, he asks, "What's in the box?"

She reaches for the box and Jiron hands it to her. "On the road I got to thinking about your shaving kit and the knife you used to use," she says to him. She opens the box and pulls out a knife, similar to the one he had used. "I was thinking that if you could do that with others, maybe we could sell them."

"Who would want them?" he asks.

"Any barber out there," she explains. "Also, those with sheep that need shearing may want them as well." She looks to him expectantly.

"It's not a matter of if I can," he tells her. "But if I will."

"What do you mean?" she asks. "I know you've been wondering how to raise money for this place, having so many to care for isn't going to be cheap. And the money you already have won't last forever."

He starts to responds when Jiron jumps in. "You're worried about people finding out, right?" he asks.

"Exactly," he says. "If I started doing this, there's no end to the number of people that would flock here. Each of them wanting me to make them something that they 'desperately' had to have."

"I understand your concern," Delia says. "I don't plan on telling anyone where I got them. Your secret is safe with me."

He sits there considering it while they wait expectantly. "If I do this, you must swear to never tell anyone where you got them," he insists.

"I swear it!" she says.

"How many do you have?" he asks.

"Ten," she replies.

Nodding, he holds his hand out for the box. "Understand that the magic that will enable them to work will come from the wielder. They have to be aware of that fact or they may get seriously hurt if they do it for a long period of time. If too much is drawn from them, they could become weakened, even die though I doubt if that is much of a possibility."

"I understand," she says, handing it to him.

One by one, he takes the knives out of the box and casts the spell on them that will allow them to cut hair but nothing else. When the spell has been set in the knife, he lays it on the side table next to his chair.

By the sixth knife, he's beginning to feel the effects of doing so much magic. At the eighth he can barely focus enough to be able to cast it properly. When he finishes the eighth knife, he sags back in his chair "Eight's going to have be it for now," he says. "I can't do anymore."

She comes over and removes the final two he hasn't enchanted yet from the box and sets in the eight that he has imbued with magic. "I'm sure this will do fine." She looks at him and says, "You look like you could use some rest."

"Yeah," he says, "I do need to rest. I don't think you understand just what that takes out of me." He gets to his feet and begins to wobble. Jiron is right there and gives him a shoulder to lean on as he helps him to his room.

When they get there, James plops down on his bed and before Jiron leaves, says, "Tell her to get another batch of crystals. The same amount as before and that should be all I will require for a while."

"Alright," he says as he moves to the bedroom door. "You get some rest and we'll see you in the morning." Before he gets the door closed, James is already asleep.

Chapter   Five

The next morning when he wakes up, Delia and her caravan have already left. When he goes to the kitchen, he finds the remnants of the meal Ezra had sent them off with. He grabs a plate and begins helping himself to the leftovers.

Tersa comes in and sees him there and says, "She wanted to say goodbye, but didn't know how long you'd be asleep. We offered to wake you up but she said it would be better for you to get your sleep."

"It's alright," he replies. "Where's Ezra?"

"She and Roland took the wagon to collect the chickens from the neighbors," she explains as she begins cleaning up. "I promised her to get this place ready for lunch and to feed everyone if she doesn't get back in time."

"Where is everyone?" he asks.

"Most of them are out collecting scraps of wood from where they're building the house and are planning on throwing together a hut of sorts out by the road. I think Jiron went into town for some reason or other."

"Thanks," he says. Sitting down with his plate, he eats while she continues cleaning the kitchen.

"Do you like being here?" he asks.

She pauses in her work and turns to look at him. "Yes, I do actually," she replies. "I miss the City something awful, but here it's nice and peaceful." Giving him a slight grin, she adds, "Most of the time."

"I'm glad," he says sincerely. "I'll endeavor to preserve the tranquility as much as I can."

He finishes his breakfast and then takes his plate over to where she's doing the dishes. "Thanks," she says as she takes it from him.

"If anyone needs me, I'll be out at the workshop," he tells her as he heads for the back door.

"That's where they look first anyway," she replies just before the door closes behind him.

Grinning at her words, he heads out to the workshop. Just before he gets there, three men step out from around the side. It's the same three men that were turned away when he was returning from town yesterday.

Oh, bother! He stops as they approach him and steels himself for the inevitable demands he knows they're going to make. *Am I going to have to build a high fence or hire more guards?*

Two of the men stop five feet from him while the third approaches. "Excuse me, are you James?" the man asks. "The wizard?"

"Yeah, that's me," he replies. "Now just how did you get on my property?"

One of the two men brings something up to his mouth and blows.

James suddenly feels a prick on his neck and pulls out a small needle dart. He brings it up to look at and can see a drop of his blood upon it. At first confused, then realizing he's being attacked, he calls the magic to defend himself. But his mind is beginning to cloud and he's unable to focus enough. His equilibrium begins to falter as he tumbles to the ground.

The man closest to him says to the others, "Pick him up. We've got to get out of here fast."

Just then the back door to the house opens up and Tersa steps out. "James, I just remembered..." she says before seeing the men standing there. She takes it all in, the sight of James lying on the ground and the three men standing next to him. An ear piercing scream escapes her as she darts back into the house. More screams echo as she races through the house and out the front screaming for her brother.

From the end of the lane where Jiron had paused a moment to talk to the guys working on the hut before heading on into town, he hears her scream. "Tersa!" he cries as he turns his horse back toward the house, kicking it into a gallop. The others drop their tools and race after.

The largest man picks up James and slings him over his shoulder. Turning away from the house, they begin running toward the forest. Tersa's screams continuing behind them as she runs through the front door.

Seeing Jiron racing back down the lane, she points to the back and says, "Three men!"

He nods and races around the house. "James!" Jiron cries out as he rounds the house at a full gallop, his horse quickly closing the gap. Seeing them carrying him away toward the forest, he yells, "They've got James!"

Without even slowing, he rides straight for them and crashes his horse into them before jumping clear. Two of the men fall to the ground, the one carrying James continues on toward the forest. Not taking the time to dispose of the two his horse had knocked to the ground, he races after the one carrying James.

The man glances over his shoulder and sees the gap between them narrowing quickly. He abruptly comes to a halt and drops James to the ground as he turns to engage Jiron. Seeing his other two partners already on the way, he worries more about defense, keeping him busy until help arrives.

Jiron closes with him, both knives at the ready. A quick glance at James shows him to still be alive, if unconscious.

He strikes out with his left knife which the man blocks with ease and then comes back in with his right which scores along the man's side. Pressing the attack with vigor, he lays into him with a barrage of blinding attacks honed through hundreds of battles in the fight pits back in the City of Light.

The man quickly realizes he's not going to win this fight and starts backing up, putting as much distance between himself and Jiron. Looking over Jiron's shoulder, he realizes his partners are just about there.

Knowing what the man is doing, Jiron continues pressing him, not allowing him the opportunity. Closing again with him quickly, Jiron launches into a series of attacks and then suddenly kicks out with his foot, shattering the man's kneecap.

With a cry of pain, he falls to the ground at Jiron's feet.

Looking back, he sees the men are almost upon James and he rushes back toward them. All of a sudden, he feels a sharp, poking sensation on his arm and he sees a small needle dart embedded in his skin. Pulling it out, he throws it on the ground as he continues moving to defend James.

His mind begins to grow cloudy and the world starts to spin. Before he realizes it, he's on the ground, not three feet from where James lies. Unable to move, he watches as the men approach, one's leading his horse.

In a world that's spinning and warping, he watches as they quickly load James up on a horse. *His horse!* He hears one of them say, "Take care of Corim, we'll not be able to take him with us."

"You can't kill me!" the wounded man cries from the ground.

"Sorry," the first man says. "But we can't let you live to tell them where to find us."

"No!" the man cries as his partner runs his sword through his chest. Quickly wiping his blade on the man's clothes, he comes to Jiron and asks, "What about him?"

"He doesn't matter," the first man says from the back of the horse. "Come on and mount up, we've not much time."

"We'll not get far with the three of us on horseback," the second man says as he swings up behind the first.

"Just need to get to our horses, then we'll be fine," he says.

As they start riding fast for the forest, Jiron hears more footsteps as Illan and the others approach. "Jorry, see about Jiron," cries Illan. "Fifer, Yern! Go back and get our horses ready, fast!"

"Yes, sir!" replies Fifer as they race back to the barn.

"Uther, I want you to follow them as best you can," he says. "Return here should they get away."

Uther nods and then races after them.

"Damn!" he exclaims as the men are already out of sight in the forest.

Coming over to where Jorry is examining Jiron, he asks, "How is he?"

"Conscious, I think he's been drugged," Jorry replies. "His eyes aren't focusing and he's not responding to anything I say. At least he's still breathing."

"Take him back to the house," Illan says. "Tell Tersa that I want to know when he regains the ability to talk."

"Yes sir," he says as he picks him up and starts carrying him back to the house.

"What about James?" cries Miko, staring at the forest where the men disappeared.

"We'll find him lad," Illan assures him. Going over to the dead man, he kneels down and begins going through his pockets.

"I know him," Miko says.

Standing up abruptly, Illan turns to him and asks, "What?"

"I know him," he says again, looking Illan in the eyes. "He's from Bearn."

"Bearn?" asks Illan incredulously. "What in god's name would someone from Bearn be doing here? And what possible interest could they have in James?"

"Lord Colerain," Miko explains. "He's had it in for James ever since we were seen on his property." When Illan looks askance at him at that, he adds, "We were there by accident, but ever since he's been trying to capture him."

"Better tell me the whole thing," he says.

Miko begins from when they got chased into the sewers and by the time he's done with the narration, Uther returns.

Seeing him approach, Illan asks, "Well?"

"They lost me in the forest, but I cut over to the road and caught up with them again just as they were riding down the road toward town," he reports. "They all have horses now, they must've had them stashed out by the road before making the attempt on James."

"Go help Fifer and Yern with the horses," he tells him. "If they're on their way to Bearn, then we're going to follow."

"Yes sir," he says and then starts running to the barn.

"You're sure about this Colerain, then?" he asks Miko as they hurry back to the house.

"Couldn't be anyone else," he replies. "Not if Corim there is involved. He and his buddies are known for this sort of thing."

"At least we have an idea where he's being taken," he says. Coming in through the back door, he finds them out in the front room where Jiron is lying on the couch. "Well?" he asks as he enters from the kitchen.

"I think it may be wearing off," Jorry tells him. "Though I can't be sure."

"Jiron," Illan says as he kneels on the floor by him. "We think they may be taking him to Bearn."

His eyes move back and forth slightly as his mouth tries to form the words.

"I know, I know," he says to him. "We're leaving now to get him back. I'm going to leave Yern here since he's wounded and you two are going to have to look after things while we're gone." Giving him a meaningful look, he adds, "If you know what I mean?"

A brief nod from Jiron shows he understands. "When Roland gets back, let him know what's going on and see if you can get Ceryn to hang out around here until we return."

Getting up, he glances at the worried look on Tersa's face and says, "He'll be fine, just drugged. I think it's the same drug they used on James. It's something you use on a mage to inhibit his ability to use magic."

"Okay," she says. "What should I do?"

"Nothing you can do for the moment," he tells her. "Just have to wait until the effects wear off."

"I understand," she says as she gazes down at her brother lying there. A slight tear rolls down her face.

He puts a hand on her shoulder and says in a reassuring voice, "He'll be fine."

From the front door, Uther says, "The horses are ready."

Turning his attention to Uther, he replies, "Tell Yern to come in here then go and get enough supplies to last for several days."

"I'll help you," offers Tersa as she moves to the kitchen.

Uther goes outside and soon Yern comes in.

"I want you to stay here with Jiron to look after the place," he tells him. "After the attack the other night, now this, we can't afford to leave this place undefended."

"I understand," he says.

Indicating Jiron, he adds, "When he finally gets up, try to keep him from following."

"I'll do my best," he says.

Miko returns from where he'd gone to get his sword. Seeing him buckling it on, Illan says, "Go on out and wait with the others. Tell 'em we'll be leaving in five minutes."

Nodding, he walks out the front door.

Turning back to Yern, he says, "One of you should stay out by the road to turn people away, the other needs to walk a perimeter around the property. Keep an eye out for any more intruders."

"Will do," Yern assures him.

Uther comes out of the kitchen with several pouches stuffed with food. "Go distribute them among the horses," Illan tells him then he moves to James' room where he opens the money chest and fills his pouch with many golds, silvers, and coppers.

He moves back out through the front room, pausing only a moment to give just a cursory goodbye before he walks out the front door. Everyone is already in the saddle, waiting for him. As he mounts, he sees Tersa and Yern coming out of the front door. "We'll get him back," he says then kicks his horse into a gallop as they race down the lane in pursuit.

"Miko," he hollers back to him as they reach the road, "I want you next to me. Before we get to Bearn, I want to know everything there is to know about it."

Miko closes the gap and rides abreast of Illan as he commences telling him about Bearn.

By the time they've caught up with Delia's caravan, Illan has practically exhausted Miko's knowledge of Bearn. He thought he'd known Bearn, but with the pointed questions that Illan had been asking him, he realized just how little he knew of the city he grew up in.

Stig's bringing up the rear of the caravan and when he sees them coming up the road, waves. The greeting he was about to give dies on his lips when he sees the grimness of their faces. Dropping the greeting, he asks, "What's wrong?"

"Follow me," Illan says as he comes up to where Delia's driving the lead wagon.

"Delia!" he calls out as his horse reaches her side.

Surprised at seeing him, she quickly brings her wagon to a halt as the others with her gather around. "What brings you out here?" she asks.

"Trouble," he replies and then proceeds to explain what happened.

"Damn!" curses Scar. "They rode by us not a half hour ago. One of them had been slumped over the saddle, but we never even imagined that it could've been James."

"Got a favor to ask you," Illan says to her.

"What?" she asks.

"I want to take Shorty and Scar with us," he says. "Jorry and Uther will ride into Bearn with your caravan."

"But you'll need us!" exclaims Uther.

"I understand how you feel," he tells them. "But from talking with Miko, it seems the most likely spot for them to take him would be to Lord Colerain's estate. And Miko says the best way would be in through the sewer entrance that he and James used earlier."

"But…" Jorry starts to object.

"It's a very narrow passage, in which James had almost become stuck when he went through it," he says. "I don't think either you or Uther will be able to squeeze through."

"You won't be able to either," Uther states.

"I know, but Scar and Shorty should be able to," he tells him. "That's why I need them. You can come in with Delia, a day or so behind us. If we're done fast, we'll pick you up on our way back."

"Shorty! Scar!" Delia calls out to them. "You're going with them." To Illan he says, "Don't get them killed."

"Do my best," he says. "Miko here says there's an inn there called the Flying Swan. If we haven't met up on the road before you get to Bearn, meet us there."

"The Flying Swan," she says. "We'll be there, could take us two days, though."

"Understood," he says. Looking back, he sees Uther and Jorry now with the caravan, their faces hanging low with sullen expressions. Shorty and Stig are now behind him, happy to be doing other things than riding along with a dull caravan.

"Let's go," he tells his men. Nudging the sides of his horse, he gets him moving quickly down the road to Bearn. A short distance later the road forks and they follow the one that continues along the Kelewan River toward Bearn.

They continue riding hard the rest of the day and when it gets close to sundown, they see a small town ahead of them on the road. It's just one of the many clusters of buildings they've passed through, usually consisting of not much more than an inn or a store for the occasional traveler.

This one boasts of not only an inn, but a horse trader. A corral with a dozen horses sits near a large building with a sign of a large bird in flight. "We'll stop here for a bite to eat and rest the horses," Illan announces.

Miko understands the necessity of stopping, but he's anxious to find James. "Don't worry lad," Illan tells him when he sees the worried look on his face. "I don't plan to be here long."

"I hope not," Miko replies.

Inside they find a dining room and take a long table, large enough to accommodate them all. After they order and are waiting for their food, Miko is gazing out the window at the horses in the corral and suddenly cries out, "That's Jiron's horse!"

"What?" exclaims Illan. "Where?"

Pointing out the window, he says, "Out there in the corral."

"You sure?" he asks.

"Absolutely," he states with conviction.

To Shorty he says, "You stay here and wait for the food." Standing up, he adds, "The rest of you come with me."

On the way out, he asks the serving girl who he could see about the horses in the corral outside. She tells him her father, Terrol, should be out there in the adjacent stable. He thanks her and they all leave the inn and head over to the stable.

They find a man currying a horse in the first stall. He looks up when they approach and asks, "Can I help you?"

"Are you Terrol, the horse trader?" asks Illan.

Nodding his head, he says, "Yes, as well as the innkeeper."

"We'd like to know where you got that horse?" he asks, pointing to where Jiron's stands in the corral outside.

"Why?" he asks, realizing something's not quite right.

"It belonged to a friend of ours and I was wondering how you came to be in possession of it?" he asks.

"Not more than an hour ago," he explains, "these men came riding up and wanted to exchange their horses for three of mine. I could tell they'd been riding hard from the haggard look of their mounts. We haggled a moment and they gave me a good price for mine, then they were off. Why?"

"Did one of them look sick?" asks Miko.

"As a matter of fact," he replies, "one of them didn't look all that good. The other two had to help him off his horse and onto the other. Is there some kind of problem?"

Illan pauses a moment and then says, "No, just curious is all."

With relief evident upon his face, Terrol says, "That's good."

Illan turns around and they head back to the inn. Once seated back around the table, he says, "They have fresh horses, we'll never catch them now."

"Why don't we get fresh ones too?" asks Miko.

"Don't have enough money," explains Illan. "Plus, he doesn't have enough fresh ones for all of us, at least none I would want."

"So what are we to do?" he asks.

"Follow as best we can," he says. "We should only be a few hours behind them by the time we get there." When the food finally comes, he says, "Eat fast, I want to be on the road in ten minutes. We're riding straight through with only brief stops."

The meal of roast fowl and tubers is filling and they're soon back on the road. Night finds them still hours away from Bearn. They ask the occasional traveler heading north about the riders ahead of them. Some remember seeing them, while others do not. From what the ones who've seen them say, they're steadily falling behind. Where they've had to have more frequent rest breaks for their tired horses the others can continue on with their fresh ones.

When the lights of Bearn begin to appear in the distance, they all breathe a sigh of relief. Tired, though not nearly as bad as their horses, they find an inn outside the walls.

"I thought we were going to be staying at the Flying Swan?" asks Miko.

Illan glances at him as he dismounts from his horse, "I've been thinking the last hour that if we're still here by tomorrow night, we've got serious problems. We need to get James and leave town fast."

Miko looks at the inn and it brings to mind another inn that James had adamantly refused to stay at because it was filthy. There're few windows and the one fellow who comes stumbling out from the front door stank to high heaven.

"You sure about this place?" he asks Illan.

"I'm not planning on sleeping here, if that's what's worrying you," he says to him. Lowering his voice, he continues as the others move closer to hear, "I just want a place where the horses can rest and be outside the gates. When we get James, there's a possibility we'll have the guards after us and I don't want the horses inside the walls if they should shut the gates."

Shorty nods his head and says, "Good idea."

"Now, you all just wait here and I'll be back in a moment," he tells them before walking to the door.

They stand there by the horses as he enters through the front door. "Think we'll get him out?" Fifer asks.

"If we have surprise on our side, then it's a good possibility," Scar says. Then to Miko he asks, "You'll be able to find the entrance to Lord Colerain's estate?"

"I think so," he says. "I remember exactly where we entered the sewers the last time. If we start there, I should have no problem."

"Good," grunts Scar.

Just then, the front door opens and Illan comes out. "Let's take the horses around back to the stables," he announces. "I arranged for two days, which should give us ample time to get James."

Taking the horses to the stables, Miko is surprised to find they're in better condition than the inn. *Suppose the horses are more important than the guests themselves.*

Finding stalls for each, Illan then tips the stableboy a silver to give them extra care and some feed. The boy begins filling feed pouches with grain as they leave the stable. Illan sees an unused lantern hanging on a peg and asks the boy if he can borrow it.

"My master would be most displeased if he were to find it missing," he replies.

Reaching into his pouch, he pulls out two silvers and hands them to the boy. "If we don't return, buy a new one," he says.

Snatching the coins, the boy nods his head and resumes feeding the horses.

Illan checks the lantern and finds it has a wick and can hear oil in the base when he shakes it. Turning back to the others, he looks to Miko and says, "Lead on."

Miko nods his head and moves out of the stables and toward the street the inn borders on.

Once out of the inn's courtyard, Miko takes the lead as he passes through the familiar streets. They don't seem quite as imposing as they once did, back before James came along. Smiling, he wonders what that gang would do now if they found him. Would they even recognize him?

At the gate, they're questioned briefly by the guards before being allowed to pass through. Miko sees the spot where he first met James that day he arrived. What stroke of fortune had made James pick him out of all those boys who were clamoring for his attention? Despite all that's happened to him, he's glad that he did.

Working through the streets they make it back to the dead end alley the boys had chased them into. The door where James had held them at bay is broken off its hinges and lies inside on the floor.

They can smell the sewers as they pass through the room to the smaller one in the back. The trapdoor covering the entrance is closed and before Miko opens it, he pauses. "There's a gang down there that doesn't take too kindly to intruders," he warns. "If they should discover us down there, it could get bad."

"Then we'll just have to be careful," Scar says.

"Don't worry," Shorty tells him, "we're probably more than they've ever encountered down there before."

"I hope so," Miko says as he bends over and pulls up the trapdoor. The smell from below hits them like a wall. Moving to the entrance, he begins to make his way down the rungs into the sewer below. Illan follows him next and finally Scar brings up the rear, closing the trapdoor after him.

Snik! Snik!

Miko sees sparks as Illan uses a flint stone to light the lantern. A glow begins to fill the tunnel as the wick catches fire. A shutter on the lamp allows him to adjust the amount of light it emits. He closes it until only a small amount escapes so as not to announce their presence to whoever may be down here.

"Which way?" he asks Miko.

"Follow me," Miko says as he takes the lead and moves down the sewer tunnel.

Chapter Six

Miko's able to remember the way fairly well, the light from Illan's lantern giving out just enough light for them to be able to see their way. He continues leading them through the sewers of Bearn until he comes to a spot where he pauses a moment.

"What?" asks Illan as he comes up to him.

"I may have gotten turned around," he admits.

"Why do you say that?" he asks.

Gesturing to the area of the sewer they're in, he replies, "There should be a body here blocking the flow, but there isn't."

"Maybe it was pushed further along during a storm, or was removed," he offers.

"Maybe," says Miko. "If you're right, then it isn't far." He continues on and sure enough, they come across a decomposing body lying up against the side of the tunnel. He glances at Illan and says, "I guess you were right."

A little further down, they arrive at a small passage leading off to the right and he continues past. Several feet beyond that they hear him sigh with relief when a crack in the wall appears in the light ahead, the one leading to the hidden rooms under Lord Colerain's estate. Stopping in front of the opening, Miko whispers, "This is it."

"You sure?" asks Fifer.

"Completely," replies Miko. "Though I remember it as being bigger."

"You've grown some since then," states Scar.

Getting a grim expression on his face, he says, "Yeah, I guess I have."

Illan comes forward and shines the lantern's light into the crack, "How far back does it go?"

"About four or five feet then it opens up onto a small storage room," he tells him. "At least that's what James thought it was. It hadn't been used in a very long time."

"Alright," he announces. "Shorty, you go in first and take a look around."

"Right," he says as he moves to the crack in the wall. Squeezing through, he finds he has plenty of room. From the sewer he can hear Scar comment with a laugh, "No way Potbelly could've fit through there!" The picture of Potbelly trying to squeeze through brings a grin to his face.

Sidestepping, he slowly reaches the other side and comes out of the other end. "I'm through!" he hollers back.

Illan hands Miko the lantern and says, "You next."

"But what about you?" he asks. "Won't you need it?"

"You'll need it more," he tells him. "Besides, I may be able to make it through."

Miko looks at him doubtfully before stepping into the crack. He's able to make it on through with little problems despite his increased size. Next goes Fifer then Scar who has the hardest time making it through. Both of them have to remove the upper half of their armor in order to make it.

When they're all through to the other room but Illan, he says, "Alright, I'm coming through." Removing his breastplate, he tries to squeeze into the crack and quickly discovers there's no way he'll be able to make it, even without his armor. "You guys will have to go ahead without me," he says when he once again stands in the sewer tunnel. "I'll meet you back at the inn where we left the horses."

"What should we do if we don't find you there?" Scar asks.

"If I'm not there when you get there, assume I'm not going to," he says. "If worse comes to worse, just get James and head back to The Ranch. If you don't show at the inn, I'll make my way back home on my own."

"Alright," replies Scar.

"Good luck," they hear his voice coming from the other side of the crack.

"You too," Fifer says, hating to leave him there alone. Turning to Miko, he says, "Lead on."

Exiting the room, they follow the corridor as it moves away from the doorway. "At the end are stairs going up," he tells them. "At the top will be a trapdoor with a barrel attached to the other side. James said it was there to better hide the entrance leading to this area."

"Makes sense," says Fifer as he follows behind Miko.

At the stairs, Scar and Fifer go up first and together are able to lift the trapdoor with ease. Everyone scrambles on through and they set the trapdoor back down.

"Doesn't look as if anyone's been here since you guys were," Shorty states as he indicates only two sets of footprints leading away from the hidden trapdoor.

"Good," Fifer says. "Maybe this way still remains secret."

"That makes this a whole lot easier," Scar adds.

Miko walks over to the door in the wooden wall and says quietly, "On the other side of this door is a hidden passage that runs within the walls of the estate. Once we're in it, we should be able to move about the estate and find where they've taken James."

"If he's even here," Fifer adds. "We're not entirely sure this is where he's being taken."

"True, but we've got to start somewhere," says Scar.

Miko closes the shutter on the lantern, plunging them into darkness and then opens the door. The hallway on the other side is completely dark, he sticks his head out and peers down both directions. Nothing but darkness.

"Come on," he says as he opens the shutter a tiny fraction to let out a small amount of light. Stepping out into the hallway, he says, "Not sure which way to go. Last time we went to the right, but I have no idea which way to go now."

"At least you got us in here," Scar says approvingly. To Fifer and Shorty, he says, "I'll take Miko here and go to the left. You guys go to the right and we'll meet back here in ten minutes.

"Alright," Fifer says as he and Shorty begin moving down to the right.

Scar takes the lantern and says, "Let me go first."

"Okay," replies Miko as he relinquishes the lantern. Behind them, he can hear Fifer mutter, "Wish we had the lantern."

Going down to the left, he follows behind Scar as he makes his way further into the house. "We need to find a crack of light that may indicate where another secret door lies," he tells him.

"But it's night," counters Scar.

"A light will indicate a room where someone is," he explains. "That's also likely to be where James is being held."

"Good thought," he says. As they move along, he periodically closes the shutter so they can better tell where light may be coming in from. When the ten minutes is about up, they spot a sliver of light coming from a crack in the wall. Excited, they move closer to it and discover a small sliding panel set into the wall.

Ever so slowly, Scar slides it open and they look through the opening into what appears to be a bedroom, an open doorway leads from the bedroom out into another room. A lit candle sits on a small table next to a bed. Scar sees night clothes for a lady laid out upon the bed. Suddenly from the outer room, a woman walks into the bedroom, naked as the day she was born. She comes to the bed and begins putting on the nightclothes.

Scar watches for a moment before sliding the panel closed. Whispering very quietly, he says, "Let's go back to the others." When he gets a nod from Miko, he leads them back.

"What did you see?" asks Miko when they've moved further away from the spy panel.

"It was a bedroom," he replies with a grin. "Nothing of interest."

"Oh."

They're the first ones back at the meeting spot and wait several anxious minutes before Fifer and Shorty return. "Anything?" asks Scar.

In the dim light of the lantern, they see Fifer shake his head, "No. We found one room with a candle burning, but no one was around."

"Us too," he says.

"Now what?" asks Shorty. "We're running out of time."

Just then, they hear footsteps approaching from the direction Shorty and Fifer had just investigated. Closing the shutter quickly, they stand there in silence as the footsteps approach. Whoever it is, they're walking in darkness so must know this way well.

Fifer is standing closest to the approaching footsteps, and when they're almost upon him he strikes out with his fist, trying to connect with the person's chin. Instead, he catches the person a glancing blow to the side of the head, causing the man to cry out in shock.

Light suddenly fills the hidden corridor as Scar throws open the shutter. The man sees them standing there, blood running down the side of his face from where Fifer had struck him. He quickly turns and begins running down the corridor away from them when Fifer tackles him and they both crash to the floor.

The man starts to call for help and Fifer knees him in the stomach, silencing his cry as the wind is knocked out of him. Before he has a chance to recover, a knife is being held to his throat and Fifer says in a quiet voice, "Make a sound and I'll cut your throat. Understand?"

Gasping, trying to get his lungs working again, the man nods. "Who are you?" Scar asks from behind Fifer.

When the man finally gets his breath back, he says, "Gregory, servant to Lord Colerain." He looks from one face to another with fear in his eyes.

"Is he here?" Fifer asks.

Shaking his head, Gregory replies, "No, he left a half hour ago."

Fifer glances to Scar and then returns his attention to Gregory and asks, "Where did he go?"

"What are you going to do?" he asks fearfully.

"Just answer the question!" Fifer says, pressing the knife more firmly against his throat.

"I don't know," he says.

"We're looking for a friend of ours who may be held captive here," Miko says to him. "Is he here?"

Gregory gives them a blank look as he replies, "No. As far as I know, there is no one here but those who work for Lord Colerain."

"Is there anyone here who would know where he went?" Scar asks.

"Your friend?" Gregory asks, confused.

"No, Lord Colerain," clarifies Scar.

"Maybe Tillon," he answers.

"Who's he?" asks Shorty. "And where can he be found?"

"He's Lord Colerain's administer," he explains. "He takes care of the estate and any business the lord has within Bearn."

"Where is he?" asks Fifer.

When he hesitates, Scar says, "If he's not going to be of help, just kill him. We don't have much time."

Eyes going wide he says quickly, "He's here. I think he's still in the office."

"Is that the room with the large picture on one wall?" asks Miko.

Surprised at him for having known that, Gregory replies, "Yes it is."

Fifer glances to Miko, who says, "That's where James and I came out of this secret passage."

Yanking Gregory to his feet, Fifer says, "Take us there."

When the man hesitates, he puts the point of his knife under his chin.

Defeated, the man says, "This way." He then turns and begins leading them down the passage. Fifer keeps a firm grip upon him and the knife hovers around his throat to prevent him from doing anything stupid.

As they approach the hidden entrance behind the large picture, light begins to be visible around the hidden door behind the picture frame.

"Miko, come here," Fifer whispers as he pauses. When Miko nears, he hands Gregory to him. "If he makes a sound, kill him."

Taking out his knife, Miko takes hold of the man and places it against his throat. "No problem," he tells him. He looks intently in Gregory's eyes, who swallows nervously when he sees the threat there.

Fifer, Shorty and Scar move over to where the hidden doorway lies. "Let's move fast before he has a chance to alert the whole house," Fifer says.

"You needn't state the obvious," replies Scar.

Flashing him a grin in the dark, Fifer asks, "Ready?"

"Yeah," Scar and Shorty both say at the same time.

Finding the latch to open it, Fifer releases it and thrusts the hidden door open as he bursts into the room. He sees a man getting up from the large desk dominating the room. Looking shocked at seeing them come out he freezes a moment in surprise. Quickly overcoming his paralysis, he makes a dash for the only door in the room.

Fifer runs to head him off when a knife flies from behind him and strikes the man in the leg. Crying out, the man falls to the floor just as Fifer reaches his side. Staring up at the tip of Fifer's sword which is scant inches from his face, the man becomes motionless as he holds his thigh in which Shorty's knife is embedded.

"Who are you?" he asks frantically, pain making his voice rasp.

To Scar, Fifer says, "Check the door."

Nodding, he goes over and opens the door a crack and looks out. Closing it, he turns back to the others and says, "Nothing."

Turning back to Tillon, Fifer says, "That's not what you should be worrying about. But whether you're going to live through this." Pausing to let that sink in, he catches a glimpse of Miko and Gregory coming out from behind the picture.

When Tillon sees Gregory with them, he gets a dark look.

Gregory takes in the look Tillon is giving him and cries out, "I didn't help them. I SWEAR!"

"Quiet!" Miko says to him.

"Now," Fifer begins, "just where might we find Lord Colerain?"

Tillon stares back at him defiantly while remaining quiet. "I see," Fifer says to him when he sees him being uncooperative. "Unfortunately, we do not have the time to play games." Motioning to Scar and Shorty, he asks, "If you wouldn't mind holding him down while I cut off a finger."

"Sure," says Shorty as he comes over and pulls his dagger out of Tillon's thigh, eliciting a cry from the injured man. Wiping it off on Tillon's clothes, he replaces it in his belt.

Scar places one knee on his chest and takes a firm hold of his right arm, holding the hand up so Fifer can get to it.

Fifer removes a dagger from the sheath on his belt and takes hold of the hand. He spreads the man's pinky finger wide and rests the side of his knife against it. Looking back down at Tillon, he says, "Now, where is Lord Colerain?"

Sweating, fear in his eyes, Tillon stares at the knife threatening his finger.

Sliding the knife slowly at the base of his pinky, Fifer produces a few drops of blood as he arcs an eyebrow in question.

"Just tell them!" Gregory implores him.

"What are you going to do to him when you find him?" Tillon asks, the pressure Scar is putting on his chest making it hard for him to breathe.

The knife backs off a fraction as Fifer replies, "A friend of ours was taken by people from Bearn and we mean to get him back. It's believed Lord Colerain is behind it. As for what we'll do, that remains to be seen, but we're not assassins. If we were, you'd be dead already."

"I don't know anything about your friend," says Tillon. "If Lord Colerain is involved with that, he never mentioned it to me."

"Where is he?" asks Fifer, taking the knife a little bit further away from the thumb.

Relaxing only slightly, Tillon says, "If he finds out I told you, my life won't be worth anything."

"I hardly think we'll have the time to talk with him, let alone tell him of your involvement," Scar adds from where he's kneeling on his chest. "Only you and Gregory over there know what's going on."

"Alright," Tillon says visibly deflating as he gives into the inevitable.

Fifer motions for Scar to get up off his chest and he pulls him up. Setting him in a chair, he has Shorty tie a cloth around his leg to stop the flow of blood. When his leg is taken care of, he says, "He's meeting someone by the name of Egger over in the abandoned linen warehouse on Strill Street. He left here about a half hour ago and didn't say when he'd be back."

Fifer glances to Miko who nods his head, "Corim, the man who was killed when James was taken, was part of the same gang as Egger."

"Good, then we're on the right track," he says. "Do you know this place?"

"Yeah," replies Miko.

Indicating Tillon and Gregory, he says, "Tie them up."

Using their knives, they cut strips from the window curtains and bind their hands and legs. "What are we to tell Lord Colerain when they find us like this?" cries out Tillon before he's gagged.

Laughing, Scar says, "Don't see how that's our problem."

After getting them completely secured, Fifer turns to Miko and says, "How far is it?"

"It's outside the walls," he explains. "In the poor section."

"Should we go back the way we came?" Shorty asks.

Shaking his head, Miko says, "No, we can make it over the estate's walls easy enough."

"Lead on then," Fifer says to him.

Going over to the window, Miko looks out for the guards patrolling the grounds. Not seeing any, he opens the window and passes through to the other side. After the others pass through, they shut the window and Miko indicates the tree he and James had used to escape from Lord Colerain's estate the previous time. "We can get over the wall by climbing that tree over there," he whispers to them.

Just then, a guard comes walking around the corner of the house. They press themselves against the side of the house and pray that they're not discovered. The guard doesn't seem very alert as he goes about his rounds. He fails to take notice of the men hiding in the shadows by the house.

When he finally walks around the other side of the house, they make a run for the tree. No cries of 'intruders' breaks the silence this night and they quickly gain the tree. With Miko in the lead, they climb up to where the limbs reach the top of the estate's wall.

Miko goes first and looks over to the street on the other side to see if anyone's around. Only two people are visible, a man and a woman walking arm in arm down the street. He indicates everyone should remain still and quiet. He watches them pass by and when the coast is clear, he quickly passes over the wall.

Once everyone is down on the street, he says, "This way." Moving out, they quickly make their way to the gates of the city.

Now in total darkness, with just a slim crack of light coming through the narrow opening from the lamp on the other side, Illan begins to move back down the sewer the way they came.

Keeping his hand along the wall, he retraces his steps, hoping to find the exact spot where they had entered. If he remembers correctly, it should be the fifth set of rungs on this side.

He steps carefully, making sure not to trip over the debris littering the sewer passage. Suddenly, from the darkness up ahead, he hears a man scream and then is abruptly cut off.

Pausing, he listens intently and tries to see through the darkness ahead but is unable to see or hear anything. Taking it slowly, aware that he may not be alone down here, he continues moving forward. Miko's words echo in his mind as he makes his way further down the tunnel:

"There's a gang down there that doesn't take too kindly to intruders," *he warned. "If they should discover us down there, it could get bad."*

His hand comes in contact with the third set of rungs since parting with the others. *Only two more to go!* He pauses every once in a while and strains to listen for any sound coming from up ahead. So far, nothing. He moves on.

Shortly after reaching the fourth set, a light begins to be seen from up ahead. Stopping, he presses himself against the slime covered side of the sewer as he waits to see what the light is going to do.

He knows that just ahead is the fifth rung, but how far he's not entirely sure. It becomes apparent the light is making its way toward him. Backing up quickly, he comes to the fourth set of rungs and quickly begins climbing them.

At the top, he finds a trap door. He pushes up on it but it doesn't budge. *It's locked!* Smashing it open would surely alert whoever is coming down the passage as to his whereabouts, not to mention whoever might be on the other side of the trapdoor. Holding still at the top of the rungs, he watches as the light continues its approach.

As it comes closer, he can see there are seven men with two women. The women have obviously just been taken off the streets above. They're crying and scared, while the men are laughing and joking among themselves.

Knowing their fate, yet being unable to do anything about it has Illan seething with impotent rage. To intervene would surely mean his death and the women would still meet the same fate.

The light comes ever closer until the group approaches his hiding place at the top of the rungs. If they were to look up, he'll be discovered.

Sweating, he holds on as the group passes beneath him and then continues past down the tunnel.

Breathing a sigh of relief, he waits until they move further away from him before returning to the floor of the sewer. Moving much faster this time, wanting nothing more than to be out of here, he hurries down the sewer passage until he finds the fifth set of rungs.

Relieved to have reached them, he climbs up and passes through the trapdoor at the top. The room is dark but looks to be the same as the one they went through before. Shutting the trapdoor, he moves out of the small room into a larger one.

Recognizing the broken door leading to the alley, he knows he found the exit he had been looking for.

Leaving the room, he passes into the alley and makes his way to the inn where their horses are waiting.

Chapter   Seven

After they passed through the outer gates into the poor section, Fifer says, "Maybe we should see if Illan's made it to the inn yet." To Miko he asks, "Is it on the way?"

"Actually, it is," he replies.

"Then let's stop there first," Scar says. "Another sword may come in handy."

"Very well," Miko says as he begins making his way through the streets toward the inn. Before they come close, a shadow disengages itself and approaches, "What happened?" it asks.

"Illan!" Fifer greets him happily. "We found out he may be in an abandoned warehouse, Miko knows where it is."

Nodding, Miko tells him, "It's not too far away."

"Alright then," Illan says. "Let's not waste any more time." He indicates Miko to lead the way and he follows right behind.

Miko takes them down a long street, the buildings bordering it becoming steadily more run down and shabby. The few people on the street don't look like the kind you would want to run across when you're alone; thugs, and others of a more disreputable nature are loitering together near one building.

The group gazes at them as they pass but make no move to waylay them.

Miko turns down another side street, moving still further away from the city walls and after another two blocks, brings them to a halt. Everyone gathers round as he says, "It's just ahead." He indicates a large building sitting a hundred feet further ahead. The only light other than the stars above is the light coming from out of its windows."

"Looks like someone's there," observes Scar. He points out a carriage with four guards standing watch beside it. "Must be Lord Colerain's."

"Yeah," replies Illan. "Let's move around to the back and see if we can get in that way."

Miko backtracks to the previous alley they had passed and takes them through to the street on the other side. Turning down the street back toward the warehouse, they approach it, this time further away from the carriage and the guards.

They quickly cross the street to the edge of the warehouse and are soon out of sight of the waiting guards. A small door stands closed two thirds of the way down.

Miko moves toward it and tries the handle. He's surprised when the handle turns and the door opens. "Thought for sure it would be locked," he whispers.

"Never question good fortune," Scar says.

"I suppose not," replies Miko as he moves to enter the warehouse. Anxious to find James, he begins to rush in when Illan places a hand on his arm and stops him. "Wait a moment," he tells him. Then to Shorty he says, "Go in and look around."

Nodding, Shorty draws one of his knives and enters the building. They wait outside for several minutes before he returns. "I didn't see him but whoever's in there is in the warehouse's office," he says. "I couldn't get close enough to see whose inside, it's on the other side of the warehouse and there're two guards standing outside the office door."

"Could you hear anything?" Illan asks.

"Muffled voices, nothing definite," he tells him.

"Four guards outside and two inside by the door," he says. "No telling how many there may be in the room with everyone else."

"What're we to do?" Miko asks him.

"Try to take out the two by the door quietly, if possible," he explains. To Shorty he asks, "Was there any other way into that room?"

Shaking his head, he replies, "Not that I saw."

"Alright then, let's go." Leading the way, Illan enters through the door and goes down a short hallway with a door on either side. The doors lead to rooms that are dark and quiet. Paying them no heed, he continues to the end of the corridor and looks out into the main storage area of the warehouse.

A large area, virtually empty but for a few scattered boxes stands between them and the office. Over to the left is the door leading out to the street, outside of which are the four guards by the carriage.

"Shorty, can you take them out with your knives?" he asks, indicating the two by the office door.

"Probably," he replies. "The first one for sure, but the second, maybe a 50-50 chance."

"That'll have to be good enough," Illan tells him. To the others he says, "Stand ready. When Shorty throws his second knife, run like hell to finish them off before they can sound the alarm."

Scar looks dubiously at the distance between them and says, "Okay, but that's a ways."

Ignoring him, Illan says to Shorty, "Ready?"

Nodding, Shorty draws two of his knifes and moves to the end of the short corridor until he's as close as he can be without being seen. Taking a couple calming breaths to center himself, he takes the first knife and after a brief pause to judge the distance, throws it toward the first guard. Before the others even realize he's thrown the first one, the second one follows.

Illan leads the charge quietly and watches as the first knife sinks into the first guard's chest. The second guard stands stunned as he watches his partner falling to the ground, at first not realizing just what had happened to him. Then the second knife strikes him off center in the chest and he falls backward into the side of the office with a thud.

Both guards fall to the ground without as much as a peep. Illan was afraid the sound of the guard hitting the side of the office would alert those within, but after a moment they realize it hadn't.

Upon reaching them, Shorty retrieves his knives, wiping them off on the clothes of the dead men before replacing them in his belt.

Illan moves to the door and places his ear against it.

"...a thief," a voice says. "I want to know who sent you."

James voice replies, "I already told you, we were there by accident and took nothing!"

Whack!

He hears James cry out as he's struck with what sounds like a leather whip or strap.

"You don't expect me to believe you do you?" asks the voice again. "You just happened, by accident, to be within a walled estate? No, I don't think so."

Whack!

Again, Illan hears James being struck.

"I'll ask you again," the voice continues. "Where is it and who sent you?"

"What is it you think I stole?" James cries out. "Is that why you've hounded me ever since that day?"

"Either tell me or you will not leave here alive!" the voice shouts at him.

"I DON'T KNOW!" screams James.

Illan glances at the others, and when they give him a nod saying they're ready, steps back from the door and raises his foot as he kicks out hard.

Wham!

Connecting with the door, the force of his kick causes it to burst inside, swinging wide and slamming hard into the wall behind it.

Illan quickly assesses the scene. James is tied to a chair in only his pants, red welts across his shoulders and back show where he's been struck repeatedly. Two other men are in the room as well, one is a well dressed man who is standing before James. The other is to the side and is holding a three foot long strap, obviously the source of the welts upon James.

The man before James has to be Lord Colerain, the quality of his clothes shows him to be a man of great wealth. He turns as the door crashes open and begins to say something when he sees them enter with their swords drawn. Pulling a knife, he moves threateningly toward James but a knife flies and strikes him in the shoulder, throwing him off balance.

The one with the strap throws it to the ground and draws his sword as he moves to put himself between the attackers and his lord. Illan strikes out and the man successfully blocks the attack but is run through by Scar who comes in beside him. Falling to the ground with Scar's sword wedged in between his ribs, he breathes a few last raged breathes before lying still. Scar then puts his foot on the dead man and yanks his sword out.

"James!" Miko cries as he enters. Coming to where he's tied to the chair, he gives him a hug.

"Easy, easy," James moans when Miko's hug brings pain from the welts.

"Sorry," he says, releasing him.

Shorty comes and cuts through the bonds with a knife as James asks, "How did you manage to find me?"

"We'll get into that later," Illan says. "Right now we've got to get out of here."

"What should we do with this guy?" Scar asks from where he's covering Lord Colerain with his sword.

They look to see him holding the wound in his shoulder where the knife had struck. Shorty comes over and retrieves his knife from where it lies on the ground next to him. Glaring at all of them, he says, "Murderers and thieves! I'll see you all executed for this!"

James gets up and stands before him, "Know this, milord. I did not take anything from you, and I am warning you to let me be!"

Lord Colerain sits up against the wall. Scar backs off slightly with his sword allowing him room to maneuver to a sitting position. "Warning me?" he asks as he glares at all of them. "How dare you!"

"Understand this," James says to him as he stares intently into his eyes. "If you should ever come against me again, I will not rest until you are destroyed, completely. I will not seek revenge against you because of what transpired here today, I simply want it to end."

Leaning closer to him, he adds in a quieter, menacing tone, "But, I cannot tolerate these continuous attacks and if I must, I will come here and raze your house to the ground. I will destroy every enterprise you have. Your very life will be forfeit!"

Lord Colerain just glowers at him from where he sits against the wall. "Tie him up and gag him," James tells the others.

As Scar and Shorty take care of it, he stands back and watches until he's secured. Then says to Illan, "Let's go home."

Fifer moves to the doorway of the office and peers out into the warehouse. He's relieved to find the guards who are standing out by the carriage haven't been alerted by the commotion within the office. "It's clear," he says.

James pauses at the doorway to glance back at Lord Colerain, and can see the hate in his eyes. He moves out of the way as Fifer and Scar bring the two dead guards into the office.

Illan indicates the hallway across the warehouse where they entered from and they begin moving in that direction. "Think what you said will stop him?" he asks James.

"I hope so, but I doubt it," he replies. "I meant what I said though, should he continue against me."

"Good," Scar says from behind him. "I don't think he realizes just what you're capable of."

"Maybe not," replies James. "And I really hope he never has to find out."

They pass down through the hallway to the door leading out into the street. Once outside, Miko takes the lead as he leads them back to the inn where their horses are waiting for them.

Moving through the dark streets, they fill him in on how they found him and what transpired at Lord Colerain's estate. He pats Miko on the back, as he praises his quick thinking and resourcefulness.

At the inn, they get their horses but realize they're one horse short for James. So he mounts behind Shorty and they move out into the night putting as much distance between themselves and Lord Colerain as they can before fatigue and exhaustion begin to take affect.

Finding a good spot off the road to make camp, they get settled in and Illan has them take turns at watch. All that is, except James, whom the others allow to sleep throughout the night. By the next morning, the effect of the drug that was in his system has completely worn off and his head is once again clear.

He tries to make his orb and when it readily appears, he immediately cancels it, confident in his ability to do magic once more.

Later that day, a little before noon, they meet up with Delia's caravan.

When Scar sees them coming into view ahead of them he kicks his horse into a gallop. With a whoop and holler he races to meet them. Potbelly sees him coming and does the same thing, much to the amusement of everyone else.

Laughing, James has Shorty break into a gallop as his group quickly catches, and then passes, where Scar and Potbelly have met in the middle. Leaving them behind, James rides up to where Delia has begun to pull the wagons off the road.

"Good to see you James," she says, greeting him with a warm smile.

"Wasn't sure for a while if I'd ever see you again," he says. Dismounting, he goes to her and gives her a hug. She returns it gingerly when she sees the welts scoring his back.

"What happened to you?" she asks, concern in her eyes.

"Well, let me tell you…" he says and then begins to relate all that had happened to him since she left. When he was done, Scar relates what happened to them and then the rescue of James. During the tale, they've set about having their midday meal and Stig is delegated the job of feeding and watering the horses. At one point, Delia produces a clean shirt from her inventory for him.

"It seems that for some reason," says James as he continues eating his rations, "Lord Colerain believes I stole something while we were there." He looks to Miko who only shakes his head. "I didn't," he says.

"I know," James assures him. "But for some reason, he thinks that."

"Do you think he'll try anything again?" asks Potbelly.

"Maybe," he replies. "Hopefully, I put worry in him about my reprisal if he does."

They finish their meal and all make ready to get underway.

"What do you plan to do now?" Delia asks him as the caravan is about ready to pull out.

"Go back and continue what I was doing," he explains. "Only be more vigilant this time."

"Good luck," she says.

"You too, lady trader," he replies with a smile.

A flick of the reins and the team begins to pull her wagon back onto the road.

Shorty and Scar have already resumed their place in the caravan while Jorry and Uther have taken their places back with James' crew.

As the two parties begin to move in opposite directions, there's a scattering of farewells until they're too far apart to continue.

Thoughts of Lord Colerain and the Empire haunt him the entire day. Will he ever be rid of people wanting to kill him? That night they find an inn to stay and since the pain from the welts have begun to diminish, he's able to get a good night's sleep.

The next morning they set out after a good breakfast of ham steaks and fried eggs. Even after allowing the horses to get a full good night's rest, they still take it easy the rest of the way back to The Ranch.

When they at last arrive back at The Ranch, they're surprised to find a teenage boy standing guard out at the end of the lane holding a spear in one hand. When he sees them coming up the lane, he takes a horn that's slung at his side and blows two quick notes.

From The Ranch, they see four horsemen come riding quickly down the lane toward the sentry. "Wonder what's going on?" questions Illan.

"I don't know," James replies.

When James and the others reach the sentry, he recognizes him as Devin, Corbin's son. He's standing there, the spear he gave him in one hand and says, "Welcome home."

"Thank you," James tells him. The four horsemen are other lads from the surrounding area. He asks, "What's all this?"

"Jiron said to tell you, 'to go up to the house and he'll explain everything'," he replies.

"Alright," he says as he turns onto the lane and heads for the house. Illan and the others follow. The town lads on the horses fall in behind at the rear and 'escort' him back to the house.

James notices another lad with a bow and a quiver of arrows slung across his back, walking the edge of the forest on the far side of the house. He glances to Illan who just shrugs, he's noticed him too.

The front door of the house opens and Jiron, Yern, Tersa and Ezra holding Arkie come out to meet them.

"Glad to see you're back safe," Jiron says with relief.

Gesturing around at all the lads, James asks, "What's all this?"

"Come on inside and I'll explain," he says. Coming over, he helps James down from his horse. He then leads him inside, with Illan following closely behind. Ezra and Tersa return within the house as well while the rest tend to the horses and see that they're settled in.

Jiron sits down in the front room, James and Illan following suit. Tersa and Ezra soon come out of the kitchen with mugs of ale for them.

"Now, just what have you been doing while I have been gone?" he asks.

"After the last attack, I felt we could use some help around here," he tells him. From the back, Roland comes out and joins them. "Actually, it was Roland's idea to ask the locals if their sons would care to help out."

"The harvest around here is about over and I knew these lads would have little to do," he explains. "Basically what they're going to do is provide security for us."

"But they're not fighters," protests James. "Against a real adversary, they'd be slaughtered."

"True," agrees Roland. "But by them being around, there will be fewer attempts like the one that succeeded in getting to you. Their mere presence will keep most of them from even happening. If something major should happen, then they will be able to give you and us warning to come to their aid."

"The whole point is not to be caught unawares again," interjects Jiron.

"Did you tell them of the danger?" James asks.

"Yes, and their families," Roland replies. "We're also paying them each two coppers a day for their services. Around here, that's a lot of money."

"How are we to pay for all that?" he asks.

"That's something I need to discuss with you later," Roland replies.

"Oh, one other thing I should mention," Jiron adds.

"What?" asks James.

He glances to Roland who grins at him and then returns his attention to James. "They stumbled across your glowing crystals out in the forest," he explains.

"And?" prompts James.

"And, they mentioned it to their families," replies Jiron. He gives James an amused smile as he continues, "It seems your reputation is growing even faster because of it."

"What are they saying about them?" he asks with trepidation.

"That you've captured evil spirits and imprisoned them," he explains.

James' jaw drops open and he exclaims, "That's absurd!" he says.

"I know, but rumor has a life of its own," he counters. "Especially when you're not here to squash it."

Sighing, James says, "I suppose so."

Illan begins laughing.

"What's so funny?" he asks him, annoyed.

"It's just the way with all things that can't be explained," he says. "Everything must be explained, one way or another. If the truth is unavailable, then good old imagination will have to do."

"Do you plan to explain it to them?" Jiron asks.

"No," he says. "I don't dare. Can't have anyone knowing what I'm doing."

Ezra pops in and announces dinner will be ready in several minutes.

Getting up, James says, "I'm going to go out and check on the crystals, then I'll be back in for dinner."

"Yes, sir," she says before returning into the kitchen.

Jiron gets up and says, "I'll come with you."

They leave through the front door and walk around the side of the house. "One lad is stationed out at the road to announce anyone coming," he explains. "He blows the horn and several riders who are waiting here spring into action and ride out to meet whoever is coming. Two notes indicate the sentry doesn't feel it's a threat, one note and everyone comes running. So far, we have had only one instance when a single note had been blown. Orry said that he blew two notes, but no one believes him. Yern made him practice blowing two notes for a whole hour."

"So Yern is in charge of our irregulars?" James asks.

"He's taken charge, yes," he replies. "I didn't want the job and he seems a natural at leading and organizing them. But now that Illan's here, he'll probably take over."

"How many do we have?" he asks.

"Eight," he answers. "They rotate in their jobs. One stays out at the lane, another three patrol the woods surrounding us. Each of those in the woods has a horn as well. Four stay by the house with horses ready to go to someone's aid at a moment's notice."

"Seems you have it well under control," he says.

"After the last two fights we've had here, it became evident we needed help," he says.

Passing by the workshop, they enter the woods and James heads toward where he left the crystals. He first goes to the area with the two that had been simply sitting and were no longer leeching from their surroundings.

He finds them still resting on the ground though they look as if they may not be in the exact same location as he left them. "I think the kids have been touching them," he tells Jiron. Glancing at him, he says, "You probably better tell them it may not be safe to do so."

"Alright," replies Jiron, "I'll do that."

He bends over and picks up the crystals, both still have a red glow within them. Both glows look to be the same intensity. One had a deeper glow than the other the last time he checked them. *Perhaps the stored power dwindles to a certain point, and then stops. Interesting.*

"What?" asks Jiron when he sees the perplexed look.

"Just that I thought one would have a darker glow than the other," he explains. He puts them into his pocket and then makes his way to the area where he put the four crystals that were going to continuously maintain a full capacity by leeching micro amounts from their surroundings.

He almost doesn't realize he's reached them until Jiron points one out to him. Smiling in satisfaction, he goes over to it and sees a soft red glow forming within its center. A careful examination of the surrounding vegetation shows only the slightest signs of withering. He's actually not entirely sure if it's a natural occurrence, or was caused by the crystal's leeching.

Checking all four of them shows the same result. Each has absorbed magic from their surroundings in such small, micro amounts that they haven't significantly affected any living thing near them. Nowhere near capacity yet because of the slow process, James is confident that given enough time, they will be able to reach and sustain full power.

Standing up from where he had been examining the last of the crystals, he gives Jiron a wide grin. "Things going okay then?" Jiron asks him.

"Couldn't be better," he says. "Let's go have dinner."

On the way back, James asks, "If all the kids are working during the day, what do you do at night?"

"They take two hour shifts," he explains. "One night on , one night off. Two are patrolling at any given time during the night. Plus, Yern and I have been taking turns keeping an eye on them, at least until they've proven themselves."

"I see," James says.

They round the workshop just as Ezra opens the back door, "I was just about to holler for you two. Time to eat."

"Thank you," James tells her.

She opens the door wide for him as he enters. Going over to the washbasin, he cleans himself up and then takes his seat at the head of the table.

Dinner is good, as always. The kids are not eating. They inform him that Ezra sends meals out to them and they eat outside. "Too many in here if I allow them to eat with us," she explains.

With all the additional mouths to feed, he's glad he made provisions for a large kitchen area in the new estate house he's having built. She may have to prepare meals for an army before too much longer. Luckily she has Tersa to help her. He may have to get even more help if the number of people here continues to rise.

After dinner, they adjourn to the front room for ale and evening conversations. Jiron and Yern remain outside with their new charges, keeping an eye on them.

James finds it hard to keep from yawning after awhile and excuses himself, saying he needs to get some sleep. Once in bed, he has a hard time falling asleep even though he's very tired. His mind continues thinking about Lord Colerain, wondering if he'll stop his relentless attempts to capture him. And just what is it that he's supposed to have stolen? Will he ever know? Eventually though, exhaustion wins out and he slips away to sleep.

Chapter   Eight

"Steady now."

A voice from outside his window wakes him up. "Hold it steady," the voice says again. Getting out of bed, he goes over to the window and sees Illan there with the eight recruits. Each of the recruits is holding a sword in their right hand at exactly a forty five degree angle. To his surprise, one of them is a girl. As he watches for a moment, one of them lets their sword droop a fraction. Illan notices and gets right in their face.

"You will hold it steady until I tell you to stop!" he yells at the lad. The recruit grits his teeth as he strains to raise the sword to bring it back into line with the others. James can see the strain and struggle in all their faces as they attempt to keep it up and in the correct position. "You are going to learn to use your sword, and by god you'll learn to use it well. The first thing you must learn is endurance." Another allows their sword to droop a fraction and he's right on top of him until it rises back in line with the others.

The girl manages to maintain the correct angle of her sword throughout the drill. The determination clear upon her face.

"In combat," Illan continues, "the first one to lose strength, the first one who can no longer swing their sword, is the first one to die!"

"Lower them," he commands.

James watches as they bring their swords down, relief evident upon their faces. Then Illan says, "Switch hands!"

"What?" one of the boys asks. "I don't use my left hand?"

Illan comes over to him and says, "What if your right arm is wounded? Are you going to tell the man trying to kill you to stop attacking because you don't fight with your left hand?" Staring straight at the boy, he yells, "Left hand, now!"

Gulping, the lad passes his sword to his left hand and joins his fellows in holding it up at a forty five degree angle.

Moving away from his window, James gets dressed and then goes out to the kitchen for breakfast. He finds Tersa and Jiron there finishing up their meal. "I see Illan has them working hard this morning," he says.

Smiling, Jiron replies, "They've been at it for over an hour now."

"May have to construct a barracks of some kind if they're going to be here permanently," says James as he sits down at the table.

Tersa gets up and brings him over a plate with eggs and tubers.

Seeing the eggs, he asks, "So Ezra has the new chickens laying already?"

"Most of them never even stopped as she was afraid of," Tersa replies, sitting back down next to her brother

"Good," James says as he takes a large bite of eggs.

"While the recruits are training, the rest of us are on patrol duty," Jiron informs him. "Illan says they must have at least three hours of practice a day, maybe more when all of us are here. They didn't really expect all this training when we first asked around for help, but it makes sense."

Nodding, James adds, "After what we've been through the last week, any and all training can only help." He eats a couple more bites in silence before continuing, "I saw a girl out there with the others."

"Oh, that's Errin," he says. "She's the daughter of some farmer on the far side of town. When her father heard we were asking for help, he brought her over to us. Said she was a hellcat and would fit right in."

"He did, did he?" James asks.

"Yeah, he did," answers Jiron with a grin. "In fact, he seemed right glad to be rid of her. But she's caused no problems and she can shoot a bow better than any of the others. You probably didn't see her yesterday because we have her mainly patrolling the woods."

"Does she want to be here?" he asks, concerned about forcing someone to do something against their will. Especially something that could endanger their lives.

"She's taken to it with great determination," Jiron tells him. "Yern says that she was wasted back on the farm and that's where she would have most likely spent her days seeing as how the Cardri army doesn't allow women recruits."

They spend the remainder of breakfast catching up on small details that have cropped up since James was gone, thankfully nothing of any real importance. Just before he's done eating, Roland comes in from the front room.

"Oh, there you are," he says to James. "I need to talk to you."

Getting up, James says to Jiron and Tersa, "If you'll excuse me."

"Of course," Jiron says.

He follows Roland as he exits the kitchen and moves toward James' room. Once inside, he closes the door and comes over to the chest and lifts the lid. What had once been a chest filled to the brim, now contains only a few coins.

"What happened?" asked James, shocked.

"What happened?" echoes Roland. "We've got construction going on and that seems to be a constant drain on our coins. New recruits for security, not to mention arming them and feeding them, plus just the maintenance of this place, it all costs. We're fast running out of money."

"I'll go down to Alexander's and get some more," he tells him.

"Do that," he says. "Also, you need to tell him that you'll allow me to withdraw funds while you're gone so I can keep this place going. I tried to while they were hunting for you, but since you hadn't made that stipulation, he wouldn't release any to me."

"Sorry, I hadn't thought of that," apologizes James. "I'll take care of that today."

"That's not the worst of it," Roland says with a worried look.

"Oh?" asks James.

"The money you have with Alexander will last awhile, but at the rate we're spending, it probably won't last more than a few months, maybe less. We have to find a source of income, one that's consistent and which we can count on."

"Do you have any suggestions?" he asks.

Shaking his head, Roland says, "No. The only one I can even think of is for you to make similar objects like your shaving knife that Delia could sell for us."

"I really don't want to do that," he says.

"I know, we've discussed it before," Roland replies. "But try to come up with something, and don't take too long about it."

"Alright," James tells him. "Anything else?"

Giving him a smile, he says, "Just that we're all glad you're back."

"So am I," agrees James.

Roland leaves him there in his room alone, shutting the door behind him as he leaves. He moves over to his window and looks out at the recruits. Jorry and Uther are demonstrating sword techniques while Illan explains them, how to achieve them and their various merits.

Errin is watching the exhibition with keen attention and is unconsciously pantomiming with her hands the motions she sees.

He leaves his room and makes his way out to his workshop. On the way, Illan sees him and waves him over. As he approaches, Uther and Jorry come to a halt and lower the wooden swords they've been using for the demonstration.

To his recruits, Illan says, "For those of you who don't know him yet, this is James, the master of The Ranch."

Eight pairs of eyes stare at him as he comes to a stop in front of them. "James," Illan continues, "these young men and lady, have all agreed to help in keeping the security and to warn of any possible attack."

"You know Devin," he says. Devin gives him a smile and a nod.

"Yeah," James replies, returning the smile, "we've met once or twice."

"The other ones are, Orry, Caleb, Errin, Jace, Nerrin, Moyil, and Terrance." He points to them one by one as he makes his way through the group.

When he's done, James nods to them all and says, "Glad to have you aboard. I just have a couple things you need to know. First of all, I do magic." Pointing over to his workshop, he continues, "Over there is my workshop and when I'm inside, don't disturb me unless it's for an emergency. It could prove disastrous. Second, I may have experiments running out in the forest. Don't touch them! Walking by them will cause no harm, but there may be some where coming into contact can be fatal."

Some of the recruits' eyes widen and their faces pale. James smiles inwardly, these must've been the ones who had moved the crystals out in the forest while he was gone. "I would be most unhappy if I had to go and tell your family you're dead because you couldn't leave well enough alone. Understand?" He gets eight nods in response. "Good!"

"Finally, I would appreciate it if you all would stop spreading rumors about me. What goes on here, I want to stay here. Anyone caught talking about anything I do to someone outside of here, will be discharged." Pausing a moment to let that sink in, he asks, "Any questions?"

Eight hands fly into the air and he says, "In case you're going to ask me about whether or not I've captured evil spirits or not, I haven't." Seven hands lower and only one remains, Errin's. "Yes?" he asks her.

"Is it true that the Empire sent a mage and fighters here to kill you?" she asks.

Nodding, he says, "Yes, that's true. I have made some enemies and they may come here seeking revenge for wrongs they may feel I have done them. But I assure you, that I never sought them out, nor did I ever instigate anything with any party. My general philosophy is live and let live, be nice to all and to help those you can."

"Anything else?" he asks. When no questions are forthcoming, he says, "Then I'll let you resume your training."

"Thank you, sir," Illan says to him.

"You're welcome," he replies and then begins moving back toward his workshop. From behind him, he hears Illan say, "Alright now! Pair up and we'll practice the techniques you've just been shown."

Glancing over his shoulder, he sees the recruits picking up the wooden swords lying beside them on the ground. Then they get up and begin pairing off. He sees Devin has managed to be paired with the dark haired Errin.

Finally back in his workshop, he closes the door and takes his seat at the workbench. They all look so young, none can be over fourteen. He fervently hopes none come to harm while they're here.

Turning back to the matters at hand, he decided to go into town after lunch to take care of his business with Alexander. What is he going to do for funds? He's not going to be able to put that off indefinitely, not from what Roland said.

He hears a wagon rolling toward the house from down the lane so he gets up and looks out the window. Ezra is returning with Miko and Fifer from town. James sighs when he sees the amount of food stacked in the back of the wagon. Expensive.

These people go through food like a horde of locust. Returning to his seat at his workbench, he decides to shelve that worry for awhile. His main concern now is the 'Fire' and getting it hidden away. In a day or two, the box he's commissioned will be completed and he will need to have everything in readiness so he can move fast to hide it for good.

He's already come up with the general idea of where to hide it. Now he just needs to figure out how to hide it from searches, especially those magical in nature. The first problem, how to supply the power for the spells needed to hide it, seems to have been solved. On the chest, he's having five crystals embedded, one on each side. Four can be responsible for the gathering of magic, the fifth needs to be able to draw on the stored power of the four to empower the spells of hiding.

What he needs to figure out now, is a way for magic to hide the 'Fire'. He finally decides to take something out into the forest and then try to locate it by magical means. All the while he'll be focusing on how the magic is locating it and try to come up with a way to counter it.

He takes one of the stools from the workshop and etches an 'X' in the top of it. Then he leaves the workshop and carries the stool about ten yards into the forest. After setting it down, he returns to the workshop and then takes out his mirror as he begins trying to locate the stool…

"Lunch!" he hears Ezra calling. Canceling the spell, he puts his mirror down in frustration. He understands better now how the magic is locating it, he just hasn't come up with a good way to actually counter it. *This is harder than I thought.*

As he gets up from the workbench, he realizes he's quite tired from all the magic he's been doing. His head aches a little and when he leaves his workshop, he has to shade his eyes to keep the sun from hurting him. Once in the kitchen, he washes up and then takes his place at the table.

"How's it going?" asks Jiron.

"Frustrating," he replies. "Just when I feel I understand, I realize that I don't."

"I'm sure you'll get it," Tersa says encouragingly. "This will just take time."

"I know," replies James. "Just not sure how much time we'll have."

"What do you mean?" she asks.

"Oh, nothing," Turning to Illan, he asks, "How's the training going?"

Shaking his head, he says, "I doubt if anyone will kill themselves with their sword, but they've just had no experience at this sort of thing. A couple are good marksmen with the bows, especially Errin, but they're hopeless with swords. Given enough time, I'm sure we can shape them up."

"It's only been a few days," Jiron says.

"True," admits Illan.

"I'm going into town today," he announces to everyone.

"I better come with you," Jiron states.

"Me, too," Miko pipes up.

"Alright," he agrees. "We'll leave right after lunch."

James is quiet during most of the meal, his mind on the problem with the spells as well as the funds needed for this place. There're lots of gadgets he could introduce into this world from his own that would turn a profit, like the steam engine or the printing press. But revolutionary ideas like those usually bring turmoil and strife among those trying to control them. This world already has enough to worry about. Maybe his trip into town will bring an idea or two.

When they finish eating, they go out to the barn and saddle their horses. On the way down the lane, James looks over to the construction site and sees they've managed to get the walls to the house up and have begun to finish the roof.

At the end of the lane, red haired Moyil stands guard, the horn hanging at his side. "Do me a favor," James says as they approach him.

"Yes, sir?" he asks.

"Don't blow the horn when we return," he tells him.

Giving him a nod, he replies, "I won't sir, promise."

"Thank you, Moyil," he says as he leaves the lane and turns onto the road.

"You know," says Jiron, "since we've gotten the extra lads, we've been bothered by fewer people."

"Good," states James. "They're a nuisance we can do without."

Once in town, they make their way to Alexander's where he arranges for Roland to be able to withdraw funds. He also withdraws another two hundred golds. Leaving Alexander's shop, he then heads over to the blacksmith to check on the status of his box.

They find Kraegan again at the anvil working on some kind of iron bar. When they pull up, one of his apprentices tells him of their arrival. Glancing over to them, he hands the iron bar to his apprentice who continues working the metal while he goes over to greet them.

"Ah, master blacksmith," James greets him.

"Here to see about your box?" he asks.

"That's right," he replies. "Just wondering if it was ready yet?"

"About two more days," he says. "All but the interior lining is completed and the man who will be doing that gets back in town this evening. Tomorrow at the earliest, but most likely the day after."

"Excellent," exclaims James. "I appreciate the update and I'll not keep you from your work any longer. Good day to you."

"Good day to you, too," Kraegan says. Then he returns to where his apprentice is working the bar.

"Are we heading back now?" asks Miko.

Shaking his head, James says, "One more stop first."

He takes them down to where Burl the chandler's shop is located and stops in front of it. As he gets down from his horse he sees Mary, Devin's mother, coming out the door carrying a bundle of goods.

"Good day, Mary," he greets her.

"Why, James," she says to him, a smile on her face. "It's so good to see you. How is Devin doing?"

"He's taking well to it," he says. "He seems to be enjoying it."

"Good," she says, almost breathing a sigh of relief. "He's always been a quiet boy and I was worried about him."

"He's doing fine," he assures her.

"He never did much care for the farm," she says. "Oh, he did well and I believe he would've made a good farmer, but his heart never was in it. I remember when you first came to us, his eyes lit up at the things you talked about. And then after you faced the demon, or whatever that was, I knew he'd never again be satisfied with farming."

"I'm sorry," he tells her.

"Oh, don't be feeling bad or anything," she tells him. "I may worry, but that's a mother's prerogative. I know a boy must find his own way, maybe this is his. At least with you, he shouldn't get into any real danger."

James glances to Jiron a second then says, "We'll try to keep him safe."

"I know you will," she says matter-of-factly. "You're a good man. But I must be off, no telling what the girls have gotten themselves into while I've been here in town."

"You take care Mary," he says.

"You too, James, it was nice seeing you," she says as she moves past him with her bundle. Down the street, he can see her horse and wagon.

Feeling better about Devin being out at The Ranch, he proceeds into the chandlery.

Burl is behind the counter and looks up as the door opens. He breaks into a smile when he sees them walk in through the door. "Welcome," he greets them.

"Good day to you Burl," James replies.

"What can I get for you today?" he asks.

"Just looking around," he tells him.

"If you need anything, just let me know," he says.

"I will," James assures him.

As they move through his shop, he looks at the goods and tries to come up with an idea, possibly a variation on what's already available. He sees bolts of cloth and other items people may want to buy, but nothing really springs to mind. Discouraged, he leaves the shop as Burl's "Come again" follows him out the door.

"Didn't find anything?" Jiron asks him.

"No," he replies. Before mounting, a thought suddenly occurs to him. He looks around at the people on the streets and a smile comes to his face. Why didn't he notice it before? Turning around, he returns to Burl's store.

Ten minutes later he leaves, Jiron and Miko laden with several bundles each.

"What do you want with all this stuff for anyway?" he asks.

"You'll see," he replies cheerfully. *Yes, you'll definitely see.*

Back at The Ranch, he has them put all the bundles in his room and then asks Tersa to join him there. Before closing his door, he asks Jiron and Miko to leave.

"Why?" Jiron asks as he's being escorted out.

"Because I like surprises," James replies, shutting the door in his face.

As he stands at the door with his ear to it, he tries to listen in to what they're saying inside.

"That's not very polite," admonishes Miko.

"Neither is shutting the door in my face," he retorts. "Shhh!" he says to Miko as he tries to hear what's being said inside. James is talking so softly that he can't make out the words.

Suddenly the door opens up and he stumbles into the room, almost colliding with his sister. "Jiron dear, be good enough to bring the bundles to my room. Thank you."

He moves aside to allow his sister to pass through the door and then he turns to see James smiling on the bed. "What?" he asks, his smile making him slightly irritated.

"Oh nothing," he tells him.

"What's going on with my sister?" he asks.

"Nothing to be worried about, I assure you," he replies. Then he nods to the bundles sitting on his bed, "Your sister is waiting for these I believe?"

Giving James an annoyed look, he picks them up and takes them to his sister's room.

"Just what are you up to?" Miko asks him from the hallway.

"Like I said, I like surprises."

From the other side of the house, James hears Tersa's door slam shut and then he sees Jiron stalking into the front room.

When he sees James looking at him, he says, "She kicked me out!"

"Why don't you take Miko and see if you can bring in some meat?" he asks.

"Alright," he says. Then to Miko he adds, "Grab that crossbow of yours and we'll see what we can do."

"Okay," he tells him as he moves to get it.

James watches him go, *I suppose I could've told him, but I do like my surprises. This won't generate a great deal of coins, but it should bring in some.*

Getting up off his bed, he heads back out to his workshop to see about resolving the hiding spell. The rest of the afternoon flies by as he works on it and by the time dinner is almost ready he thinks he may have it. But he is so tired from all he's done that he decides to wait until morning before attempting it. No sense in taking chances when he is this tired.

After dinner, Tersa lets him know she's done. While they're all in the front room relaxing, he has her bring it out.

"Finally!" exclaims Jiron.

They all wait expectantly while she goes to her room to get the big secret. When she returns, she has in her hands, an object. It's about a foot in height, with two stubby arm and two stubby legs as well as a mouth sewn on and two eyes.

"What is it?" asks Roland.

"A teddy bear," James explains.

"What's it for?" he asks.

"Tersa, give it to Arkie," he says.

Bringing it over to where Arkie sits in Ezra's lap, she holds it out to him.

They all stare as he looks at it and then tentatively reaches out and grabs hold of it. Brining it closer he looks at it and then hugs it. He finds the soft material Tersa had used for its outer shell feels quite soothing against his skin and the stuffing within is soft and comfy.

"That's what it's for," he says. "It's for kids, small kids mostly. Where I come from, every child has many of such things."

"You going to sell them?" asks Illan.

"Delia will, I'm sure," he says. "Tersa will get a copper each and the rest will go to The Ranch to help keep it going and pay for the supplies."

"You're not going to be able to charge much for them," Roland says.

"Probably not," admits James, "but it's a start." He looks to Arkie who has snuggled up with the teddy bear and has a most content look upon his face.

"Thank you," Ezra says to him.

"You're welcome," he replies. In a world where every woman can sew, there may not be a great market for this, it's true. But hopefully, initially, it will sell well. If nothing else, it will bring the children happiness.

Chapter   Nine

The next morning, Arkie is inseparable from his teddy bear. Wherever he goes, he drags it along behind. "That was a good idea," states his father as he watches him toddle across the floor. He glances up to James, who has just left his bedroom.

"He does seem to like it," he agrees. Moving into the kitchen, Ezra gives him a quick breakfast before he heads out to the forest where the stool marked with the 'X' lies. He casts the spell of concealment upon it he worked out last night before dinner.

Once it's cast, James returns to the workshop and picks up the mirror lying on his workbench. Concentrating hard, he attempts to locate it. The image settles upon the spot where he knows it to lie but sees a black spot where it should be.

That's no good! Whoever is looking will know where it is even if they can't see it! Canceling the spell he sits back and considers the problem once more. He needs to prevent someone's magic from even knowing where it is, not just being unable to see it. *Maybe warp the magic around it, so whatever spell is cast will pass it by as if it wasn't even there? Perhaps.*

Excited by the idea, he tries to come up with a way for it to work, keeping in mind that the box will need to be able to absorb magic from the surrounding area in order to sustain the spells. If the magic is unable to be drawn to the box by the crystals due to the effect of the concealing spell, then he's got a problem.

He considers the problem and then a thought comes to him. *Is there a difference between magic at large in the natural world, and magic that is being manipulated by a mage? Could there be some slight alteration that he can exploit to make this work?*

The difference could be likened to a river and a lake. A river being the force driven by a mage, and the lake being the static magic in every living thing.

So intent is he in trying to figure this out, that he doesn't even realize it's getting close to noon until Ezra sends Miko out to retrieve him for lunch. "But I've almost got it!" he exclaims to Miko.

"She said to get you or we don't eat, so get you I will," he says. "It'll wait a few minutes longer James, you need to keep up your strength."

Feeling slightly light headed from the intense concentration he's been doing all morning, he says, "You may be right. I think I could use a break."

"What do you say we go and take a bath after lunch?" he suggests. "You haven't taken one for several days, that's not like you."

Suddenly feeling quite dirty, he says, "You're on." He walks with him back to the house where Miko holds the door open for him.

With a quick, "Sorry" to everyone, he takes his seat and the meal commences. Afterward, he and Miko, along with Illan and Jiron go out to his bathing pool.

They settle in and are ten minutes into it when they hear someone approaching. He hears Miko give a short intake of breath and looks up. There stands Errin several feet away and she's looking in their direction with a smile on her face.

"Get along with you!" Illan hollers over to her from where he sits naked in the water.

Giving them all a mischievous grin, she continues with her patrol and soon disappears in the trees. They can hear her begin to whistle a merry tune.

"She's got more pluck than any of the others," Illan tells them.

"I have to agree," adds Jiron. "Definitely more dedicated and takes to instruction better than the rest."

"Women can be fierce fighters," comments James. "Why, where I come from they tell of a band of women, Amazons they're called and…" For the rest of the time they spend in the bathing pool, they argue the various merits and handicaps of having women fight. The consensus seems to be, that though they don't figure into the armies of this world, they can be good fighters.

After they get out of the bathing pool, James heads back to his workshop, resolving to figure this whole thing out before going to bed tonight.

"Need any help?" Miko asks when he sees the direction James is heading.

"No," he replies. "Not with this, anyway. Thanks."

"Alright," he says. "Might go and see if I can't bag some rabbits, Tersa asked me earlier if I could."

"Why?" he asks.

"She said their fur would be good for her teddy bears," he explains.

Nodding, James says, "They would at that." Leaving Miko behind, he makes for his workshop. *Good to see she's taking a real interest in this.*

Entering his workshop he begins working on the problem. It takes him the rest of the evening and almost the entire following day before he gets it to work. Ezra had sent Miko to fetch him for dinner but he didn't even bother answering his call, so engrossed was he. She finally relented and allowed everyone else to eat and was mollified by Miko bringing him out a large platter of food to the workshop.

When exhaustion finally takes him, he falls asleep at his workbench. In the morning when he wakes up, he's disoriented at first, not realizing where he is. Then he recognizes his workshop and resumes working.

Just before dinner of the third day, he has everything set. He's taken one of his crystals that had been charging and places it upon the stool in the woods. The crystal has been infused with spells which he believes will hide the stool from any type of magical searches.

Holding his breath, he picks up his mirror and lets the magic flow as he concentrates on finding the stool. The mirror remains normal, the image never even so much as flickers.

Excited, he puts more and more magic into it as he steps up to more intense searching. Still, the mirror remains blank. Finally, he's putting so much magic into it that his head begins to hurt and his vision starts growing hazy. Suddenly, the image in the mirror begins to shimmer and with a loud crack, the glass in the mirror shatters.

"Yeah!" he yells as he stands up quickly. But the intense use of the magic has weakened him greatly and his legs fail to hold him. Crashing to the floor he lies there, bruised but smiling. *It worked!*

The door to the workshop opens up and Fifer comes in, sword in hand. Seeing James lying on the floor and the shattered mirror on the workbench, he begins to sound the alarm.

"It's okay," James croaks from where he lies on the floor.

Pausing, Fifer comes closer to hear him better and asks, "What?"

"Don't worry," he tells him. "Everything is alright."

"You don't look alright," he says, returning his sword to its sheath.

Jiron rushes into the workshop and Fifer says, "He's okay."

Giving James a cursory glance, he asks, "Do too much again?"

James nods as Fifer helps him to his stool before the workbench. Sitting down, he rests an arm on the top to keep himself steady. "I had to," he explains. "I had to see if it would work even with everything I had working against it." Giving them a smile, he adds, "And it did!"

"Congratulations," Jiron says. "Now, let's get you inside to rest."

"No, no, no," protests James. "I'm not that bad off, just give me a moment to catch my breath. I need to go see what happened to the crystal which was hiding the stool I was searching for."

"We'll go with you," Fifer says.

"If you want," he tells them. "But I'm okay."

After resting a moment to regain some of his strength, he gets up and finds his legs are still a trifle wobbly. Jiron lends him a hand and they make their way into the forest to where the stool sits.

The crystal sitting on top of it, the one whose spells prevented him from seeing the stool in his mirror, still has a barely discernable glow within it. It would seem the effort to counter what James had been doing took almost all of its power. Had James possessed more power, then the crystal would've exhausted its internal supply and the spell would have failed.

James cancels the spells of concealment that are still active in the crystal and replaces them with the slow leech spell. He then takes it over to where the other crystals are sitting in the woods absorbing power. The other crystals have a deep crimson glow within them, indicating they have maxed out their capacity.

Leaving them there, they return to the house where Ezra has dinner almost prepared. She's setting a bowl full of steamed tubers on the table when the door opens and turns to see him being helped in through the door. Taking in his condition, she gives a small shake of her head.

He flashes her a grin as they help him through to his room where he collapses on the bed, feeling completely drained.

As they leave, he says to them, "Tell Ezra I'll not be joining you for dinner."

Jiron pauses at the door and replies, "I'll tell her. You just get some rest." He closes the door and leaves James by himself.

Too tired to even attempt to get out of his clothes, he tries to get comfortable and allows sleep to claim him.

The morning drill of the recruits again disturbs his slumber. *Going to have to ask Illan to take it somewhere else.* He just lies there listening to him instruct them in proper defensive techniques for awhile, too comfortable to get up despite having slept in his clothes.

I did it. I can now hide the Fire with the concealing spell. Feeling very good about himself, he relaxes and tries to put the rest of his cares out of his mind. The money situation continues to plague him, disturbing the inner tranquility he was trying to achieve.

With the money he has now, both here and at Alexander's, he can keep this place running for several months with no undue hardship. However, he's got to figure out a way to generate a steady, reliable source of income that will last for years. The teddy bears will bring in some, but not nearly the quantity he's figuring to need.

Finally giving into the inevitable, he swings his legs over the side and sits up on the bed. The room starts spinning and he has to remain still for several minutes before it stabilizes. A slight headache and a trace of fatigue is all that remains from the exhaustion he experienced the day before.

Holding onto the bedpost for support, he stands up and the dizziness returns, but only for a second before subsiding. He slowly changes out of the clothes he slept in and into a fresh clean set Ezra has laid out for him on his chest.

Once dressed, he opens the bedroom door and makes it out to the kitchen where she provides him with a plate with eggs and a ham steak.

"Thank you," he says. The aroma coming off the plate makes his stomach cramp and he realizes just how hungry he is.

"You shouldn't go without eating," Ezra tells him. Sitting down across from him, she begins peeling tubers for their midday meal.

Finishing the bite of ham, he replies, "I know. But I needed rest more than food last night."

"Are you done with whatever you are trying to do?" she asks.

"I think so," he says. "I shouldn't be doing anything too draining for awhile."

"Good," she says. Then she pauses in her peeling and looks at him with concern in her eyes, "I worry about you."

He gives her a reassuring smile and says, "I know you do. I'll try to be more careful."

Before he's finished with his breakfast, the sound of a wagon coming down the road can be heard. Stuffing the last of the eggs and ham in his mouth, he goes to the window and looks out to see Kraegan the blacksmith, driving a wagon toward the house. One of his apprentices sits in the back with the iron box he commissioned.

Leaving the kitchen through the backdoor, he goes out to meet him. When Kraegan brings the wagon to a stop, James says, "You're done!"

"Just got it back a short time ago," he says as he climbs down. "Thought you may be wanting it so brought it out myself."

James comes forward and shakes his hand as the apprentice brings the small iron box down from the wagon. It's little more than six inches wide and tall, should be just right for the Fire to sit securely within. He can see the crystals are embedded in the sides and top just as he requested.

"Where do you want it?" he asks.

James gestures over to his workshop and says, "In there would be fine." He then turns and leads them over to it.

"Been having trouble?" Kraegan asks.

"Why do you ask that?" he replies as he approaches the door. Opening it up, he stands back as the apprentice carries the box in through the door.

He points over to where Illan, Uther and Jorry are working with the new recruits. "That and the guard I encountered out by the road," he says.

"A little," James tells him. "People keep coming by to see what I'm doing. Annoying."

"I can understand that," he tells him.

To the apprentice, he points to the floor near his workbench and says, "Just put it down there." Once he's set it down, James tells him, "Thank you."

"Go and wait at the wagon," the blacksmith says to his apprentice.

His apprentice says, "Yes sir," and then leaves the workshop.

James comes over and inspects the box, running his fingers over the crystals. He nods his head when he finds them securely embedded, they don't even wiggle a tiny fraction. Opening the box, he feels the soft inner lining where the Fire will rest. It's just large enough for it to sit securely within. Closing the lid, he sees a small keyhole in the top near one of the sides.

"Here," Kraegan says.

Glancing over his shoulder to the blacksmith, he sees him holding out a small key. Closing the lid, he places the key within the lock and turns it. After removing the key, he tries to open the lid and finds it securely locked. Placing the key in a pocket, he stands back up and turns to the blacksmith. "Very nice work," he says.

"Is it what you wanted?" the blacksmith asks.

"Yes," replies James. "Exactly. Now let's go back to the house and I'll get you the rest of what I owe."

Leading the way, he takes him in through the house and has him wait in the kitchen.

"Would you care for anything?" Ezra asks him.

"No thank you," he tells her.

James moves into his room and opens the money chest. Taking out a sack of coins, he removes all but what he needs for Kraegan. He adds two silvers as well as the promised bonus of ten extra golds for quick delivery and then closes the chest.

Coming back out to where he's waiting, he places the sack of coins on the table and then they proceed to count them. When Kraegan sees the extra two silvers, he nods his head and puts the coins back in the sack.

"I appreciate the speed in which you managed to complete the job," he tells him.

"Always try to, if I can," he says as James leads him out the back door to where his wagon waits. The apprentice has already taken his position in the back.

Getting up in the driver's seat, Kraegan says, "Good day to you sir."

"You too, master blacksmith," replies James as Kraegan turns the wagon around and heads down the lane to the road. On his way back to his workshop, he sees Yern out practicing with his sword as he works to regain the strength he lost after being hit in the shoulder. He's moving his sword in a complex pattern as he moves around the ground. His red hair is matted against his face by the sweat his exertions are producing.

Coming over to him, James says, "How's your shoulder?"

Yern brings his workout to a stop as he turns and replies, "Much better. It doesn't hurt so much anymore and I've regained much mobility and strength."

"Good," he says. "I was wondering if you could find Fifer and meet me in the workshop?"

"Why?" he asks, rubbing the sweaty hair from out of his face.

"I have something I need you to do," he tells him.

"I think he's out by the road," he says. "I'll see if Jiron will take over for him and we'll be there in a few minutes."

"Alright," replies James.

Yern goes over to a bucket of water and washes the sweat off of his face before going to find Jiron.

James turns back and continues to the workshop. Once inside, he picks up the box and places it on his workbench, it's not nearly as heavy as he'd been anticipating. He spends several minutes in further examination of it, checking to make sure there are no cracks in any of the crystals, even to the point of sending his senses to inspect them internally.

Finding no fractures that he had been afraid would've happened during the construction process, he brings himself out of the crystals just as Yern enters the workshop with Fifer close behind.

"What did you need to see us about?" asks Fifer.

"I need you two to go on a trip," he tells them. He then fills them in on just what he wants them to do and answers their questions as best he can without revealing too much to them. Once he's sure they understand, he leads them back to the house and into his room where he opens the money chest and takes out two small bags of coins. Handing one to each, he says, "I'll be meeting you there in less than a week so don't take too long."

"We won't," Yern assures him.

They then proceed to the stable where they saddle their horses and are soon heading down the lane to the road. Pausing only a moment to speak with Jiron, they then turn and gallop down the road toward town.

Back at the workshop, James is inspecting the box further when Illan walks in. "Saw Yern and Fifer leaving," he says.

"I asked them to do me a favor," he explains. "They'll be gone for a while."

"Might I ask where and what for?" he asks.

James nods and then fills him in on what he plans on doing. When he's done, Illan asks, "Think it will work?"

"I hope so," he says. "If it doesn't, I don't know what I'll do."

"When do we leave?" he asks James.

"Day after tomorrow," he replies. "There're still a couple more things I need to do before I'm ready." He turns back to the box and resumes his inspection.

"Very well," says Illan and then turns to leave the workshop.

"Oh, one more thing," James says quickly before he leaves.

"Yes?" Illan asks as he glances back from the doorway.

"Could you find someplace else to do the morning drills?" he asks. "They keep waking me up."

Giving him a smile, he says, "Sure, no problem. Didn't realize they were bothering you."

"Thanks," says James. As Illan walks out of the workshop, he thinks how glad he is to have good reliable people with him.

He leaves the workshop and enters the forest where he collects the crystals he's had out there absorbing magic. They all look fully charged, each having a deep crimson glow. Taking them back to the workshop, he begins the final stage in preparing the box for the Fire.

There are five crystals embedded within the box. He endows three of them with the concealing spells, one which will leech magic from its surroundings, and the last one will be an extra reservoir of magic. His original idea of only having one concealing crystal had been scraped. After his experiment with the stool, he figures to need three so as not to lose too much power should it become necessary.

The way he has it set up, only one of the concealing crystals will be completely active at any given time. The other two will standby and only join the first when they detect someone searching for it. The concealing crystals will in turn continually draw their power from the reservoir crystal whose only function is to provide a single source of power for them to draw from.

The reservoir crystal will get its power from the leeching crystal which will continuously draw sufficient quantities from its surroundings to keep itself at the maximum, thereby powering all the rest as well.

James takes the crystals that have spent the last several days absorbing power and transfers their power into the leeching crystal, one at a time. As he begins the transfer of power, the crystals on the box each begin to emit a soft red glow as they slowly fill with power.

He hears a knock at his door but ignores it.

"James," Miko's voice is heard from the other side. "Lunch time."

"Can't right now," he says. "In the middle of something serious."

"But…" Miko begins.

"NOT NOW!!!" he shouts as his concentration begins to waver from the interruption. Miko must've gotten the idea for the knocking ceases and he is no longer bothered. He returns his full concentration to the matter at hand as the first of the crystals whose power is being absorbed into the box completely loses its glow.

He then directs the flow to draw the power from the next crystal with a deep crimson glow just as he hears a barely audible…**Crack!** The first crystal which he completely drained now has a hairline crack running through the middle of it. *Interesting.*

The second crystal's glow steadily diminishes until it, too, is completely drained. Shortly after he's started on the third one, again he hears a…**Crack!** Again, a hairline crack has appeared in the second drained crystal. By the time he's done with all the crystals, three of them now have hairline cracks within them, while the fourth has completely split in two.

Thinking he'll worry about the cracking of the crystals later, he turns his attention back to the box. The crystals embedded in the sides and top of the box all have a crimson glow, not quite as deep as it would be if they were fully charged.

Taking the box outside, he takes it into the forest and places it on the ground. Leaving it there with the leeching spell activated to continue charging the crystals, he returns to the workshop where he picks up the mirror he brought out earlier to replace the one he shattered the day before. Concentrating hard, he tries to find the box. But just like the last time with the stool, he's unable to get a picture. He increases the magic usage and concentration, yet still the mirror remains blank.

Backing off, he finally cancels the spell and sits back. Exhausted and tired, yet feeling good about his accomplishments, he knows the box is unlikely to be found by magical means. Unless an incredible amount of magic is used, but that doesn't seem too likely.

There's one more thing he wants to do before they go and hide it. Getting up from his stool, he sees the moonlight coming in through the window. A lit candle sits on his workbench which had been giving him enough light to work by. *Just when did I light that?* Surprised at how long he must've been at it and how engrossed he must've been to not even remember lighting a candle, he leaves the workshop and goes into the house where Ezra provides him with a plate of leftovers from dinner.

He can hear the rest of them out in the front room where Tersa is favoring them with a song. Her voice is really quite good but it makes him realize how much he misses hearing Perrilin sing. *Wonder what's happening with him and if he's gotten into any more trouble.*

When he finishes eating, he moves into the front room with the others who just give him a concerned look. "I'm okay," he assures them. "I was just in the middle of something requiring my undivided attention and time just sort of got away from me."

"Here," Tersa says to him. "Come sit by me."

He takes a seat next to her as she begins another song, this one a fast paced ditty that he's heard many times. It's one of his favorites which is probably why she's singing it now.

After another song and an improbable story of how Uther and Jorry had managed to be invited to attend a hunting party in search of a band of thieves which, according to them, they slew all by themselves, he excuses himself for bed. The rigors of the day have taken their toll and he's barely able to keep his eyes open.

Lying in bed before sleep finally takes him, he thinks about the last thing he wants to accomplish before setting out the next day. A warning system to alert him should the box be disturbed.

Chapter Ten

The following morning finds James back in the workshop right after breakfast, fully rested. True to his word, Illan takes the training session to the other side of the house, as far away from his window as possible. For the first time in days, James is able to sleep himself out.

Before him on the workbench are two of the crystals from his bag. He plans to use one for his warning system and the other as a possible defensive measure against anyone other than himself touching the box.

He infuses them with the leeching spell and takes them out to the forest where he'll leave them until tomorrow in order to have them somewhat charged before he begins infusing them with the desired spells. Spells which he still needs to figure out.

The warning system should be fairly easy. Reaching down to the bag of crystals, he pulls out two more. One will be the transmitter and the other a receiver. The transmitter crystal will be set near the box at its final destination. It will sit dormant until at such a time as someone, or something disturbs the box. Then it will send a burst of power which will come to the receiver crystal.

When the burst of power enters the receiver crystal, he'll have it set up where a dormant spell within the receiver crystal will activate. The crystal will then glow a brilliant red, alerting him that the Fire has been disturbed. Whether he'll be able to do anything about it at the time is uncertain, but at least he'll know something's going on.

He works on trying to come up with exactly the right spells for this to work. By lunchtime they're pretty much finalized, he just needs to test it. He's just imbued the crystals with the spells when someone knocks at the workshop door.

"Come in" he hollers and Ezra enters with a plate of sandwiches and a mug of ale.

"Thought you might be busy and I didn't want you missing any more meals," she tells him as she puts the food before him on the workbench.

"Thank you," he says.

Giving him a brief nod and smile, she leaves the workshop and shuts the door behind her.

Taking a sandwich in one hand, he lets each of the crystals leech some power from him until they begin emitting a very soft red glow. Canceling the leeching spells, he then sets about testing his theory.

The receiver crystal has been set with a certain signature that the transmitter will home in on when it sends out its burst of power. When the actual crystal is placed within the box's final resting place, he'll fine tune it a little bit more so the power will flow in pretty much the right direction.

Picking up the receiver crystal, he takes it into the house and places it within the money chest sitting in his room. Shutting the lid, he returns back to the workshop. He activates the transmitter crystal and feels a brief tingle as it sends most of the power it has to the receiver crystal. It still has a faint glow within it, he put limits on how much can be expelled by the crystal. Since he won't have access to the box once it's hidden, he doesn't want to run the risk of any crystal becoming completely depleted and cracking.

Leaving the workshop, he heads back to his room and opens the lid. The receiver crystal is now glowing, just as he hoped it would. He cancels the spell on the crystal and the glow disappears. Smiling with great satisfaction, he takes the crystal and leaves his room.

Back in the kitchen he asks Ezra where Miko is and she tells him he's likely out back with Roland. "Thanks," he says to her before heading out the back door in search for him. The unmistakable sound of wood being chopped reaches him as he steps outside. He sees them over in the area Roland has been using for splitting logs.

Roland puts a round section of log in front of Miko who then takes the tool they use in these parts for splitting logs and strikes it with all his might, sinking the wedge half deep within the wood. The tool has a long handle just as a regular axe but the head is fashioned differently. On one side is a six inch piece of slightly curved, wedge shaped metal and on the other is a flat block of metal that can be used as a sledge hammer.

Miko lifts the log splitter with the piece of wood still attached and then slams it back down on the stump as hard as he can. When the wood impacts with the stump, the tool sinks into the wood further, splitting it apart. Roland takes the pieces and tosses them over to a large pile of wood that's already been split into firewood. He then places another round section of log on the stump as Miko readies to swing the log splitter.

"Excuse me," he says as he approaches.

Miko swings and embeds the wedge side deep within the wood. Before lifting the wood to finish splitting it, he looks over to James and asks, "Care to lend a hand?"

"No, but I could use your help though."

He again lifts the wood and slams it down on the stump which almost completely splits the piece of wood apart. Taking the wood in his hands, he pries the two pieces apart and tosses the smaller one over to the wood pile before setting the larger piece back on the stump.

"How?" he asks as he strikes the wood again, this time splitting the piece in two with one blow.

"If you can spare him Roland, I need him to ride into town," James says.

"Sure," Roland replies as he comes over to take the log splitter from Miko. "Thanks for the help," he says to Miko.

"No problem," he says as he follows James over to the stables.

"This won't take too long," he assures him. "What I want you to do is ride into town or maybe even past it." Holding up the receiver crystal he says, "I'm going to try to have this crystal light up from a distance. As you ride, hold this in your hand. When you see light coming from within it, turn around and come on back."

Seeing the doubt in his eyes as he glances to the crystal, he adds, "It won't hurt you. You won't even feel anything."

"What do you want to do this for?" he asks as he hesitantly takes the crystal.

James almost laughs at the way he's holding it. You'd think he had a deadly snake or something in his hand. "Just an experiment is all," he explains. As much as he likes and trusts Miko, there're just some things he doesn't need to know about.

"Alright," he says. "When do you want me to leave?"

"Right now if you wouldn't mind."

"Sure, just let me get washed and I'll saddle my horse," he tells him.

"Thanks, I appreciate it," he says. "I plan on letting you ride for an hour or so before the crystal begins to glow. I want to see how well it does over a distance." He watches a moment while Miko walks over to the washbasin out by the kitchen to clean up before heading back to the workshop. *Now for the defense of the Fire.*

He mulls it over back at his workbench for several minutes before he hears Miko's horse racing down the lane. Glancing out the window, he sees him turning out of the lane and heading into town. Turning back to his work, he continues contemplating the best types of defensive spells he could put in the crystal.

The spells can't be such that they may pose a risk to the box or the Fire. They need to be more selective, but powerful enough to thwart any attempt to steal it. Of course the spells should be tailored to the environment where the Fire will be as well. Somehow incorporating the strengths of the area where it will lie to aid in its defense.

Throughout the rest of the day, he comes up with ideas and then scraps them. Nothing seems to work the way he plans. He takes a short break for dinner but then is right back to work afterward. When the light outside begins to fade, Ezra comes out and places a couple candles in his workshop to give him light to work by. So engrossed is he in what he's doing that he barely even realizes she's placed the candles until long after she's left.

Finally, exhausted and mentally fatigued, he looks at the defensive crystal sitting before him. All the spells he thinks he needs are infused within. All it'll take now is to power the crystal and then finally activate the dormant spells within once the Fire is properly hidden.

Getting up from his workbench, he stretches and begins to head to his room where he intends to crash hard. Almost to the door to the kitchen, he abruptly stops as a thought suddenly occurs to him. *Miko! I forgot all about him!*

It must be well over five hours since he sent him off to check on the receiver crystal. Rushing back to his workshop, he finds the crystal and activates it. He feels a short tingle as it sends its signal to the receiver crystal.

Feelings of guilt fill him as he leaves the workshop and heads to his room. *Poor Miko, wonder how far he'd gotten.*

The town of Osgrin had long since disappeared behind him when the crystal finally begins emitting the light James had told him about. *Finally!* Bringing his horse to a stop, he pauses as he looks at the crystal in his hand. A soft reddish glow is coming from deep within it. *Wonder how he does that?*

Putting the glowing crystal in his pack, he turns his horse around and heads back to Osgrin. *An hour, indeed. Been more like five!* Miko's starving and figures James is just going to have to wait a little bit longer. He plans on finding an inn somewhere in Osgrin where he can have a bite to eat before heading back. If he didn't think James would want to know about his crystal, he would get a room and head out in the morning.

The lights of Osgrin appear ahead of him out of the dark and when he passes the outskirts he comes across a two story building with a sign depicting a pig on a spit roasting over a fire.

A wonderfully delicious aroma is coming from the building, roast pork is what it smells like. Stopping in front, he ties his horse to one of the rails outside and makes his way through the front door.

The place is packed and the only table left to him is all the way in the back, a small table only large enough for one or two people. He signals one of the serving girls on his way over and she arrives shortly after he takes his seat.

"Welcome to the Cooked Hog" she greets him, a warm smile upon her face. "My name's Celia. Is there anything I can get for you?"

"I'd like some of whatever it is that smells so good," he tells her. "And a mug of ale, too."

"What you're smelling is our specialty, roast pig," she tells him. "It's only half a silver and comes with some vegetables as well as a half loaf of bread."

"Perfect," he says as he hands over the coins.

Taking the money, she says, "Back in a moment."

He sits back and looks out over the other patrons as he waits for his meal. Sitting around the table next to him are five men, mercenaries by the looks of them. Scattered throughout the common room are others, perhaps ten in all. Most likely they're guards from some caravan who's stopped here in Osgrin for the night.

Celia comes out of the kitchen a minute later bringing over his meal. She sets a large plate with sizzling slices of roast pork before him, their juices running all over the plate. Arrayed around the edges of the plate are several of the favorite local tubers everyone seems to like. On the table next to it, she places half loaf of bread and his mug of ale. "Is there anything else you'd be requiring?" she asks.

Taking out his knife and grabbing the fork which had been supplied, he cuts off a large slice. Shaking his head, he stuffs the pork in his mouth as she turns and walks away. The juice runs down his chin and he wipes it off with his arm. Taking the bread, he discovers it's still warm as he tears off a chunk and dips it in the juice on the plate before eating it. He never did that before until he saw James do it one time. Ever since, he's rarely eaten just plain bread.

From the table of mercenaries next to him, he hears something that makes his blood run cold. One of them just spoke in the Empire's language before the mercenary sitting next to him stops him.

"Not here," the other man whispers. "Use only their tongue!"

"Right," the first man says.

Miko glances over to them while trying to appear that he isn't. Now that he's paying closer attention to them, he can easily tell they're from the south. The slight darkening of the skin and their facial characteristics all say they're from the Empire. They're not as prominent in these men as in others he had been around when he was in the Empire and would most likely not be noticed with just a cursory look. But after what he had been through, he's not likely ever to mistake them again.

James. They must be here after James. He continues eating, more slowly this time and tries to listen to their conversations. Most of what they're saying is barely audible and he can only make out fragments of what they're saying.

"…just to the north of here…"

"…will kill him. That's what…"

"…soon. Maybe tomorrow, not sure…"

"…get it done and return home where…"

They're here to kill James! He wolfs down the rest of his meal quickly and takes the bread with him to eat on the road. Getting up from the table, he tries not to make eye contact with the men as he moves past them toward the door.

A hand grabs his arm and he almost pulls out his sword before he realizes it's Celia. She looks expectantly at him as she asks, "Wouldn't you like to stay around a little longer?"

"What?" he asks her, confused.

"I get off in an hour," she explains, giving him a look that stirs his blood. "We could go somewhere if you like."

"Sorry," he says as he removes her hand from his arm. "But I really have to be going." Turning back to the door, he leaves a very disappointed Celia behind as he exits the Cooked Hog. Untying his horse, he quickly mounts and gallops out of Osgrin. He's got to return to The Ranch and warn James!

Three and a half hours later, the lane leading to The Ranch appears before him. In the moonlight he's able to make out the recently erected guard shack next to where the lane begins. As he approaches, a shadow detaches itself from within the guard shack and suddenly, a lantern's shutter is opened, bathing him in light.

"Miko!" he hears Uther's voice exclaim as the lantern's light turns away from him. "Didn't think you would be returning till morning."

"We've got trouble," he tells him and then gives him a brief rundown of what he overheard back in Osgrin. "You'd better keep extra alert."

"I will, and thanks," he tells him.

Kicking his horse, he races down the lane to the house. Not bothering to tie his horse, he jumps down and rushes inside and slams open James' bedroom door.

Startled awake, James wakes to find Miko framed in his doorway. Figuring him to be mad about having him ride for hours, he begins to say, "Miko, glad you made it back. "Sorry about…"

Interrupting him, Miko says, "James, there're men from the Empire in Osgrin!"

Sitting up, all thoughts of having forgotten about Miko earlier vanish. "What?" he exclaims. "When?"

Roland comes to the door behind Miko and asks, "What's going on?"

"Miko says there're men from the Empire down in Osgrin," he explains to him.

"Are you sure?" Roland asks.

"Absolutely," he replies. "After the time I've spent around them, I can recognize their speech."

About this time, Illan and the others show up with their weapons. "Uther just came and told us we're about to be attacked," he says.

"Everyone quiet!" James shouts. All talking ceases as they turn their attention to James. "Now," he says to Miko, "tell us what happened?"

Miko runs through the whole story, trying not to leave out even the most insignificant detail. When he's done, he glances from one face to another and then settles on James. "What are we going to do?" he asks.

"Illan?" James asks, looking at the veteran soldier.

"Since we know the are coming, we can be prepared," he says. "That's half the battle." To Jorry he says, "Wake up the new recruits and send them out into the forest, tell them what's going on and to keep their eyes open. After that, join Uther out by the road. One by the shack, and the other a little ways away so if they come down the road, they won't see both of you."

"Right!" he says as he bolts down the hallway to the front door.

Turning to Miko, he asks, "You say there were ten of them?"

"There were five at the table next to me," he tells him. "I saw another five scattered throughout the inn."

"So ten," he says. "With the element of surprise gone, we should be able to take them on with no trouble." To Jiron he says, "Take a horse into town, if you don't find them on the road then head on into Osgrin and see if you can locate them. They probably haven't left Osgrin yet and with any luck, they'll stay the night there and not head out till morning."

"They were at the Cooked Hog," Miko tells him. "They may be staying the night there."

"Thanks," he says as he hurries out to the stable to get his horse.

"What should the rest of us do?" asks Roland.

"Nothing much else to do until we know where they are," he says. "Go back to bed."

"But how can I sleep knowing we could be attacked at any minute?"

Giving him an exasperated look, Illan turns to James and says, "You stay here, get some sleep if you can. You too Miko, you're dead on your feet now. You'll be no use in a fight if you're too tired."

"What about you?" James asks.

"I'll be outside, keeping an eye on everything," he tells him. "Don't worry about a thing, we'll know if something's about to happen before it does."

"If you say so," Miko says as he goes to try to get some sleep.

Illan hurries to get his armor on and then goes outside where James can hear him barking out orders to those patrolling the woods. Returning to his bed, he lies there thinking about the upcoming attack. At least they know what's going on first this time. Maybe it wasn't just chance that had him forgetting about Miko? Perhaps another had taken a hand in it? His mind finally calms down enough so he can fall back asleep.

He wakes early the next morning and gets out of bed fast. Leaving his room, he finds out that nothing out of the ordinary has happened during the night. Jiron hasn't returned yet and that has Illan worried.

"Should we send someone after him?" he asks Illan when he learns Jiron has yet to return.

"Can't afford to," he says. "Should they launch an attack here, we'll need everyone we have."

"You're right of course," admits James.

"I'm going to start rotating them in for some rest and food," Illan tells him as he heads out to the woods and the new recruits on patrol there.

Worry for Jiron still nags at him so he goes out to his workshop where he gets his mirror. Laying it out in front of him on his workbench, he concentrates on Jiron. As the image begins to coalesce, he sees him riding his horse hard along a road. Enlarging the view, he's still unable to determine exactly where he is. *Probably on his way here.*

Putting the mirror away, he leaves the workshop and sees Jace coming in out of the forest. Moving to intercept him, he asks, "Is Illan still out in the forest?"

Jace looks at him, brown eyes widening at being addressed by him. Pushing aside the lock of hair that's forever curling down in front of his face, he replies, "I think so."

"Thanks," he tells him then heads into the forest.

He finds Illan further in where he's talking with Errin. When he sees James coming, he says one last thing to Errin before she heads off into the forest. He then turns and walks toward James.

"Jiron's on the road, riding hard," James informs him. "Couldn't determine exactly where though." As Illan comes abreast of him, James turns and walks with him out of the forest. "I'm thinking he's coming back here to give us word about the mercenaries."

"Most likely," Illan agrees. "We'll know soon enough. When he returns, we'll have a better idea what's going on and then we'll know what we're going to need to do."

As they exit the forest, they see Ezra standing out by the kitchen door. When she sees them, she signals for them that breakfast is ready. James gives her a nod and heads over there.

"I'll be along in a few minutes," Illan tells him. "I just need to find Moyil and then I'll join you."

"Alright," James says. Illan angles away from him to proceed around the house as they draw near. The sound of hammering can be heard from the construction sight as the builders resume working on the house. He wonders if it's a good idea to have them here with what may be coming their way. Perhaps it's better to give the appearance of normalcy so the attackers won't think they're ready for them.

Entering the kitchen, he finds Jace, Orry and Devin seated at the table, first time any of the recruits have sat there. They're all waiting for him, Ezra must've already instructed them in the proper etiquette when eating at the master's table. Once he's seated and has begun to spoon eggs on his plate, they begin grabbing serving bowls and platters.

"Seen anything?" he asks them after swallowing his first bite.

"Nothing," replies Devin.

"What's going on exactly?" Orry asks.

Glancing at him, James replies, "I've made some enemies and we've gotten word some may be on their way to try to kill me."

"That's dumb," Jace exclaims.

"Why is that dumb?" James asks him.

"Trying to kill a mage, I mean," he says. "One spell from you and they're toast." The other recruits nod their heads at what he said.

"It's not as easy as that," he explains to them. Just then, the door opens up and Illan walks in. "Did you find him?" he asks him.

Illan takes his seat and while he begins filling his plate, he replies, "Yes I did, everyone's accounted for." He glances around the table and when he doesn't see Miko, asks, "Is he still sleeping?

James nods his head. "He was up pretty late last night."

Just then, they hear the sound of a horse racing down the lane toward the house. "Jiron!" he exclaims as he comes to his feet and practically runs through the front room to the door. He hurries outside as Jiron brings his horse to a stop.

Dismounting, Jiron comes over to him and says, "I found them."

"Where?" Illan asks from the doorway before James can get the words out.

"They spent the night in Osgrin and headed out this morning," he tells them. "It didn't seem that they were in all that much of a hurry, though. When I saw they were taking the road to Trendle, I came back as fast as I could."

"How many were there?"

James motions him to come inside as he answers. "Twenty one. The party that left Osgrin had eighteen men at arms as well as two wagons. Couldn't tell what was in the wagons, but one was being driven by a single man, the other had a man and a woman."

"A woman?" Illan asks as they return to the kitchen where they all take their seats at the table.

"Yeah," Jiron replies as he begins helping himself to the food. "She didn't have the look of a fighter."

"Maybe a mage?" James asks.

Shrugging, Jiron says, "Maybe."

"I want you and young Devin here to go back and find them," Illan tells Jiron. "If anything develops that we need to know about, send Devin back."

Devin gets an excited look in his eye when he hears that he'll be going with Jiron on a 'mission'.

Turning to James, Illan continues, "I think we should stand everyone down seeing as how an attack is not imminent."

"You know best," he says.

The rest of the meal goes fairly quickly, Jiron hurries and eats so he can return to find them. As soon as Devin is done, Illan has him go out to the stable and get two horses saddled and ready for when Jiron is finished eating.

After Devin's left, James says to Jiron, "You be careful."

"I will," he assures him. "They've probably not come too far along by now, the wagons are going to slow them down. They're most likely going to reach Trendle sometime before nightfall." Scooping up the last of the food from his plate, he stands up and makes to leave.

"Good luck," Illan says to him.

"Thanks," he replies and then goes outside to where Devin sits on his horse waiting for him. Once mounted, they quickly ride down the lane to the road where they break into a gallop as they head toward the advancing party.

Chapter   Eleven

They caught up with the men and wagons an hour past Trendle. Jiron and Devin continued at a gallop past the mercenaries. When they were far enough beyond them that they were no longer visible, they turned around and followed them at a discreet distance, keeping them just within visual range.

"What are we going to do?" Devin asks.

"Follow them and see what they plan to do," he replies. "When we know, I'll have you ride back and alert the others as to what's going on."

Devin nods his head, excited at the prospect of being the one to bring back word.

The group continues traveling at a steady pace, reaching Trendle several hours past noon. Without pausing they make their way through town and continue on past, crossing over the river Kelewan. At a clearing a mile past the river they pull off the road and appear to be settling in for the night.

"Don't you think it's too early for travelers to stop for the night?" asks Devin.

Glancing at him, Jiron nods and says, "Yes, unless you've reached your destination." He looks at the group settling into the clearing, his unease growing. Once Jiron has determined that they definitely plan to camp there, he sends Devin back to The Ranch with word. Leaving his horse a good ways away, he moves closer and finds a concealed spot from which to keep an eye on them.

The clearing they're in is one in which Delia has used on occasion with her caravan whenever she stopped for a visit. Lately though, she's just gone to The Ranch itself with her wagons.

Tents begin to spring up and two campfires are made, one near the wagons and the tents the civilians are using. The other is further away where most of the mercenaries congregate.

After watching the clearing from the cover of the trees for several minutes, he sees Ceryn, the forest warden in these parts, walk out of the trees on the other side of the camp. Jiron immediately gets ready for trouble but none is forthcoming. The civilians hail him as he enters their camp and waves for him to come over and sit by their fire. *Strange.*

Ceryn shakes his head, and says something to them, but Jiron's just too far away from them to be able to hear what's being said. The woman suddenly stands up and gives Ceryn a hug and a peck on the cheek. A few more words are exchanged before Ceryn begins leaving the camp as he makes for the road.

Jiron quietly makes his way through the trees as he moves to intercept Ceryn. Before he even reaches the edge of the treeline, Ceryn says, "You can come out now, Jiron."

Surprised that he even knew he was there, Jiron comes the rest of the way out of the trees and joins him on the road.

"So, what brings you out spying?" Ceryn asks as he gestures behind them to the camp. He resumes walking down the road away from the clearing with Jiron right beside him.

"We were told they meant to come and kill James," he explains.

Stopping dead in his tracks, Ceryn turns his full attention on him and asks, "Who told you that?" The expression on his face is one of slightly controlled anger.

"Miko," he replies.

"Miko?" Ceryn asks. "James' friend?"

"That's' the one."

"Now why would he think that?" he asks.

Jiron then relates all Miko had told him of the conversations that he'd overheard back in Osgrin. When he's done, Ceryn begins breaking out in laughter as he again continues down the road.

"What's so funny?" Jiron asks as he moves to stay with him.

"That war party you think is encamped back in that clearing is in fact a betrothal one," he says, smiling.

"What?" Jiron asks, now quite confused.

"They're escorting the young lady to Wurt where she'll be married to the son of an old friend." He holds up his hand to stop any more questions as he continues. "She's sort of my niece in a way, though not blood related or anything like that," he explains. "This union has been arranged for many years."

"But they're from the Empire!" he states.

"True, but that doesn't make them evil," he says. "They're just people."

Jiron walks for a minute in silence as he assimilates all this information. Then he starts to laugh, "Wait until I tell them about this."

"I'd love to go with you to see their reaction," Ceryn tells him, "but I'm already overdue at the mayor's home. I just had to swing by here to say hello and give her my best wishes."

Still chuckling, Jiron says, "Thanks for telling me about them." With a wave, he leaves Ceryn on the road as he makes his way through the forest back to where his horse is waiting. *Wait until James and Illan hear about this. They'll probably skin Miko alive!* Then he starts laughing all over again.

Upon reaching his horse, he mounts up and heads back to The Ranch. He comes out of the forest and makes his way onto the road, then heads back to Trendle. Once over the bridge, he takes a short cut around the town along a little known way through the forest, finally coming out near James' workshop.

The place seems surprisingly quiet, he looks around and doesn't see anyone. Not wanting to take the time to unsaddle his horse, he ties it near the back door to the kitchen and goes in.

"Wait until you guys hear…" he stops what he was saying when he sees Ezra and Roland sitting at the table with little Arkie playing with the teddy bear on the floor beside them. "Where is everyone?" he asks.

"Went to find you," Roland says.

Tersa comes in from the other room when she hears his voice. "Thank goodness you're okay!" she cries as she runs over and gives him a hug.

He disengages from her and asks, "What's going on?"

"When Devin came back and told everyone where the men from the Empire had camped," Roland explains, "Illan took everyone and headed over to deal with it. He felt it prudent not to wait for the attack, but to fight while we have the advantage of surprise."

Suddenly overcome with dread, he asks, "They're going to attack them?" When he sees everyone's nod, he swears and then runs out the door to his horse.

"What's wrong?" Tersa cries out as she follows him out.

"They're not here to attack!" he exclaims. "They're on their way to a wedding. The woman is the bride."

"Oh, no!" she cries out.

Jiron vaults onto his horse and races down the lane to the road. This way is much faster at a gallop than the short cut would've been. At the end of the lane, the ever present guard isn't there either. Illan must've taken everyone with him. *Don't attack!* he cries out silently. Then, from over where the clearing lies, he can see bright bursts of light exploding in the air.

James! No!

As they ride through town, James asks Illan for the third time, "Are you sure we need to attack them?" It took some convincing from Illan for him to even agree to this venture.

"If they are here to kill you, then attacking with the element of surprise is our best bet," he explains. In fact, he's explained this more than once since leaving The Ranch for the clearing. Everyone knows of James' reluctance to kill, but there are times when it's necessary.

They ride through the center of town, the locals stop what they're doing when they see who it is. Some of them call out to their new recruits who just sit taller in the saddle, basking in the notoriety of just being in the same company as 'the mage'.

James hates the stares, but knows there's not a whole lot he can do about it. When word gets out about this escapade, there'll probably be even more in the way of gawkers coming by The Ranch.

Once past the town, they increase their speed and ride quickly until they're about a half mile away from the clearing where Devin told them the party was encamped. Illan has them stop and walk their horses a ways into the trees before tying their reins to the branches.

"This way no one will come along and 'borrow' our horses while we're dealing with the assassins," Illan explains.

They move back to the edge of the trees by the road and follow it toward the clearing. When they begin to see their campfires ahead of them, Illan has them move into the trees. Taking it slowly and quietly, they make their way through the trees toward the clearing. As the clearing begins to be visible through the trees, he has everyone stay where they are while he and James approach closer. Getting within several yards of where the trees end at the clearing, they stop and crouch down as they watch those within the clearing.

The mercenaries are congregating around the far campfire while the two men and the lady stay by the one near the wagons. They can hear them talking in the speech of the Empire, but neither James nor Illan understand it.

"They don't look like they're preparing an assault," James whispers.

"No, they don't," Illan says.

One of the men begins preparing their dinner as he brings out a large cook pot and fills it with water from a barrel in the back of one of their wagons. Setting it on the fire, he returns to the wagon where he obtained the water and removes a large, bulging sack. Removing his knife, he opens the sack and pulls out a large tuber and then begins slicing it into the cook pot.

Over at the other campfire, similar preparations are in progress as well. Most of them actually have their armor removed and stacked on the other wagon.

"Do you think Miko could have been mistaken?" James asks Illan.

"I don't know," he says. "I still don't like the fact they're from the Empire."

"Cardri's not at war with them," James reminds him. "They could just be traveling through, or even merchants."

Illan doesn't look convinced. They sit there a couple more minutes observing them when from behind them, they hear a twig snap as Miko approaches.

James glances to the clearing, fearful they may have heard. With relief, he doesn't see any indication that they heard.

"Well?" Miko asks as he joins them.

"Are you sure they were coming after James?" Illan asks him.

"Yes, I am," he replies. "Why?"

James gestures to the clearing and says, "Just look at them." When Miko looks, he continues, "They're not acting as if they plan to attack. I also haven't felt anything that would lead me to believe one of them is a mage."

"Did they actually mention James by name?" asks Illan.

Miko thinks back and then shakes his head, "No, not by name. But they said they were going to kill someone to the north. Who else could it be?"

"I don't think they plan anything here," James says, glancing to Illan.

"I tend to agree," Illan says, giving Miko an annoyed look. "But to be on the safe side, we should leave someone here to keep an eye on them just in case."

Suddenly from the campsite, the woman calls out and one of the mercenaries gets up and goes over to a wagon. He reaches in and picks up a small wooden chest and begins carrying it over to her.

All talking ceases as James and the other two watch what's going on.

The guard's foot suddenly snags on an exposed root, causing him to lose his balance and the chest flies out of his hands. The woman gasps as the chest hits the ground, the lid flying open. A dozen small tubes spill out, three of which land in the fire.

"No!" she cries as she dives away from the fire.

James gets to his feet, his eyes riveted on the tubes in the fires. Suddenly, one of them explodes in a green flash sending embers flying in all directions. Another one goes off and they watch as a trail of sparks rises into the sky and then explodes in a brilliant yellow ball.

"Magic!" he hears someone behind him exclaim.

The trees near the edge of the camp begin to catch fire from the embers thrown by the first explosion. When the third tube explodes, it sends a yellowish-orange spray of sparks toward one of their wagons. Its canvas cover begins smoking as many pinpoint fires spring to life.

The woman scrambles back to the spilled tubes and hastily replaces them in the chest while her guards rush to remove the now burning canvas from the wagon.

Without even thinking, James runs toward the edge of the clearing and begins stomping upon the growing flames, trying to put them out before they spread. Illan and the others join him as they use feet, shirts, and water bottles to slow the fire.

The guards succeed in getting the canvas off the wagon just as it bursts into flames. Throwing it to the side, it lands in the middle of the clearing where it's quickly consumed.

Smoke fills the clearing from the fires that are beginning to be brought under control. The woman closes the lid on the chest after the remaining tubes have been placed inside and that's when she notices James' group at the edge of the clearing stomping on the remnants of the fire.

She calls out and her guards, some with swords drawn, place themselves between her and James.

"James," Miko says next to him, bringing his attention to the clearing and the gathered guards.

A quick glance shows the remaining flames are being dealt with effectively by the others. Stepping out from the half burnt bushes he takes three steps within the clearing and stops. "Hello," he says.

"What are you doing here?" she asks from behind her guards. The guards who haven't drawn their swords all have their hands on the pommels in the event James' group proves hostile.

"Just happened by and heard the explosions," he tells her.

"Indeed," she says. Her eyes flicker to the others as they come to join him having put the rest of the fires out. She looks to be about ready to say something when she turns her head toward the sound of a fast approaching horse.

James is surprised to see Jiron riding hard to the clearing. "They're not here to attack!!" he cries out as he enters the clearing. Coming to a stop between them, he says, "They're on their way to a wedding!" He suddenly pauses and takes in the scene; burnt canvas, smoldering brush around the edge of the clearing, and a wagon which looks to have been charred slightly.

The eyes of the woman grow cold when she hears that. "Attack?" she exclaims. "Is this why you are here? You think us assassins?" Her eyes bore into James and a growling can be heard coming from her guards.

"At first, yes," he admits. "We'd heard rumors that you were from the Empire and grew concerned. When we came here and observed you, we realized the rumors were false and were about to leave when your fire exploded."

She stares at him a moment as she contemplates his words, then she turns her attention to Jiron and asks, "How is it you know we are going to a wedding?"

Jiron looks somewhat sheepish under her glare and replies, "I ran into Ceryn and he told me."

"Are you friends of Ceryn's?" she asks.

"Yes," replies James.

Her expression softens slightly, then looks back to James, "Why did you think us here to attack you?"

"We were at the fall of the City of Light where a friend of ours had been taken captive," he explains. "We freed him, but killed some slavers doing it. Hearing those from the Empire were here, we feared your presence might indicate a reprisal."

Nodding her head, she says, "I see." A few brief words in their language to the guards and they relax. All but two return to where they were, the remaining two staying nearby.

"That was quite an explosion," he comments. "By the way, my name is James and these men are my guards." He gives her a slight bow.

"I am Allana," she says. "These were meant for my wedding. I'm glad they all weren't destroyed."

"What are they?" Miko asks, indicating the chest at her feet.

"They are a gift from my uncle," she tells him. "They are used in celebrations by the Illuminator's Guild. Though I am not one of them, my uncle is a high ranking member and allowed me these for my wedding. Since it is going to be here in Cardri, there's little chance of word getting out."

"I'm sorry we intruded upon you," James tells her. "We shall go now, and best wishes to you and your groom." He indicates for Illan to get the others moving.

"Thank you," she says.

Leaving the clearing behind, they make their way back to where their horses are waiting. "The Illuminator's Guild must have powerful magic," comments Miko.

"Not really," replies James. "What those tubes were would've been called 'fireworks' back where I come from."

"Fireworks?" asks Jiron.

"That's right," he explains. "It's just something relatively harmless that people use to make bright lights and noise."

"Oh," says Miko. "Do you think we could get some?"

Turning to Illan, James asks, "Ever heard of anything like that before around here?"

Shaking his head he says, "No, not around here. Though I have heard talk of something like that before, but I didn't really believe it."

After reaching their horses and are riding back to The Ranch, James considers the ramifications of what he just learned. *The Chinese used fireworks for a thousand years before the military aspects of gunpowder were realized. Should the same thing happen here, it would turn this world upside down.*

Deciding not to open that particular Pandora's Box, he keeps all this speculating to himself. An idea is one of the most powerful instruments ever devised. For once an idea gets out, there's no going back.

By the time they get back to The Ranch, everyone is beginning to give Miko a hard time. James listens to it for awhile before putting a stop to it. "Leave him alone, guys. He made a mistake, but for the right reasons."

Miko gives him a look of gratitude as the others quit pestering him. Once they're back at The Ranch, James says to Illan, "We're leaving in the morning. See that everyone is ready to go."

"Will do," he assures him.

The front door to the house opens up and Roland and the girls come out. "What happened?"

"False alarm," he tells them. "Seems Miko was mistaken, they were on their way to a wedding."

"A wedding?" Roland asks incredulously. Laughing, he asks, "How could he make that kind of mistake?"

Shrugging, James says, "He feels bad enough about it as it is, try not to bother him too much."

"Alright," agrees Roland.

"I'll be out at the workshop for the rest of the day," he tells him. "I'm taking Illan and the others somewhere for probably about a week. The new recruits will be staying here with you."

"Very well," he says as James turns and heads over to the workshop. Sitting on his desk is the crystal he'd infused with the defensive spells the day before. He still has the two crystals out in the woods charging, one from which he will transfer the stored power it contains into that of his defensive crystal.

He looks down to the sack that had once been bulging with crystals sitting on the floor by the workbench. Reaching down, he picks it up and only finds two crystals remaining. Taking the larger of the two, he infuses it with the receiver crystal spells and then places it on a shelf over against the wall. *Have to get this set up better so it will be more visible and less likely to get lost or broken.*

The box to hold the Fire is prepared with all the spells it will require. The defensive and warning crystals are out in the forest charging, he just needs to transfer the power of one and infuse the other with its spells. The receiver crystal is ready and positioned. All that's left is to dig up the Fire tonight and place it in the box before they set out in the morning.

Leaving the workshop, he sees Miko and Roland over by the woodpile chopping more firewood. Suddenly, a scream rips through the air as he sees Uther and Jorry come running toward Miko.

"We're under attack!" cries Uther.

"Oh, help! Heeeeeeeelllllllp!" wails Jorry.

James sees Illan grinning at their antics, but Miko has a grim look upon his face. He knows it's him their making fun of. Doing his best not to smile, for they are pretty darn funny, he moves away from the workshop and goes over to them.

"Stop that right now!" he yells at them.

They come to a stop and look his way as the grins begin to fade from their faces.

Coming closer toward them, he continues, "I asked you not to bother him about this and I meant it."

"We were just having a little fun, is all," Uther explains.

Illan begins making his way over to where James is confronting Jorry and Uther.

"I don't care if you were," he says. "It will end, now. Do you understand?"

They both nod their heads.

James glances to Illan as he joins the others and adds, "We are a team, all of us here. We've been through too much together to treat each other in this manner. I will not tolerate it in my presence or on my property."

"Yes sir," says a chastised Jorry.

"We didn't mean anything by it," Uther says. Then he looks over to where Miko is standing with the axe in his hand and says, "Sorry Miko."

Miko just nods then goes back to chopping wood. His next strike is a bit harder than it had been before. James can see him working his anger at being the brunt of a joke out on the wood.

"Now, don't you gentlemen have something better to do?" he asks them.

"Yes they do," Illan tells him. "Follow me please." Jorry and Uther fall in behind Illan as he leads them off to the barn. James watches them for a moment and when they reach the barn door, Illan has them pick up a rake and shovel.

Illan glances back at him and gives him a wink as Uther and Jorry proceed to muck out the barn. James glances over to Miko who's noticed where they've been put to work and he sees a slight smile begin on his face. The next chop of the axe sounds more normal as his anger begins to subside.

Heading back to the house he's told by Ezra that dinner is still an hour away. Not having anything pressing to do, he sits in his favorite chair by the window in the front room as he relaxes until it's ready.

Tersa comes out of her room shortly after he got himself settled and brings over a small brown object. It's a rabbit shaped stuffed animal. "I thought perhaps children would enjoy something like this as well," she tells him as she offers it to him. "Miko caught some rabbits today, and after their skins are ready, I'll try using their fur as well."

Looking it over, he nods and hands it back to her. "Looks like you've really taken to this whole project."

She sits in a chair next to his and replies, "It gives me something to do and if it helps out, then all the better. I like sewing, and making these lets me feel useful."

"I know what you mean," he says. "You'd make a good seamstress."

"You think so?" she asks.

"Of course," he assures her. "The stitching you've done on the teddy bears I've seen thus far is quite excellent."

"Thank you," she says, blushing slightly. Getting up, she adds, "I just wanted to show you what I've been doing." When she sees his nod, she returns back to her room.

James once more gazes out the window as he lets his mind wander. He'll be glad when the Fire is hidden, that's the major worry on his mind. After that, find someway to sneak into Saragon to look for clues as to the whereabouts of a priesthood that disappeared centuries ago. He really doubts if there is anything left that would tell him anything, but what else does he have to go on? *How long have I been here and I still know very little about why I'm here?* At times he wonders if he'll ever go home again.

Chapter Twelve

He moves through the house in the dark of night, light from the moon overhead filters in through the windows giving everything a surreal feel. Snores can be heard throughout from those asleep in the various rooms. He walks softly so as not to risk waking anyone as he makes his way to the kitchen. Moving extra cautiously through the darkened room, he maneuvers around obstacles by touch until his hand comes into contact with the unmistakable shape of the door handle.

Turning the handle, he opens the door slowly to prevent it from making any noise that might disturb those asleep in the house. Slipping outside, he quietly closes the door behind him. He pauses there a moment when he catches movement from the corner of his eye. The night's sentry is moving out in the dark, going about his patrol. Which one of the newcomers is hard to tell.

Whoever is walking guard duty this evening fails to notice him as they continue on by. He holds still, barely daring to breathe until he sees the sentry pass around the far side of the workshop. Moving quickly, he makes his way to the barn where he locates a shovel. Pausing a moment to make sure the guard hasn't returned yet, he quickly crosses over to the chicken coop.

The chickens are all roosting inside the coop area, the outer pen is empty. Lifting the latch on the door leading to the pen, he opens it and slips inside where he secures the latch closed.

Moving to the center of the pen, his foot accidentally kicks over a water trough and he can hear some of the chickens within the coop begin to rouse from the clatter it made. He holds still and quiet until the chickens once more settle down and is about to start digging when he sees the guard's silhouette approaching.

He waits until the guard once more passes out of sight and then places the end of the shovel to the ground. Pressing down firmly with his foot, he digs out a chunk of dirt. He places it next to the hole and then scoops four more times before the guard again can be seen approaching. Remaining still, he watches as the guard passes by no more than a dozen yards away. After the guard again passes out of sight, he continues digging. The pile of dirt next to the hole steadily grows as he digs deeper until his shovel finally hits something hard.

Widening the hole a little more, he reaches down with his hand and can feel the top of the box buried there. Using the shovel as a pry bar, he removes the box from the ground. It's a small wooden box, not very big. After pausing one more time to wait for the guard to pass by, he then fills in the hole with the pile of dirt. He places the watering trough he had knocked over earlier on top of the recently excavated ground to camouflage what he's just done. He then picks up the box.

With the box tucked under his arm, he leaves the chicken coop and makes his way back to the side of the house just as the guard again comes into view. Pressing himself to the side of the house, he remains hidden in the shadows until the guard is no longer in sight.

Moving to the edge of the house, he glances around the corner and watches as the guard continues on his rounds. When the guard passes around the far corner of the house, he runs quickly over to the workshop where he opens the door and enters. Shutting the door behind him, he glances out of the window. The shadows cast by the moonlight are all that can be seen outside. Sighing with relief, he moves over to the workbench where he sets the box.

James is relieved no one saw him remove the Fire from its hiding place. The less the others know of what he's doing and what he's planning, the less they can inadvertently tell somebody else. It still bothers him that he needs help in the hiding of the Fire and that those that help him will know exactly where it is. But unless he wants to be like the Pharaohs of Egypt who had everyone killed that had a hand in the building of their tombs and knew its secrets, he'll just have to live with it.

Picking the iron box the blacksmith delivered earlier off the floor, he sets it on the workbench next to the one containing the Fire. Opening the iron box, he widens the space in the interior cushioning with his hands to receive the Fire. He then takes a small pry bar and removes the lid to the wooden box containing the Fire. As the lid comes off, he can see a barely perceptible glow coming from within. Just looking at it makes his skin crawl. He'll be glad when this thing is secured away forever.

Remembering the warning the shade of the long dead priest of Morcyth had given him, he takes two small sticks of wood he left lying on his workbench earlier. Taking one in each hand, he places them against the sides of the Fire and slowly draws it out of the box. Holding firmly and carefully, he transfers the Fire over to the iron box and settles it within the protective covering. Once it's in, he uses a stick to fold over the covering until the glow can no longer be seen.

Closing the lid, he locks it with the key. Picking up the iron box, he takes it over to the side of his workshop and places it under a larger box to wait until morning when he will finalize all the necessary spells before they leave.

Going back to the window, he looks out and waits until he sees the guard again move around the far side of the house. He quickly leaves his workshop and runs to the kitchen door. Slipping in quietly, he shuts the door and begins to return to his room when he sees a shadowy form, framed in the doorway leading further into the house.

"James?" he hears Miko's voice asks in a whisper.

"Yes," replies James. "It's me. What are you doing up?"

"Something woke me," he says. "It felt like I needed to do something."

That's when James notices he has his sword in his hand. "What?" he asks. "What did you need to do?"

"I don't know anymore," he says. "It's gone."

Coming forward, James lays a hand on his shoulder and says, "Then let's go back to bed."

"Alright," agrees Miko as he turns around and allows James to escort him back to where he sleeps.

When he's finally back to bed, James goes and wakes up Jiron. Not saying anything, he indicates for Jiron to follow him back to his room.

"What's going on?" he asks when James' bedroom door closes behind them.

James fills him in on what he's just done. Of everyone there, he's the one he trusts with this information the most. Then he tells of finding Miko, how he was acting and what he said. At the mention of the sword in his hand, Jiron says, "Was it the Fire that called him?"

"I can't think of what else it could've been," he replies. "I don't think it would be wise to take him with us to hide it."

Shaking his head, Jiron says, "You may be right. He won't like being left behind though."

"I know, but what else can we do?" he states. "Also, I'd like you to keep an eye on him tonight, just in case."

"Alright," agrees Jiron. "I'll do that."

"Good. We're going to leave first thing in the morning after breakfast. I still have a couple things to do in the morning, but they shouldn't take me too long."

"See you then," he says as he opens the bedroom door and slips out.

Once the door shuts behind him, James lies down on his bed and thinks about Miko. *It must still have some control over him. The sooner I get rid of it the better.*

When the sky first begins lightning with the coming of the day, James gets up and finds Jiron still sitting up in the front room looking tired. "Anything?" he asks.

Shaking his head, he says, "He stayed asleep the whole night. He's still in his bed now."

"Good," replies James. "Get some sleep if you can. I'm going to finish what I need to do before breakfast."

As Jiron goes back to where his pallet lies, James enters the kitchen and finds Ezra already there beginning to prepare breakfast for everyone. Arkie lies asleep on a blanket in the corner. "Good morning," he says as he passes through to the door.

"Good morning," she replies.

Leaving the kitchen through the back door, he makes his way out to the woods to collect the two crystals that have been charging the last two days. Over by the barn he sees Illan putting the new recruits through their morning drills. James has heard rumors they're glad Illan is going to be leaving for awhile and that their morning drills will be put on hold.

The crystals are still exactly where he left them, each having a fair sized glow within them. Not exactly maxed out, but still not too bad. Taking them back to his workshop, he begins the final stages of transferring power and setting up the spells.

Taking one of the crystals, he transfers the stored power it has to the defensive crystal. The spells contained within the defensive crystal he leaves inactive. He doesn't plan to activate them until the box lies in its final resting place. The other crystal he infuses with the spells which will light up the receiver crystal which will remain here in his workshop.

Taking the receiver crystal down, he sets the spell of the transmitting crystal to seek out this particular one and send almost all of its stored energy to it. This in turn will cause it to light, warning James that something is not right with the Fire.

When all the spells for all the crystals are just the way he wants them, he replaces the receiver crystal back on his shelf. The transmitting and receiver crystals go into his pouch and he picks up the iron box, carrying it back to the house. He takes it into his room where he sets it on the floor by the end of his bed.

A noise causes him to turn around and he sees Miko standing there. "Everything ready?" he asks James.

"Yes," he replies as he searches for any sign that the Fire is effecting him. When he doesn't discern any oddities about his behavior or facial expression, he says, "Sit down for a moment." Miko moves into the room and sits on the bed next to him. "I need you to stay here while I go do this."

"Why?" he asks, hurt already beginning to show on his face. James sometimes forgets that inside this 'man' is actually a young boy. Who, though he has the outward characteristics of a man, still hasn't matured within yet.

"I feel you shouldn't be anywhere near this," he says, indicating the iron box, "than you have to."

His eyes flick toward the box where they pause a moment before returning to James. He can see warring emotions going on within him until finally he says, "I understand."

Just then, they hear Ezra call them for breakfast. James claps him on the shoulder and gives him a grin. "Don't worry, I'll be back soon."

"I hope so," he replies.

They leave his bedroom and head out to the kitchen where Ezra has everyone that's leaving with James crammed in at the table. Thankful that his seat is at the head of the table where there isn't any room for another, he sits down and the meal commences.

"Miko will be staying here while we're gone," he tells Roland. "You might need more than just the new recruits if something should happen again."

"We'll be okay," Roland tells him. "With them out patrolling, it would take quite a bit to take us unawares."

"True," says James.

Illan glances to Miko and says, "I set up a schedule for drills and duties. If you could take charge of our ragtag bunch, I'd appreciate it." When Miko looks somewhat sheepish, he asks, "What?"

"I can't read," he admits as his face turns slightly red in embarrassment.

"No problem there," Roland says, jumping into the conversation. "I can help you read it, after that it should be no problem."

"Thanks," Miko says gratefully.

"Perhaps I could even begin teaching you to read," offers Roland.

"Excellent idea," James says. "In fact, I'd appreciate it if you could start a class with some of the brighter new recruits, as well as Miko."

Nodding uncertainly at the idea, he says, "I could do that, say with another three or four." Turning his attention to Illan, he asks, "Know anyone who might be a good candidate?"

Illan glances from Roland and James as he considers it. "The brightest one is Errin," he finally says. "She would most likely take to it the best. Other than her, maybe Nerrin and Caleb."

"Okay then," James says, smiling at Roland.

Roland doesn't look too happy adding this to his regular workload, but he'll not gainsay it.

"Make sure you keep my workshop locked and off limits to everyone," he warns him. "I have a few things in there that shouldn't be messed with."

Roland actually laughs before he says, "I doubt if we'll have anyone going in there. Everyone's sort of scared of what might be secreted inside the 'Mage's' workshop." When James looks questioningly at him he continues. "Ever since you had that explosion in there, they keep their distance. Even on patrols they give it a wide berth."

"Good," he states.

When he sees Jorry and Uther have finished their second helping of everything, he says to them, "We'll be leaving shortly, if you two gentlemen wouldn't mind getting the horses saddled for us?"

"Sure," Jorry says as he and Uther get up to head out to the barn.

Once they've left, he says to Roland, "I'm really not sure how long we'll be gone, hoping not more than a couple of weeks. Just keep things together here until we get back." Looking to Illan he asks, "Ready?"

Nodding, he gets up and follows James to his room. He picks up the iron box containing the Fire and asks, "You sure this is going to work?"

"I hope so," he replies. "We can't keep it here, it's too vulnerable. Not to mention the repeated attacks that will come because of it." Going to his chest, he takes all but a few golds' worth of coins which he leaves for Roland's use. Putting the coins in his belt pouch, he says, "Let's go."

Illan precedes him out of his room with the chest under one arm. Out front, the horses are already waiting for them. When the others see them exit the house, they begin mounting.

James has a small blanket in his hand and wraps the chest in it before they secure it behind his saddle, effectively hiding it. Once it's secured, he swings into the saddle and glances at the others, making sure they're all ready to travel. The recruits who aren't out on patrol are gathered to see them off.

"While I'm gone, Miko will be in charge of your training," Illan says to them. A groan can be heard coming from more than one as they realize they're not going to have it easy while he's off with James. "Anyone not giving him his all, or causing any troubles will have to answer to me when I get back." He gives each one an intent gaze before asking, "Understand?"

As one they say, "Yes, sir."

"Alright then." Turning to James, he gives him a nod.

Roland, Ezra and Tersa are standing just outside the door. Tersa comes to her brother and gives him a hug saying, "You be careful."

A little embarrassed over the display of emotion in front of everyone, he replies, "I will. Don't you be worrying about me." He then gives her shoulder a soft, reassuring pat.

"We'll be back as soon as we can, just have a little business up north to take care of," James says to Roland who only nods in reply. "Let's go," he says to those going with him as he turns his horse and begins going down the lane. The construction on the new estate is coming along nicely. Supposedly it'll be done sometime in the next couple of months. He never thought they could do it that fast, but seems they've been able to enlist the help of craftsmen who aren't otherwise occupied.

At the end of the lane, they find Devin at the guard shack. "Back in a few weeks," he says to him as he passes by.

"Where you going?" he asks.

"North," he replies as he turns onto the road going northwest.

When Devin has long since disappeared behind them, Illan asks, "Do you think it wise to tell them where you're going?"

"Yes, actually I do," replies James. His plan is to take the Fire north for some miles before activating the concealing spells infused within the crystals in the hopes of misleading whoever might be keeping a magical eye upon it. He knows they're hunting for it, and it just stands to reason that someone would be continuously watching it magically in the event he tries to move it. If he had activated the crystals before leaving The Ranch, they might still believe the Fire remains there and that would continue to bring danger to those who remained. But now, his hope is they'll believe he is moving it north, away from the Empire to better keep it from them. Which would seem logical.

So for most of the day, they will continue north, all the while allowing whoever may be watching the opportunity to discover the move. By telling those remaining at The Ranch he plans to go north, he hopes they may inadvertently relate that to an Empirical agent, thus corroborating the fact it's going north.

All that morning they press on as the road winds its way around the edge of the Kelewan Forest. Shortly after noon, they come to a crossroads where the road forks, one branch continuing to follow the edge of the forest north while the other one goes almost due east.

James takes the one which continues following the forest northward. By the time night falls, they've reached the small town of Wurt which lies on the southwest shore of Crystal Lake. The town is slightly larger than the average village, docks can be seen upon the water with many small and medium sized craft moored to them.

"Fishing is the main business here in Wurt," Illan tells him as they approach the outskirts of the town. "Not much else to it really, but the lake has fish in abundance so they do fairly well."

They pass through into the heart of Wurt where they find a large, three story building with a sign depicting a fish sleeping in a bed. "The Sleeping Perch," Jiron announces. When he sees the questioning look in James' eye, he adds, "Delia mentioned it. She said it's a good place to stay."

"Then let's stay here tonight," he says. Pulling up to the front, he and Illan dismount and go inside where they find the proprietor and arrange for rooms and stalls. James takes the box to his room and remains there with it throughout the night. In shifts, the others take turns standing watch outside his door in the hallway until morning.

The proprietor notices the guard at his door and when he asks about it, is told that James has been robbed at inns before so always has a guard posted outside his door. This explanation seems to placate him and he doesn't bother them anymore.

Several hours after the sun has gone down, explosions begin to sound off in the distance. Bright flashes of light draw him to his window as he watches. His door opens and Illan and the others rush into his room, swords at the ready.

"We're under attack!" Jorry exclaims.

James glances back at them with an amused smile as he shakes his head. "No, we're not." Gesturing out his window just as another flash lights up the night, he adds, "It's just the wedding of the woman we almost attacked back by Trendle."

"What?" asks Uther as he sheathes his sword.

"Remember those tubes she had in that chest?" he asks. "The ones that exploded when they went into their fire?" When he sees them nod their heads, he continues. "They're called fireworks, at least where I come from they are, and are used for celebration. She must've just been married."

"Oh, right," Jorry says as he comes closer to the window to watch the spectacle. Another flash, this one green in color, challenges the night for supremacy. But then it slowly dies as the night once more asserts its control.

The fireworks last another ten minutes before finally stopping completely. Everyone files out and leaves James once more alone. He makes sure the chest is sitting right next to his bed on the floor before turning in. Tomorrow, he'll activate the spells.

The morning dawns brightly and they're soon up and back on the road. Before he left his room, he'd activated the concealing spells and monitored everything for several minutes before he was sure that each crystal was functioning properly.

When they leave Wurt, much to the amazement of the others, he takes the road south. The others ask him about it and he gives them vague replies at best. Finally, Illan tells them to shut up and stop their bothersome questions.

Several miles further down the road, Uther suddenly exclaims, "James!"

Glancing over his shoulder, he asks, "What?"

"Behind you!" he replies pointing to the old blanket covering the box. A red glow can be seen coming from within. Afraid of what this might mean, he stops and gets off his horse. Removing the chest from his horse, he sets it on the ground before taking it out of the blanket. The crystals are all glowing.

Glancing up and down the road he sees no one around. "Into the forest, now!" he cries as he picks up the box and runs through the edge of the trees. *Can't let anyone who may pass by see what's going on.* Not even looking back to see if they're obeying him, he hurries deeper within the forest. Once he's well hidden from the road, he sets the box down and sits on the ground facing it.

As Illan and the others approach, he says to Illan, "They're hunting for it." The crystal supplying the power to the concealing ones is being drained rapidly.

"What are you going to do?" Illan asks.

"What's going on?" asks Uther.

"Quiet!" commands Illan.

James ignores them as he calls forth his magic. He immediately can feel a malignant power trying to find the Fire, the sheer amount of magic being used is staggering. Channeling his own magic into the power crystal, he attempts to keep the concealing spells active.

The one searching for the Fire suddenly dramatically increases the amount of magic being used, causing James to gasp as more of his own power is being sucked out of him to maintain the spell.

Illan and the others watch on as the glow of the crystals begins to intensify. They see James begin to pant and beads of sweat form as they drip off his forehead as he tries to thwart the attempts of the seeker.

Suddenly, the trees around them begin withering, one actually cracking down the middle. "What's happening?" exclaims Jorry.

"It's James," explains Jiron.

"What's he doing?" cries out Uther.

"I don't know," he says, shaking his head. "But he'll not be good for much when this is over."

"Form a perimeter around him," Illan barks out. "Jorry, you go out to the road and keep watch. Jiron, stay next to him and do what you can for him. Uther, keep the horses under control. We can't afford to have them running off."

As they hop to it, he glances at the box in wonder as the glow from the crystals continues to grow.

No longer able to use his own nearly depleted inner stores of power, James has had to tap other resources. Drawing the power from the trees and the other vegetation around him allows him to be able to maintain the spells.

The amount of power used is staggering! Never could he have imagined such an unrelenting torrent of power. Malignant evil can be felt emanating from the source of the power, itself almost as hard to counter and deal with as the seeking magic.

Just as he did back when he fought that evil presence when he first came to this world, so too now does he again create conduits from the vegetation to deliver power to the crystals.

Concentrating as hard as he is on maintaining the flow of power to the crystals, he fails to notice just what effect it's having around him. Trees and plants are dying rapidly, some even give a 'pop' as they crack open and crumble to the ground.

Suddenly, whoever was seeking the Fire, stops. James cancels the conduits quickly and almost feels fried as a backlash of power burns through him. Crying out, he falls backward into Jiron's arms and slumps into unconsciousness.

Chapter Thirteen

"Now what?" asks Jorry as they gather around Jiron who's cradling James' head in his lap. A large circle of devastation radiates outward from James and the box, almost reaching the road.

"I don't think we should stay here," Jiron says. "Until he wakes up, we'll not know if they found out where we are."

"I agree," Illan says. Indicating James, he says to Jiron, "Better get him on his horse, tie him if you must. The rest of you, get mounted."

Uther lends a hand with helping to secure James on the horse. Illan takes the old blanket and again wraps the box before securing it behind James' saddle. When everyone is mounted and ready to go, he turns to Jiron and asks, "Do you know exactly where he planned to go?"

"Trademeet," he says. "Though we shouldn't go through Trendle on the way back, we don't want anyone knowing we've turned around."

"Good point," he says. "Let's move." They come back to the road where Illan turns them to the south as they follow it back around the forest.

Several hours past noon they return to the fork in the road with the branch leading due east. He turns them that way. "How's he doing?" he asks Jiron.

"About the same," he replies. "He's not going to look like he's improving until he actually regains consciousness."

"Let me know," he says.

"I will."

Near nightfall, James begins moaning and thrashing around on his horse. Jiron moves next to him and somehow manages to calm him down. By that time, they have all stopped and gathered around him.

Illan looks to Jiron with a concerned look on his face.

"We need to find a place to rest for the night," Jiron tells Illan. "I don't know what that was, but he never did anything like that before."

"Okay. Next place with an inn, we're stopping."

The next place happens to come along an hour later. Just a bunch of buildings along the side of the road, not much more than a place catering to travelers who weren't able to reach the next town.

No sign hangs out in front of the inn and the place looks a little worse for wear. Several horses, along with a small caravan are tied around back. This place doesn't even have a decent stable for the horses. If it wasn't for James' need for a good night's rest, Illan would've passed this place by.

"Uther, go in and see if they've got at least three rooms for us."

Nodding, he gets down from his horse and enters through the front door. Returning shortly, he says, "They've got the rooms, cheap too."

"Jorry, take the horses around back and stay with them," he says. "I don't trust a place with no stable."

Not looking happy about it, he says, "Alright."

"Don't worry, we'll all take turns watching the horses," he assures him.

As he leaves with the horses around back the rest go in through the front door. Uther and Jiron carry the unconscious James between them. Illan goes and confers with the innkeeper while the others stay near the front door. An exchange of silvers produces three keys for rooms upstairs. When they carry James through to the stairs leading up, the innkeeper gives them a curious look but otherwise says nothing.

Once in their rooms, they lay James out on one of the beds. Illan sets the box on the floor next to him before leaving to make sure the rest get squared away properly. He returns a short time later and says, "I'm arranging for all of us to eat in our rooms. I'll have something sent up for you two." When Jiron nods from where he sits next to James on the bed, he asks, "How is he?"

"Don't know," Jiron replies, worried. "He's still breathing."

"That's something," says Illan. "There'll be someone posted outside your rooms all night. So if you need anything, or if there's any change, let us know."

Nodding, he says, "Sure." After Illan has left, he looks to his friend and wonders just what's going on in there.

A smoky haze covers a landscape burnt and dying. Unseen, the desolate wailing of tortured people comes to him as he walks through what once must've been a beautiful forest. Broken and charred trees lie scattered about, dark shapes move through them.

The dim light coming through the smoke hanging over him gives an unholy feel to his already dismal surroundings. He jumps and starts at every slight shadow and sound, ducking behind burnt out husks of trees when he catches a glimpse of shadows moving in the distance.

Moving cautiously, he makes his way through the dead forest and comes across what looks to have been a cabin of some sort. Some of the walls are still standing though the roof has long since collapsed from a long ago fire.

The fear which has been his constant companion ever since coming here now grows even stronger. Compelled, almost against his will, he begins moving toward the cabin. As he draws closer, a shadow moves across the doorway and then is gone.

Pausing only a moment, he continues on his way to the doorway. Wanting to stop, fighting the need to continue, his steps are sluggish but still he comes closer. At the doorway, he somehow manages to overcome his overpowering need to enter the cabin and comes to a stop. Fear. Fear the likes he's never experienced cuts through him like a knife, sapping his will, his strength.

Again, the shadow moves within, this time further back from the doorway. The sight of the shadow spikes his fear and he longs to turn and run, if only his legs would obey him.

The muscles of his leg begin to contract as they move his leg forward against his will, passing through the doorway. He watches as his foot touches the floor within the cabin. Cold hate suddenly washes over him as he looks up at the shadow, now aware of him. Evil, pure evil radiates from the eyes within the shadow. The yellow, glowing eyes.

He senses, more than sees the shadow reaching out for him. His will all but gone, he can no longer withstand the compelling need to come to the shadow, even though he knows it's to his doom.

Stepping through the doorway, he's suddenly grabbed from behind and yanked out of the cabin. A screech erupts from the shadow as its prey escapes from its clutches.

James stumbles backward and turns to see Igor there. A resounding slap across his face and he comes back to his senses. "Come on!" Igor yells at him as he turns and begins running away from the cabin.

The presence of evil behind him suddenly grows and a quick glance back shows the shadow is moving quickly to take him. Fear again erupts within him but is no longer overpowering as it had been before. With renewed strength, he runs to follow Igor.

A white light flashes from Igor and slams into the shadow, producing another hellish scream. To James' horror, answering screams can be heard coming from all around them.

"What are they?" he shouts to Igor as he catches up with him.

"You'd call them demons," he explains. "Not exactly what you think, but it's the closest comparison that you'll understand. Now shut up and run. There's only one place we can leave here and there's a chance we may not be able to reach it in time."

"Why?" James asks.

"We don't belong here," he replies. "Me especially. The gate won't last forever."

From behind them, he can see several shadows have now joined with the first in pursuit. Igor suddenly stops and turns to confront them. White light again shoots out and strikes the shadows, generating wails of pain and outrage.

Igor grabs him again and propels him onward. "These are relatively harmless, but all this commotion could attract something we would really rather avoid."

"Like what?" James asks.

Igor ignores him as they continue running. Periodically he stops and slows down their pursuers with another flash of light before resuming their flight. "There it is!" he says.

Ahead of them, James can see a bright arch shining in the darkness. Surprisingly, there're no shadows close to it. "Won't that attract them?"

"No. They're unable to see it," he says. "If they're close enough, they might feel it though." He glances to him as he says, "Especially the more powerful ones."

The wailing behind them increases as more of the shadows join their fellows. Suddenly, a deeper growl can be heard. Materializing before them is a ten foot tall figure of horror. Roughly man shape, but that's where the similarity ends. Its body writhes and ripples as it continuously changes form. It has no head, just two protrusions sprouting up from its main torso, like horns or tentacles.

A scream of fear erupts from James as he comes to a stop, terror freezing him into immobility. Igor gasps when he sees it. Turning back to James, he quickly rubs his thumbs over James' eyes and says, "You've got to make it through that arch. Do you understand?"

Glancing behind Igor, he sees the monstrosity advancing toward them. A stinging slap brings his eyes back to Igor. "Don't look at it. Concentrate on the arch and only the arch! Make for it, it's your only chance."

Sudden realization strikes him, "What about you?"

"You've got to make it through!" he yells. "Now go!" Turning, Igor faces the monstrosity as he moves to intercept it. A white light flashes and strikes it, causing it to slow its pace momentarily, but then it resumes. The light seems to have less of an effect on this creature than it did on the shadows.

James looks to the arch, the sight of it giving him renewed determination. Getting his legs moving, he runs toward the arch. He feels the presence of the monstrosity, its gaze upon him when another blinding flash of light, this time brighter and more intense than before, strikes it. A roar of pain and hate reverberates through the air as it stumbles backward a step.

He quickly glances to Igor who's now wielding a blindingly bright sword as he strikes out and slices into the creature. A wave of dark power comes out of the creature, striking Igor, throwing him back a step. Igor sees him pausing there. "Get through the arch!" he yells as he moves to strike out at his opponent.

Again, James runs as fast as his legs will move toward the arch. As he reaches it, he can feel a calming aura emanating from it. He looks back at the fight just as the monstrosity connects with Igor and knocks the shining sword from his hand. "Flee! NOW!" he hears as bolts of white strike the creature.

Suddenly on the other side of the arch, he sees another monstrosity approaching. In terror he dives through the arch.

A scream rips through the night, jarring Jiron out of sleep. The door bursts open and Jorry comes in, sword in his hand. They both look to find James sitting up in bed, the look of absolute terror on his face.

"James!" cries out Jiron as he comes to his side. To Jorry he says, "Get Illan." As he leaves the room, Jiron sits next to James and says to him, "James, you're okay. You're safe."

His eyes begin to focus on Jiron and his surroundings as they start to lose the wild look they had. "Oh my god!" he exclaims as he lies back down on his bed. Slowly, his pulse calms down and the fear he experienced begins to subside. He looks again to Jiron sitting there on the bed next to him and then to the door as Jorry returns with Illan.

"What happened?" Illan asks.

"A dream, I hope" croaks James. Then to Jiron he says, "Got any water?"

Getting up, he goes over to their packs and brings him a water bottle. James takes it and almost downs the whole thing. "Thanks," he says as he returns the near empty bottle to him.

"Are you okay?" Illan asks, concerned.

"I think so," he replies. "Just tired."

Illan turns his attention to where Jorry waits in the hallway and says, "He's okay." Jorry nods his head then closes the door as he keeps watch in the hallway.

"Where are we?" asks James.

"Somewhere to the west of Trendle," replies Illan.

"We started to head to Trademeet," explains Jiron. "We thought it best to not be seen passing through town so are taking a more roundabout way."

"Good," James says, nodding. "Has the box been glowing any while I've been out?"

Shaking his head, Illan replies, "No, nothing."

"That's good news," he says. "I doubt if I could counter another attempt so soon."

"Who was trying to find it?" asks Jiron.

"I don't know, probably one of Dmon-Li's followers I'd expect. Whoever it was used an awesome amount of power. It was all I could do just to maintain the concealment spells."

"Just get some rest," Illan says as he begins heading for the door. "Are you going to feel up to traveling in the morning?"

Nodding, he says, "Whether I do or not, we need to get this done."

"Alright," he says, opening the door. "See you then." He passes through the door and they can hear him saying something to Jorry before his footsteps are heard going down the hallway to his room.

Jiron gets up from the bed but James grabs his arm and says, "Jiron, I don't think it was just a dream."

Sitting back down, he says, "Why do you say that?"

James then relates to him the events as transpired on that other world, about the shadows, Igor and finally the monstrosities. "I don't know what it was, but it felt too real to be a dream," he concludes.

"It sounds too farfetched to be anything but a dream," states Jiron. "But you would know better than anyone else. What could it mean?"

"I don't know and that's what's bothering me," he replies. "If it wasn't a dream, was it a foretelling of the future? Or maybe I entered another level of existence? But what really has me worried is what happened to Igor. He was losing the battle when I passed through the arch. Is he gone?"

Jiron just sits there with him as he works through it. "Maybe you should try to get some sleep," he finally says. "It's not going to be answered tonight and you'll need your rest tomorrow morning."

Stifling a yawn that suddenly tries to break loose, he says, "You're right."

Jiron gets up off the bed and goes over to the other. Lying down, he blows out the candle on the nightstand.

James can hear his breathing relax as he slips into slumber, but he is far too worried to be able to fall asleep quickly. His mind continues wrestling with what happened and the implications of it as well. Finally though, exhaustion wins out and he falls asleep.

The morning finds him rested and feeling better, the terror of the night before all but gone. His memories of that time are no longer as sharp and clear as they had been when he originally came out of it. Pushing it to the back of his mind, he focuses on the task at hand.

He notices the box on the floor by his bed and picks it up, placing it next to him. A close examination of the crystals reveals no cracks and that they have a glow to them showing they still have power. Hoping not to go through the struggle he went through in the forest, he places the blanket back over it.

Jiron is still sleeping so he gets dressed quietly and opens the door. Jorry is standing there on the other side of the door and is startled when the door opens behind him.

"Are you okay?" he asks as he steps aside to let James by.

"Better, anyway," he replies quietly with a grin. "Just going to go downstairs and see about getting something to eat."

"Alright," says Jorry.

He makes his way downstairs to the common room and finds a table near an open window. The morning breeze feels good as he waits for the serving girl to finish with two men at another table. Looking outside, he sees Uther out by the horses. Doesn't look like he's doing much more than just hanging out next to them. Curious.

By the time the serving girl finishes with the other two men, he's joined by the rest of his crew. Jiron carries the blanket covered box and takes the seat next to him, placing the box on the floor between them.

After breakfast has been ordered, James asks, "Exactly where are we?"

"Somewhere east of Trendle, as best I can figure," Illan explains.

"Hmmm…" James thinks a moment and then says, "If we head due south, we'll come to the river. We'll just need to find a spot to cross and then make our way to Trademeet."

"What are we going to do there?" asks Jorry.

James taps the box and says, "Get rid of this."

"How?" he asks.

"You let me worry about that," he tells him.

Once breakfast comes, they eat quickly, Illan has an order of eggs and tubers sent out to Uther by the horses. When James asks, he tells him he didn't trust a place without a stable so stationed a man out there to keep an eye on them all night.

When they're done, they leave the inn and go out to their horses where Jiron helps James secure the box behind his saddle. Once secured, they mount and head out of the small collection of buildings. They leave the road as they make their way cross country to the south.

The day passes fairly uneventfully, those traveling behind James continue casting glances toward the box to see whether the glow will return or not. Much to the relief of everyone, especially James, the crystals remain dormant.

As the sun begins its descent toward the horizon, they see the river coming up ahead of them. James has them continue to follow it as it flows to the south. "If Bearn is up ahead, we can cross there."

"Aren't you worried about running into Lord Colerain?" Jiron asks.

"I don't plan on taking us through the city, just around the outside of it," he explains. "It's doubtful if we'll encounter him or anyone else who knows us."

"Let's hope not," Uther says.

The skyline of Bearn appears ahead of them a couple hours before nightfall. He forgot the bridge sits in the middle of town. They'll not be able to circumvent the city as it sprawls on both banks of the river.

"Guess we have to go through," Illan states. "Or continue further downriver to the next one."

"There is a ferry we might take," he tells them. "Not sure just how far it is though."

"What do you want to do?" Jiron asks him.

James pulls out a hooded cloak from his baggage and slips it on. A little hot but at least it covers his features well enough. "That might work," says Illan. "As long as no one takes a close look, you should be fine."

"Lead on," James says.

They approach the outskirts of town and pass through the outlying buildings before coming to the gate. A brief questioning by the guards and they're waved on through. "Just head straight through," James tells Illan. "I believe this road leads directly to the other side."

Riding their horses at a walk through the crowded city streets, it takes them a little over an hour to reach the gate in the eastern wall. The sun is almost to the horizon as they draw near the gate. Just before they reach the eastern wall, they can see the guards beginning the process of closing the gates for the night. "Let's hurry!" Illan says to the others as he kicks his horse into a trot.

"Hold the gate!" he hollers to the guards there. One of them looks their way and cries, "Hold!" to his fellows. They wait for them to ride through the gate before closing it.

"That was close!" Jorry exclaims.

"Yeah!" agrees Uther.

Riding along the road through the outlying buildings, they eventually leave the edge of town. Another hour and they find a spot to make camp.

During the night, James is awakened by Uther who's on watch. The box is again glowing as someone seeks to find the Fire contained within. James immediately casts out his senses to aid the crystal but finds the power behind the search is lessened quite a bit.

The others are awakened by Uther while James is concentrating on the box. He glances to them and says, "It isn't nearly as strong as it had been the last time. It almost feels fainter, like it's only the fringe of the spell."

"Maybe it's being directed elsewhere," suggests Illan.

"That's possible," agrees James. "If so, it looks like this might actually work. You guys go ahead and get some rest, I'm going to keep an eye on this until whoever is trying to find it stops."

Though they lay back down, none of them are able to return to sleep as long as the crystals on the box glowed. When a half hour later, the crystals finally subside back to their normal glow, everyone relaxes and begins drifting off to sleep.

The following morning, after a quick meal, they resume their way east to Trademeet. The travelers they meet are mainly merchants, with the few odd travelers thrown in. They ride quickly with only short breaks to give the horses a rest before continuing on.

By the end of the day, they come to a crossroads where they learn from a fellow traveler that the north road will take them to Osgrin and then on to Trendle. An inn and a couple other buildings have been constructed here and they decide to stop for the night.

The inn is of good quality and has a stable with a stableboy who lives in a small room in the back to keep an eye on things. A quick supper and James hits the bed, he's still not completely over the ordeal of the day before. The night goes by quickly and he wakes up almost feeling back to normal.

They have a quick meal in the common room before heading out on the road, the box again secured behind James' saddle. They take it quick, really wanting this whole thing over.

An hour or so after they start, they come to a fair sized town sitting at a crossroads. They discover it's called Guellin, a town whose main source of trade is wool and wool products. James could've figured that out by the number of sheep farms they came across along the road as they drew near.

The road heading south would take them to Willimet if they were going in that direction. Willimet! Just hearing the name makes him seethe after the way that woman treated him. If he wasn't in such a hurry, he'd go down there and demand his money back. Not to mention that she begin telling the truth about what happened and stop all this demon possession talk. That's probably what's driving the curious out to The Ranch.

Leaving Guellin behind, he comes to the realization that this may be a good place to procure some wool stuffing for Tersa's teddy bears she's making. Have to talk to Delia about that.

The road ahead of them begins to have fewer and fewer travelers as they progress until it's just the odd caravan coming to or from Trademeet. From what one caravan master said, Trademeet is still over a day away unless they want to kill their horses getting there, which they don't.

By the time the sun begins to dip below the horizon, they're still out in the middle of nowhere. James says he's not that exhausted and that he could go another couple hours in the hopes of finding an inn. So they press on and two hours after night had fallen, they begin to see the lights from a small town ahead of them.

Finding an inn, they get settled in and after a meal in the common room, head to their rooms for the night.

The next morning, clouds can be seen coming in from the west. James sees the approaching storm as a blessing which will hopefully give him some relief from the hot summer sun beating down upon them. By noon, the clouds have blanketed the sky and a short while after that a drizzling rain begins falling, making everyone uncomfortable. Except James, who finds this a welcome relief to the sun. Since coming here, he's managed to get quite a tan. They plod on through the rain the rest of the day until they see Trademeet appear on the horizon ahead of them.

Chapter   Fourteen

Upon reaching the outskirts, James announces, "Fifer and Yern should be here somewhere."

"So this is where they went to?" Uther asks.

Nodding, James continues, "I had them come ahead of us to procure some things we'll need, as well as scout around."

"I would think they'll be in a tavern somewhere getting drunk," Jorry says.

"This place is pretty big, may take us awhile to find them," Illan tells him.

"I realize that," says James. "If I would have known of a place here, they could've met us there, but I didn't."

They begin searching the taverns and inns along their way. Finally, after searching in over ten places, they find them sitting at a table, each with a buxom young woman on their knee.

When Fifer sees them walk through the front door, he has the girl get off his knee as he says to Yern, "Looks like the fun is over." Seeing Yern's confused look he indicates the door.

"Damn," Yern curses under his breath. "Sorry my lovely, but duty calls," he tells the girl in his lap as he gently removes her from his knee.

"There you layabouts are!" Uther exclaims at them as he comes to their table.

Giving him a grin, Fifer says, "You have poor timing my friend. Couldn't you have waited an hour more?"

"An hour?" Jorry asks laughing. "It wouldn't have taken you that long."

James comes forward and asks, "Did you get everything?"

"Yes we did," replies Fifer. "It's out back in the wagon."

"Wagon?" asks Uther.

James turns to Uther and says, "See if there are a couple more rooms available for the night." When he nods and moves to find the innkeeper, James says to the others, "Let's talk about this somewhere more private."

Uther returns shortly with two keys and says they've got stall space for their horses. Illan has him and Jorry take the horses out to the stables while the rest of them go up to their rooms with the box.

Once the horses are taken care of, and everyone is crammed into one room with the door shut, James asks them, "Is the Pass open?"

Shaking his head, Yern says, "No. From what we've been told, the area on the other side is still too volatile and they're not allowing anyone to cross over."

"But, we may have arranged a way for us to be allowed up the mountain, though," adds Fifer.

"How?" James asks.

"The last few days we sort of made friends with the guard in charge of this side of the Pass," he explains. "We told him that we come here every year to fish up in the Pass, along with some friends of ours. I believe we convinced him we don't plan on crossing over so he said as long as we give him our word to stay on this side of the way stop at the summit, we can proceed up the Pass."

"Excellent!" exclaims James. "That's better than I was hoping for. And you definitely got everything I asked for?"

"Yep," Fifer says, nodding. "It's all in the back of the wagon. Most of the stuff we got real cheap, seems the merchant's around here are having a bad time now that no more traffic is coming through the Pass." He hands James a coin filled pouch, what's left of the coins he gave them when they left The Ranch.

"I can understand that," says James, taking the pouch. "Well, since all is in order, I suggest we get some sleep and head out early."

"Hope this rain stops," Jorry moans as they begin to file out on the way to their rooms.

"Would you stop your complaining!" Uther commands.

James smiles as he hears their bickering continue down the hallway. Jiron again shares the room with him and he says, "I know you plan to hide it somewhere around here, but is it a good idea to do it so close to the Empire's forces?"

"I know what I'm doing," he says. "It'll take them some doing to find it where I plan to put it."

"I hope so," he says as he blows the light out.

As James lies there in the dark trying to sleep, he suddenly notices the crystals of the box begin to glow brighter again. This time, he hardly has to use any of his own power to sustain the spells.

Whoever is seeking it, is directing their search far from here. Thank goodness. It looks like his misdirection earlier is definitely going to work. If they should concentrate directly on the area where the box is when he's gone, it's over. But they'll have to be pretty lucky to do that.

The rain is coming down harder the following morning as they make their way to the barricade blocking the entrance to the Pass. A contingent of guards stand watch and one comes forward as they approach.

"So, you still plan to go up there and fish in this weather?" he asks Fifer with a smile, the rain pelting them as they exchange words.

"Sure do," he says. "Should be back in a couple days."

"Bring me one," the guard says.

"Will do," he says.

The guard hollers over to the men at the barricade and they swing a section of it clear to allow the wagon James is driving through. They stare questioningly at the boat tied down in the back, but just stand back as he rolls on by. Once they're all through, the barricade is again replaced.

As they trundle along the road up the pass, the rain continues its downpour. The many waterfalls along the road are fat from the recent rains adding even more spray to soak the already drenched party.

James reminisces about when he and Miko had traveled this same route. He smiles at the wonder Miko had shown at the spectacles of nature along the way. When they reach the bridge by the one big waterfall, he pauses a moment to watch it as it cascades down the side of the mountain.

The others just look at him strange while he sits there on the wagon, remembering Miko as a lad before the Fire changed him. Saddened, he flicks the reins and the wagon once again rolls forward.

It's close to dark when they reach the plateau with the abandoned keep. "That's where we want to go," he tells them.

"In there?" asks Uther incredulously. "That place doesn't look like it could keep anything secure anymore."

Smiling a sad smile, he replies, "You'd be surprised."

They move forward and he has them go around to the back where they secure the horses and the wagon. When he starts to untie the boat from the back of the wagon, they look at him like he's crazy.

"Give me a hand, would you please?" he asks them. Coming to his aid, they help him get the boat off the wagon and set it on the ground. In the bed of the wagon, they find packs, bulging with equipment along with a couple small sledgehammers.

Taking one of the backpacks, he slings it over his shoulder and says, "We need this stuff too." Everyone comes over and either takes a pack or a sledge hammer. Much to his chagrin, Uther gets stuck with both.

Going back over to the boat, James says, "Now, those of you with just the packs, help me with this."

Illan, Fifer and Jorry come over and help him lift it. "We need to take it around front and carry it inside."

"You heard him," Illan says as they begin to carry the boat around. When they come to the front door, Uther and Yern open it wide to enable them to enter. Inside is very dark so he creates his orb and has it settle on his shoulder.

James directs them down the hallway with the now more decomposed corpse. Stepping carefully, they carry the boat down the hallway to the broken door leading to the basement.

He indicates they should rest the boat on the floor for a moment. He takes the orb off his shoulder and carries it over to the door where he looks down the broken stairs. Still looks the same. *Wonder if the stuff is still under the stairs?*

Turning back to the others, he says, "We need to get the boat down to the room below. There's a flight of stairs, but they're broken and unlikely to hold everyone's weight at once."

"Then what are we going to do?" Yern asks.

"I'll go down first and you can lower the boat down to me." To Fifer he asks, "Which pack has the rope?"

"They all do," he says. "We weren't sure just how much you would need so we got a lot."

"Good thinking," he says. "While I make my way down to the bottom, one of you tie a rope to the boat. Then when I say so, slide it down the stairs slowly until I have it settled on the floor below."

Creating a second orb, he leaves it with the boat and then begins to descend the rickety and broken stairs to the room below. He notices the circle on the wall, the first trigger which will open the secret door, as he makes his way down. Once on the floor, he hollers back up for them to send the boat down. While he waits for them to begin lowering the boat, he checks under the stairs and is pleased to find all his equipment still there, looking as if it's remained undisturbed.

Jiron comes to the top of the stairs and then the boat begins making its way through the doorway as he guides it toward the stairs. The stairs groan when the weight of the boat settles upon it and begins to slide down. James moves back to the bottom of the stairs where he can watch and guide the boat coming down.

Those in the hallway hold onto the rope while they slowly allow the boat to slide down the stairs to where James is waiting. From his vantage point at the top of the stairs, Jiron is able to direct those in the hallway.

"Easy," he says to them as inch by inch the boat makes its way down. "Almost there."

When the boat draws near, James takes hold of it and guides it the rest of the way to the bottom. When the front end touches the floor, he pulls on the boat until it's completely off the stairs and resting on the floor.

"That's good!" Jiron hollers to those in the hallway and then begins making his way down to James. The others enter and begin following him down.

"Stop!" James cries up at them when he sees they're about to all come down the stairs at once. "The stairs won't support you all," he tells them. "You need to come down one at a time. And Uther?" he asks. Once he has Uther's attention, he says, "See if you can find a thick piece of wood out in the woods, about three feet long." He uses his hands to show the size he wants.

"What do you want that for?" he asks.

"Just do," he replies.

Illan turns to him and says, "Take Jorry with you, and be quick."

Uther and Jorry leave to do as requested. Once Jiron has reached the bottom, Illan begins to descend. The stairs groan badly in one spot and he even hears one of the boards give a little crack. Continuing carefully, he makes it to the bottom.

Looking around the room, he says, "There's nowhere to go."

"Yes there is," James says as he moves to where the entrance to the secret door in the wall is located. Tapping on it, he says, "Behind here is the old escape route from this keep. It leads through an underground cavern to an underground river that eventually leads to the river at the bottom of the canyon."

"And you plan to hide that," he asks, indicating the box containing the Fire, "somewhere down there."

"Precisely," he says.

"Why do you need the boat?" he asks.

"I don't plan to hide this in an easily accessible location," he explains. "But rather somewhere that would make it very hard to get, even if someone should learn of its location."

Illan nods as he glances around the room.

From the hallway at the top of the stairs, they hear Jorry and Uther coming back. They're talking to one another and when they enter the room they both begin to descend the stairs at the same time.

Illan notices them and cries out, "One at a time!" but is too late.

The stairs give out with a loud crack and the top section upon where they're stepping suddenly collapses and Uther falls forward, hitting the step just after the section that fell, and smashing though it with a grunt. They fall ten feet and land on the equipment James and Miko had left there from their earlier visit.

James and the others rush over and he asks, "You guys okay?" Pulling some of the broken stairway off of Jorry, they find them with only a few minor scrapes and cuts.

"Nothing broke," Uther says as Illan helps him to his feet.

"Same here," says Jorry.

Now that they're all together, James lays out the plan to them. Taking a few of the items out of the backpacks, he explains how they're to be used and so forth.

"Once we're done, Jiron and I have something we need to do so won't be coming back this way," he explains. "You will need to return through here and take the horses and wagon back to The Ranch." Pointing to the stashed equipment that now lies under the debris of the fallen stairs, he adds, "And take that equipment with you as well."

"Where will you two be going?" Fifer asks.

"Saragon," he tells them.

"Are you crazy?" Yern exclaims. "That place is in enemy hands. How are you going to get in there? And why?"

"As for how we'll get in there," he says, "there's a way." Pulling out the medallion, he holds it out to them and continues, "I still need to understand why this was given to me. The only place left for me to find out is in Saragon, it was the home of the last High Priest of Morcyth. Ollinearn, from the City of Light said that it's possible he might've gone there before they disappeared. It's all I have to go on."

"You be careful," Illan says.

"Oh, I plan to be, rest assured," James tells him. "Now, to open the secret door."

"Uther, on the wall along the stairs you'll find a circle engraved into it," he says. "Go up there and stand by until I tell you to press it. There are three triggers and they have to be pressed in the correct order."

"Sure thing," he says as he moves to climb the stairs, this time using great caution. He makes it almost up to where they end at the break before stopping and turning around. He gives them a thumb's up indicating he's found it and ready.

"Illan, if you will take this," James says as he picks up the broken piece of the door jamb he used last time. Handing it to him, he points out the double circle on the ceiling. "After Uther presses the circle by the stairs, you press that double circle on the ceiling. Then I'll step on the triple circle on the floor and the door should open." Glancing around at everyone, he says, "Got it?"

When he gets a nod from Uther and Illan, he says, "Okay Uther, press your circle."

Uther presses his circle and then nods to Illan. Illan then raises the broken door jamb and presses the double circle in the ceiling. Once he's begun lowering the broken door jamb, James goes over and steps on the triple circle in the floor.

From where the secret door is located, they hear a soft grinding noise as the door slowly begins to open. To Jorry, James says, "Take that piece of wood you brought down here and lay it in the doorway to keep it open. You'll need it open if you are to come back this way."

Jorry picks up the wood and goes over to the door where he wedges it in to prevent the door from closing.

James waits a minute for the door to begin to close, but the piece of wood successfully keeps it open. "Good," he says. "Through there is a narrow passage which should be wide enough to carry the boat through sideways. After that is a cavern with ample room."

"Okay boys," Illan tells the others, "You've got the boat."

Yern, Fifer, Uther and Jorry all take a side and lift the boat off the ground. Jiron moves into the passage with James right behind. "There's a bundle of old torches here," he hollers back to Illan. "Grab a couple to use on your way back."

"Good idea," he says.

With a groan, the four guys flip the boat on its side as they move to the opening in the wall. It's quite a tight fit, but they manage to maneuver the boat through the opening and shuffle with it down the passage. From the rear, light flares up indicating Illan has found the bundle of torches and has lit one.

When they at last exit the narrow passageway and are in the cavern, they flip the boat back upright again. Moving the boat through the stalagmites rising from the floor and the pools of water is much easier than it had been getting it through the narrow passage.

Jiron, who had been scouting ahead with one of James' orbs of light, comes back. "There's a broken down bridge ahead, spanning a very deep chasm," he tells them.

"I know," says James. "That's the way we've got to go."

"How in the world are we to get that boat across?" he asks.

"What do you mean?" interrupts Uther from where he's carrying the boat. "What bridge?"

"You'll see," replies Jiron.

Shortly, the light from James' orb illuminates the beginning of the rickety bridge hanging precariously across the chasm.

The guys carrying the boat stop and set it on the ground. "It'll never hold us carrying the boat across," states Fifer. "It'll collapse!"

"I never said we'd be carrying it over," he tells them.

"Then just how do you propose to get it over there? Magic?" asks Uther.

Shaking his head, he says, "No, I'll need all I have for a little bit later on. Somewhere in one of the packs are three large eye rings. We need two of them now." They rummage through the packs and produce the two eye rings.

James takes out the long rope from within his own backpack. After making sure it's long enough, he hands one end of it to Fifer. Taking the other end, he gives it to Jiron and says, "Take this over to the other side."

Nodding, he ties the rope around his waist before beginning to cross the bridge. As he makes his way over, James turns to Yern and says, "You take one of the eye rings and sledge hammer over across the bridge after he's cleared the other side. Then you and Jiron need to hammer it into the stone securely."

To Fifer he says, "Tie the other end of the rope to the forward section of the boat."

He notices Illan already has a long piece of rope and is securing one end to the rear of the boat. "I think I see what you're planning to do. You've been planning this long?" he asks.

"Ever since I found that," he says, pointing to the box carrying the Fire. To Uther and Jorry he says, "Take the other eye ring and hammer it securely into the stone on this side.

"Okay," Uther says as Jorry takes the eye ring and sledge hammer over to within three feet of the edge of the chasm. Soon, hammering can be heard coming from both sides as they put the eye rings into the stone.

Seeing that Fifer has the end of the rope secured to the bow of the boat, he tells him to cross over to the other side. By the time he arrives there, the hammering has stopped. "Now," he hollers over to the other side, "slip the rope through the eye of the eye ring." When they've accomplished that, he has them stand to one side as they grasp the rope. He sees that Illan already has the rope that's tied to the rear of the boat threaded through the eye ring on this side.

With Jiron, Fifer and Yern on one side and Illan, Uther and Jorry on the other, he has them firmly grasp the rope and take in the slack. "Now, when I holler 'GO!' I want you on the far side to pull slowly and steady while those on this side maintain the tension on the rope as the boat goes over. Use the eye rings for leverage and it shouldn't be too difficult. Everyone understands?"

Once he gets the affirmatives from those on both sides, he yells, "GO!"

Jiron's side begins to slowly pull the boat toward them while Illan's on this side continues to maintain the tension. Inch by inch, the boat moves toward the edge of the chasm. *If this doesn't work, I don't know what I'll do.*

Suddenly, the prow of the boat clears the edge and soon the rest of it follows. He can see the strain of those on his side as they try to maintain a steady rhythm of hand over hand and still keep a firm grip.

He watches as the boat slowly makes its way across the chasm. When it's a third of the way across, he hollers, "Doing good!"

Halfway across and the two teams still maintain the tension, though the boat has dipped a little into the chasm. The team on the other side continues to steadily reel in the boat.

Two-thirds of the way, and everything is still moving steady. It has dipped still further into the chasm, but continues making its way across. Finally, the bow comes to within a foot of the other side. Yern lets go of the rope as he steps to the edge and reaches out to help get it up over the lip of the chasm. Pulling with the help of those behind him, the boat finally slides onto the other side.

James can hear a groan of relief as the men on his side release the rope. Hollering over to the other side, he says, "Pull the rope the rest of the way across." Jiron waves back at him as he goes to the boat and begins reeling in the rope that is tied to its rear.

"Just need to get the rest of us across now," he says to Illan.

"You go first," he tells James. "Then I'll send them across one at a time."

"Very well," he says. Shouldering his pack, he moves to the bridge and works his way across to the other side. "You guys alright?" he asks Jiron and the others when he gets there.

"Arms are sore, but otherwise fine," Fifer tells him.

Jiron's there, rubbing his shoulder, the one that had been hit by the crossbow back in Lythylla. "Shoulder hurt?" he asks as he comes over to him.

"A little," he admits with a grin. "Too much strain I guess. It'll be fine in a few minutes."

"We'll have a break when everyone else gets over here," he tells him. Over on the bridge, Jorry is making his way across while Uther and Illan stand on the other side waiting their turn. One by one they make their way across until they're all together once more.

"Let's take a few minutes to rest and have a bite to eat," he suggests.

"Good idea," Jorry and Uther say at the same time which makes the others start laughing.

As they break out their rations, Yern asks, "What's up ahead?"

"Up ahead is another small passage which opens up on a vast cavern," he explains between bites. "That's where it gets interesting."

"You mean, more interesting than what we just went through?" asks Jorry.

Nodding, James finishes a mouthful of food before continuing. "At the end of the passage, a narrow stairway leading down has been carved out of the rock. It descends for several hundred feet before coming to a stone platform next to an underground river."

"Is that where you'll be needing the boat?" asks Illan.

"That's right," he tells them. "You're going to hold the rope against the rushing of the water, preventing Jiron and me from being sucked along with the torrent. I'll hide the box somewhere in the tunnel, and when I'm done, you just release the rope and let us go."

"Isn't that going to be dangerous?" Fifer asks.

"Some," he admits. "But Miko and I came through here earlier this summer and survived."

He can see those around him have their doubts about his plan, but he can't think of anywhere that would be as good a place to hide it as here. Who would even think to look in such a place?

"You all must swear to keep the secret of where this is hidden all the way to your graves," he says. Looking from one to another, they nod saying they'll never tell. "I'd hate to think what would happen should this ever be found."

"You can trust us," Illan says. Glancing at the others, he says, "Right?"

"Sure." "Right." "You can count on us."

When everyone is through having a small bite to eat, they shoulder their packs and the four again lift the boat. With Jiron in the lead, they cross the remainder of the cavern until they come to the narrow passage.

Flipping the boat again on its side, they carry it into the passage. The floor of the passage is slick with slime, water runs along the bottom in the same direction they're going. At the end of the passage, the roar of a waterfall can be heard from somewhere in the distance.

Jiron goes to the edge and says, "I'll go down and help with the boat as you lower it down."

"Good idea," agrees James.

Nodding, Jiron takes the stairs and soon all that can be seen is the glowing of the orb as it descends into the darkness below. As the men with the boat approach the end of the passage, they suddenly hear Jiron's voice holler from below. "James! You need to see this!"

"Wait here," he tells the others before he descends the stairs to see what Jiron is talking about.

Before he reaches the bottom, he sees Jiron still standing on the stairs. His breath catches in his throat when he sees what it is that Jiron is talking about. There is no longer a stone platform. The water level has risen from the rains and now has completely covered the platform.

"What are we to do now?" Jiron asks over the thunderous roar of the waterfall.

James stares at the water a moment then throws the orb toward where he and Miko had left through the tunnel on the boat last time. The orb arcs through the air and before it hits the water, they can see the opening where the water is rushing out.

There's barely enough room for the boat, in fact, there may not be enough at all.

"What do you think?" he asks Jiron. "Can we make it through in the boat?"

"Man, I don't know," he says shaking his head. "It could be possible. Depends on how much our weight will cause the boat to sink into the water."

From up above, they hear Illan holler, "What's wrong?"

"We better go up and tell them," James says. Jiron nods his head and they begin to climb back up. Once up there, they explain the situation to Illan and the others.

"Do you still mean to go through with this?" he asks.

"I have to," he stresses. "This is more important than I can say."

"Alright, what do you want us to do?" he asks.

"Fifer, you and Yern make your way down to the water lever," he explains. "Take the last eye ring and a sledge hammer. As close to the top of the water as you can, pound in the eye ring then return here."

"You got it," he says as they get the equipment and head down the stairs. Jiron hands Fifer his glowing orb for light before they go. They watch as the orb makes its way down into the darkness. Soon, the sound of them pounding the eye ring into the stone wall can be heard. Shortly after the sound stops, they return back up to the others.

"All done," Fifer tells them as he hands the orb back to Jiron.

"Thanks," he says. "Now, to get the boat down there." He thinks for a bit before continuing. "We'll lower the boat gently until it rests upon the water. Then well put the rope tied to the stern through the eye ring. The rest of you will have to remain on the stairs holding it while Jiron and I get in."

"Once we're in, slowly let out the slack in the rope until we're within the tunnel and I give you a signal to hold it still. At that point, I will be placing the box within its hiding spot."

"What's the signal?" Uther asks.

"I'll make one of my orbs appear," he explains. "When the orb disappears, that'll be the signal to let the rope go. After that, you make your way back out. Make sure you allow the secret door to close, no sense announcing to anyone coming in there that it's there."

"Alright," Illan says. "How long will it take you to make it back to The Ranch?"

Shrugging, he says, "I can't even begin to guess on that. But if we're not back in a couple weeks, start worrying."

Illan just nods.

"Everyone ready?" he asks.

When everyone nods their head, he has Jiron move to the bottom of the stairs to aid the boat in reaching the water safely.

Once they get his holler saying he's ready, they start lowering the boat over the edge. It seems like they're lowering it forever before tension in the rope slackens and they hear Jiron holler up that it's on the water.

"Secure it to the eye ring while we come down!" he hollers down to him.

"Okay!" they hear back in a second. "Come on down."

They make their way down to where Jiron stands on the step just above the water, the boat resting on the surface near him. The rope attached to the front of the boat is secured to the eye ring.

Giving Jiron the rope tied to the back, he waits while Jiron switches the rope securing the boat to the eye ring. When he's finished, the boat is now pointing in the correct direction.

Handing his pack which contains the box to Jiron, he has him put it into the bottom of the boat. Jiron is about ready to get in when he tells him to wait until the others are in position and gripping the rope.

"You ready?" he asks them.

"Go ahead," Illan shouts down to him from where he's anchoring the rope.

Nodding to Jiron, he waits while he gets into the boat, then climbs in after him. He indicates the two oars secured to the bottom of the boat and tells Jiron to take one. "Use it to keep us from the walls as best you can."

Jiron removes one and indicates he's ready. To the ones on the stairs, he hollers, "Okay!"

Slowly, the boat begins to move out into the rushing torrent on its way to the outflow. The light from Jiron's orb begins to illuminate the entrance to the outflow. "Man, we're not going to fit in there!" he cries out to James. The opening looks even smaller than it did before. Water crashes on both sides of the opening sending fountains of spray up into the air, soaking them in ice cold water before they even get close.

When they're within several feet, they discover that they will in fact be able to make it through, though the ceiling of the tunnel will be but inches from the top of the boat. They'll have to practically lie down in the bottom of the boat to keep from hitting their heads.

As the bow of the boat begins to enter the tunnel, James looks back to those on the stairs holding the rope. The light from Illan's torch illuminates him and Uther who stands just below him from where it lies on the step above. Foot by foot, the tunnel swallows them until the light from Illan's torch can no longer be seen.

"Hold on!" Illan cries out to them as they continue letting out slack for James and Jiron to move even further into the tunnel. He looks behind him and sees there's only about another ten feet before they run out of rope. Still, James' signal has not appeared.

Uther's hands have begun to bleed from where the rope is cutting into them, but still he holds on. "Can't hold on much longer!" he cries up to Illan.

"Yes you can!" he hollers back. Suddenly, an orb appears before them.

"That's it!" Illan cries out. "Hold it steady while he does what he needs to."

Keeping the rope still is much harder on their muscles than controlling it as the slack had been let loose. They hold it there for five minutes before Fifer yells up to Illan. "The eye ring! It's sliding loose!"

"How long?" yells Illan back to him.

"Seconds!"

"When it goes, let loose or you'll lose your arms!" he yells to the others.

"What about James and Jiron?" cries Uther.

"There fate will be in the hands of the gods!" he hollers back.

Suddenly, the orb disappears just as the eye ring lets loose. They let go of the rope and watch as it gets sucked into the tunnel. "Good luck James," Illan says quietly to himself before they begin climbing back up the stairs.

Chapter   Fifteen

As they inch their way along the tunnel, the boat continuously scrapes the sides and ceiling of the tunnel. Water periodically sloshes into the boat from where it hits the sides, and the bottom has already filled with two inches of water. When Jiron mentions it to James, he tells him the added water isn't that bad, that it will enable them to ride lower in the water and hopefully not scrape so much.

It seems they've been a long time within the tunnel before James finds what he's looking for. Suddenly, the light from the orb reveals a gap in the ceiling above them. When the gap reaches the middle of the boat, James releases the magic and the orb appears back with the others, signaling them to hold fast.

The boat abruptly stops its forward progress and James takes the orb as he inspects the cavity in the rock above. It's about two foot in diameter and several more feet deep. The light from the orb shows it is just a vertical opening with no place to set the box and crystals.

He feels Jiron tap him as he shouts to be heard over the sound of the rushing water, "You better hurry, not sure how long they'll be able to hold us here!" Lying on his back, he has one of the oars pressed to the side of the tunnel in an attempt to hold them steady.

"I know," he hollers back. Picturing in his mind what he wants to do, he lets the magic flow as chips of rock begin to fall from one side of the top of the cavity, three feet above the rushing water. A hole begins to form as more and more of the rock is broken away. It takes a couple minutes to clear a spot large enough and level enough for the box.

"Hand me the box," he hollers to Jiron who takes it out of the pack and gives it to him. Setting the box within the just cleared opening, he checks a final time to make sure all is as it should be with the spells and the crystals. When everything checks out fine, he takes the warning crystal and the defensive one out of his pouch and sets them next to the box within the cavity. He activates their spells and then removes two small spikes and a small hammer from his pouch. Then taking the pack, he wedges it into the cavity next to the box, effectively blocking the opening.

Using his small hammer, he pounds one spike through the pack into the bottom of the opening, and another through the pack into the top of the opening, thereby preventing anything from inadvertently falling out.

"Ready?" he asks Jiron as he comes out of the cavity and lies back into the bottom of the boat.

Jiron removes the stabilizing oar from against the wall and flips himself over until he's lying on his stomach. Glancing to Jiron he nods.

When he gets the nod, he cancels the orb signaling the others to let them go, and they're suddenly rocketed through the tunnel. Lying on their stomachs with their heads facing the bow and holding onto a bench for dear life, each prays to survive this wild ride.

The boat continuously strikes not only the ceiling but the walls as well, the continuous jolting makes James nervous. His eyes suddenly widen as a crack appears in the side of the boat near him as one of the boards begins to splinter. He looks in horror at the crack and when the boat again strikes the side of the tunnel, the crack widens as the board beneath it breaks as well.

From up ahead, he can hear the sound of the water begin to change. Another strike against the side and he hears a crack from the rear of the boat and suddenly his feet are drenched as water fills the boat rapidly.

"James!" cries out Jiron as the sound ahead of them gains in volume.

"Just hold on!" he cries. "This is going to be rough!"

Suddenly, they're airborne as they're propelled over the waterfall. James holds his breath in anticipation of striking the water. When they do, the boat completely disintegrates.

A piece of the destroyed boat stabs him in the arm as he's thrown into the water. The iciness of it takes his breath away as he breaks the surface, gasping for air. The pain in his arm is tremendous and when he feels with his other hand, finds a piece of wood has completely passed through and is sticking an inch out both sides.

"James!" he hears in the dark, his orb having disappeared when he hit the water and broke concentration.

"Over here!" he hollers as he treads water. Another orb springs into being and he sees Jiron swimming toward him. Not far off is half of the boat floating upside down in the water. He starts swimming as best he can with one arm toward it.

Jiron sees what he's making for and angles his way over to reach it. He reaches the remnant of the boat first and takes hold of the side as he begins bringing it to James. When he meets up with him, he holds it steady as James works himself up onto it. "What happened to you?" he asks when he sees the piece of wood sticking out of his arm.

"Piece of the boat got me when we hit the water back there," he explains. Legs still submerged in the water, he at last has a secure hold on the boat with his good arm and isn't likely to sink again into the water.

"Let me look at it," Jiron tells him. James winces in pain as he inspects where his left arm near the shoulder has been punctured. "Doesn't look like it hit the bone, just went through the muscle." He looks James in the eye and says, "You know it needs to come out. If you move around too much with it in there it's going to do more damage to the muscle."

"Okay, do it," he says as he grits his teeth.

Jiron takes the piece of wood and slides it back out the way it had come in. James cries out from the pain and almost slips off the overturned boat before Jiron grabs him and steadies him.

When the piece of wood is out, he throws it into the water and then tears off a piece of James' shirt which he ties tightly around the wound to prevent anymore blood loss. "You should be fine, it came out cleanly," he tells him.

James can only nod as he becomes nauseous from the pain. Now weak and shaky, it's all he can do just to hang onto the boat with his one good arm.

"How do we get out of here?" Jiron asks. The light from James' orb doesn't illuminate very far and all he sees is water.

"If we move away from the waterfall behind us," he explains, "we'll eventually come to where the water leaves the cavern and flows to the river outside."

"How far is that?" he asks.

"I don't remember exactly," he replies.

"Just hold on and we'll get there," he tells him.

Nodding, James holds on tighter as Jiron begins kicking with his feet, moving them further away from the crashing of the waterfall.

When they've progressed enough that the sound of the waterfall begins to diminish behind them, Jiron hears the sound of teeth chattering beside him. Glancing over to James, he can see that he's shivering badly from being in the cold water. "You okay?"

"N-n-n-o-oo," he says, trying to control his chattering teeth. "J-just c-c-c-old."

Cold himself, he's even more worried about his friend. He at least has the benefit of moving to keep his body temperature up. "Kick your feet," he suggests. "That might help keep you a little warmer."

Shortly, splashing can be heard from where James begins kicking his feet. Suddenly, he cries out as he loses his one armed grip on the remnants of the boat and slides into the water.

Jiron lets go of the boat and quickly moves to help him keep afloat. James feels cold to the touch as he assists him in getting up on the boat again. Holding the boat with one hand, he uses the other to pull James back up to where he can again grab and hold on.

"Sorry," he apologizes to James. "You just hold on while I try to get us out of here."

James tries to respond but the dunking in the water has left him so cold, he can't even talk.

Jiron begins swimming even harder, he needs to get James out of the cold water before he dies. From up ahead, the orb's light reveals a small island. Not very big, but large enough to accommodate them and allow James to get out of the water. Turning the boat slightly, he moves them in the right direction. The boat runs aground as it comes next to the island. Grabbing hold of James, he helps him get to his feet and onto the island.

James is pointing back to the boat and says, "B-b-b-b…"

"Get the boat?" Jiron asks. When he sees James nodding vigorously, he glances back and sees the remnants of the boat beginning to slip away from the island. Moving quickly, he takes hold of it and pulls it up onto the island next to them.

Coming over to James he sees him lying there shivering. "F-f-f…"

"Fire?" he asks. "You want me to make a fire?"

James nods his head.

Looking around the island all he finds to burn is the boat and they'll need that when they leave the underground lake. "There's nothing to burn but the boat," he tells him.

Shaking his head, James says, "S-s-spark!"

"Spark?" he asks and James again nods his head.

Not completely understanding, he takes out his flint and begins striking it against a rock. After the third time when sparks appear, a flame roars to life out of thin air. Hair smoking from where the fire had connected with his face, he falls backward in startlement.

Getting himself back together, he sees James has his eyes closed and is inching his way toward the fire. "How'd you do that?" he asks.

James gives a slight shake of his head and keeps his eyes closed. When he's close to where the fire is burning, he stops and begins warming up.

Jiron comes close to the wonderfully warm flame as he thaws himself out. He had begun to be about as cold as James and even felt his teeth start chattering.

They sit around the flame for several minutes before James' teeth stop chattering and he opens his eyes. Sitting up, he scoots a little closer to the fire.

"Better?" Jiron asks him.

"A little," he replies, the warmth from the flame has calmed his chattering jaw. "But I can't keep this up too much longer."

Jiron just looks at him questioningly.

"I'm using pure oxygen to sustain the fire," he explains. "Remember back in Councilman Rillian's office when I had used up all the oxygen and we couldn't breathe? Well the same thing is happening here. Since this cave is enclosed, it's not going to have an unlimited supply. It should have plenty for awhile, but once we're warmed up a bit, I'll have to stop. Then we'll need to get out, fast."

"I hear you," Jiron says. "Just where is the exit from here."

Pointing back to the sound of the waterfall they sailed over, he says, "We came from that way and if I remember right, the way out is further away from it, past this island."

"It's going to be another cold swim," he says.

"I know," he admits. "But if we have a brief respite here to warm ourselves, we'll make it."

They sit in quiet as they bask in the warm glow of the fire. James finds that even his clothes are beginning to dry. When he finally feels warm through and through, he looks with trepidation at the water and says, "Shall we?"

"Best to get it over with," says Jiron. "It's not going to get any warmer."

"Ain't that the truth," agrees James.

Canceling the flame, they're once more reduced to just having the light from the orb to guide them. The coldness of the cave again begins to suck the warmth from their bodies even before they get into the water.

They push the remnant of the boat back out into the water and that first step into its icy grip takes James' breath away. Jiron holds the boat steady while James gets as far up onto it as possible before pushing it further out into the water. Then keeping a firm grip on it, he kicks with his feet and propels them away from the island, maintaining a direction which will keep the sound of the waterfall behind them.

The coldness of the water sucks the warmth from them rapidly. "If you get rid of the orb, maybe we'll be able to see the light shining in through the exit."

"I doubt if there'll be any," explains James. "It was almost dark when we first entered the old keep. And what with the rain, it's unlikely there would be any moonlight."

"That's right," he says.

"I'll try though." Suddenly, the orb disappears and they're thrown into complete and utter darkness. The sound of the now distant waterfall and the splashing of Jiron's feet lends an eeriness to the dark. Giving their eyes a chance to adjust to the dark, they look around but no light is forthcoming.

After being in the dark for ten minutes, James again creates the orb. His teeth are beginning to chatter, though not nearly as bad as the last time. If they don't get out of this water, they'll both be in trouble from hypothermia.

"There!" Jiron exclaims."

"What?" asks James. "Where?"

"Over to our right," he says. "I saw a light?"

James looks in that direction and says, "I don't see anything."

"I tell you I saw something," he insists. "It was just a momentary flash, but it was there."

"Then let's check it out," says James.

Kicking to angle their boar toward where he saw the flash, he propels them with renewed vigor at the prospect of being out of the water.

"There! I saw it too," cries out James in gladness.

As they come closer, other flashes become apparent as well. Once they're close enough for the light from the orb to illuminate the area, they discover the source of the flashes are several gems embedded in the side of the cavern.

"Gems!" exclaims Jiron.

Red, green and yellow stones of varying sizes sparkle in the orb's light. "There must be a fortune here!" James says.

A slight rock outcropping from the wall runs along the water's edge, allowing them to leave the water and follow it as they continue to hunt for the exit. It extends past the limit of the orb's light in both directions. It isn't very flat or stable looking, but it's still better than being in the frigid water.

Jiron moves them close to the ledge and then helps James onto it before climbing up himself. A large red gem sparkles in the orb's light near him. Taking out his knife, he pries out the gem and holds it up to the light. Glancing to James he says, "This might be the end of your worries about coins for the Ranch."

Giving his friend a smile, he says, "I think you're right. Let's take some and get them appraised. If they're worth a lot, we'll come back from time to time and harvest more."

"Wonder how many are here?" Jiron asks. He then proceeds to remove several more of varying size and color, each looking to be worth quite a bit.

"Don't know," admits James. Looking around at all the flashes of light outside the orb's radius, he adds, "It looks like hundreds, maybe thousands." A serious shiver hits him and he says, "But we need to get out of here."

"I agree," says Jiron. The boat has begun to float away from the wall. "Should we get back in the water or try to make it along the wall?"

The thought of going back into that iciness is more than he can bear. "I say wall," he decides.

"Then let's go," says Jiron. "Which way?"

Pointing to their right, he says, "I think it would be down that way, though I'm not completely sure."

Shrugging, Jiron says, "One way's as good as another." He leads the way as they carefully move along the uneven outcropping of rock. The footing is treacherous, sometimes there is very little for them to cling to and at times have to step into the water in order to continue onward.

James is finding it more difficult since he doesn't have the use of his left arm to maintain a grip on the wall during the worst areas. But with Jiron's help, he's able to make it.

During one rather difficult spot, James suddenly smells the scent of the forest. "We must be getting close," he tells Jiron. "I smell pine trees."

"I do too," agrees Jiron as he helps him over a steep section of stone jutting up before them. Just after that, they start feeling a faint breeze, and a few more yards further down, they find the opening where the water is flowing out of the cavern.

They'll have to wade into the flowing water in order to pass through the opening. The water is moving quickly from the cave and hidden rocks under its surface make for unstable footing. Taking it carefully, Jiron helps James as they make their way down from the outcropping of rock and into the water.

Passing out of the cave into the undergrowth beyond, they notice a slight rise in temperature. Still not warm by any means, it's still preferable to that which was within the cave. The rain is still coming down and if anything, has actually increased since earlier in the day.

"We need to find some shelter," James says to Jiron. "Or at least a large tree to stay under."

The orb doesn't give them much light to see by, the rain and trees preventing its light from extending any great distance. James is reticent to increase its brilliance, he doesn't want to attract the attention of someone who might be in the area.

Once past the cave mouth, they climb out of the water and trudge their way through the bushes and small trees lining the edge of the water. With relief they come across a good sized tree which has a relatively dry space beneath its overhanging branches.

Thankfully, they enter the protective space it provides and then set about gathering what firewood they can. Most of it is wet, but with the help of James' magic, they manage to get the wood burning. Jiron sets other damp pieces nearby to dry before being added to the fire.

"Good to be out of there!" says James.

Nodding, Jiron agrees. "Let me look at that arm of yours again," he says. As James holds out his arm, he unties the bandage and examines it. "It's a little red around the opening and some blood is still oozing out. I think I got all the wood out, won't really know for a day or two."

"I hope you did," James says as Jiron secures the bandage tight around the wound once more. Infections are one of the things he hopes to avoid. Wounds which turn septic in this world could mean the loss of a limb if not outright fatal.

What rations that were in their belt pouches have been ruined by their trip through the water. Their packs were lost when the boat had disintegrated and are now probably at the bottom of that lake. James had kept his water bottle in his pack so all they have is the one on Jiron's belt, which isn't very big. But that's the least of their concerns right now.

"How long should we stay here?" Jiron asks him.

"I'm not really sure," he says. "We could probably make it along the river as it continues through the ravine in the daylight. But once we reach the far side, we'll need to move at night. The Empire will most likely have patrols in the area looking for spies and infiltrators trying to sneak through."

"Why don't you get some sleep," suggests Jiron. "I'll watch the fire and wake you sometime past midnight."

"Okay," he says. "But make sure you do wake me. I don't want you to be too tired tomorrow because you wanted to allow me to sleep."

"I will," he assures him.

Really too tired to argue very much, James lies down and is soon asleep.

True to his word, Jiron wakes him up for his shift and gets some sleep. By the time the dark of night begins to turn into the grey of morning, James wakes him up and they get on their way.

The rain is still coming down though has tapered off a bit since last night. The cloud cover remains absolute with not even a trace of blue breaking its way through. They follow the stream as it continues down to where it joins with the main river making its way into Madoc.

The main river is flowing quickly, having been swelled by the rain of the last two days. Walking is easier here as the water has periodically overflowed its banks and washed away smaller vegetation leaving a few large trees which had been able to withstand the rushing water.

Throughout the rest of the day, they make their way alongside the river, slowly coming to the far side of the pass. Near the end of the day, the mountains begin falling away and the road leading down from the pass becomes more visible above them.

"We better camp soon and cook our dinner before the light fades completely," suggest Jiron.

"Good idea," agrees James. "We don't want to advertise our presence here to those up by the road."

They find another sheltering tree beneath which Jiron starts a fire while James goes out into the cold water with a sharpened stick to get their dinner. After spearing two large fish in succession, he brings them back to the fire. The pain in his shoulder has worsened due to the strain of catching the fish. It's definitely easier to catch fish with two good arms rather than one.

He rests his arm and warms himself by the fire while Jiron prepares the fish. "You wouldn't think it was summer as cold as that water is," James says.

"Summer's almost over," comments Jiron while he readies the fish. Once he has them skewered on sticks, he hands one to James who holds it over the fire to cook. The smell of the cooking fish makes his stomach cramp and he realizes he's not eaten for awhile.

"The last time Miko and I had come this way," he tells Jiron, "Cardri had a force up ahead at the end of the pass. They had also begun constructing a defensive barrier, I suppose in the event the Empire proved hostile to them."

"That should make it interesting for us to get through," he replies. "Maybe we could make it to the other side?"

Looking at the fast flowing river, James has his doubts about the feasibility of that idea. "I don't know," he says, hesitantly. "Let's see what awaits us further down the river first. We may be able to make it past without having to cross."

"As you wish," says Jiron. Taking his fish off the fire, he checks it and finds it not quite done. Replacing it over the flames he sits back and relaxes.

The rest of the evening passes uneventfully. As the sun dips below the horizon and the light begins to fade, they put out their fire so as not to alert anyone to their presence. They again share the watch throughout the night and when the sun begins to rise, they set out for the end of the pass.

The rain had stopped sometime during the night and by midmorning the clouds begin breaking up. James welcomes the sunshine and enjoys the warmth it brings him. Sleeping without a fire on the cold ground had kept him shivering through most of the night.

Above them on the mountainside, the road leading from the pass continues its descent down to the plains on the far side. By midafternoon, it's close enough for them to be able to make out soldiers traveling upon it. Most are moving toward the Madoc side of the Pass.

Early evening finds them close to the end of the Pass. From ahead of them, the scent of smoke wafts toward them from numerous campfires. "There must be a sizeable force up ahead?" Jiron whispers to James during a short break.

"There were around a hundred there the last time," he says. "No telling how many there might be now."

"We should await the coming of night before moving ahead," suggests Jiron. "We're just getting too close."

"I agree," responds James. They find a good spot to rest while they wait for night. James falls asleep for several hours until Jiron awakens him when it gets completely dark.

"Time to go," he says to James.

"Right."

Staying close to the river, they make their way carefully toward the end of the pass. After an hour of trudging along the bank of the river, they begin to see light from several campfires in the distance through the trees ahead of them. "Wait here" Jiron says as he moves forward to reconnoiter.

James waits by the river and watches as Jiron's shadow merges with the darkness on his way to the camp ahead. After what seems a long time, Jiron returns. "Well?" James asks him.

"It's not good," he says. "They built a wooden wall across the entrance to the Pass, and it extends to the edge of the river. There's no way we can get through on this side without going over or through the barricade."

"Which would mean alerting them to our presence," adds James.

"And I don't think they'll treat us kindly if we're discovered sneaking around," he says. "More than likely, they'll treat us as spies, probably kill us on the spot."

"Then it's the river for us," James says, not sounding too thrilled about the prospect of another dip into the cold water.

"They have a camp on the other side as well," he says. "Though there are not as many, probably just enough to keep the Empire from sending small parties around or through the lines."

"How about the river itself?" he asks.

"They don't have that blocked off," he says, "but they do have watchers on the wall stationed close to the river. I think they're more worried about boats coming up the river than out of the pass."

"I would think so too," agrees James. He sits there and thinks awhile, knowing what he's going to have to do but dreading it. After trying and failing to come up with an alternative plan, he says, "We'll need to float down the river."

"There're plenty of logs on the bank of the river," states Jiron. "We could tie a few together and use them to keep us afloat."

"We don't have enough rope to construct a raft," counters James.

"I don't mean a raft," he explains. "I mean just enough to hang onto while we float in the water. It'll be cold, but we shouldn't drown."

"Might work," agrees James. "Do we even have any rope?"

Jiron grins as he lifts his shirt and shows him a coil of thin rope that's wrapped around his waist.

"Where'd you get that?" he asks.

"Back in Trendle," he tells him. "When I knew we were going to hide the Fire, I got it. Knowing you, I figured it would be needed." James can sense that he's grinning at him in the dark.

"Okay, let's do it," he says. For the next hour, they comb the bank of the river and locate several logs which will work. Tying four of them together with the rope, they soon have a makeshift raft.

"Ready?" asks Jiron.

"No, but let's go anyway," he replies. Helping Jiron push the raft into the water, he follows it in and takes hold with his good arm.

Jiron maneuvers them to the center of the river and they float silently toward the barricade. The number of men stationed in this area has indeed greatly swelled from before. A large encampment with several buildings has sprung up where the original site had been. The wall Jiron mentioned is thirty feet high with a platform running along the top allowing archers an area to stand where they can rain arrows down on attackers.

A thousand men or more are encamped on the side of the river where the road leaves the pass and another couple hundred on the other side. A hundred feet before they reach the wall, a rope spans the river. Sitting next to the river by the main encampment is a ferry which they must use to transfer men and supplies from one camp to the other. "Looks like they mean to stay here awhile," whispers Jiron.

"I would have to agree with you," replies James.

Now coming to where the river passes by the wall, they duck down in the water with nothing but their heads above the surface. At the end of the wall is a guard set to keep watch on the river but is currently talking to the man next to him. As fortune would have it, he's facing the other way, away from the river.

The river takes them past the wall and into Madoc, now Empire territory. Before the encampment behind them completely disappears another one springs into view ahead of them.

A vast army is spread across the plains. Sprawling on both sides of the river, campfires by the hundreds can be seen. Though no wall has sprung up to ward off Cardri's men, they do have a series of sentries stationed on the Cardri side.

As they approach the Empire's encampment, a soldier moves to the river and fills his canteen right when they pass. James holds his breath as the makeshift raft sails past without the soldier even noticing them. When the soldier gets back up and returns to the camp, they both breathe a sigh of relief.

The river continues to take them through the encampment, and they see a large series of tents on the pass side. These tents are much grander and on a larger scale than the hundreds of others that dot the landscape. These must be the tents of the commanders of this force.

At the rear of the encampment is a great host of horses, at least five hundred strong. *What would they need with such a large force here? It doesn't make sense, the fighting with Madoc is much further north.*

At last, the river takes them past the end of the encampment and they pull themselves more out of the water as they watch the light from the campfires slowly disappear behind them.

Chapter   Sixteen

"Why do you suppose they have such a large army back there?" asks Jiron once they've put sufficient distance between themselves and the Empire's forces.

"I don't know," replies James. "It doesn't make much sense though."

"Think they're planning to invade Cardri?" he asks.

"I don't think so," he says. "From everything I've seen and heard the last few weeks, I don't believe they would be able to sustain a war with Cardri. They're spread way too thin."

After floating another few minutes, James indicates the north bank, "Let's get out of the water."

"But isn't Saragon further south along the river?" asks Jiron.

"Yes," he replies. "But we're too exposed here in the river. When morning comes, anyone glancing in this direction is sure to see us."

"Good thought," says Jiron and they commence angling toward the northern bank. Dripping wet, they leave the river and do their best to wring the water out of their damp clothes.

"Shall we follow the river?" Jiron asks.

"I was considering it," he says. "Though let's stay some distance away to avoid being seen. And first chance we get, we'll need to acquire some horses." Looking to Jiron, he asks, "How far is it to Saragon?"

He shrugs as he says, "Don't know. Never went very far out of the City of Light."

Finished with emptying the water out of his boots, James laces them back on before getting to his feet. The squishing in his boots is a real problem. Besides being uncomfortable and annoying, he's afraid of getting foot rot.

"You ready?" he asks Jiron.

"Just a moment," he says as he goes over to their raft and begins untying the rope. Once he gets the logs untied, he pushes them back in the river where the current takes them and they soon disappear down the river. He ties the rope back around his middle again and then turns to James, "Now we can go."

Setting out, they begin to move along the bank of the river, steadily moving away until they can just barely see it in the moonlight. Keeping the river on their right, they make their way to the south for several hours before the lights of a town appear ahead of them.

As they approach, they're able to tell that the lights they are seeing are coming from campfires spread throughout what's left of the city. The light reveals the city is all but destroyed. A once sizeable town has been reduced to a broken, charred remnant of its once former glory.

"Pleasant Meadows," James tells Jiron in a hushed whisper.

"What?" he asks.

"Pleasant Meadows," he repeats. "At least I think it is. Miko and I had come across people fleeing the Empire's sacking of the city before coming to the City of Light. This town ahead of us could very well be it."

"I've heard of it," Jiron tells him. "They used to make good knives there, though it doesn't look like they do anymore."

"No," agrees James.

Patrols are riding the perimeter and sentries can be seen positioned throughout the town. "Why would they need all that for a town so far behind their lines?" asks Jiron. "Unless there's something there they're protecting?"

"I don't know, maybe" agrees James.

"Perhaps we should investigate," suggests Jiron. "It might be important."

"It could also prove dangerous," counters James. "We don't need to get ourselves killed without a good reason. Besides, how would we even get in there? They have the whole place cordoned off pretty well."

"I don't know," he admits.

"Jiron, we have more important things to worry about right now," insists James.

"Okay," he says as he looks at the town longingly. His curiosity is definitely getting the better of him.

"Now, let's make our way around to the other side, but keep your eyes open for an opportunity to acquire some horses."

Moving away from the river, they circle the town, giving the patrols a wide berth. The opportunity doesn't present itself to acquire horses by the time they've arrived on the other side of the town.

The sky begins to lighten as they leave Pleasant Meadows behind. "We'll need to find some place to hole up until night again," announces James.

"Haven't seen anything yet," Jiron replies.

As they continue along, the sky continues to brighten until the sun finally crests the horizon. They come across an orchard and move within the trees to better hide themselves. The fruit hangs heavy on the branches, testament to the fact that the farmer is no longer around to pick it.

James pulls one down and munches on it as they continue to move through the orchard, Jiron does the same. From out of the trees ahead of them, a blackened structure appears. Burnt down and destroyed, it probably used to be the home of the farmer whose orchard this is. Fortunately it still has two of its four walls remaining. "This could afford us some protection," James offers.

"True," agrees Jiron.

They advance on the house slowly, keeping a constant look for anyone who might still be in the area. Jiron draws James' attention off to the side where three skeletons lie, their meat having been picked clean by scavengers. "Don't think we have to worry about the farmer coming back," he says gravely.

James nods as they continue their approach. In the corner of the house where the two remaining walls meet is a dresser which seems to have escaped the worst of the fire. The only damage it sustained was some scorching by the heat as well as some damage when a crossbeam had struck it when the ceiling collapsed.

It takes a few minutes, but they get an area cleared away in the corner large enough for them to lie down and get some rest. Taking turns at watch, they spend the rest of the day there in the corner of that burned out farmhouse.

Having taken the second watch, Jiron walks through the orchard around the farmhouse as he keeps an eye out for intruders. A noise causes him to stop in his tracks as he cocks his head, trying to locate where it had originated. The noise comes to him again. He plasters himself against the nearest tree as he looks off through the orchard.

Moving through the trees are five men on horseback, soldiers of the Empire. And they appear to be heading straight for the farmhouse where

James is still sleeping. Moving quickly, he races for the farmhouse, trying his best to remain unseen by the horsemen.

Suddenly, a cry erupts as one of them catches a glimpse of him running through the trees. A glance back shows the horsemen quickly moving to overtake him. "James!" he yells as loudly as he can. Dodging between the trees, he alters his course to lead the horsemen away from the farmhouse. "James!" he cries again.

A knife appears in his right hand as he races through the orchard. From behind him, the men on the horses are calling to him in their language, but whether or not they're ordering him to stop, he can't tell.

His meandering flight through the trees has succeeded in leading the horsemen away from the farmhouse. One of the horsemen behind him cries out as he falls off his horse, his right shoulder blasted away by one of James' slugs.

The remaining horsemen abruptly come to a halt as they try to discover from whence this new attack is coming from. Jiron looks back at the horsemen and can see further behind them where James is standing by the broken wall of the farmhouse, as he cocks his arm back to unleash another of his deadly missiles.

Now with both knives in his hands, Jiron turns back and races to attack the mounted horsemen. The odds improve again as another soldier is knocked off his horse by the force of a slug blasting out of his chest.

The soldiers turn as one and race toward James, intent on seeking retribution for the death of their comrades. Their swords in hand and war cries on their lips, they ride to kill this lone man standing by the burnt out farmhouse.

Jiron races behind them, falling behind as he sees them rapidly closing the gap between them and James. Another soldier is taken out as a slug exits what used to be his skull, his companions don't even stop. Hell bent on James' death, they kick their horses into even greater speed.

Crumph!

The ground under them suddenly erupts, horses scream in terror as they're thrown into the air. Bones snap and break as the horses fall back to the ground, smashing their riders beneath them.

Jiron reaches the scene, but the battle is over. The soldiers lying under the horses no longer move as the animals thrash and cry out. Taking up one of the soldier's swords, he's quick to put the injured horses out of their misery.

He looks up to see James approaching. "You okay?" James asks him.

Nodding, he replies, "I'm fine." Looking around at the dead men, he continues, "Wonder what brought them into this orchard?"

"Who knows?" replies James. He goes over and takes the reins of one of the remaining horses and says, "At least we have horses now."

"True," agrees Jiron. Going over to another horse wandering around, he takes its reins and walks back over to where James is going through the pouch of one of the soldiers. "Looking for something?" he asks.

"Never know," he says as he gets up and moves to another lifeless body where he opens its pouch as well. "Could be something that may tell us what they were doing here."

Jiron walks over to another one and goes through its pouch, but all he finds are some coins which he adds to the ones he's already carrying.

When James finally stands up from inspecting the last of the dead soldiers, he says, "Nothing."

"Really didn't think you'd find anything," comments Jiron.

"Me either, actually," he admits. "I just couldn't leave without checking."

"Right, you never know."

The sun is almost to the horizon, so they decide to wait until it becomes darker before they head out through the orchard. Back at the farmhouse, they have a meal of apples and some cheese they found in a sack with other food items behind one of the saddles. Each now has two canteens and some rations, though neither has much.

As twilight settles in, they mount and begin riding through the orchard, once again on their way to Saragon. Traveling by horse allows them to put miles behind them much quicker than they had been able to on foot. James worries about the soldiers killed back at the farmhouse and what that may mean when their bodies are found. Hopefully, they won't think to look further into Empire controlled areas for the killers, but rather search in the other direction.

Throughout the night, the stars shine bright, giving them some light with which to see. The moon rises several hours later, allowing them even better visibility.

To their right, the river turns to follow a more southerly direction than it had north of Pleasant Meadows. Though the road beside it remains empty, they dare not trust that it will remain so. Keeping a wide distance from the river, they ride parallel to it as they continue south.

Several times they encounter lights ahead of them, forcing them to circle around before continuing on. Camps of soldiers, none with more than ten, are scattered about the countryside. Makes no sense to James, but who knows why anyone does anything.

Near dawn, they come across another farm that had been abandoned when the Empire entered this area. The farmhouse is still in good condition so they bring the horses into the front room to keep them out of sight. In one of the rear rooms, they find beds to sleep on while awaiting the coming again of night.

Sitting around the table in the kitchen, they have a dinner of rations and apples. They did find a loaf of bread left behind when the farmers left. But the amount of green and grey on it kept them from eating it. "How do you plan for us to get into Saragon?" Jiron asks.

James looks to him and says, "Back when Miko and I first came through the Merchant's Pass, there was a refugee camp at the way stop for the people of Madoc who fled the coming of the Empire. We met a couple men with their families there who shared our fire and food that night."

"One of the things they told us was how they managed to escape from Saragon when it finally fell. One said, '*My grandfather used to be a smuggler way back when he was a younger man and had showed me an old smuggler route into the city that he said no one, not even the Governor knew about. Silas and I found it and used it to get our families out past the walls. The tunnel came out in a pile of old stones a dozen yards from the river, almost two miles north of the city.*'"

"Think it's still hidden?" he asks.

"Hope so, can't imagine why it wouldn't be," he tells Jiron. "The problem is going to be in finding it. A pile of old stones two miles north of the city could be hard to find. At least he said it was a dozen yards from the river, which should help in narrowing it down some." He takes another bite and then adds, "We'll probably have to hunt for it in the daylight, I doubt if we'll find it in the dark."

"Which means we'll run the risk of being spotted," Jiron states.

"True, but we'll try to minimize that as best we can," he assures him.

Jiron offers to take the first watch today for which James is grateful. The magic earlier in the day had tired him out some but not nearly as bad as it used to. He must be growing stronger in magic or his body is just getting used to it and its effects.

Lying down on the bed, he's soon fast asleep. Sometime past noon, Jiron wakes him for his turn. And then later, when the sun dips below the horizon, James awakens him and they continue on their way as twilight deepens into the dark of night.

They ride quickly once the moon rises, giving them ample light to see their immediate surroundings. Early in the evening, lights from another town appear out of the darkness ahead of them. "Do you think that's Saragon?" Jiron asks.

"Hard to tell," James answers. "From what I've heard of Saragon, it is or rather was, an important town to southern Madoc. This one doesn't look big enough."

"You may be right," Jiron says. They swing wide of the town and go around it.

Halfway around, James feels the tingling which always accompanies another doing magic. In the dark it's difficult to determine who or where it's coming from. The tingling only lasts a minute or two before stopping. Once they've passed the town and its lights have long since disappeared behind them, he tells Jiron about it.

"At least it wasn't directed at us this time," he says.

"True," agrees James as they continue riding on into the night.

The terrain begins to turn gradually hilly, and they find they have to move between some of the hills in order to parallel the course of the road to their right without actually riding upon it.

The moon arcs overhead as they ride hard to the south in search of Saragon. Just what he expects to find there, he doesn't know. But to the core of his being, he knows he has to go there.

During the final conclave of the Priests of Morcyth, the High Priest had fasted and prayed for a long time. At the end of which, the priests up and left, leaving no word about where they went and taking nothing with them. It all seems rather strange to James that they wouldn't have taken something with them. With the followers of Dmon-Li eradicating them, he can understand about not telling the world their destination. That makes perfect sense.

But Ollinearn in the City of Light had found a passage which told the birth place of the last High Priest had been in Saragon. From that time, he knew he would be going there. Somewhere in that town there has to be a clue or something to reveal where they went.

When the sky begins to lighten with the coming of the morn, a large city appears out of the distance before them. A formidable wall encircles the city, several sections or which having been reduced to rubble during an earlier battle. The city itself sprawls across several hills to the north of where two rivers meet. It looks to be entirely in the crook made by the meeting of the two rivers. From where James sits, it looks to have once been a very defensible area. The Empire must've brought in mages to take the walls down, that's the only explanation.

"This must be Saragon," states Jiron.

"I would tend to agree," adds James.

Coming to a halt at the top of a hill overlooking the town, they scan the horizon for enemy forces. Between them and the town lies an encampment of several hundred men, riders can be seen going from one point to another.

"I sure hope you can find that entrance," Jiron tells him. "I don't think we would have much luck making it past all those men."

Nodding in agreement, James indicates they should get down off the hill before they're spotted. Moving back down to the bottom, he dismounts. Jiron follows suit.

"The man said the entrance was two miles to the north of Saragon, hidden in amongst a pile of stones by the river," he says. "I would think that other river over there would be the one he mentioned. The one we've been following is more to the west."

"That would stand to reason," he says. "Maybe we should leave the horses here and work our way through the hills over to the river."

"In broad daylight, that's going to be chancy," James replies. "But sitting here for hours would be just as bad." Walking his horse over to a nearby tree, he secures the reins to it. Jiron brings his over and secures it as well.

"If we keep between the hills," Jiron says, "I think we might be able to get over there without being spotted."

"Let's do it quickly then," says James.

Jiron nods as he heads out with James right behind. It's a couple miles of hills they have to work through in order to reach the river. Keeping low, they're able to cross the distance within an hour while remaining unseen.

At the river, they look with chagrin at a stretch of broken stone over two hundred yards long. "We'll never find it!" exclaims Jiron.

"We don't have a choice," insists James. "Let's start looking, most likely we'll find it at the base of a hill or among some trees."

Nodding, Jiron says, "That does narrow the scope down some."

Getting busy, they begin combing the area, concentrating mainly within the parameters set up: within a couple yards of the river, by a hill or among some trees. "I think I found it!" exclaims Jiron after a half hour of searching.

James looks over and sees him at the base of a hill that looks as if it had collapsed sometime in the past. Several trees and bushes have overgrown the area, masking the entrance. He goes over to where Jiron stands next to a large boulder.

"I can feel air moving from behind here," he tells James as he joins him.

James checks it out and sure enough, he can smell the musky odor of the earth coming from behind the large boulder. "Can we move it?" he asks, indicating the boulder.

"I would think so," Jiron replies. Putting his shoulder against it, he begins to push as James adds what strength he can from his one good arm. The other one has steadily improved, but remains too tender to allow him to use it for this.

The boulder begins to move and then the top rocks to the side revealing an opening with a downward slanting passage behind it. James looks to Jiron with a big smile on his face, "Told you."

"Okay, so you did," he admits.

Looking around, they make sure no one is in the vicinity before slipping into the passage. Once they're both within the tunnel, Jiron manages to pull the boulder back into position, again hiding the entrance. Light suddenly floods the passage as James' orb appears on the palm of his hand. He takes the lead with the orb held out before him.

The passage is narrow, barely wide enough for them to stand side by side let alone walk next to each other. As they move forward through the passage, they encounter water. The floor of the passage has been flooded, maybe by rains or maybe by just seeping through the ground from the nearby river.

After several yards of first encountering the water, it deepens to the point of where their boots are completely submerged in it. "This better not get much worse," comments Jiron.

"Whoever built this should've anticipated something like this happening," says James. "The river will at times overflow its banks and this place would then be completely submerged."

Sure enough, they come to an area further ahead with a grate in the side of the tunnel where the water is draining away. "See," says James when they come to it. "Stop worrying."

"Wasn't worrying," Jiron replies defensively. "Just stating a concern."

Continuing past the grate the water level of the passage remains constant all the way through. It's a wonder smugglers would've used such a way to get their goods out of the city. Of course, back in that guy's grandfather's day, this passage was probably better maintained than it is now.

It seems a long time before the passage again begins to ascend back to the surface. James realizes they are again moving to the surface when the water level in the passage begins to drop. After several hundred more feet, the floor of the passage passes out of the water and they're once more walking on dry ground.

Not too much further past where they are again on dry ground that the passage ends abruptly at a brick wall. No handle or latch is visible for opening whatever door this may be. James hunts around for loose bricks, or ones that seem loose. So confident at first of being able to solve this riddle, he soon becomes more and more worried that he's not going to be able to figure it out as time passes.

Bored, Jiron leans against the brick wall at the end of the passage while he waits for James to finish searching the walls for the hidden mechanism. As his weight comes full against the brick wall, it suddenly swings open with a slight squeal of rusty hinges. Off balance, Jiron stumbles through the opening and falls to the ground on the other side, coming up quick with a knife in his hand.

"Found it!" he says to James with a smile.

As James leaves the tunnel, the light from the orb reveals they are inside what used to be a basement. The place reeks of charred wood, the ceiling having recently collapsed due to a fire that had raged through here, burning most of the wood.

Above them, light filters down through the rubble and wreckage that used to be a building. James extinguishes the orb, as the light filtering down gives them plenty with which to see.

Jiron holds very still as he listens for a sound that may indicate someone is nearby. "Stay right here," Jiron tells him.

He moves carefully through the rubble, trying not to disturb anything that may cause the wreckage above them to come crashing down upon their heads. He works his way to the other side of the room where a stone stairway still stands. At the foot of it, he turns to James and motions for him to come over to him.

When James reaches his side, he whispers, "I'll go up and see what's going on. Just wait here and I'll be right back."

"Okay," James says. Waiting there at the bottom of the stairs, he watches as Jiron moves to the top and then with a quick glance back he motions for James to remain where he is.

James watches as he moves away from the top of the stairs. Several minutes pass by before Jiron reappears and comes back down to where James is waiting for him.

"Well?" asks James.

"Up there is pretty messed up," he explains. "We are going to need to be really careful, the whole place looks unstable and about to cave in at any minute."

Nodding, James says, "I see. We're going to need this to remain open so we can get out of here."

"Exactly," agrees Jiron. Pointing up the stairs, he says, "Once to the top, we have to cross through the wreckage before we'll be able to reach the street. I couldn't see any better way, so we'll just have to step very carefully." He looks to James and asks, "Understand?"

Nodding his head, he says, "Yes."

"Follow me and try to go where I do," he tells him.

"Okay."

Jiron again moves to the top of the stairs, this time with James right behind him. When he gets to the top, James understands what he was talking about. The walls near them are still partially standing and no way to leave the building. The only way out is across the broken, burnt floor to where a wall has collapsed outward when the roof had caved in.

"Ready?" asks Jiron. When he gets a nod from James, he steps out onto a blackened piece of wood that used to be a support beam for the ceiling.

James waits until Jiron has completely navigated it and is on another section before following. Piece by piece, Jiron leads them closer to the hole in the wall. Suddenly from the street outside the building, they can hear footsteps approaching and they hold still upon their precarious perches.

The footsteps come close and James watches as several soldiers pass right in front of the hole in the wall they've been trying to reach. Had they but looked within the hole, they would've seen Jiron standing there on a section of the collapsed ceiling not six feet from them.

When their footsteps can no longer be heard, Jiron resumes moving until he reaches what remains of the floor beside the hole. Jiron steps to the hole in the wall, knife in one hand, as he looks out upon the street running outside the building. When James joins him he says, "Looks clear."

"Alright," replies James. "Let's go."

The building across the street from them still looks to be in good shape. Jiron gestures with his head toward it and raises an eyebrow questioningly. James nods his head in reply and after again making sure no one is on the street, they race across the street to the doorway.

The door proves to be locked and they have a heart thumping few minutes standing there exposed in the street while Jiron works on the lock. Finally, they hear a click and the door swings open. Rushing in, they close the door behind them.

Chapter   Seventeen

The room they find themselves in looks as if it had been ravaged by looters. Tables overturned, items from shelves thrown carelessly on the floor, and even a chair shows signs of being searched. The back of it has been sliced open and most of its stuffing lies scattered across the floor.

"They sure did a number on this place," James says. Looking around, he picks up a book which has been torn apart. From the intricate design on the cover and the few pages he scans through, it seems a work of art. Saddened, he drops it back to the ground.

From where Jiron is looking out a window he nods without commenting. "Looks like they have slave gangs working to clear the streets," he says after another minute.

Coming over to the window, James looks out and sees a dozen slaves with two guards further down the street where they're clearing away the rubble. Several wagons stand ready next to them for the debris of the collapsed and ruined buildings they're removing from the street. "Maybe they plan to stay here awhile?" he guesses.

"Probably." Jiron then glances at him and asks, "Now that we're here, how are you planning on discovering any information?" Gesturing to the slaves outside, he continues, "We'll be seen sure as anything if we spend any time out there."

"I know," he replies. "Any information would be hundreds of years old. We need to locate buildings that have been around for centuries and somehow find a way to search them."

"That could include over half the town!" Jiron exclaims. "It might take us weeks to be able to search all the buildings that would entail. And that's only if they're not currently occupied by the Empire's forces."

"We should probably work at night," James says as he breaks out in a yawn. "Less chance of being spotted."

"I agree," replies Jiron. "We could use some rest. I'll take the first watch. Don't think I could fall asleep right now anyway."

A tired James nods, not wishing to argue the point. He turns a couch back upright before lying down. Jiron standing before the window looking out is the last thing he sees before closing his eyes.

It's almost night before James wakes up. "You didn't wake me!" he says accusingly to Jiron where he still stands by the window.

"Wasn't tired," he says. "You looked like you needed it."

Getting up, James walks over to look out the window. "Anything happening?" he asks.

"No," he says, shaking his head. "The slaves continued all day clearing the rubble. A short time ago the wagons left and they were taken away."

The street outside looks deserted in the deepening shadows. The light is beginning to fade as the sun hits the horizon. Jiron points down the street off to the west and says, "The only really old looking buildings I could see from here are down that way. One has the look of a temple, though in its present condition it's hard to be sure."

"Then let's check it out once the light has completely faded," James tells him.

"Maybe I should go alone?" he suggests.

"No," replies James, rejecting the idea. "I need to go. There could be something there you'll not recognize but that I will."

"As you wish," he replies. He then nods when he remembers the bronze plaque they found in the complex back in the swamp and how James had recognized its significance.

For the next hour they wait by the window as the light continues to fade until darkness completely envelopes the city. Jiron then opens the door, peering out to make sure the street is deserted. When he finds no one about, he moves into the dark street with James right behind him.

Keeping to the shadows, they move slowly down the street in the direction of the church Jiron had indicated earlier. If there was indeed an old church there, there may also be others in the immediate vicinity.

No patrols walk the streets of Saragon. They've been in control of it for so long they no longer need worry anymore about hold out survivors from the time of the city's fall. This makes it easy for them to move quickly without being seen.

A noise in the night freezes them in their tracks. Keeping still against a wall bordering the street, they wait for a moment, listening. When the sound doesn't repeat itself, they continue on.

Coming to an intersection of streets, Jiron pauses a moment to make sure the cross street is empty of soldiers. Looking down both ways, he then motions for James to follow as he darts across to the other side.

"We're almost there," he whispers as they work their way further down the street.

A great shadow looms in the darkness before them. Its spire, once tall and majestic now lies broken on the street. The smell of charred wood permeates everything, a fire had raged through here not very long ago, a week or two maybe. James glances in through a broken doorway of the building they're moving along. The light from the stars above reveals a burnt out husk. What function the building held before the fire, can no longer be determined.

Jiron points to the building across the street and says, "That's the temple I saw."

"Let's go then," James tells him eagerly.

A quick look down the side streets and then they race across to the temple's double entry doors. The one on the left is askew and slightly ajar. Squeezing through, they make their way inside. Jiron jumps when a small light appears in James' hand.

"Sorry," James says, orb glowing softly in his hand.

"No one's going to detect that are they?" he asks.

"I don't think so," he assures him. "I haven't felt anyone do magic since coming here."

The interior is definitely that of a temple. Though it has been stripped and looted, it still has the unmistakable look of a place of worship. In the minimal light the orb is putting out, it's hard to tell just who had been worshiped here. "Where do you propose we look?" Jiron asks.

"I'd think in the basement below," suggests James. "It's unlikely that had this been a Morcyth temple at one time, anything would have remained where the average person would be. The new occupants would've stripped off any old insignias and replaced them with their own."

The temple is filled with rubble, portions of the ceiling as well as half a wall have fallen in. The debris covering the floor makes their footing unstable. They split up as they search for access to the lower levels, if there are any.

"Over here!" shouts James from where he's searching near the back. Behind a fallen column lies a stairway going down.

Without waiting for Jiron to join him he moves down the stairs, taking care not to trip over the debris that has fallen upon them. As he makes his way down, the glow from the orb reveals where the stairs end at a corridor moving to the left and right. Glancing back to make sure Jiron is following him, he turns to the right and proceeds cautiously down the corridor.

Not very far down the corridor, he finds a body in the middle of the corridor. Hacked to pieces, it lays in a pool of dried blood. From the vestments the dead man is wearing, he looks to have been a priest of some sort.

Jiron comes close and after a brief examination says, "Asran. This temple must've been to the god Asran."

"Asran?" asks James questioningly.

Nodding, he indicates a symbol of a plant encircled by a ring of interwoven leaves embroidered on the dead man's clothes. "Asran is the god of nature, of growing things." Glancing to James he adds, "A very important god to farmers and the like, can't believe they would kill even priests, especially these."

"From what I've seen of the Empire's soldiers, nothing surprises me anymore," he says.

Throughout the hallways and rooms they find more of Asran's slain priests. In one room, they find coffers smashed open where the soldiers had looted the temple's treasure. A dozen slain priests lie just within the treasure room where they had died defending it. Shaking his head, James just continues on.

Room after room they search for anything which may indicate Morcyth or the Star of Morcyth, but fail to find any. "I don't think we'll find anything here," Jiron says as they reach the furthest room from where they entered the temple.

"I'm sure there are others close by we can check before it gets light," states James.

"Most likely," replies Jiron.

As they make their way back toward the stairs, they hear from up ahead of them the sound of footsteps coming down the stairs. James immediately extinguishes his light as they duck into a side room. Holding still, they listen as the footsteps reach the bottom and begin to come their way.

It sounds as if there are two people coming, the light from their torch beginning to illuminate the hallway outside the room where they wait. The ones approaching are talking amongst themselves and Jiron glances to James when they realize it's the speech of the Empire they're using.

In Jiron's hand, James sees the light from the approaching torch reflecting off the blade of a knife. He pulls a slug from his belt and then gives Jiron a nod as they ready themselves.

The footsteps continue to come closer but then suddenly turn into the room just prior to theirs. The torchlight greatly diminishes as the bearer passes into the room. Jiron motions for James to wait while he goes and sees what they're doing in the other room.

He moves to the edge of the doorway and looks inside to find them going through the shattered remains of some priest's living quarters. They're tossing things out of drawers as well as the chest by the foot of the bed in their search for anything that may have been overlooked by previous looters.

Jiron comes back to James and whispers, "They're busy looting. We might be able to slip by without them noticing."

Nodding, James motions for him to lead the way.

Coming into the hallway, Jiron pauses a moment to check within the room where the Empire's soldiers are looting and then motions for James to follow him.

Moving quickly, they pass by the room and hurry down the hallway without being seen. Upon reaching the stairs, they glance back and see that the guards are still busy looting. They ascend the stairs and move on to the next building.

Coming back from their third night of seeking signs of Morcyth, they enter the home they've been using as a base of operations since the first night. Except for the slave work crew clearing the streets, this part of town has been relatively quiet. The majority of the soldiers and civilians from the Empire are congregated in what used to be the Government Quarter of the city.

Sitting down against the wall, Jiron looks to James and says, "I don't think we are going to find anything."

"We can't give up," he insists. Taking out a portion of his remaining rations, he takes a bite before continuing. "Somewhere in this town, there has to be something which will tell us where the priests went."

"Why?" Jiron asks. He's asked this same question daily since the first night turned up nothing. "Just because the last high priest was born here doesn't mean he came back here."

James just gives him a look of frustration, "There just does."

"We're running out of food," he tells him. "And I just hope no one discovers the bodies of those guards we left in that cellar, the hunt will be on for sure." Yesterday, while they were searching through an old building, three soldiers had stumbled upon them and were disposed of quickly. They stashed their bodies in the building's cellar and then stacked old boxes and crates around them to better hide them.

The morning light continues growing as the sun peeks over the horizon. Shortly the sound of the slave gang can be heard approaching as they come to continue working to clear the streets.

Today, the work gang comes to just in front of the building where James and Jiron are hiding. Jiron glances out the window and sees them beginning to clear the rubble away from where the wall from the building next to them has fallen out into the street. It had been one of the ones gutted when the fire had raged in this area.

They decide to move upstairs to avoid accidental detection should anyone wander into their building. Directly above them they find a room with a window which overlooks the area where the slaves are clearing away the debris.

Taking turns at watch, they settle in to await the coming of darkness when they can once more resume their search. As Jiron had taken the first watch yesterday, James takes it today.

There are times when it's hard to keep yourself awake when you have nothing to do, especially when you are unable to do anything for fear of being discovered. James sits near the window taking advantage of the slight breeze coming through. His mind wanders to a life which now seems so long ago.

He thinks of his grandfather and grandmother, both had always tried to do their best, but he was at that age when nothing anyone told him meant anything. Homesickness strikes him and he wonders if he'll ever go home.

Dave. Just what is Dave doing? He must be worried sick about him, as he supposes everyone who knew him is right now. If he ever does make it back, will role playing games ever mean the same to him again? After having lived it? He wishes that some day he'll get the chance to find out.

The sound of the men outside working continues to give him some added distraction, albeit not very much. There's only so much rock clearing you can watch at a time. Every once in awhile he can catch a snippet of what they're saying, for the slaves are the former citizens of Saragon and thus, he can understand them.

From down below, he can hear one of the men sneeze. Such an occurrence has been common, what with all the dust being raised by the removal of the rubble.

"Gesundheit," he hears another of the slaves reply.

He continues to reminisce about home when his mind turns to Meliana. Oh, Meliana. The way he felt when she had held his arm while he walked her home is still strong. How she swayed while they danced, her laugh when he said something whimsical. She's been in his mind a lot lately, perhaps when he gets back to Cardri and all this Morcyth business is concluded, maybe he'll find a way to return to Corillian and find her. See if there's actually something between them.

Suddenly, his mind snaps back to the here and now. *Gesundheit?* Did he hear that correctly? A chill runs through him at the realization that that is not a word native to here. *That's a word from home!* Since coming to this world he's not once heard that particular expression.

Going to the window, he peers down and sees the same slave gang that he's seen the last few days since they arrived. A dozen men of varying ages, from early teens to even one old grandfatherly looking individual, none of which immediately stand out as the one who spoke.

He continues to watch them and after a half hour, the scene repeats itself. Someone sneezes and the grandfatherly individual says "Gesundheit." Excited, he keeps a close eye on the old guy. The other slaves near him help him out. He does less than everyone else due to his age, but the slaver must allow it for no recriminations are forthcoming from him.

Every once in awhile the old man sits down and takes a break while the others continue working. From what Miko had told him of his experiences with slavers, he was surprised the old guy is being allowed to rest. *Guess different slavers work differently.*

Waking up Jiron, he tells him what's been happening and the significance of that old man saying the word he said.

"You think he's from your world?" he asks incredulously.

"Yes," he says with conviction. "I can't think of any other reason he would say that." When Jiron looks at him skeptically, he adds, "If I can be here, others can too."

"True," agrees Jiron. "But there's still no reason why he has to be from your world. He could've picked that word up anywhere. Or it could even be a different word that just sounds similar."

Shaking his head, James says, "No. He said it at just the right moment under just the right circumstances. Not once, but twice."

Jiron gives him a silent look for a moment before saying, "Okay, then. What do you plan to do?"

"Help him," he replies.

"How?" he asks. "If we take him with us, he'll just slow us down and then we'll all be either dead or on a slave gang." Going to the window, he glances down to the old man below who's still sitting on large piece of broken wall close to their building, wiping the sweat off his face with a rag. "Look! He can't even keep up with clearing away small rocks and wood. There's no way!"

"I know," concedes James. "But I have to at least talk to him. I've got to know for sure."

Jiron gives him another long look and then glances back down to the street. The old guy has once more joined his fellow slaves in removing the rubble. "Where he sat is near one of the windows on the bottom floor," he says. "Maybe he'll sit there again and you can whisper to him out the window."

"Good idea!" agrees James excitedly.

"Just be very quiet," he warns. "You don't want to attract the notice of the slavers."

"I know," James assures him.

Moving back downstairs, they position themselves by the window near where the old man had rested. They occasionally glance outside to see if the old man will sit back down near them. A half hour later, he pulls out his rag and once more goes to sit on the large piece of wall not three feet from the window where James waits.

Once the old man has sat down, James whispers out to him, "Don't make a sound. I'm in the building behind you." He sees the old man's shoulders stiffen a fraction as his words reach him. "Do you understand me?" he asks.

The old man nods his head as he wipes his face.

The slavers who're overseeing this group are over by the main party of slaves and are pretty much ignoring the old guy. James asks, "Are you from around here?"

He rubs his face with his rag and then turns his head toward the window where James is and replies just loud enough to be heard, "Born here."

That was definitely not the answer he was expecting. Glancing at Jiron, he sees him shrug. Turning back to the window, he whispers, "I heard you use the word 'gesundheit' when that other man sneezed."

Nodding, the old man asks, "Do you know what it means?" There seemed to be a slight tremor in his voice when he asked the question.

"It means, health, or good health," he replies, wondering why he would ask such a question.

The old man freezes for a second then again wipes his face with the rag. He sits there quietly for several minutes until James begins to think he might've forgotten about him.

"Why did you ask?" questions James.

The old man shakes his head as one of the slavers looks over in their direction. Getting up, the old man returns to help the other slaves in removing the rubble.

"What was that about?" asks Jiron when James moves away from the window.

"I don't know," he replies. "But when I told him what it meant, he reacted to it." Sitting down against the wall under the window, he adds, "Something's going on here."

Jiron munches on some of his rations as he watches James mull over what happened. "I have to find out what."

He waits by the window the rest of the morning and afternoon. Though the old man takes several rest breaks in that time, he doesn't do it near their window. James catches him casting looks over toward the window from time to time as he works. Finally, when the sun is getting low in the sky, he comes and sits back down by the window and asks, "You here tomorrow?"

James whispers back, "Yes."

The old man nods as the slavers holler for the slaves to gather together for the return to the slave compound. As the old man gets up off the piece of wall, he points to it and then points to a spot closer to the wall before going to join the others.

James watches as the old man shuffles along with the others back down the street. When they've moved out of sight, he turns to Jiron and says, "We need to move that section of wall closer to the window."

"Why?" he asks.

"The old guy indicated we should," he replies. "It may enable us to communicate better tomorrow. Less chance of being overheard."

"No. I mean why bother talking to him?" Jiron corrects.

"When I told him what it meant, he seemed surprised that I knew," he clarifies. "He also asked if I was to be here tomorrow. Why would he say that?"

"To tell the soldiers and have us arrested," suggests Jiron.

Shaking his head, James says, "He could've done that any time today. No, he wants to tell me something."

"You may be reading more into this than there is," Jiron insists. "He could just be a lonely old man who wants to talk with someone who's either not a slave or a slaver."

"Maybe," James skeptically admits. "Only one way to find out though. If he is just a lonely old guy, I'll say no more about it."

"Okay," he agrees.

They wait until it gets dark and then make their way out onto the street to where the section of wall the old man had sat on lies. Struggling with all their strength, they're able to move it over to where it almost touches the wall beneath the window. "That should be close enough," Jiron says after the section of wall is in position. They use their feet to eradicate the marks on the ground they made when moving the slab of wall.

Nodding, James adds, "We should be able to hear each other well without having to speak too loudly."

"Are you planning on searching other buildings tonight?" he asks him.

Shaking his head, he says, "No, I'm too exhausted."

"Then go ahead and get some sleep while I keep watch," he volunteers.

"Thanks." They return into the building where James lies down and falls right to sleep. Jiron doesn't wake him all night, and even manages to get a few hours of sleep as well. True, he was taking an awful chance having no one on watch, but they've been there several days now and no one has yet to come by except for the slave gang.

The next morning, the sound of the slave gang approaching awakens James. He moves to the window where Jiron is already looking out at their approach. "Do you see the old guy?" he asks.

"Yeah," he replies. "He's in there with the others."

They watch as the slaves and slavers approach and then begin working in the same area, clearing the rubble. It's an hour or so after their arrival when the old guy makes his way over to the now much closer section of fallen wall. Sitting down with his back to the window, he produces the same dirty, stained rag to wipe the sweat off his face and neck.

"You there?" James hears him whisper.

"Yeah," he whispers back.

"How did you know what that word meant?" he asked.

"It's used a lot where I come from?" replies James. "Why?"

"You're the first one ever to know," he explains. One of the slavers glances over in his direction, but then after a moment resumes the conversation he's having with another.

"Does that mean something to you?" James asks.

"Yes," replies the old man. "As far as I know, my family has been the only ones to have used it. Have been for hundreds of years."

"Oh?" prompts James.

He glances over to the slavers to make sure they're not watching before continuing. "Seems one of my great-great- I don't know how many grandfathers had been told that someone would come who would know the meaning of it. That we needed to be aware and ready."

"Ready for what?" he asks.

Just then a slaver looks in the old guy's direction and he gets up to join the others in picking up rubble.

James almost screams in impatience. Knowing he's got a while to wait, he sits anxiously next to Jiron under the window. What the man said keeps running through his mind.

The time seems to pass excruciatingly slow before the slave gang takes their noon meal. When the sound of them clearing away the rubble ceases, James peers out to see the slaves lining up to get their food and water. After receiving his share, the old guy comes back over to take his place on the section of wall by the window.

"You there?" he whispers just after he sits down.

"Yes," replies James. "What were you to be ready for?"

"You," he replies. "Didn't think I'd be the one to live to see it." Taking a bite of his food, he chews a moment then continues. "Thought the secret our family kept would die with me. You see my son and grandson both perished when the Empire took Saragon, I'm all that's left."

At the word 'secret', James' pulse quickens. "I'm sorry for your family," he says, offering his condolences.

"Me too," he replies sadly. After taking a drink of his water, he says, "Anyway, what's done is done. Who told my ancestor has been lost, but what was told was not."

"What was he told?" asks James. He can feel his heart pounding in his chest in anticipation.

"That a day would come when one of us was approached by a man who knew the meaning behind the word 'gesundheit'," he explains. "We were told 'To hold the secret safe until such a time. Great tragedy would foretell his coming and the one the man approached would feel as if all hope is lost'."

"You can be sure, many times throughout the past, my forefathers have faced tragedy and some had felt that all hope had been lost. Each time they expected the one to come as had been foretold to them. But each time none came."

"Through the years, it's become more of a story than something any of us actually expected would be fulfilled. Since it was a favorite of the kids, we told it often so never lost it." A sad smile comes to him as he reminisces about his own son and grandson as he told them the story.

"What was the secret?" prompts James when the old guy remains quiet for several minutes.

Snapped out of his reverie, he says, "It's never made much sense to us, and let me tell you we've tried to figure it out for centuries."

"What was it?" asks James eagerly. "Did it have something to do with Morcyth?"

"Morcyth?" questions the old man. Shaking his head, he says, "I don't think so. Wasn't he a god or something a long time ago?"

"Something like that," answers James.

"There're three verses. The first ones goes…"

When the Fire shines Bright
And the Star walks the Land.
Time for the Lost
Will soon be at Hand.

At the mention of the Fire shining bright and the Star walking the land James and Jiron look at each other. A gleam of recognition can be seen in both their eyes.

"The second verse is:"

At the foot of the King
Bathe in his Cup.
Pull his Beard
To make him sit Up.

"Doesn't make much sense does it?" he asks.

"No," agrees James, "it doesn't." He glances to Jiron who looks just as confused at the second verse as he does.

"And the last one goes…"

Seven to Nine
Six to Four.
Spit in the wind
And open the door.

"That's it," he tells him. The slaver in charge of the slaves starts to holler for them to resume their work. "I have to go."

"Thank you," says James.

"I'm glad I was able to fulfill the charge laid upon us," he says as he slowly gets to his feet. "Probably be best if we don't speak again."

"Thank you again," he says as the old guy walks back to the other slaves. He just nods his head in reply.

They move away from the window and further into the house where they can talk without running the risk of being heard by those outside.

"What do you think it means?" Jiron asks him once they've reached the inner room.

Excited, James replies, "The first verse has to refer to the Fire of Dmon-Li and the Star of Morcyth."

Nodding, Jiron says, "Yeah, I figured that out already."

"'Time for the lost will soon be at hand'," says James. "That I'm not sure of."

"Could it mean the missing priests of Morcyth?" asks Jiron.

"Maybe," he says, shrugging. "The rest of it doesn't make much sense. But that's the way with things like this. They can't make sense until it's time for them to make sense. Otherwise people will act prematurely."

"Sounds reasonable," comments Jiron. "So, is this what we came here for?"

"I would think so," replies James. In his own mind, the feeling of completion is there. "It's possible there could be more, but I doubt it."

"Then we should get out of here," states Jiron. "Better wait until it's dark though and go back the way we came."

"Wonder if the horses are still there?" says James.

"Doubt it," he replies. "They'd be starving by now and probably have broken their tethers. We'll have to see about getting some more after we get out of here."

"Very well," James says. "Best get some rest before we leave. Could be awhile before we get anymore."

They move upstairs where the beds are and Jiron offers to take the first watch. While James is sleeping, he thinks about what they've just learned and tries to make sense out of it.

Chapter   Eighteen

James looks out of the second story window while Jiron is sleeping. The sun had long since fallen below the horizon and the city is shrouded in night. Off in the distance he can see the lights where the occupiers have taken up residence.

The words the old man had spoken keeps returning to him again and again. They make no sense, but like he told Jiron, that's the way of these things. He was surprised to find what he came here for in the memory of an old man. But sitting here thinking about it, it makes a sort of sense.

If it had been hidden physically here in Saragon, then it would have needed to been marked in such a way that it would be recognized. That would've meant the Star of Morcyth symbol or something else which assuredly would've drawn the attention of those who know and understand the significance of such.

But to have it secreted in such a way that he practically had to stumble upon it, and to use a word only he or someone from his world would understand, enabled it to remain hidden all these years.

He can feel the hand of Igor in this. Just as he had trained Jiron and put him in a position to become part of his quest, so must he have also placed this snippet of information in the hands of the old guy's family centuries ago. He can't help but wonder if there may have been similar snippets left with different people here in Saragon in the hopes he would stumble across at least one of them. Maybe he'll ask Igor the next time he sees him. Thinking back to the time he spent in that other world, dimension, whatever, he wonders if he'll even have the chance. Igor may not have survived the attacks of those creatures.

A noise behind him causes him to turn where he sees Jiron getting up from the bed. Noticing how dark it is outside, he asks, "You ready to go?"

Coming away from the window, James says, "Yeah. Let's get out of here."

Stretching, Jiron begins to move out of the room and to the stairs leading down. He passes down the stairs then over to the doorway across from the collapsed, burned out structure. Beneath which lies the entrance to the secret smuggler passage they used to enter Saragon.

Taking a moment to ensure no one is on the street, he dashes across to the burned out building, James follows right behind him.

Pausing a moment, he turns to James and says, "Remember, it's not very stable so walk where I walk and try not to be on the same section as I am. Our combined weight could cause it to collapse."

"I understand," agrees James.

The moon overhead gives them some light with which to see by. Jiron begins making his way through the broken structure, taking the same path he used the last time. The first part of the path leads across a beam lying over an open section in the floor. Stepping carefully, he begins to cross.

James waits outside until he's cleared the beam, then he steps out upon it and follows. Taking it slow, he stops when he feels the beam begin to shift under him. Grabbing another section of the collapsed ceiling for support, he steadies himself until the beam ceases its shifting. Once the beam again becomes stable, he continues moving along it until he reaches the next one.

Suddenly, they hear a groan and the entire framework they're upon collapses. James is thrown from his precarious perch and tries to grab onto a section of what used to be a part of the ceiling. He takes a firm hold of it but it breaks off and he falls through the wreckage all the way to the floor, landing on his back. His breath is knocked out of him and it takes him a minute or two for him to get his lungs working again.

The section Jiron was on had remained somewhat stable. Holding onto a beam lying slantwise near him, he was able to prevent falling. "You okay?" he hollers down to where James lies upon the floor.

When he doesn't receive an answer, he begins making his way down, fearing the worst. From the direction of the street, he hears the sound of several people approaching just as the fragile structure gives out with another groan and another section collapses.

This time, the beam he's standing on gives way. Reaching out, he grabs hold of a neighboring beam just in time to prevent himself from falling. Hanging there from the beam, he sees the light from several torches approaching. Holding very still, he hopes to remain unnoticed by the men approaching.

Voices talking excitedly can be heard as they draw closer to the collapsing building. The light from their torches soon begins to illuminate the wreckage as half a dozen soldiers come to investigate the cause of the collapse. He can hear their excited conversation as their light begins to illuminate the building.

The light from their torches at last falls upon Jiron as he's hanging there and one of them cries out when he sees them. Two of them have crossbows and they take aim at him. One of the soldiers says something commandingly to him in the Empire's language.

When he doesn't answer or react, he changes to the common tongue and says, "Come out of there!"

Looking at two crossbows leveled at him, he glances down to the floor and gauges his chances.

"Don't think about it!" the soldier exclaims when he sees him debating about his chances of making it to the floor. "Come out now and you won't be hurt."

Jiron quickly realizes he'll never make it without being fired upon. He swings his leg up and begins climbing back to the top. The structure groans and another piece on the other side of the building collapses before he makes it all the way out. Once back out to the street, the soldiers quickly bind his hands behind him and remove his knives.

"Move!" says the soldier who had spoken to him before, as he pushes Jiron to get him moving. They begin marching him down the street, toward the lights of the main encampment.

James looks up from his position where he's hiding in the shadows on the floor as Jiron is taken away. Feeling helpless but unable to do anything about it at the moment, he waits for the soldiers to move further down the street. When the light from their torches disappears, he begins making his way up through the unstable wreckage back to the street. Fortunately the settling the structure had done during the last two collapses seems to have made it more stable and he's able to make it to the street with little difficulty.

When he at last makes it out of the ruined building he can see the party of soldiers with Jiron further down the street. Running as fast as he can, he races to catch up with them. They're still many blocks away from the area where the Empire's forces are located. He's got to get him away from them before they arrive, a small group he can handle, the main force could prove more difficult.

Jiron's captors don't seem to be in any hurry in taking him back to their encampment and it's easy for James to catch up with them. When he comes near, he slows his pace to avoid making any more noise than necessary. He remains far enough behind them so the light from their torches won't give him away.

He concentrates on Jiron's bonds and they break apart as he releases the magic. Jiron's arms jerk a fraction before he catches himself and holds them together to maintain the illusion he's still secured.

James follows them from a distance as he readies several of his slugs. *More death and destruction! Will it ever end?* After seeing the dead priests in the temple to Asran, he has less compunction about killing Empire soldiers than he used to. He just prays that he never gets numb to the killing, or worse yet, gets to liking it. Before releasing the slug, the thought crosses his mind of the woman who'll be waiting at home for the husband who'll never return. Or the children who will never see their daddy again. *He hates war and everything to do with it!*

But, he has no choice if he's to save Jiron. Sometimes situations in life only give you the choice between bad and worse.

Jiron was startled when his bindings snapped and almost wasn't able to recover in time to prevent them from falling to the ground. Back at the collapsing building, he had been afraid that James might have been seriously injured, or even dead from his fall. But when his bonds broke, he knew he was not only alive, but following them.

The soldier marching next to him has his two knives sticking out of his belt. He readies himself for what's to come next. They walk for several more yards and nothing happens. *Come on James! What're you waiting for!*

Then suddenly, one of the two soldiers bearing a crossbow cries out as a slug erupts from his belly, spraying blood and gore on those ahead of him. The leader of the group shouts commands as the other crossbowman is taken out with yet another slug.

Jiron tackles the one with his knives and quickly retrieves them. A quick slash across the man's throat and he's taken out of action. Rolling, he moves away from the soldiers just as another crashes to the ground, a gaping hole where his chest used to be.

The leader throws down his torch as he and the other remaining soldier flee down the street into the darkness. Just before they leave the area illuminated by the torches on the ground, another slug flies out, taking out the soldier. The leader disappears into the darkness, the sound of his running feet and shouts echoing as he flees for his life.

James appears out of the darkness and asks, "You okay?"

"Fine," replies Jiron. "You? I was worried when you fell."

"Just had the wind knocked out of me was all," he assures him. "We better get out of here."

From further into town, a horn begins blowing. Other horns from all around them sound in reply. "That tears it!" exclaims Jiron. Turning, he leads them back to the collapsed building.

Lights can be seen moving along streets in the distance as soldiers make their way toward their location. Horns continue to sound, making it seem as if the entire city is mobilizing to hunt for them.

Arriving at the structure, Jiron steps out upon the beam and begins to make his way across to the next when it gives out with a groan and collapses. James reaches out and catches hold of him just as the entire structure gives way and collapses.

James falls to his knees as Jiron's weight pulls him to the ground. Jiron falls hard against the wall of basement just beneath James and grabs hold of the edge. Pulling hard, James hauls him quickly back to the street.

"Thanks," Jiron says as he gets to his feet.

"Don't mention it, let's just get out of here."

The total collapse of the structure has blocked off their escape route. If they had time maybe they could dig their way through it, but not with soldiers on the way.

"Come on!" Jiron yells as he begins running away, sure that any pursuit will begin in this area. They've got to get out of here fast. Racing off down the street, they don't get far before they see a mob of soldiers enter the street three blocks away from them. The soldiers turn and begin making their way toward them.

Coming to a quick stop, Jiron grabs James and pushes him down an adjacent alley before the oncoming soldiers have a chance to spot them. Moving quickly they race for the other end of the alley.

As they draw near the end of the alley, it's suddenly lit from the light of torches held in the hands of more approaching soldiers. Pressing themselves against the side of the alley, they wait until the squad passes and then enter the street behind the marching soldiers, running the way the soldiers had just come from.

More lights appear ahead of them. "In here!" Jiron looks back to see James at an open doorway, motioning for him to follow. Running back, he moves through the doorway right after James and shuts the door.

They move quickly through to the back of the house, the light from the torches moving out on the street giving them ample light with which to see by. Before Jiron opens the backdoor, James grabs his arm and stops him.

"What?" he asks, turning around to face him.

"We need to figure out just where we're going to go," he insists.

"There's only going to be so many ways out of Saragon," Jiron says. "And you can bet they'll have them all covered with as many men as they can spare."

"So how are we to get out?" he asks.

"Hopefully we can find a gate that's not too well manned and force our way through," he explains. "With all the commotion going on, we'll not be able to sneak our way out."

"No, you're probably right," he agrees. "We should head for the part of the city where they've set up camp. I doubt if they'll think we would head in that direction."

"As good as any way, I suppose," replies Jiron. "Have you felt anything that might indicate a mage in the city?"

Shaking his head, James says, "No, not yet."

"That's good," he affirms.

Moving to the back door, he opens it a crack and finds the alley outside to be dark. Slipping out with James right behind, they head toward the Empire's camp within the city.

Light from the search parties and soldiers hollering out to one another can be seen and heard on neighboring streets. The bulk of the searchers seem to be heading back toward where they were first spotted. Horns continue to sound throughout the city.

Jiron takes them down another side alley which ends at a major thoroughfare. Peering around the corner, he sees search parties down both sides of the street. "Not this way," he says to James. Turning to go back the way they had come, they see light approaching the end of the alley.

Stopping and pressing themselves to the side of a neighboring building, they watch as the light continues to approach the alley. Suddenly, the soldiers appear at the end of the alley and turn into it, coming straight for them. "Run!" exclaims Jiron as he bolts back down toward the thoroughfare with James right behind him.

At the sight of them running, the men behind give chase as one of them sounds a horn, alerting the city that they've been found.

Bursting out onto the thoroughfare, Jiron sees men running toward them from both directions. Not even pausing, he crosses over to the alley on the other side and continues to flee.

Crumph!

The end of the alley bordering the thoroughfare suddenly explodes as the buildings facing it begin collapsing, effectively blocking the alley and preventing their pursuers from following. As they exit the far side of the alley, a billow of dust belches forth from the collapsing of the buildings behind them.

The street the alley opens on is wide and currently unoccupied. "Head to the wall!" James cries to Jiron.

Taking but a moment to check which way lies the shortest distance to the wall, he turns to the right. There ahead of them, the wall looms high over the tops of the buildings. They can hear the screaming and shouting of soldiers from behind them, as they pour into the street from a junction further back. Glancing behind them, Jiron guesses there must be a hundred or more soldiers back there.

Ahead of them in the street is a large square with a fountain that had seen better days. At one time it used to have four tiers where water would rain down from one to the other. Now, it lies all but broken, only a small section of what used to be the top two tiers remains.

As they come toward the square, four soldiers enter from a side street and charge. A slug takes one out before they even have a chance to close the distance. Jiron moves to intercept as a second slug takes out another.

The first to engage Jiron strikes out with his sword. Jiron deflects it to the side as he follows through with a thrust using his other knife, taking the soldier in the chest. Kicking the dying man off his knife, the soldier flails into his partner, throwing him off balance.

Jiron moves in quickly and takes the remaining soldier out. As the last dead body hits the ground...

Crumph!

...the street behind them explodes upward. Looking back, he sees a dust cloud in the torch light as bodies rain back down to the street. Pursuit momentarily halted from that avenue, they turn and continue toward the wall.

"How are you doing?" he asks James, worried that the magic may be making him weak.

"So far I'm doing alright," he tells him.

"Good, I'd hate to have to carry you out of here!" he says with a grin.

"I wouldn't care for that either," he replies.

They race further on, horns still sounding behind them, but are eerily quiet before them. James figures most of the pursuit has been directed back behind them before he started doing magic and letting them know their whereabouts.

The wall now looms large before them. The street they are on comes to the base of the wall and they are forced to either turn left or right. Both ways look the same, so they turn to the left and race along the wall, hoping to find a way out.

Out of the dark ahead of them, they begin to see light as they approach the gates. Coming to a stop, they see arrayed before them, over a hundred men as well as a dozen or more crossbowmen. Five other crossbowmen man the walls above the gate.

"Man, what are we going to do?" Jiron asks him.

"I don't know," he admits. "The magic I would need to use to clear that away would leave me unconscious if not outright kill me."

They make to turn around when from behind them, the force that had been stopped by the exploding street now boils into view behind them. When the soldiers see them standing there, a cry goes up and horns begin to sound as they charge.

The force at the gate, now aware of their presence, forms into ranks as they make a wall of iron across the street. The crossbowmen ready their crossbows.

Crumph!

The ground behind them erupts, throwing the leading edge of the charging men in the air in the hopes of slowing them down. It does, but only momentarily.

James readies a spell for the group by the gates when their lines begin to buckle and he sees the crossbowmen on the walls turn and appear to be firing at their own forces. Whatever the reason, he changes his tactics and begins peppering the crossbowmen on the walls with slugs and they begin to fall.

"Look!" cries Jiron as he points to the force in front of the gates.

James turns his attention to them and sees them fighting with men in slave rags. *The slaves!*

"Come on!" Jiron says as he races to the gates and the fighting going on there.

James runs behind him as he sees a group of twenty slaves bearing nothing but makeshift clubs and scavenged weapons, race toward the gatehouse. The crossbowmen on the ground see them and a flight of bolts cuts down half before they make it.

The ten or so left reach the gatehouse where they overpower the two guards there and are soon inside. Two of the slaves lay dead at the gatehouse door.

James glances down the street behind him and sees the force there that had been stopped by the erupting of the street now making their way around the blasted area and continuing the pursuit.

Hundreds of slaves pour into the ranks of the defenders by the gates. The group of crossbowmen, who had so recently mowed down the men on their way to the gatehouse, are now chopped to pieces or bludgeoned to death by men bent on revenge.

Suddenly, the gate opens up just as the last remaining soldier before the gate falls. A cry erupts and is quickly dampened by a man, an old man. Shouting out orders, he forms them into a line to meet the oncoming soldiers.

James looks his way and for a moment their eyes lock. He gives James a grin and a nod before resuming the marshalling of his forces.

"James! We've got to go now!" yells Jiron, trying to be heard over the noise of horns and men shouting.

"But they'll be killed!" counters James.

"They know that!" replies Jiron. "They're not doing it for their freedom. They're doing it for revenge on those who destroyed their town and killed its people." Grabbing him by the shoulder, he propels him toward the widening gates. "And one is doing it so you can get out of here! Don't let them have died in vain."

Before passing through the gate, he glances back just as the two forces meet. The slaves are no match for the soldiers, but have the numbers in their favor. He sees the old man out in front of his men, sword held high and time seems to slow as he engages with the nearest soldier.

He runs the soldier through and pulls out his sword to ward off the blow of the next, but isn't fast enough. James watches as the soldier's blade strikes off the old man's left arm. Before he has a chance to strike the old man again, the old man runs him through the chest where his sword becomes lodged. Then he passes out of sight as another slave comes to take his place in line.

A slave comes up to them and says, "Get out now! We can't hold them off for long!"

"What was the old man's name?" James asks the slave as he's being pulled through the gates by Jiron.

"Derrion," the slave replies as he and others push to close the gates.

With a resounding thud, the gates close and they can hear the locking mechanism secure the gates.

"Now let's run!" Jiron cries out.

They turn to run and come to a stop when they see twenty horsemen arrayed before them. Without even a pause, James releases the power.

Crumph!

The center of the line of horsemen erupts upward from the force of the explosion. The horses not caught in the blast rear up, some unseating their riders. Jiron races forward to meet them before they have a chance to recover. James follows as slug after slug flies through the air, taking out more of the remaining horsemen.

Jiron closes with one of the unhorsed soldiers and blocks his attack with both knives while kicking out and connecting with the man's knee. Bones snap as the man cries out in pain. Leaving him there to writhe on the ground, Jiron moves toward two horses milling around without riders.

Crumph!

Another explosion erupts, throwing more men and horses into the air.

Jiron almost reaches the horses before another unhorsed rider closes with him and strikes out with his sword. Catching it on crossed knives, Jiron pushes outward and throws the man backward off balance. Moving in quickly, he strikes out and scores two quick thrusts, one which punctures a lung. As the man falls, Jiron runs past and reaches the horses.

Vaulting up onto one, he turns it around and sees James beset by three soldiers. A flare of light and one soldier is thrown backward as the other two continue their advance. James is beginning to look very tired.

Taking the reins of the other horse, he kicks his into a gallop and rides directly at the men advancing upon James. They fail to see him coming in time and he rides right over them, bowling them over. "Get on!" he shouts at James as he brings the horses to a stop next to him.

More soldiers are advancing upon them from all directions as James gets into the saddle. A sound of turning gears and the gates behind them begin to open as even more soldiers start pouring through.

Once James is securely in the saddle, Jiron kicks his horse into a gallop again and they race away from the city into the night. Behind them, they see hundreds of soldiers pouring out of the gates but quickly fall behind.

The road they find themselves on follows the river as it flows on their left. After getting his bearings, he realizes this is the same river they had followed on the way down to Saragon. And up ahead of them is a large force of men and a mage, perhaps even now waiting for them.

Chapter   Nineteen

As they follow the road in the dark, James can't get the death of the slaves off his mind. A tear runs down his cheek as his emotions begin getting to him.

"You okay?" asks Jiron after they've ridden in silence for awhile.

"Just thinking of Derrion and the others back there, sacrificing themselves so we could escape," he says sadly.

"I wouldn't think of it that way," replies Jiron. "They were fighting for their freedom, whether in death or in life. No man who has known freedom can long suffer slavery, they are either broken spiritually and are no longer the men they once were. Or they fight and die."

James rides in silence as he thinks about what Jiron had told him.

"How or why they came to aid us, we'll never know," Jiron continues. "I would expect something like this has been planned for some time, seeing as how they escaped their pens so readily. You just gave them the excuse." When James glances over to him, he adds, "This was going to happen anyway, I expect. So don't take it so personally."

Sighing, James says, "I suppose you're right."

"Of course I am," he insists. "If you take personally the decisions of others, you'll be carrying the weight of an enormous amount of guilt. You didn't ask them to fight and die back there, they volunteered knowing full well what their fate would be. I honor their choice to die as men, not slaves."

Taking a deep breath, James gets his emotions under control and replies, "Maybe Perrilin will make a song about them?"

"Probably," he agrees. "People like songs about hopeless struggles for a good cause."

"I'll tell him all about it next time I see him," he says. He feels better having decided a course of action with which he can honor their sacrifice.

"Now," says Jiron, "we have to figure out how to get back to Cardri." Glancing to James he adds, "Providing of course we're going back to Cardri?"

"Yes," replies James. "We're going home."

"Good," states Jiron. "By morning we should be at that town up ahead with the bridge we passed on the way down. Somehow, we need to cross it."

"Let's push a little harder so we can make it before dawn," suggests James. "Hopefully we can make it across before it gets light."

With that, they both increase their speed to a gallop. Over the course of the next several hours, they alternate speeds between a fast gallop and a trop for optimum speed while at the same time saving their horses' strength. They could well need it when they get there.

An hour into their ride, Jiron asks, "How far away can you sense magic?"

"I don't know," replies James, "half a mile or so, maybe a mile. Why?"

"Oh, I was just thinking of that mage you said you detected at the town north of the one we're heading for," he explains. "I was worried he may have sensed what you did back at Saragon."

"I doubt it," James assures him. "I didn't do anything very strong."

"That's a relief," he says.

After several more hours of riding, the sky to the east has begun to lighten with the approach of dawn, and still the town has not appeared. Worried about not making it in time, they increase their speed.

It isn't until the sun crests the horizon that the town finally appears before them in the distance. "Now what?" James asks.

The town still has a garrison of soldiers, a hundred or so from the looks of it. Two stand guard on the bridge, dashing their hopes of easily making it across undetected.

"We could still try," suggests Jiron. "If you blew up the bridge after we crossed it, it wouldn't matter whether they discovered us or not. They would be unable to follow."

"True," he says. "But something that big would most likely alert whoever was up in Pleasant Meadows."

"That's over a day away," counters Jiron. "Whether he did or not would doubtless make a difference. We'd be over in Cardri before whoever it is could get here to do anything anyway."

"Very well," he agrees. "But I'm going to need a moment close to the bridge to make it work."

"I'll give you that moment," he tells him.

As they approach the outskirts of town, they slow to a normal pace so as not to draw attention to themselves. Some of the soldiers begin to take notice of them coming up the road but don't seem to be too concerned. After all, they're coming from the south which is totally controlled by the Empire. And what enemy in their right mind would casually ride up to a garrisoned town in broad daylight.

As they near the first building, a soldier hails them with a smile and a friendly wave. "Now!" says Jiron and they kick their horses as they turn off the road. The soldier's smile quickly vanishes in confusion as he watches them begin racing around the town toward the bridge. He yells something to them as they race away and then raises a horn to his lips.

Rounding the last building before the open space between the town and the bridge, they hear a horn sound behind them. The guards on the bridge look their way and see them riding fast toward them. They form up at the foot of the bridge and one of them calls something to them, most likely a command to stop. When they fail to heed his command, he and the other soldier draw their weapons and stand ready to greet them.

"Do what you have to," yells Jiron. "I'll take out the guards."

Riding hard, Jiron pulls ahead of James and aims his horse straight for the two waiting soldiers at the foot of the bridge. They stand to block his path, one again shouting something unintelligible at him. Just before he reaches the beginning of the bridge, the two guards dive to the side to avoid being caught under his horse's hooves.

Bringing his horse to an abrupt halt, Jiron vaults from the saddle and his two knives are in hand before he lands on the ground.

The guard on the right sees him coming toward him and strikes out with his sword. Jiron deflects it and follows through with his other knife, barely missing his shoulder as the man twists away.

From behind him, he hears the other soldier approaching and sidesteps quickly just as the soldier's sword pierces the space he had just vacated. Lashing out with his foot, he catches the man behind him in the chest and knocks him backward.

Pressing the man in front of him, he feints a thrust at the man's face. When the soldier raises his sword protectively, he strikes out with his other knife and takes him in the belly. Crying out, the man steps backward where he hits the railing of the bridge and then tumbles over into the river below.

Jiron hears the splash as he turns to face the remaining man. From town, a large group of soldiers are on the way, as well as several mounted horsemen riding hard from the center of town. More horns sound as they begin marshalling their forces.

Twisting to the right, he avoids an overhand hack by the soldier and then lashes out with his right knife, scoring a long cut on the man's forearm.

"Ready!" he hears James yell and a quick glance shows him getting back on his horse.

Striking out with his foot, he knocks the soldier off balance as he races for his own horse waiting nearby. Jumping into the saddle, he kicks it into a quick gallop as he and James race off the other side.

He looks back to the bridge just as the horsemen gain the center and then…

Crumph!

…the entire central span of the bridge explodes outward, throwing stone, horses and men into the air. They pause a moment to wait for the dust to clear and when it does finds that James has created a twelve foot gap in the bridge.

The soldiers on the other side come to a startled stop as debris begins raining down upon them. Jiron watches as a dead, mangled horse falls and crushes two soldiers who hadn't moved quickly enough.

"That should do it," he says to James.

Looking tired, James replies, "I hope so."

Getting their horse back up to speed, they follow the road as they leave the town and the broken bridge behind them.

Two men stand before the large basin of dark water. An image plays across its surface, a ruined bridge and two men on horseback riding away. One man is armored head to toe with a large sword hanging at his hip. Cruel eyes gaze from within the dark helm, rage practically oozing from every pore of his being.

The other man next to him wears a red robe, the hooded cowl hiding his features. He can feel the rage of the man next to him and prays that it will not be directed at him.

Suddenly, the door to the room where they stand before the basin opens and one of the armored man's acolytes enters.

"Prepare the army," the helmed man says.

"Yes milord," the acolyte replies before leaving and closing the door behind him.

"Are you sure that's him?" the voice from within the helm says.

"Yes, milord," replies the cowled man. "His magic is singularly unique. We've never been able to ascertain why."

The mage. The bearer of the Star! The one who defeated Abula-Mazki! One who seems to travel at will within the Empire, yet none can stop him. Hate and anger radiate from the armored man with a palpable force as he gazes at the figure riding away from the ruined bridge.

As he turns to leave the room, he says, "Keep me informed of his progress."

"Yes, milord," replies the cowled man. Turning back to the basin, he continues to watch the two riders.

Leaving the room, the man in armor sees the commander of his army waiting for him. "Send riders to Kirak and Zuri. Tell them the mage has just destroyed the bridge at Cerinet and may be coming their way. They're to stop him from reaching Cardri at all costs."

"Yes milord," the commander says. He turns to go and carry out his Lord's order.

Watching the commander leave, the man in armor looks out over the preparations the host before him makes for getting underway. With a vow to his dark god, the man moves to take charge of the army and destroy this harbinger of doom. *He must not reach Cardri!*

Two hours after leaving the bridge, they still haven't seen any sign of enemy patrols. They left the road an hour ago, angling more toward the mountains in the hopes of finding better cover in which to hide. They'll have to follow the mountains around to the south in the hopes of finding a viable way across.

To the north is Pleasant Meadows which holds an army that may or may not be on the way. To the east is more enemy territory, plus it brings them further away from Cardri and home. The last time they tried to get across the Silver Mountains in this area, they were fleeing from a forest fire which James had inadvertently started while battling forces pursuing them from the town of Mountainside. They had stumbled across a rope suspension bridge which spanned a deep gorge and barely made it across before the inferno behind them consumed it. With the collapsing of the bridge, that way is no longer viable.

Over the Silver Mountains to the west lies a giant cloud, smoke from the fires still raging to the north. When they draw close enough to be able to see the devastation the passing of the fire had wrought they realize the shelter they hoped to gain from the forest upon the mountains is no longer possible. The trees are burnt husks, a forest of black spires reaching to the sky.

"Since the fire's moving north, the trees to the south of Mountainside may still be untouched," states Jiron.

"Perhaps," agrees James. "I'm just hoping another garrison hasn't been sent there yet. Could make things more interesting than I would want."

"We'll see," he replies.

They come to the road running alongside the mountains as it winds its way through the gently rolling hills at their base. Turning south, they follow the road for awhile before James says, "We need to find somewhere to rest. My horse is beginning to droop."

"Mine too," he says.

Ten minutes later, they come to where a series of hills rise more steeply. Moving off the road, they find a space behind one of the hills which will prevent them from being spotted by anyone traveling upon the road.

Leaving the saddles on the horses in case a quick getaway is required, they find some grass and water for their steeds before settling in themselves. Taking turns at watch, they rest throughout the rest of the day.

At one point, a rider is heard riding fast from the north. Jiron moves to the top of the hill overlooking the road. The rider turns out to be a lone soldier leading a spare mount. He watches him race past their hiding spot and quickly disappear down the road to the south.

Nothing else of note happens before the sun goes down and they're on their way once again. Following the road in the dark isn't too hard, what with the stars overhead and after an hour or so, the moon as well.

They stay to the road as they continue moving through the hills, they need the speed it will afford even though it may mean encountering unfriendly forces. From up ahead, they begin to see lights from a town. "Must be Mountainside," suggests Jiron.

James nods in agreement as they slow down and approach the town with caution. Before coming close to the outlying buildings they leave the road and make their way around the outskirts.

"Something doesn't feel right," whispers Jiron after they've progressed a little ways around the town.

"What do you mean?" asks James as he looks around to discover what he's talking about.

"There's no one on the street," he says. "Not even soldiers, and that seems strange."

"It is the middle of the night," replies James. "Everyone's probably in bed or about to be."

"I don't know," he says. "It's not that late."

Keeping their eyes open, they continue to circle around the town, leaving plenty of room between them and the outlying buildings. James pays a closer attention to the town and he begins to understand what Jiron's talking about. Nothing is moving on the streets of the town. The lights coming from the windows don't even have the occasional silhouettes of those within moving around. It's as if the whole town is deserted.

Suddenly from ahead of them, shutters of a dozen lanterns are removed and they're bathed with light. "Stay right where you are!" a voice from out of the lights commands. "Move, and you'll be fired upon."

"James?" questions Jiron quietly.

"Wait!" he replies.

A man moves out from the dark, an officer of the Empire's army and approaches them. "You are under arrest," he says.

"On what charge?" asks James.

"Being enemies of the Empire," the officer replies.

James begins laughing. The officer looks at him like he's lost his mind. "What's so funny?" he asks somewhat annoyed.

"I don't think so," replies James as a shimmering field suddenly springs up around them. To Jiron he says, "Take him, please. Make sure you don't kill him."

As Jiron swings down from his horse, bolts begin striking the barrier and bouncing harmlessly off. The officer draws his sword as he begins backing away from Jiron until his back encounters the barrier.

Turning around, he touches it in fear, realizing he's trapped inside. Spinning around, he stands ready to defend himself.

"Drop your sword," Jiron tells him, "and you won't be hurt."

Light suddenly erupts all around them as brightly glowing orbs appear in the sky, illuminating the entire area. A cry erupts from the gathered soldiers surrounding them. In the light, they can see there are only about thirty or so soldiers surrounding them.

Trapped within the barrier, as well as the display of magic in the sky around him, drains the officer's will to fight as he looks into the eyes of Jiron. Lowering his sword, the officer remains quiet as Jiron removes it from his hand.

From the back of his horse, James says to the officer, "Tell your men to drop their weapons or I'll kill them all right here, right now!"

"You'll never get back to Cardri!" says the officer defiantly.

"How do you know that's where we intend to go?" asks Jiron, somewhat taken aback at his knowledge.

The officer glances from one to the other before replying. "A rider came through here earlier saying you two may be coming this way," he explains. "He stopped here only briefly before continuing on, alerting our forces to the south of your presence. They'll be ready for you."

"Damn!" exclaims Jiron. He glances back to James who arcs an eyebrow questioningly.

Jiron shakes his head as James repeats his demand for the officer to order his men to drop their weapons. "I'll not ask again," he threatens. When the officer hesitates...

Crumph!

...the ground a little way away from the edge of the barrier explodes upward, peppering the nearby soldiers with dirt and rocks. There were no soldiers in the vicinity, James only wanted to demonstrate his power in the hopes of resolving the situation without bloodshed, if possible.

The officer looks at the hole in the ground, thankful that none of his men had been there at the time. Defeated, he calls out to his men.

James watches as their weapons begin falling to the ground. "Now, have them begin moving back that way," he says, indicating back down the road to the north.

The officer again calls out and his men begin walking toward the north, some moving quicker than others.

"What are you going to do with me?" he asks.

"Nothing," replies James. "I'm not a killer, despite what you may have heard. Once they're far enough away, we'll leave." He sees the surprise in the officer's eyes at that. Leaning forward slightly, he adds, "If you follow us, then I will kill you." His serious expression leaving no doubt that he will follow through on his threat.

Jiron gets back on his horse and watches as the soldiers continue moving away to the north. He glances to James and can see sweat beginning to form. The exertion of continuing the shield, the orbs in the sky and all they've been through the last few days are starting to take a toll.

James sits and waits while the men move further away from their weapons. When they've gone far enough to suit him, he says to the officer, "Please don't follow us. I would really hate to have to kill you and your men."

The orbs wink out, plunging the entire area into darkness once more. On the ground around them, a few of the lanterns that were left by the departing soldiers still give off some light, so they're not completely in the dark. He was about to cancel the barrier when he suddenly feels the tingling sensation forewarning of nearby magic. Then the feeling spikes and from the north he sees a red glowing blob flying straight for them.

"Look out!" he cries as it hits the barrier.

Magic is sucked out of him in staggering quantities in order to keep the barrier stable. The red blob begins oozing down the side when the barrier suddenly gives way. The red blob, no longer held up by the barrier, falls directly on the officer.

With a scream of agony, the officer is enveloped by the blob and James looks in horror as the red substance begins dissolving his flesh away.

"Ride!" he yells to Jiron and they turn their horses south, riding as fast as their horses can go.

"What was that?" asks Jiron as he bends low over the neck of his horse to gain as much speed as he can.

James is unable to answer as spots begin to dance in front of his eyes and he fights merely to stay conscious. That took far too much out of him.

"James!" cries Jiron next to him. "Stay with me man!"

The coolness of the rushing air gradually brings him away from the edge of unconsciousness. Behind him, he knows whoever was the source of the red blob is still doing magic for the tingling stays with him.

"We've got to get out of here!" he tells Jiron when he again has control of his voice.

"Why?" he asks. "What was that?"

"I don't know what it was," he replies. "But the magic felt familiar. I think it was another warrior priest, though I'm not for sure."

"Damn!" he exclaims.

The sound of pursuit follows them as an unknown number of riders chase them in the dark. Suddenly, the tingling sensations spikes again and he yells, "To the right!" They both swerve to the right just as another of those blobs strikes the road where they would've been if they had kept going straight. A slight sizzle can be heard from where it hit the ground.

Behind them, dozens of riders can be seen in the moonlight behind them. And they're closing quickly. "Do something!" yells Jiron.

James is having a hard time thinking, his mind is already tired from when the barrier had initially been struck. "To the left!" he cries as the tingling sensation once more spikes. Swerving to the left, they barely get out of the way before the blob hits the road a few feet from them. *That was too close!*

An image springs to mind of another time when they were being pursued on horseback and he had created holes in the ground to slow their pursuers. Concentrating hard, he begins creating a patchwork in the ground behind them of foot deep holes that will entrap and break the horses' legs.

From behind them in the dark, they begin to hear screams of horses as they encounter the holes. The tingling which had been constant since leaving the town abruptly stops.

"I think that slowed them down," he tells Jiron as they continue racing through the night. "I can no longer feel the presence of magic back there."

"Think you killed him?" Jiron asks hopefully.

"I would think that's highly unlikely," he replies. "Most likely his concentration was broken when his horse collapsed after stepping in one of those holes."

"Is that what you did?" he asks.

"I hate hurting the horses, but I didn't know what else to do," he replies in regret.

"You did what you had to do," he says, trying to assuage his guilt over what he did to the horses. They ride on for a few minutes before he says, "This isn't going to slow them down very long."

"I know. They'll be after us as soon as they get more horses," he says. "Which shouldn't take very long."

"If we follow this road far enough I think we'll come to the town Bindles," Jiron says. "You remember that town we first came to after leaving the mountains last time?"

"I remember," he says.

"There was a road there going west along the southern edge of the mountains which may lead us to Cardri," explains Jiron.

"If we can reach Cardri," James tells him, "whoever is back there won't dare to continue following us unless they're willing to risk war."

"Let's hope he takes that into consideration."

James continues attempting to sense the working of magic behind them as they ride, but so far, nothing. Sometime after leaving Mountainside behind them, they reached the end of the fire ravaged area. The mountains on their right again have a full forest of trees upon them, enough to shelter them from anyone traveling along the road.

"Maybe we should get off the road now," suggests Jiron. "Remember that officer back there said a rider came through and warned them about us. Anyone further ahead will be alerted and looking for us." Glancing to James he adds, "We don't want another ambush like the last one, not with that other force hot on our heels."

"Good idea," agrees James.

Moving off the road, they begin making their way up the mountain and into the shelter of the forest. After putting a mile or so between them and the road, they decide to make a brief camp. The horses are on the verge of exhaustion and both of them could do with a few hours of rest before heading out again.

Jiron takes the first watch and after letting James rest only three hours, he wakes him for his turn. "Don't fall asleep!" he warns. He knows James is incredibly tired, but he needs sleep too.

"I won't," James assures him. Getting to his feet, he begins walking around the camp in order to remain awake. After his second pass around, he glances over and sees Jiron has fallen asleep. The night here in the forest is anything but comforting. Every shadow, every sound, startles him in expectation of enemy soldiers coming for them.

After what seems several hours, the sky to the east begins to lighten and he realizes he's wandered some distance from their camp. Using the sound of the horses to guide him, he makes his way back.

Snap!

Behind him he hears the sound of a twig breaking and quickly turns to find someone standing there, arrow knocked and aimed right at his heart.

Chapter   Twenty

"What do we have here?" she asks with a grim expression.

James is slightly surprised to find the archer is a woman, a young one at that. She couldn't be more than seventeen or eighteen. Dressed in greens and browns, she blends in well with the forest, her long auburn hair tied in a ponytail. No telling how long she had been in the vicinity before making her presence known.

"My name is James," he replies. "A wanderer."

"Spy of the Empire no doubt," she says. "I should just kill you right where you stand." She pulls the bowstring back a fraction of an inch.

"I'm not a spy!" he asserts, trying to prevent the arrow from being released.

"No one wanders these woods in times like these unless they're up to no good," she says.

"Believe me," he says, "I am no servant of the Empire." He glances briefly over to where their camp lies. The horses are visible where they're tied but there's no sign of Jiron. Scanning the woods behind the woman, he sees him working his way quietly through the trees to get around behind her.

"What business do you have here then?" she asks.

"Merely trying to get back to my home in Cardri," he tells her.

"Perhaps," she says.

Jiron is closing the distance quickly, now no more than ten feet behind her. James sees one of his knives in his hand as he sneaks up behind her.

"One more step," she says loudly, cocking her head to the side, "and I'll kill your friend." When Jiron comes to a halt, she glances back to him. Nodding to James, she says, "Go over and stand by your friend. Now!"

Jiron doesn't resheathe his knife but does what she says and makes his way over to stand next to James.

"So, two wanderers," she states.

"We are no friends of the Empire, you can rest assured lady," Jiron says to her. "In fact, we're trying to escape from them." He gives her a serious look and then continues, "We all need to be getting out of here. A large force has been tailing us since yesterday and could be in the area at any time."

"I saw the force you mentioned earlier," she tells them. "It went past earlier as it made its way south."

As James stands there with the arrow pointing menacingly at him, he begins to once more feel the tingling of magic being worked in the area. "Jiron," he says nervously. "I feel it again."

"Where?" he asks looking around, the danger from the woman now ignored.

"I'm not sure, but it's getting stronger," he replies. "They may be heading back."

Jiron moves to return to the horses when the woman says, "Stay right there! I don't know what kind of trick you're playing here, but it's not going to work."

"This isn't a trick," insists James, fear growing in his voice. "A mage of some power is out there, and he is drawing near."

"You expect me to believe that?" she asks. "I don't think so."

Further down the mountain, the sound of a large number of individuals can be heard as they forge their way through the brush. She glances down and her eyes widen when she makes out the unmistakable sight of Empire soldiers heading their way.

Seeing them too, James says, "Now do you believe us?"

Nodding her head, she relaxes her bow and quickly replaces her arrow in the quiver behind her shoulder. As James and Jiron begin running toward the horses, she says, "Leave them!" When they both look at her, she continues, "They'll just slow you down in the forest. Follow me." She then slings her bow behind her shoulder as she turns and begins running through the trees.

Jiron looks to him and James only shrugs. Breaking into a run, they follow her as she races through the undergrowth. "Where are we going?" asks James when they finally catch up to her.

"I know a trail that will take us through the mountains," she tells them. "It comes out near the fortress of Kern on the Cardri-Empire border."

"How long will it take?" Jiron asks.

"About three days perhaps longer," she replies. "Longer still if we can't shake the pursuit."

The sound of their pursuers gradually diminishes as she takes them further up into the higher elevations. They all remain quiet as they work to navigate the sometimes steep and narrow way. Boulders and fallen trees have to be circumvented and at times scaled in order to continue.

They come to a cliff face with a small trickle of water running down its side. Turning to them, she says, "We have to climb up to the top of this." Indicating a section of the wall, she adds, "Start here, it affords the best hand and footholds than anywhere else."

She reaches out and takes hold of a crack and begins the ascent. When she's gone about ten feet, Jiron looks to James and asks, "You want to go next?"

"You better, I might end up falling and I wouldn't want to knock you down in the process."

"It's only about thirty feet," states Jiron. "You can make it."

Looking dubious at the prospect, he steps to the wall and begins following her with Jiron's help. Once James has gone far enough to allow him room, Jiron steps to the wall and begins his ascent.

When James is halfway up, he hears her voice from where she's standing at the top of the cliff, "Hurry up."

"Do you see anyone coming?" Jiron shouts up to her.

She looks out for a moment then replies, "No. All I can see is the tops of the trees. They could be just right below and I wouldn't know it."

"Great!" he hears Jiron grunt below him.

As he reaches the top he sees her hand reaching down to help him up the rest of the way. Taking it, he's soon up over the edge and lying on the top. Arms and legs shaking from the ordeal, he just lies there a few moments until he sees Jiron's head crest over the top.

She reaches down to help him as well, but he just shakes his head as he makes the rest of the way on his own.

"We can have a short break here," she tells them as Jiron gains the top.

James sits up and reaches into his belt pouch where he pulls out the pitiful remnants of what use to be rations, oh so long ago. Grimacing, he takes a bite out of the stale fare and looks up to see her grinning at him. "What's so funny?" he asks.

"Just your expression when you bit into that," she explains with a slight laugh. She pulls out some jerked beef and hands him several strips. "Here, you can have some of mine." When she sees Jiron's hungry looks, she gives him some as well.

"So what are you doing out here?" Jiron asks as he takes the offered food. He keeps a constant lookout for any approaching soldiers, but it looks like for the moment they may have lost them.

Her expression turns grim as she says, "Surviving. I used to live in Mountainside before the soldiers came. Fortunately I was out hunting in the mountains when they showed up and was spared the ravages they inflicted on my family and friends."

"That's too bad about your family," James says.

"Yes. I miss them dearly but we can't live in the past," she says wistfully. "Now I stay up here where they can't find me. Been doing alright so far, though I hope they get pushed back into the Empire so I can go home. If there's even a home to return to."

"We were just through there and it looks like most of it is still standing," explains Jiron. "Some of the buildings were burned down by the fire, but most of them appeared in good condition."

"Strange thing about that fire," she says. "It just started up out of nothing. I was in the forest that day and there wasn't any lightning or such to spark it. Though I heard a whole lot of soldiers got burnt in it. That was good news."

Jiron glances at James who just shakes his head. He doesn't want her to know more about them than is absolutely necessary. "So you just stay in the woods?" he asks. "How are you able to manage?"

Giving him an annoyed expression, she asks in reply, "What? Do you think I'm some helpless little girl who can't take care of herself?"

"We'll, no," he replies. "It's just that…"

"It's just that I'm a girl," she finishes for him. "If I were a man, would you even ask such a question?"

Face reddening, he looks to Jiron for help but finds him smiling, enjoying the predicament he's gotten himself into. "No, it's not that at all. Where I come from, women are considered equal to men in all things. What I was getting at was that the soldiers might've discovered you, or something."

"I don't let them 'discover' me," she informs him. She gets up and says, "I think it's time to go." Without even waiting for a reply, she moves out through the woods at a quick pace. James and Jiron have to scramble to catch up with her.

James glances to Jiron who only gives him an amused smile.

That night when they stop for the night, James is about ready to die. The pace she kept the rest of the day had been unrelenting. No stops and he had to practically run in order to keep up with her. When she announced here is where they would be spending the night, he just collapses.

Coming over to him, she asks, "Tired?"

Nodding, he says breathlessly, "Yeah. Not used to so much climbing. Plus the air is thinner up here."

"The sun's going to be down soon and we don't have time to rest," she tells him. "You need to collect enough firewood to last through the night while I get dinner." While stringing her bow, she adds, "It gets very cold up here when the sun's down." Once her bow is ready, she moves away from him and disappears in the trees.

Jiron comes over and gives him a hand up. He looks to where she disappeared in the trees and says, "I like her."

James gives him a grin and says, "You like all the girls."

Shaking his head, he says, "Not like that. But we better get busy if we'll have a fire going and enough wood collected before she returns."

Groaning, James gets his already stiffening legs moving again as he begins gathering small branches and sticks. When he has an armful, he returns and deposits it in camp where Jiron goes about lighting a fire. Four more trips are required before Jiron determines they have enough to last through the night.

About that time, she returns with two small animals and proceeds to clean and dress them for the fire.

While she's doing that, James asks her, "You never even told us your name."

She looks up from the rabbits and says, "Aleya."

Jiron comes over to her and says, "I'm Jiron."

A quick nod and then she returns her attention back to the animals.

Jiron just stands there not sure what to do, a simple nod was not the reply he expected. There's just something about her that both annoys and attracts him. Finally realizing he'd been standing there like an idiot, he goes over and sits near James across the fire from her.

"How much further is this fortress?" James asks her.

"Another two days," she replies. She points to an imposing ridge to the west and says, "We should reach that ridge by tomorrow night. It's all downhill from there on."

A deep valley separates them and their destination. The ridge is quite high and steep, higher in fact than where they sit now. James looks at the prospect of trying to climb it with trepidation.

She notices how his face has fallen as he stares out across the valley. "Don't worry," she tells him with a reassuring smile, "it's not going to be that bad. There's an old stairway that was cut into the ridge a long time ago which leads all the way to the top."

"A stairway?" Jiron asks.

"A series of steps that wind their way up to the top," she explains. "From there you can see the Fortress of Kern nestled in the hills below, which sits at Cardri's southern border. An old road leads down from the top of the ridge and comes out somewhere near Kern. Never actually had the occasion to cross the ridge before. From there you two can go on your way."

"What about you?" Jiron asks.

"I'll go back to where you found me," she replies. "Not much else for me now." Having finished dressing the animals, she impales them upon sticks and hands them to Jiron and James. "You boys can do the cooking, if you don't mind."

"No, we don't mind," Jiron says as he takes the sticks from her and hands one to James.

James takes the stick and tries to hide the amused grin that's threatening to spread across his face. Jiron seemed just a little too eager to do as she requested, not to mention the speed with which he'd gotten up from where he'd been sitting once he knew she needed something. Even if that something was taking the animals from her for roasting.

As the flames begin licking the carcasses and the fat drips with a sizzle to their ravenous heat, she eyes them speculatively. "Just what does the Empire want with you guys anyway?" she asks.

"What do you mean?" James asks her with a sidelong glance to Jiron.

"That was no mere patrol that chased us up into the mountains," she explains. "They had already gone past, but then returned and entered the trees just where you happened to be. How do you explain that?"

"Just a lucky guess?" stammers James.

The look she gives him says she doesn't believe it was 'a lucky guess'. "They knew right where you were," she continues.

"They did, didn't they?" says James suddenly thinking. *If the warrior priest is using the same technique with a mirror or other magical device to keep track of us, we're in serious trouble.* He glances to Jiron and can tell he's having the same thought.

"Now, come on," she demands. "What's going on?"

James pauses as he considers what, if anything, she deserves to know. "It's true, the Empire wants us in a bad way. We've recently spent some time deep within its borders and caused some trouble."

Jiron chuckles and adds, "You got that right."

"You see, a friend of ours had been captured during the fall of the City of Light and we went to retrieve him," James explains. "Ended up killing a few soldiers and destroyed some buildings. Now we have a mage or something behind us who's trying to prevent us from reaching Cardri."

"I see," she says.

They watch her for awhile to see what, if any, her reaction may be to what he had just said. After sitting quietly in contemplation for several minutes, she glances to Jiron and says, "You better turn that, it's starting to blacken."

Realizing he's been staring at her and not paying any attention to the animal he's roasting, he pulls it off the fire and examines it. The charred sections aren't too extensive so he just turns the stick and begins roasting the other side. He catches her looking at him and he blushes slightly.

Seeing his friend blush surprises James. He's never seen him flustered or embarrassed in the presence of a woman before, always has been cool and collected.

Later that evening when they begin settling down for sleep, James offers to take first watch. He notices that she keeps a knife in her hand as she lies down to sleep. Most likely in case either one of them try to force their attentions on her during the night.

James can't help but thinking about the army behind them. He doesn't believe they gave up on them, but there has been no sign of them since they initially fled into the forest. He would have thought they would have caught up to them by now. Not even the faintest trace of the tingle which indicates magic in the area has come to him.

He walks around the camp to keep awake, occasionally throwing another log on the fire to keep the cold of night at bay as best he can. During his second trip around the camp, he sees Jiron get up from where he'd been lying and come over to him.

Jiron indicates for them to move away from camp with a nod of his head and they move out away from the camp so they won't wake Aleya. When the darkness of night envelopes them, Jiron stops and asks, "Do you think that warrior priest behind us is still there?"

"I don't know," replies James. "I haven't felt anything since we fled into the mountains. Usually I can always feel something whenever one of them is around, at least I did when around Abula-Mazki. Why?"

"It just doesn't feel right," he says. "All the other times they've pressed with great vigilance, but not this time."

"I know, it's got me worried too," admits James. "But whatever the reason, I'm just thankful they're not trying to kill us right now."

"True," he agrees. "Can you find out where they are with that mirror thing you do?"

"Not now," he explains. "I wouldn't dare. If by chance they had lost us in the forest, then all I would be doing is sending a beacon telling them exactly where we are. Besides, in the trees it's hard to locate anything the way I do it."

"Alright," he says, somewhat disappointed.

"Go back to sleep," James tells him. "I'll be getting you up soon enough."

Jiron nods as he returns to his blanket on the ground.

The following morning she again sets a quick pace. "I'd like to reach the beginning of the stairs before nightfall," she explains.

"Why?" James asks her.

"There's a good spot there to make camp and that will ensure we'll be well rested when we begin the climb tomorrow," she tells him. "It's a long ways up."

Jiron grins when James gives out with a groan, pats him on the back and then hurries after Aleya as she disappears between the trees.

James follows his friend and they quickly catch up with her. The downward slope leading to the floor of the valley is gradual and he finds it quite easy to navigate. At one point during the morning, they begin coming across blocks of stone that look to have at one time been part of a structure.

"There are ruins throughout this valley," she remarks after passing several clusters of them. "Sometime way in the past there used to be a city here."

"Wonder what happened to it?" James asks.

"Who knows?" she replies.

The path they've been following slowly begins to resemble a road of sorts, though it's completely overgrown with vegetation. If it wasn't for the fact it runs straight and is relatively level, he wouldn't even have know it existed.

As they continue progressing further into the valley, the ruins become more pronounced. Aside from the moss covered stones they at first had encountered, they now begin to come across pieces of statues and other sculptures whose features have been worn away by time.

One large statue of what might once have been a man had long ago fallen across the road. They have to scramble over it in order to continue.

"This road we're on leads directly to the beginning of the stairs," she tells them.

At one point they must've reached what used to be the city center of that long ago town. From out of the vegetation on the side of the road, broken walls can be seen. None are very high but the number of them suggests this had been a populated place at one time. In what could've been the courtyard of a building of importance, they find what has to be the remains of a once exquisitely crafted fountain. It doesn't look so much as worn with time as being smashed to bits with hammers or something similar. James wonders what could've happened here. Within what would've been several city blocks of the courtyard, other evidence corroborates the theory that this area was destroyed intentionally rather than by time.

About midday, she calls for a lunch break near a fallen column.

Glad for the rest, James settles down on the column while they have a quick bite. The rest break is all too short before she once more gets them moving. A little after noon they reach the bottom of the valley.

In the distance ahead of them, the stairs begin to be visible. At first a jagged line going up the side of the ridge, then as they move closer, they are better able to make out the individual steps.

It isn't long before the road begins going up the other side of the valley. "It isn't that far now," she tells them. "About another couple of hours and then we'll be able to rest before the big climb tomorrow."

"Good," huffs James. Going uphill is decidedly less easy than going down. He maintains the pace she sets and by the time they get to the campsite, his legs are feeling quite numb and it's all he can do just to keep putting one in front of the other.

Jiron on the other hand seems completely unaffected by the rigorous pace set by Aleya. When they come to a small ring of stones which has served as a fire pit in the recent past, Jiron sets to collecting wood for the fire while James collapses on the ground. Aleya again goes in search of dinner.

After collecting enough wood to last through the night, Jiron builds a fire in the fire ring. They have a good sized blaze going before long and they sit and wait for the return of Aleya. From where their camp lies, they're able to see the beginnings of the steps leading up to the top of the ridge. It must have taken some doing to carve them out of the side of the mountain like that. A level space had been cleared before the steps, seven tall spires of stone stand as sentinels.

The light slowly begins fading as the sun falls further behind the ridge to the west. After a half hour they begin to worry about her. "She should've been back by now," Jiron says, concern in his voice.

"Yeah, she's never taken this long," agrees James.

Standing up, Jiron calls out. "Aleya!" When no answer is forthcoming, he says, "I'm going to go search for her."

"I'll go with you," James says as he gets to his feet.

With Jiron in the lead, they head out of the camp, following the same general direction that Aleya had taken. Her footprints are readily visible in the soft dirt and they're able to follow them quickly.

"Help!" they hear her cry from up ahead.

"That's her!" exclaims Jiron. Knife in hand, he rushes forward with careless abandon, James right behind.

"Aleya!" he cries out as he races through the brush ahead of them.

A large log has fallen across the game trail that she had been following and without even slowing, Jiron vaults over it.

Aaaiiiiiiiieeeee!

James comes to a quick halt when he hears Jiron cry out. Coming to the log, he picks up a rock from off the ground and cautiously peers over the top. A steep ravine falls away on the other side and he sees Jiron picking himself up off the ground from where he landed after sailing over the log. Several new scrapes and cuts are testament to the haphazard way in which he landed on the far side.

Just beneath the log, he sees Aleya lying upside down on the edge of the ravine, her bow lying below her down on the bottom. From the angle she's laying, it looks like her foot has gotten wedged in between some roots and hanging upside down like that, has been unable to free it.

"What happened?" James asks as he cautiously makes his way over the log.

Looking rather embarrassed, she says, "I was climbing over the log when my foot slipped in between these roots and I lost my balance and fell."

Jiron comes up from the bottom and supports her shoulders while James works her foot out from between the roots. As her foot slips free, Jiron helps her to stand.

Testing it with her weight, she says, "I don't think it's broken." They help her back up to the top after which, Jiron returns to the bottom of the raving to retrieve her bow. When he returns it to her, she gives him a smile and says, "Thank you."

"You're welcome," he replies.

"You didn't hurt yourself when you flew over the top did you?" she asks.

"No," he says.

"We thought you were in trouble," explains James.

"I appreciate you coming to find me," she says.

The light is starting to fade so she returns with them to the camp where they have another meal of cold, stale rations. Still, it's better than nothing.

Chapter   Twenty One

Standing there the following morning at the beginning of the stairs with the seven stone spires rising around him, James looks with trepidation at the climb he's about to embark upon.

Jiron comes up behind him and lays his hand on his shoulder. "It's not going to be so bad," he says.

"I hope not," he replies.

Stepping upon the first step, Aleya glances to them and says, "There are several areas along the way where we can rest if you need to, but we really should try to make it all the way to the top by nightfall."

Sighing, he says, "Lead on." He approaches the stairs with Jiron beside him and begins the climb. Aleya takes the steps at an even and steady pace.

After only a hundred feet, he begins to feel the strain of the climb as his legs start protesting. And when they come to the first resting spot the builders had constructed for the weary traveler, he collapses on the ground. His legs are already tired and beginning to burn from the exertion.

A broken pile of stone shows where a bench had once rested long ago. James doesn't care, he just lies down on the flat ground to the side of the stairs and hopes his legs calm down before they resume the climb.

Jiron goes to the edge of the overlook and gazes out across the valley. "We've already come a ways," he says to James.

Coming to stand beside him, Aleya takes in the panorama of the valley laid out before them. "Beautiful," she says. "If I'd known it was like this, I would've done this long ago."

After he's rested a moment and his legs have stopped their aching, James gets to his feet and comes over to stand next to them. Indeed, the view is breathtaking. Looking hard, he can make out the ruins nestled in amongst the trees. If he didn't know they were there, he probably wouldn't have noticed them.

"James!" Jiron exclaims as he points to a clearing near the middle of the valley.

Squinting against the morning light, he's able to make out shapes down there. Hundreds of them moving in their direction. "I guess they didn't give up."

"No," comments Aleya, "It doesn't look like it." Grabbing her bow from where it sits propped up against the broken pieces of the bench, she says, "We better move."

Resuming the climb with renewed determination, James doesn't get very far before he begins feeling the tingle of someone doing magic. It's not very strong but it's there. A shadow blots out the sun for just a moment and he looks up to find clouds rolling in at an unnatural speed.

"What's going on James?" Jiron asks from where he's paused several steps ahead of him, looking at the sky.

Turning his attention to Jiron, he says, "He's calling clouds to the area."

"Why?" he asks.

"Don't know," he replies. "But I doubt if it's for our benefit. We better get up and off these stairs fast."

Aleya is further up and has paused when she realizes they've stopped. "Come on!" she hollers back down to them. "We're halfway there."

With a groan, James gets his fatigued legs moving.

Sitting at the top of the ridge is what looks to be a broken watchtower, probably at one time having stood guard over this way into the valley. By the time they've reached the next rest area, soldiers can be seen at the bottom of the stairs where they're beginning the ascent. Above them, the ruins of the watchtower stand silent vigil over the events below.

The side of the ridge begins to rise more severely as the stairs continue to wind their way along its face. One more rest area between them and the top, Aleya has already reached it and is waiting there for them to catch up.

James is having a hard time, his legs are beginning to become leathery from the incessant climbing. When Jiron is about to the rest area he glances back down to find James still quite a ways below them. Down at the base of the stairs is a veritable swarm of black shapes waiting their turn to begin ascending the stairs in pursuit.

He rushes back down to where James is huffing and puffing. Grabbing his arm he cries out, "We don't have all day!"

"I know," James wheezes, thankful for the aid. With Jiron's help he manages to make it to the rest area and collapses.

"We can't stay here!" Aleya confronts him as he lies on his back, trying to get his wind back and calm the complaints his legs are sending him. Above them, the cloud cover is steadily increasing as more and more stream in from every direction. Within the dark, churning mass above them, they begin to see bursts of light as lightning flashes. The wind begins to pick up as it whips against their exposed position on the ridgeface.

Flash! Boom!

Suddenly, a bolt of lightning strikes the ridge not far from them. The concussion of the blast knocks Aleya and Jiron to the ground. The spike in the tingling sensation just prior to the flash tells James this was no accident. Struggling against his protesting body, he gets up off the ground as the others do the same.

"He's calling the lightning!" James yells to Jiron. The wind whipping the side of the ridge almost taking his words away.

"Who is calling the lightning?" Aleya yells, both anger and fear present in her voice. She looks from one to the other, "Just who are you two?"

Putting his arm under James' for support, Jiron helps him as they begin climbing the rest of the way to the top. Aleya follows behind them, arrow knocked in her bow, more for comfort than actually thinking it will be useful in this wind.

She grabs Jiron's shirt and asks, "What is going on?"

Over his shoulder, he yells to be heard over the wind, "We got a Warrior Priest of Dmon-Li after us!"

"What's that?" she asks, never having heard of one.

"Tell you later," he yells.

As they're moving further up the steps, James has been trying to determine which way the polarity for the lightning is going. He finally believes he has it figured out when the tingling spikes yet again.

Concentrating on a point twenty yards to the side, he releases the magic and creates a severe polarity discrepancy.

Flash! Boom!

Again, the lightning flares from the sky. The bolt strikes the spot where James had increased the polarity to attract it. As the concussion knocks him down, a memory comes to him of a time back in school in Miss Anderson's Weather and Climate class when Dave had complained about having to learn about polarities. He can still hear him moaning, *'When am I ever going to need this stuff anyway?'*

Picking themselves back up, James glances back to the mass of men swarming up the stairs. He knows the warrior priest is down there with them and hopes he doesn't figure out how James is redirecting the lightning. *You're going to have to do better than that!*

Jiron again lends a shoulder as they once more press for the top. The stairs here for the last hundred feet are ascending up an almost vertical slope. The sides are almost sheer, the drop below easily over a thousand feet.

Chink!

Something strikes the steps near James' foot. "Above us!" he hears Aleya cry out.

At the top of the stairs, a line of crossbowmen stand arrayed, their crossbows aimed at them. Another crossbow bolt strikes the cliff face right next to Jiron. Fortunately the whipping of the wind is making it all but impossible for them to maintain any sort of accuracy.

Aleya raises her bow and fires, but the wind is blowing too hard for it to maintain a true path and her arrow is blown off course. The crossbowmen above them have the wind going their way, so even if they have limited accuracy, they at least have the added speed and distance.

As one, James watches them raise their crossbows to fire. Releasing the magic, he creates a barrier to ward off the bolts just as another spike in the tingling sensation occurs. Dividing his attention, he tries to maintain the barrier as they release their bolts while at the same time creating another disparity in the polarity to draw off the lightning.

Flash! Boom!

The lightning strikes the ridgeline further away than the last time, yet the concussion still manages to knock Aleya off her feet.

As the bolts fly toward them, James maintains the barrier. Aleya looks at the barrage of bolts coming their way, and even though the wind will reduce their accuracy, that many on the way can't be anything but bad. Seeing her death coming toward her, she watches in shock as they seem to strike something and are deflected away.

Jiron looks at the crossbowmen above them who're raining down bolts as fast as they can load them. Then he glances below him where the soldiers there have already reached the first rest stop and are closing the distance rapidly to the second.

He turns to James and yells over the roar of the wind, "Can you distract those on top for a moment or two?"

Aleya overhears him and asks, "How can he do that?"

Ignoring her, James says, "Maybe. It's all I can do just to keep deflecting the lightning and maintain the barrier. What do you plan to do?"

Leaning close so he can hear, Jiron lays out his plan.

James looks at him and nods, "I think I can help with that, just give me a moment."

"Okay," says Jiron. Then looking down at the men coming up the stairs he says, "But don't take too long." Turning to Aleya, he says, "Stay with him. Keep him safe, he's our only hope."

"What do you mean?" she cries out.

"He's a mage!" he explains.

Her eyes widen as they look anew at James. Nodding her head, she takes out her knife and comes to stand near him.

When Jiron sees the nod from James, he begins moving to the edge of the stairs.

Flash! Boom! Flash! Boom! Flash! Boom!

Three consecutive bolts of lightning strike the ridgeline, throwing the crossbowmen to the ground. A scream of terror can be heard as one of them is knocked off the ridge and falls past them on his way to the bottom.

Jiron begins climbing out onto the sheer cliff face, moving quickly with hand and foot holds. He steadily makes his way out from the stairs, moving precariously as he tests each grip before continuing on.

Another tingling spike and James creates yet another polarity disparity and the bolt strikes further up the stairs. The concussion rocks them and he looks in fear at Jiron who's hanging a thousand feet above the valley floor.

When the bolt hit, he lost one handhold and had hung there fearing he'd lose the other but had managed to regain his lost handhold. Taking only a moment to calm his shaking nerves, he again begins moving further out along the cliff face. A quick glance back at the stairs shows James on the ground with Aleya standing protectively over him. Bolts are cascading around them as they strike the barrier before being deflected away.

Moving quickly, he works his way further along the cliff face away from the stairs. The strong gusts of wind which seem to almost be slamming into him make his grips upon the cliff precarious at best. When he finally judges that he's gone far enough, he stops his lateral movement and begins climbing up, hoping to gain the top of the ridge behind the crossbowmen.

Flash! Boom!

Another bolt of lightning flashes down and strikes the cliff face further away from him than the last one, this time not causing him to lose his grip. Glancing down a moment, he sees the soldiers coming up the stairs have already reached the second rest stop, halfway to where James lies exposed on the steps under the barrage of bolts.

The number of crossbowmen above them had been reduced by half when the bolts of lightning struck in their midst, only eight now remain. Two of the crossbowmen suddenly lay their crossbows down and draw their swords as they begin coming down the stairs toward James and Aleya. Their fellow crossbowmen continue firing bolts.

Aleya replaces her knife in her belt when she sees them beginning to come down the stairs toward her. Removing her bow from where it's slung across her back, she places an arrow to the string and takes aim at the two soldiers approaching. Even with the wind whipping as hard as it is, if they come close enough, she's not likely to miss.

Seeing her there with bow in hand causes them to pause. One of them runs back up to the top and returns with two shields, one of which he gives to his partner. Holding the shields out before them, they once more progress toward James and Aleya.

James is panting now, the exertion of maintaining the barrier as well as redirecting the lightning is taking its toll. He had already been bordering on exhaustion from the climb, and all the magic he's had to do since is bringing him to the brink of unconsciousness.

Another spike and he increases the polarity disparity further up the stairs near where the two soldiers are coming down toward them.

Flash! Boom!

The lightning strikes near them and the concussion of it throws one from the stairs as he falls screaming to his death below. The other is thrown off his feet and begins tumbling down the stairs toward where Aleya waits with her bow. When he comes within range, she lets loose her arrow and watches as it flies straight toward him, striking him in the side. Before he has a chance to recover, she lets loose with another, taking him full on in the back, severing the spinal column. With a cry, he comes to a stop and she can hear his moans and wailing from where he lies on the steps. Paralyzed, all he can do is lie there as his lifeblood slowly drains from him. After several minutes, his cries cease and all that can be heard is the wind whipping the side of the ridge.

As Jiron reaches the top of the ridge, the ruins of the old watchtower loom above him. Only a few feet of level ground separates the walls of the tower and the edge. Peering over the top, he finds no one near. They're all over by the top of the stairs, raining bolts down upon James and Aleya.

Pulling himself up, he takes but a moment to assess the situation before drawing his knives and advancing upon the five remaining crossbowmen.

Flash! Boom!

Another bolt strikes further down the ridge face as he comes up behind the men. He pushes two screaming over the side before engaging with the third man. A quick strike drops him to the ground, the last two crossbowmen turn to see him upon them.

A bolt flies within inches of his face as one quickly takes aim and releases. Throwing their crossbows to the ground, the soldiers draw their swords and advance upon him. The first one strikes out as the second moves to flank him.

Crossing his knives, Jiron grabs the descending sword between them and kicks out at the soldier's groin. Twisting the sword at the same time as his foot connects causes his opponent to lose his grip on the sword. A quick twist with his knives and the sword goes flying over the side of the cliff.

The second man who was flanking him, screams a war cry as he hacks down with an overhand strike. Twisting to the side, he narrowly avoids being cleaved in two. As he twists, he strikes out at the first man and catches him in the shoulder with one knife before bumping him with his shoulder.

Crying out from the pain erupting in his shoulder, the soldier stumbles back off balance and goes over the cliff. His scream echoes as Jiron turns to face the final attacker.

Having missed with his first strike, the man again tries to bull his way through Jiron's defenses with brute strength. Slashing at him with both hands gripping his sword, he knocks one of Jiron's knives to the ground as Jiron tries to deflect the soldier's attack.

Barely deflecting the strike at the cost of one of his knives, Jiron lashes out with his foot and catches the soldier in the chest, knocking him backward. Following him, Jiron grabs the man's hand that's wielding the sword and prevents him from being able to attack.

He knees the man in the stomach hard, causing him to bend over and then follows through with another knee to the face. The soldier's head snaps back as blood begins to cascade from his now broken nose.

Jiron pauses a moment and watches as the man staggers back a few feet. He wobbles a moment before falling backward to the ground.

Coming over to where the man lies prone on the ground, he sees that his neck is bent at a crooked angle and his eyes are staring off at nothing. Nudging him with his foot to make sure he's dead, he then goes over and retrieves his knife before moving to the top of the stairs.

Aleya and James are already on their way up. He's leaning heavily upon her as they make it up one step at a time.

Flash! Boom!

Another bolt of lightning strikes the cliff face near them, knocking them to their knees. Below them the soldiers have now reached the third rest area and are pushing upward quickly.

Taking the steps two at a time, Jiron comes down and helps Aleya in aiding James the rest of the way to the top. "Come on!" he hollers over the wind. "We've got to hurry!"

Flash! Boom! Flash! Boom!

Two quick bolts strike near and he can hear an audible groan from James as he works to deflect them. Falling to their knees from the concussion of the blasts, Jiron looks to James and sees that his face is pale and drawn from the effort to keep them safe. Getting back to his feet, he picks him up and carries James the remaining few steps to the top.

"Horses!" Aleya hollers, pointing over to behind the ruined watchtower.

The crossbowmen's horses are tied in a group. "Thank god!" he exclaims as he carries James over to them. He suddenly comes to a stop as he remembers how James had stopped Abula-Mazki back at the catacombs.

Setting him down, he hollers, "James!"

Eyes opening, he's surprised at how bloodshot they are. "Remember back at the catacombs?" he asks. "Remember how you brought them down on top of Abula-Mazki?" Getting a nod from him, he continues, "Can you do the same thing here?"

A weak, "Maybe," comes from him as he again closes his eyes. "Get us as far away from the edge as you can." That last statement almost too soft to be heard over the roar of the wind.

"Go get us some horses and meet us over there," he says to Aleya as he indicates a spot far from the edge. As she nods and moves to comply, he yells, "And hurry!"

Lifting James up, he begins carrying him far from the edge of the cliff face. Aleya soon joins them with four horses. "We're away from the edge," he tells James as he lays him on the ground. A brief nod is all the response he gets.

Taking two of the horses' reins, he says to Aleya, "Hold onto them tight. No matter what happens, don't let go!"

"Why?" she asks. "What's going to happen?"

Before Jiron has a chance to reply, the ground begins to shake and the horses start neighing as their eyes roll with fear. "Hold them tight!" he cries. "We can't let them go!"

Several soldiers reach the top of the stairs and are thrown to the ground as the cliff begins shaking. A loud crack can be heard as the ground begins trembling even harder. Then suddenly, three feet from where they stand with the horses, the ground splits in two. A roar the likes neither of them have ever heard before comes from all around them as the gap grows wider, slowly at first and then more rapidly.

When the gap is over three feet wide, the side of the gap away from them suddenly drops away, the ruins of the watchtower toppling over as the ground disappears from beneath it. A tremendous roar, even louder than before assaults their ears as the cliff face comes away, taking a good portion of the ridge, as well as the soldiers upon the stairs with it.

Jiron has all he can do to keep the two horses he's holding from bolting away. Aleya loses the battle with hers and the reins are ripped out of her hands by the rearing of the terrified horses. The two horses, now free, run away from the noise. One ends up going the wrong way in its fear and plummets over the cliff side while the other races down the trail leading away from the top on the other side.

When the rumbling finally stops, Jiron moves over to the new edge of the ridge and looks down to where the stairs used to be. Below them is a massive dust cloud, obscuring everything more than several hundred feet below the top. Where the stairs had been is now just virgin, jagged rock. All those soldiers who had been upon the stairs must now be lying down at the base, buried beneath hundreds of tons of stone.

Coming away from the ledge, he sees Aleya staring at them with fear in her eyes. "What are you two?" she asks him.

"I don't think we'll have to worry about pursuit from there for awhile," he tells her as he goes back over to where James is lying. He's unconscious, but otherwise appears fine.

"You didn't answer my question," she says with an edge to her voice.

Glancing over to her, he finds an arrow knocked and aimed right for him. Getting up, he turns toward her and says, "As for me, I'm just a pit fighter out of the City of Light. I hooked up with James here shortly after it fell to the Empire and we've been together ever since."

"What about him?" she asks, indicating the comatose James with her bow.

"You can ask him when he wakes up," he tells her. "Which won't be for several hours I'm figuring. Watch him for me will you?" Completely ignoring the arrow aiming at him, he turns and begins moving down the trail to find where the horses had run off.

Lowering her bow, she asks, "Where are you going?"

"To get the horses," he replies. "If you would have held onto them tighter, I wouldn't have to. Be back in a bit."

She lowers her bow completely as she watches him move away down the trail. Replacing her arrow back into her quiver, she slings her bow across her back and looks at her red, bleeding hands. When the horses had ripped out of her grip, the reins had taken some of the skin with them.

Walking over to the edge of the cliff, she looks down at the dust cloud below. It's beginning to clear away and she can see the enormous pile of rubble at the bottom. It may be her imagination but it looks like there are still survivors down there trying to dig out their companions. The exact number is obscured by the enormous dust cloud filling the valley below.

Stepping back from the cliff, she sees James lying on the ground. The sight of him sends fear through her, she doesn't know why. Earlier during their trip together, he'd been an amiable and likable fellow. But after what she had just seen him do, the mere sight of him terrifies her. She comes nearer to him and nudges him with her foot almost as if she needs to believe he's real. A groan escapes him when she nudges him, causing her to jump backward a foot in fright.

From the trail she hears the sound of Jiron returning with a horse. She doesn't know what to do, being in company with such people. One tears down a cliff and the other scales a sheer drop of a thousand feet and then takes out the entire force at the top.

Jiron secures the horse with the other two and then notices how she's standing as if she's about to flee. "Relax," he tells her with a smile. "Help me gather some wood so we can have a fire."

When she still doesn't move, he comes over to her and says soothingly, "Truly, we won't harm you. And while you are with us, we will not allow others to harm you either. Though we do seem to attract the attention of the worst sort of people."

He leaves her to her thoughts as he begins combing the area for firewood. After depositing his second load near James, he sees her take her bow from off her shoulder and says to him, "I'll get something for dinner."

"That's a good idea," he replies as he returns to the area by the few trees up there for another load. The clouds above had begun to clear ever since the cliff fell. Soon, blue can be seen and off to the west, the sun is beginning to descend close to the horizon.

The area around them is sparsely dotted with trees, mainly just rock and the occasional bush. Off to the west, the ridge they're on slopes down until it finally dwindles into hills. Nestled in the hills lies a large fortress. *Must be Kern that she mentioned earlier. And beyond it lies Cardri!*

Chapter Twenty Two

Jiron has the fire going by the time Aleya returns with but a single rabbit. "I think all the noise must have scared off everything else," she explains.

Taking the rabbit from her, he says, "I'm sure this will do nicely."

She glances over to James where he lies by the fire. Wrapped in a couple blankets to keep the chill away, he looks down right peaceful lying there. "How is he?"

"He'll live," replies Jiron as he begins getting the rabbit ready for the fire. "This actually happens quite often when he does what he calls, 'over the top' magic. He'll sleep through the night and most likely wake up in the morning."

Taking a seat next to him, she sits quietly while he skins and guts the rabbit. When he at last has it on a stick and roasting over the fire, she says, "After what I saw earlier, I can understand why they want you so bad."

He gives her a grin. "That's not the half of it," he says to her, but doesn't elaborate further.

"Do you think it's wise for us to stay here?" she asks. When he glances at her she continues, "I mean, the archers that were up here must've come from somewhere. I understand there's a large force of the Empire's soldiers down by the fortress, they've been there ever since the invasion of Madoc."

"If an army is on its way here," he explains, "we would meet it all the sooner if we went down the mountain." Gesturing over to James, he adds, "If we give him a chance to rest and regain some of his strength, then we stand a better chance of surviving the encounter."

Nodding, she returns her gaze to the fire and watches it dance and pop as she thinks about what he just said. "What do you plan to do if you should make it back to Cardri?" she asks after a few minutes of silence.

"That all depends on James there," he tells her. "I'll be staying with him for awhile, strange things are afoot and he seems to be in the middle of it all. I don't know what the gods may have in store for him, but it should prove interesting." He takes the rabbit off the fire and inspects if briefly before returning it to the flames.

"You could come with us if you like," he suggests to her. Before she has a chance to reply, he adds, "Since the way back to your home is currently unavailable, that is."

"I may do that," she replies after unconsciously glancing to where the stairs used to be.

They sit side by side, the proximity of each other lending them comfort. The clouds have completely disappeared by the time the rabbit is ready to eat. Saving out a large portion for James when he wakes up, Jiron divvies the rest of it between him and Aleya.

After they've finished eating, he suggests taking the first watch while she gets some sleep. "I'll wake you sometime after midnight," he tells her.

"Very well," she says as she gets a blanket from one of the horses and lies down next to the fire.

Jiron moves out of the light to better preserve his night vision as he begins to slowly circle the camp. Every once in awhile he catches himself staring at her as she lies there sleeping, the light from the fire dancing across her face.

He moves through the trees further away from the camp and stares out over the valley to the west where the Fortress of Kern lies. Once James finally awakens, they're going to have to make it there somehow. If what Aleya says is correct, they'll have an army to get through somewhere between here and there.

Moving to the other side of the ridge where the stair used to be, he sees down amidst the rubble that once was the side of the ridge many lights. From their number he figures there still to be a sizeable force left. *Too bad we didn't get them all!* It's highly unlikely they'll be any more of a threat for awhile. The cliff's too high and vertical for the average soldier to scale and they have a long way to walk to get out of the mountains.

The morning dawns sunny, not a cloud in the sky. Jiron wakes to find Aleya already having killed their morning breakfast and can smell it from where it's roasting on the fire.

"Good morning," she says when she notices him sitting up.

"You too," he replies. Nodding to James, he asks, "How's he doing?"

"Still sleeping," she tells him. "He hasn't awoken yet. Is that normal?"

Shrugging, he says, "I really wouldn't know. But there have been times when he didn't wake for awhile. Once he took almost two days to come out of it." Seeing her concern, he adds, "But we'll not wait that long. If he's not up by noon, I plan to wake him up. As you said last night, there could be more forces on the way."

"I was thinking about that last night," she says. "If they would've sent a rider to warn the forces by the fortress back when we first entered the mountains, then it's possible they could've gotten to them in time to send the crossbowmen up here to block off our escape route."

Nodding, he replies, "That would make sense. It did seem kind of odd that we weren't pressed very hard in the mountains. They knew where we were going, or at least had a good idea, so they didn't want us to move too quickly and reach here before their forces could get into position to greet us."

"So that would mean," she says, "whatever forces are near Kern, will be waiting for us." After a moment, adds, "If they're not already on their way."

Nodding, Jiron gets up and says to her, "I'm going to check down the trail, just in case. Keep an eye on him, okay?"

"Sure," she replies. She takes out what was left over from the rabbit last night and begins eating. She plans on saving what's cooking over the fire for James when he wakes up. As she eats, she watches Jiron disappear down the trail into the forest. She thinks about the turn her life has taken the last few days. Glancing at James, she wonders what she's gotten into and where it may lead her.

Once she's done eating, she begins hunting through the woods for sticks just the right length. If one meets her needs, she picks it up and continues in her search for more until she has a dozen.

Returning back to camp, she takes her pack, along with the sticks, and settles down on a fallen log close enough to keep James in sight. Using her knife, she carefully carves off all excess protrusions and evens the stick out. If one is too long for her needs, she trims it with her knife until it's absolutely perfect.

Two of the sticks have to be discarded after discovering flaws while she was trimming them. When the remaining ten sticks are arrayed next to her, she reaches into her backpack and pulls out a neatly rolled up envelope of leather. Unrolling it, she examines the feathers she acquired days before James and Jiron arrived. She already has them separated into sets of three, each set of exact length, breadth, and width.

She takes one set from within the envelope and sets them on the log next to her before picking up the first of the ten sticks. Using her knife carefully, she cuts slits into the wood at one end and slowly and meticulously inserts the feathers into the slits. Once all three feathers are embedded securely within the wood, she sets it down and picks up the next stick, repeating the process. One after another, she continues until all ten sticks are fledged.

Before rolling the envelope back up, she checks the remaining feathers and sees she has enough for a little over a dozen more arrows. *Going to have to hunt for more soon.*
Placing the rolled up envelope back in her pack, she then pulls out a leather pouch with a drawstring securing the top closed.

Opening the drawstring, she carefully upends the pouch and pours arrowheads out onto the log. She has many different types and styles, even some crossbow bolt heads which she could use in a pinch, though they wouldn't be greatly effective.

Picking up one of the sticks which has been fledged, she finds a matching head which will work and then secures it onto the end. Once she's made sure the head is secure and won't fly off when the arrow is released from her bow, she sets it down and picks up the next one.

As she works on the arrows, getting them ready for what she's sure will be a deadly run to Kern, she wishes she had acquired more of the heads when she had the chance. But how was she to even have known she was to be in such a situation as she finds herself in now.

Sighing, she just works on the arrows until she has ten lying on the ground at her feet. Putting the unused arrowheads back into the pouch, she closes the drawstring and replaces it in her pack.

She gathers the ten arrows and carries them over to her quiver where she places them with the ones already within it. Twenty two arrows are now in her quiver. She'd like more, but she made that mistake before. Grinning, she remembers a hunt with her father.

She had been so young and wanted to show him how well and how fast she could fletch an arrow. So she worked at it until her quiver had been jam packed with them. When she showed the quiver to her father, he gave her a smile and told her how good she was. Oh, she was simply aglow from his praise.

Then it happened. From out of the trees ahead of them, a wild boar had emerged and charged. She reached into her quiver for an arrow, but they were so tightly packed in there that it was hard to get one out. So she pulled hard on an arrow and suddenly, the entire contents of the quiver had come out, arrows flying in all directions.

Placing the single arrow left in her hand to her bow, she sighted on the charging boar just when an arrow from her father flew past and struck it in the neck, killing it. She can still remember the embarrassment at seeing thirty five arrows scattered about from where they had all been pulled from her quiver. The amused smile her father gave her at the time had brought her great embarrassment and shame. But later on, the experience became one of fondness and amusement at the little girl who had packed her quiver too tightly.

Oh how I wish you were here now, father. But that can never be, he was one of those who died when the Empire arrived that fateful day at Mountainside. Some of the men, her father included, tried to fight them off, but there were simply too many of them. If she hadn't been on one of her solitary hunts up in the mountains at the time, she most likely would have died with him. There are times when she wishes she had.

Her mother she hardly remembers at all, having died when she was young. But from the stories her father told her, she must have been a strong woman. Had to have been to keep him in line as her father always liked to joke about.

She hears Jiron returning down the road and turns with a smile which quickly vanishes from her face. It wasn't Jiron she heard but soldiers of the Empire. Three of them are coming toward her, their longswords out and ready. One of them says something to her in their language, most likely commanding her to 'not do anything foolish'.

Screaming at the top of her lungs, "Jiron!" she quickly grabs her bow and an arrow out of her quiver. Backing up, she puts arrow to string and threatens the approaching men.

They come to a quick halt when the arrow points at them. Her quiver of arrows is now between her and them, all she has is the single arrow currently in her bow. She could easily kill one but the other two would be on her before she could do anything.

One of the men puts his sword away and holds his hands up in a non-threatening manner. His voice becomes soothingly as he begins inching his way closer to her.

Three? Is that all they sent from the forces by Kern? Can't be, but there are no others behind them. A noise behind her causes her to quickly glance backward and she sees a soldier scramble over the edge of the cliff.

They're climbing up from the valley below! What could possibly have forced them to dare such a treacherous climb?

Other men can be seen on the top of the ridge as well, moving toward where she holds the three men at bay. She glances from the three men then to the others approaching. Four others are on their way toward the standoff.

Suddenly from behind the three men, a fast moving shape comes out of the forest, and light glints off of a blade in each hand as Jiron stabs two of the men in the back, severing their spinal columns.

She lets fly her arrow and takes the lead soldier who had been advancing upon her square in the chest. The man flies backward from the force of the arrow and lands atop the other two men, dying on the ground.

"See to James!" Jiron cries as he moves to attack the others advancing upon them from the edge of the cliff.

She sees him, a man with two knives, facing off against four men with swords. *Such courage!* Moving quickly, she reaches the campsite and her quiver of arrows. Taking up position next to the still unconscious James, she slings her quiver across her back and puts arrow to string.

To her surprise, when she turns to aim at the men Jiron is fighting, one of his attackers is already lying still on the ground. Lining up another of his attackers, she releases her arrow and strikes him in the chest, spinning him around. Before he even falls to the ground, she has another arrow knocked and released, taking out another man.

Left with only one opponent, Jiron launches into a series of lightning fast attacks which the soldier is ill equipped to defend against. As his knives dance, blood starts flowing from many wounds until he manages to sink his blade into the soldier's chest. Kicking out with his foot, he knocks the man off his knife then quickly turns and surveys the area.

A cry by the cliff edge draws his attention as an arrow strikes a man who just gained the top and knocks him backward over the side. His screams gradually diminish as he plummets to the ground far below.

"Get the horses!" he hollers to Aleya as he moves to James. Kneeling down next to him, he shakes him and yells, "James! Wake up!"

James' eyes flash open and he sits up. Pain erupts in his forehead and he holds his head in his hands to quell the pain. He glances to Jiron through eyes barely open from the pain and asks, "What's going on?"

Pointing to the cliff edge, he replies, "They're coming up the side of the cliff. We've got to get out of here."

Another cry is heard from a man with an arrow protruding from his left shoulder. The pain from the wound isn't even slowing him down. The soldier continues toward them as Aleya lets fly another arrow, this time hitting him square in the chest, dropping him to the ground just as two more clear the cliff's edge.

Slinging her bow behind her, she races over to the horses, quickly unties them and leads them back to where Jiron and James are waiting. Taking up her bow again, she starts picking off the men as they clear the top.

As Jiron helps James into the saddle he asks him, "How do you feel?"

"Like, can I do magic?" he asks back.

Jiron nods his head.

"Wouldn't want to," he says. Then he glances back to the edge of the cliff and sees three more men clear the top. More are coming over than Aleya can pick off. "But can if I must."

Once he's in the saddle, Jiron mounts up and hollers over to Aleya who had just killed another soldier, "Time to go!"

Quickly slinging the bow across her back, she grabs the saddle and in one fluid motion settles into the saddle. The quiver slung next to her bow has been greatly depleted during the assault. Only half a dozen arrows remain.

Kicking their horses into a gallop, they race off down the trail. Behind them, more and more men continue reaching the top. Jiron glances back just before they disappear in the trees and counts over two score men have already made it to the top, their numbers steadily increasing.

They slow the horses down after putting some distance between them and the soldiers behind them. The trail they're on is hardly more than a game trail, at one time it looks like this may have been a roadway leading from the watchtower overlooking the valley to somewhere near where the Fortress of Kern now lies.

"That was some shooting," praises Jiron. "You're good."

"Thanks," replies Aleya. "My father was a good teacher with the bow. He always said 'Be fast, but shoot true. Speed without accuracy is fatal.'"

"True words," nods Jiron.

The trail continues to wind down the mountain as it switchbacks first one direction, then the other. James breaks the silence and asks, "How long was I out?"

"Since early last night," replies Jiron. "I would've let you rest longer, but circumstances dictated otherwise."

"Understandable," states James.

"Last night we were talking," he tells James, "and we came to the conclusion that any forces down below us are going to be looking for us to come down off of here."

He thinks about that as they ride in silence a minute and then says, "Any ideas on what to do about that?"

"Not really," he replies.

Aleya joins the conversation and adds, "We won't really know what to do until we find out where they are."

James nods his head, "True. Hopefully we'll see them before they see us."

"I've only got six arrows left," Aleya speaks up.

"Can you make more?" James asks her.

"Sure," she replies. "It's really not that difficult, just time consuming. To fletch sufficient numbers, I'd need several hours and more arrowheads."

"Which we're not going to have," he says. "Can you fight?"

"I never really had occasion to before," she says. "My father said my bow would deter anyone from bothering me."

Jiron glances at her and says, "Just stay near me and I'll protect you."

"I may just do that," she replies, giving him a smile.

The trail continues its descent through the trees, at one point they came across an overgrown pile of stone that looks to have once been a building at some point. The ceiling has long since caved in and grass and trees are growing in amongst the rubble. James notices the architecture is somewhat similar to that which was found in the valley on the other side of the ridge.

Knowing the soldiers behind them are most likely still in pursuit, they decide against stopping, except for the most immediate calls of nature. When noon rolls around, they break out rations and eat in the saddle. By this time, they've come quite a ways down from the top, the exact distance is hard to tell due to the thickness of the forest.

Jiron has begun to regale her with tales of their exploits as they make their way through the forest. He was just beginning the one where they had gone through the underground caves in the Merchant's Pass when a crossbow bolt embeds itself in a tree right next to him.

Another one flies out and strikes James' horse causing it to rear and throw him from the saddle. Then all hell breaks loose when a cry goes up from ahead of them and men begin swarming toward them out of the forest.

Crumph! Crumph!

Two massive explosions send men, dirt and trees up into the air. Jiron comes over to where James is getting up off the ground and reaches down a hand.

Taking the proffered hand, James vaults up behind him on his horse and with Aleya riding next to them, turn off the trail and begin racing downhill through the forest. "If we can make it out of the forest and into the hills, we may be able to reach Kern before they can get us."

"Are you sure?" Aleya shouts.

"About that, yes," replies Jiron. "About getting to the hills before they catch us, no."

Either way, they're making a run for it.

Moving as fast as the terrain and trees will allow, they race for their lives. Jiron swings around a rather large tree blocking their way and runs directly into a patrol of six soldiers. Riding straight through them, he hears his horse cry out as a soldier slashes out with a knife and cuts a deep gash along its left hindquarters.

Aleya stays right with them and they soon leave that patrol behind. His horse begins faltering and glancing back at the wound, can see where the blood is flowing freely down the horse's flank. He realizes his horse isn't going to last much longer and brings it to a halt.

"What's wrong?" she asks as Jiron and James begins dismounting. Then the horse turns and she sees the deep gash and the trail of blood flowing down its side. Nodding, she dismounts as well.

"Looks like we're on foot from here," states Jiron. Looking to Aleya he adds, "There's no way your horse will support all three of us for long. Go ahead and get out of here, there's no sense in you dying too."

"You'll stand a better chance with an archer than just by yourselves," she tells him. "You aren't getting rid of me so easily." She sees the protest building behind his eyes and adds, "Besides, where am I going to go?"

Giving in to the logic, he gives her a grin as he replies, "I was hoping you'd say that, but I had to give you the option."

"Can we stop all this jibber jabber and get out of here?" James asks impatiently.

Heading downhill, they make their way as fast as possible through the undergrowth of the forest. Aleya keeps one of her remaining arrows in hand for a quick draw should the need arise.

Up the hill behind them, they can hear the sound of many people crashing through the forest in pursuit. Horns begin sounding behind them and are soon answered by horns both in front of and all around them.

"They've got us encircled!" Jiron exclaims.

"Continue down," insists James. "It's our only chance!"

Rushing headlong toward the waiting soldiers they each know must be down there, James suddenly notices a stream that abruptly appears out of a clump of fallen trees. Not understanding why it should nag at him, he comes to a stop.

"What're you stopping for?" Jiron asks as he comes back to where James is standing near the fallen trees.

"This stream is flowing out of these trees," he says. "But it doesn't flow into them."

"So?" he asks, scanning around for hostiles.

James begins making his way to the base of the pile as he continues, "Doesn't it seem odd for a stream to suddenly appear like this?"

"No," replies Aleya, joining in. "It's probably being fed by an underground spring."

"Maybe," replies James. He hears Aleya's startled intake of breath as his orb materializes in his hand. Holding it out, he peers within the pile. "It looks like there may be space enough in here for all of us. Maybe we could hide until the coast is clear."

Aleya suddenly stands up, draws back her bow and lets fly an arrow. A soldier further up the hill cries out as the arrow impales itself in his side. "They're coming!" she cries out as she draws back another arrow and lets fly.

Crumph!

The ground further up the hill by the advancing soldiers erupts, slowing the advance and filling the air with a great cloud of dust. "Come on!" James cries out as he extinguishes his orb and then works his way within the pile of fallen trees. The others follow and Aleya just clears the outer edge before soldiers begin racing past.

From their hiding spot, they see dozens of soldiers running past in pursuit. Holding still and remaining quiet, they pray the soldiers don't think to look within the pile. After the last soldier disappears into the forest, they breathe a collective sigh of relief.

"Let's give it a minute before we leave," whispers Jiron. "Give them a chance to get further away."

"Good idea," says James. He sits there in a most uncomfortable position as they stare out at the forest, trying to ascertain if anyone is about. Aleya is between him and the outside, and again something doesn't seem right.

Her hair is blowing as if in a slight breeze, but the pile they're in should block any breeze from getting to them. He wets his finger and then holds it out to determine where the breeze is coming from. In amazement he realizes the breeze is blowing out from the rear of the pile. Which should be impossible as the rear of the pile is against the side of the mountain.

His orb springs to life and he looks closely at the far side of the pile. The stream is originating from there as well. Moving carefully, he starts working his way further to the rear of the pile.

"What are you doing?" Jiron asks as soon as he begins moving.

"Just wait here a sec," he tells them. "I want to check something out." Moving carefully so as not to disturb the integrity of the pile of trees, he makes his way further toward the back. After a few minutes of slow moving, his orb finally illuminates an opening, three feet in diameter, which is the source of the water. The breeze which had ruffled Aleya's hair is also coming from there as well.

Making it to the opening, he holds his orb to allow the light to shine in and discovers the opening extends further back into the hill. The entire length his orb illuminates is a uniform three feet in diameter and the sides looks to have been bricked to hold their shape.

He goes back to the others and tells them what he's found. "It looks like an outflow for an ancient sewer or maybe for drainage," he explains. "There's a breeze coming out of it as well, so that means there has to be another opening somewhere deeper within."

Just then, another force of soldiers can be heard approaching and they hold still. Fifty soldiers move quickly down the hill, following the same route as their fellows had earlier. One of them lifts a horn and blows a staccato before they move out of sight.

"You sure it's safe?" asks Aleya.

"No," replies James. "And it might not lead anywhere, but it has to be better than being out there right now."

"True," agrees Jiron. He begins moving to the rear of the pile and says, "I'll go first." Coming to the opening, he takes James' orb from him and gets on his hands and knees as he begins crawling in through the opening.

Once his feet have cleared the opening, James glances to Aleya and says, "Ladies first."

"Whatever," she replies as she gets on her hands and knees to follow Jiron. Positioning her bow and quiver on her back and out of the way, she enters the opening.

James waits until she's disappeared into the tunnel before he too gets down and begins to enter.

Chapter   Twenty Three

"Jiron," James says after they've crawled for several minutes.

"What?" he hears him reply from further ahead.

"Why is it, that no matter where we go, we always seem to be crawling around in some sewer?" he asks.

His laugh echoes back to him. "I don't know man," he replies. "Just lucky I guess."

After crawling for what seems like half a mile, he hears Jiron holler, "I'm through!"

"What's there?" Aleya asks him.

"I'm in a small room with two feet of water," he replies. "Might be some kind of drainage system from the looks of it. A set of rungs lead up about twenty feet to what looks like it might be another passage."

James looks down the drainage tube and sees the back end of Aleya silhouetted by the light from the orb. Another minute of crawling soon has both he and Aleya standing in the room with Jiron, both soaking wet.

The room is about fifteen feet square and slightly taller. Water pours into the room from numerous openings in all the walls, save the one with the rungs leading up. The water itself seems fairly clean.

Aleya checks her bow quickly as Jiron begins ascending the rungs. "Wait here," he tells them as he climbs up to the passage above. Upon reaching the top, he peers over the edge then turns to them waiting below and says, "Looks like it goes down a ways."

"Alright," hollers James, then to Aleya he says, "After you."

Finding her bow still to be in good shape despite having scraped along the narrow passage as she crawled, she slings it behind her shoulders and grabs one of the rungs. After she climbs up several feet, James follows.

When James crests the top, he glances down the long dark passage that Jiron mentioned. At least this one will enable them to follow it without crawling. Shivering slightly from the chill in the air, he indicates for Jiron to proceed.

Holding the orb in front of him for light, he begins moving down the passage. "Wonder what this place used to be?" he asks.

"Who knows?" replies James. "Could be anything." Taking a closer look at the walls, he adds, "Whoever built this, made it to last a long time. This stone still looks in good condition."

"I doubt if anyone's been down here in a long time," pipes up Aleya.

"I agree," says James.

The passage they've been following suddenly ends at a stone stairway, spiraling up. Without even pausing, Jiron takes it with the others following close behind.

The stairs circle around twice before ending at another passage similar to the one below running left and right. Jiron glances down both ways then turns back to the others. "Can't see anything other than corridor either way," he tells them.

"Take the right," suggests James.

"Okay," he replies before stepping out to the right. Moving quickly, it isn't far before they come to another corridor branching off to the left. "Keep on straight," he hears James say behind him. Nodding, he continues on past the new corridor. He shines the light from the orb down it but doesn't see anything of note.

A little further down, the corridor opens up to a square room. It's a rather bare room, an old tapestry hangs upon one wall but is so faded and tattered by time that whatever it once depicted is now lost forever. On the left side of the room lies the opening of another corridor.

Suddenly, James starts when he sees a pair of red, glowing eyes stare at him from the other corridor. Then the eyes disappear and a rat scurries into the room. His overactive imagination seems to be working in high gear.

Ever since coming here, he's had a feeling of foreboding, though he can't quite say why. He doesn't sense anything magical in nature, no tingling or anything like that, just a feeling of unease, as if this place doesn't want to be disturbed.

There's got to be a way out of here, other than the way they had come. Jiron crosses the room to the other corridor and enters. He continues holding the orb in front of him as he moves down the corridor. The only thing they encounter is the occasional rat or other small animal which has made this place their home.

James is somewhat comforted by the fact living things have made their home here. If there was a malignant presence here, nothing living would've chosen to stay.

They come across another corridor on the left again but the light once more fails to reveal anything of interest. "If we fail to find a way out up ahead," James tells them as he indicates the passage they've been following, "then we'll come back and try the passages we passed by."

"Good idea," Jiron says as he continues down the corridor.

James can't help but think that if this was an adventure he was running, the players would never have passed up anything which might've held possible treasures. But this is real life and he just wants to get out of here. The last time they'd been in a similar situation, Miko had almost been killed by a trap set to guard a handful of crystals. That's the last thing they need right now.

They pass another passage and again, nothing could be seen when they shine the light from the orb down it. Thirty more feet and the left side of the passage opens up to a room, twenty feet wide by forty feet long. Several rotting tables sit within the room, the chairs which once sat around them now all but disintegrated.

Pausing a moment to investigate, James has Jiron bring the light over to one of the tables and he takes a good look at it. He reaches out his hand to touch it, and when he touches it, a section of the table breaks off, falling to the floor where it crumbles apart. "Rotted," he tells the others. "Looks like termites or some other sort of insect's been feeding off this for centuries, or used to. There's no sign of them now."

"This place must have been here for a very long time," offers Jiron.

"I would think so too," agrees James. "I would also think that it has remained unknown to the locals, otherwise it would be used by smugglers and thieves if by no others."

"Any idea yet who used to be here?" he asks.

"Not yet, no," replies James.

"I don't like the feel of this place," announces Aleya from where she stands at the edge of the light.

Glancing at her, James nods and says, "I feel that way too." Then to Jiron he adds, "We better get moving."

Nodding, Jiron moves out and they return back to the corridor and continue down to the left. Just after they leave the long room with the tables, the corridor opens again on a room of similar dimensions. This time, the length of the room is ahead of them rather than to the right.

Two small niches on either side of the room hold busts of men. Upon closer examination, it's hard to tell from what nationality they belonged. At the far end of the room, they find another winding stairway leading up.

Getting a nod from James, Jiron moves to the stairs and begins climbing. Just after the first turn, they come across a human skeleton lying spread-eagle on the steps. The clothes that the man had once worn have long since disintegrated into rags.

Stepping carefully, Jiron moves past the dead man and then pauses when a light blossoms to life behind him. Looking back, he sees James with another orb bending over and poking through the dead man's garments with a knife. After just a moment, he stands up and shakes his head, indicating he didn't find anything.

Jiron turns back to the stairs and resumes the climb up. At the top, they find another room similar to the one below, only this one doesn't have niches with busts of men. Several worn tapestries hang along the sides of the room, the scene depicted by one can still be somewhat made out.

Most of the scene has long since faded away, all that is discernable are two men, kneeling before the figure of a third. The two men are dressed in rags and shackled, what the man whom they're kneeling before is wearing or looks like is distorted by the tapestry's poor condition.

Jiron looks to James who shrugs. "Weird," he says as he indicates for Jiron to continue.

The only way out of the room is a single corridor running to the left at the far end. They don't go very far down before they come across a cave-in. Partially buried under the rubble, they discover two more human skeletons. The corridor is completely blocked by the cave-in.

"Poor guys," they hear Aleya say when she sees them.

"I wonder what happened here." Jiron says.

"So do I," replies James. "Guess we'll have to go back down. Let's hope there's another way out."

"What about secret doors?" Jiron suddenly asks.

"With the Empire's forces above us, I don't dare try to find any with magic," he explains. "I doubt if we would find one otherwise, though you never know."

With Jiron leading the way, they return down the stairs to the lower level. Passing back through the room with the busts, they take the corridor to their right which they have yet to explore.

As they move down it, they encounter several more tapestries, all of which are in such bad condition that whatever they once portrayed has been lost. They don't walk far before the light from the orb illuminates a large door set into the right wall ahead of them.

"Wonder what's on the other side?" Jiron asks as he moves toward it.

"I don't know," replies James. "But we better find out."

Jiron goes up to it and pulls on the handle. The door moves only slightly before stopping. "I think it's stuck," he replies as he hands the orb to Aleya.

Taking the orb hesitantly, she takes a close look at it, almost as if she expects it to burn her palm.

"Give me a hand," Jiron says to James.

Coming over, he grabs the large handle with Jiron and they both pull with all their might. A loud grinding sound of rusty hinges fills the corridor as the door slowly works itself open.

When the door finally clears the door jamb, a puff of stale air wafts from the room. They continue pulling until the opening is wide enough for them to squeeze through. Taking the orb back from Aleya, Jiron holds it out into the room as he looks inside. "Looks like someone lived here," he says.

Moving through the doorway with the other two right behind, he finds three well preserved beds along with chests at their ends.

"The fact that the door remained shut all this time must have aided in the preservation of this room," explains James.

Aleya comes over to one of the chests and moves to open it.

"Stop!" cries James, but is too late. She opens the lid and he braces himself for something bad to happen. When nothing does, he opens his eyes and finds her staring at him.

"What?" she asks.

"There is no telling what could happen in a place like this," he explains to her. "Best to leave things alone."

Giving him an exasperated look, she reaches in and pulls out a set of robes. From the cut of them, they look like ceremonial priest robes. She holds them out to him and says, "Looks like this place might have been a temple."

Coming over to her, he takes a closer look at the robe. It's rather plain but of very fine quality. Looking within the chest, he discovers the robe was all there is. "Come on," he says to them, "we still need to get out of here."

Aleya lays the robes on the bed before she follows them back out of the room.

Continuing down the corridor to the right, they arrive at a junction just past the room they left. The corridor ahead is blocked with rubble from a cave-in and is impassable. To their left, another corridor moves off into the darkness.

Moving down this new corridor, they go about fifty feet when on their right, a set of ornately decorated double doors appears. When James' gaze first settles upon the doors, his feelings of foreboding increases. Aleya seems to feel something as well.

"Wait," James says as Jiron moves to open the doors.

Stopping, Jiron turns and glances back at James. "What's wrong?" he asks.

"Not sure, exactly," he replies. "It's just that there's something about this place that gives me the willies."

Looking at him in concern, he asks, "Do you want me to open these doors?"

Nodding, he says, "We have to. The way out could be in there." As Jiron reaches for the handle, he adds, "Just be careful."

"I will," he assures him. "I've come to trust your feelings." As his hand comes close to the door handle, he pauses just for a second. The worries James has about this place are beginning to affect him as well. Then he reaches out and takes hold of the handle to the right door and pulls.

Where the previous door had been all but rusted closed, this one moves easily on silent hinges. As the door begins to open, light from within the room fills the corridor. Jiron shuts the door quickly when he sees the light coming out and turns to James. "What should we do?" he asks, worried.

"Open it slowly," he tells him. "I don't feel magic or anything like that, and I seriously doubt if anyone is still inside."

"Then where's the light coming from?" he asks.

"Open the door and find out," Aleya tells him. "Or stand aside and let me do it." She begins moving toward the door when Jiron holds out his hand to stop her.

Taking a deep breath, he slowly pulls open the door. Aleya has an arrow knocked and even James has unconsciously pulled a slug from his belt. As the door opens, the light from within again spills out into the corridor and James cancels the orb as he no longer needs its light.

They gasp when the door finally opens enough for them to see what lies within. To their right and left are two rows of three wide columns stretching all the way to the ceiling. A large open space lies between the two sets of columns.

Four large braziers are evenly spaced, forming the points of a square within the open space between the two rows of columns and from these is where the light is originating. A flame burns atop each of the braziers, casting sufficient light to illuminate the entire room.

Within the square formed by the flaming braziers is a raised circular pedestal, five feet in diameter. Rising two feet off the floor, it dominates the room.

"What is this place?" breathes Aleya from behind him.

"I don't know," replies James. "Considering the robe you found in that other room, it could very well be a temple of some sort. This could be the room where the priests would perform their rites."

"How are the flames still burning?" Jiron asks. As he begins moving into the room, James grabs his arm and stops him.

"I should go first," he says.

Nodding, Jiron moves aside as James passes him on his way into the room.

He moves slowly and cautiously toward the closest of the burning braziers. They are about a foot in diameter and when he comes closer can see they're partially filled with what looks like some kind of oil. The braziers themselves are stone and their base runs all the way to the floor. Turning to the others, he says, "It's possible there could be a storage tank with the oil somewhere and they're being fed from it through pipes."

"It must have one massive storage capacity for them to still be burning after so long a time," Jiron says as he comes to stand next to James.

James just nods his head as he moves toward the dais. He comes to a stop and gasps when he sees what's inscribed upon the face of the dais.

"What?" asks Jiron before he too, notices.

Aleya comes to them and asks, "What's wrong?"

Upon the dais is a symbol they've seen before, three dots forming the ends of a triangle with lines running between them, yet not touching them.

"Then that would mean this was once one of his temples," Jiron says.

"It would have to be an old one," he replies.

"Who's temple?" asks Aleya. "What are you talking about?"

Pointing to the dais and the symbol inscribed upon it, James says, "Dmon-Li. One of his warrior priests that we ran across a while back had been bearing this symbol."

"But what can it mean?" Jiron asks. "Why would this temple have been abandoned?"

Looking to him, James replies, "We really don't know that for sure, do we? The lights here would indicate something has been going on, though just what I can't for the life of me figure out. But whatever the reasons, we've got to get out of here, and right now."

Turning around James makes a beeline for the door. Once outside, he again creates the orb as he presses on down the corridor away from the room with the dais. The light coming from the room suddenly goes out when Jiron closes the door behind him.

Now he understands why this place has bothered him so much since they arrived. The presence or maybe the old signatures of evil which must have been practiced here still resonate within the halls.

"What's wrong?" Aleya asks when she stops James by taking hold of his arm.

Turning to look at her, he says, "Dmon-Li is the god whose warrior priest has been pursuing us," he explains. Casting a quick glance to Jiron, he returns his gaze back to her as he adds, "For reasons we can't go into right now, suffice it to say it would be extremely bad for us to be found by them."

She studies him for a moment before nodding her head.

Jiron rushes past James as he once again takes the lead. "Just cursory looks from here on out," James says from behind him. "We no longer have the luxury of satisfying our curiosity."

"I hear you," he replies.

The corridor ahead of them suddenly ends at another corridor cutting across the one they're in. Jiron automatically turns to the right and continues moving. Shortly they come to a set of winding steps on their left going down. "I think this is the way we came up," he announces, pausing for only a second.

"I think you're right," agrees James.

Leaving the steps behind, they continue down the corridor and come to a branching corridor to the right. Jiron pauses a moment and glances back to James.

Shaking his head, he says, "This just leads down the other side of the room with the dais in the middle. Remember the doors that were on the other side?"

Nodding, Jiron turns back and continues moving down the corridor. Another thirty feet and it opens up into what James is beginning to realize as 'anchor' rooms, rooms of similar design lying at the corners of a level. He always had them in his dungeons, but never really thought they would be used in actuality.

Another corridor exits the room to their right. Passing by two pedestals with statues of demonic creatures, they quickly cross the room to the other corridor. Once the room is behind them, they go down twenty feet before yet another corridor branches off, again to their right.

"Just keep going," says James. "I think there will be another stairway leading off the room at the end."

"Now how do you know that?" Aleya asks.

James shrugs and says, "Just sounds reasonable. It's how I would have done it."

She shakes her head and continues following Jiron.

Sure enough, they pass two more right hand branching corridors and come to the fourth 'anchor' room. This one is completely bare. Across the room from where they enter lies the stairway James foretold.

Aleya looks back at him and he gives her a grin. "Always trust his instincts," Jiron says.

"I can see that," she says.

Moving across the room, Jiron takes the stairs and they wind up to the next level. When they reach the top, James says, "Wait!"

The others stop as they turn their attention to him. "Do you feel that?" he asks. He holds his hand out in front of him as a smile comes to his face.

"A breeze!" Jiron exclaims. "That means a way out!"

"Exactly," agrees James, nodding his head.

The light from the orb shows the room to be just like the 'anchor' rooms from down below, only this one has but a single corridor running off to the right. Several faded and tattered tapestries adorn the walls.

Not taking the time to closely inspect them, they cross the room and enter the corridor. Jiron leads them down fifty feet before it branches, with passages going either to the right or continuing straight ahead. He pauses a moment until he determines the breeze is originating from the corridor to the right. Pointing to that passage, he glances back at the others and says, "It's coming from this direction."

James nods and says, "Lead on."

Turning down the right corridor, he continues fifty feet or so before coming across an area of the corridor which has been blackened by fire. Three skeletons lie in the middle of the floor, all are wearing what at one time could have been an exact match to the robes found in the room below.

Coming to a stop, James examines them a moment and then takes a good look at the corridor itself. "It looks like fire killed them, but there's nothing here to burn," he says.

"Magic?" suggests Jiron.

"Maybe," he says. "A temple such as this had to have made its share of enemies, I'm sure."

"What, you think the priests were eradicated by someone?" asks Aleya.

"Possibly," reasons James. "It's the only explanation which seems to fit." A glint from the midst of the three corpses catches his eye and he leans forward for a closer look.

"What are you doing?" asks Aleya nervously. Her nerves have been on edge ever since they first entered this place and being around the dead priests hasn't calmed them down any.

Taking out his knife, he begins moving the rags and bones away, "There's something here."

"You shouldn't disturb the dead," she warns. "It isn't good."

James suddenly stands up with a chain dangling from the point of his knife. An amulet is attached to one end of it.

Coming closer to take a better look at what he found, Jiron suddenly gasps when the face of the medallion comes into the light. He glances to James.

"I thought so," he says. Holding it up, they all see the three points with the lines running between them. "The sign of the warrior priests, or at least something to do with them."

Taking it from his knife, he takes a closer look and says, "I once had an amulet exactly like this one that I bought from a merchant in Cardri." Removing it from his knife, he places it within the pouch at his waist. "I'll not lose this so readily this time," he announces.

"Why take it?" asks Aleya.

"Never know if it's going to come in handy or not," he tells her. To Jiron he says, "Now, shall we continue?"

"Yeah," he replies. "Let's get out of here!"

As they continue past the dead priests, Aleya says, "You know, if that is the sign of these priest, why didn't everyone have them?"

"Maybe it was only given to a priest once they achieved a certain level of the temple hierarchy," suggests James. "Simply having one may have afforded them some privilege or it could've been a sign of rank or trust as well. We may never find out conclusively."

The tingling sensation of another doing magic suddenly comes to James. It isn't very strong and it feels like it's far off, probably the mage up on the surface hunting for them. Whatever the reason, he doesn't mention it to the others, he can tell Aleya remains quite agitated about being in here. No sense giving her more to worry about when nothing can be done about it anyway.

They come to another junction of converging corridors branching off to the right and left, or they can continue on straight. Shining the light from the orb down the left corridor reveals another impassable cave-in. To the right the corridor extends further into the dark, as does the one continuing on straight.

A moment's hesitation is all they need before feeling the breeze once again coming from straight ahead of them. Not worrying about the corridor to their right, they continue on down the corridor ahead of them.

From where Jiron leads, he suddenly says, "I think there's light coming from up ahead." Glancing back at James he adds, "Douse the orb."

"Right," agrees James as the orb disappears, plunging them into darkness. It takes their eyes a few moments to adjust before they can make out the faint light from up ahead that caught Jiron's eye.

As they move closer, their excitement mounts as they realize it is in fact sunlight coming in from the outside. The corridor is blocked by a cave-in except for a small opening near the top.

Jiron climbs the rubble pile and looks through the opening. Turning back, he whispers excitedly, "I see trees out there!"

"Can you make the hole bigger?" asks Aleya, anxious to get out of the underground temple.

"I think so," he replies. Soon rubble begins to cascade down from the top as he begins widening the opening.

"Jiron," James suddenly says, interrupting his excavation.

Glancing back at him, Jiron pauses in his labor and asks, "What?"

"Maybe we should rest here until night and continue this once the sun goes down," he suggests. "Then we could get out without anyone noticing."

Aleya gets a panicked look in her eyes at the prospect of spending any more time in this old temple which is now more of a tomb.

James lays his hand on her shoulder as he says soothingly, "We'll be okay. We're right next to the opening." He can tell she has a strong desire to simply get out of here, but her expression begins to soften as she realizes the logic of his suggestion.

Nodding, she says, "I guess we could all do with a rest before trying to reach Kern."

"That's the spirit," he says, giving her a big smile.

As Jiron comes down from the top of the pile, he says, "If it hadn't been for all we've already come through, I wouldn't want to stay down here either."

"You've seen worse?" she asks.

"Oh yeah," he says, coming close and sitting down next to her. "I'll tell you about it sometime when your imagination won't run away with you."

"That bad, huh?" she asks, unconsciously scooting slightly closer to Jiron.

"Oh man, yes," he says with a laugh. "You get into interesting situations if you stay long enough with James."

They sit down along the sides of the corridor and break out what little rations they have left. Most of what they had from last night is still on their horses. James sits along the wall on one side of the corridor while Jiron and Aleya sit on the other.

"I'll take first watch," offers Jiron after everyone's done eating. "You two try to get some sleep."

"Very well," agrees Aleya. Resting her head against the wall, she closes her eyes and tries to relax.

James stretches out against the wall, lying on his side and trying his best to use his arm as a pillow.

Jiron sits there next to Aleya and listens to her breathe as she slowly slips away to sleep. He's never felt this way about anyone before. Oh sure, he's had his share of girls, but none had ever touched him as this one has.

Once Aleya at last succumbs to sleep, she begins tipping to the side until her head at last rests on Jiron's shoulder. He moves slowly and works her head down until it's resting on his lap. Using his fingers, he gently moves the hair off of her face and watches her as she sleeps.

Chapter   Twenty Four

Jiron's tired. He'd let the others sleep while he kept watch the entire time. It isn't that he didn't want to rest and allow James a turn at watch. It was just that every time he tried to get up, Aleya had stirred so he settled back down so as not to disturb her.

When at last the light had faded from the opening at the top of the rubble blocking the corridor, he waits another hour until night has completely set in before waking the others. He almost doesn't want to, Aleya using his lap for a pillow gives him a warm fuzzy inside.

Shaking her shoulder gently, he says, "Time to go." When she fails to wake up, he shakes it a little more vigorously and repeats himself a little louder. "Let's wake up!"

Coming awake, she sits up and at first begins to panic in the dark until James' orb appears to dispel the dark. "You stay awake the whole time?" James asks him.

Nodding, he replies, "Yeah. You two seemed to need the sleep more than I."

Aleya produces three strips of jerky and hands each of them one. "This is the last I have," she tells them.

"Thanks," they say in unison as they rip a piece off and begin to chew the hard, stale meat.

Leaving his orb with the others, James climbs to the opening at the top and gazes out. He can't really make out anything outside in the dark of night. Some light filters down through the trees from the stars overhead, but it doesn't do more than make indistinct shadows.

"I don't think anyone's out there," he says. Finding a hand sized flat rock, he begins scraping away the debris, enlarging the hole.

"Just be careful," Jiron tells him. "Don't make too much noise, or someone may hear you."

"I will," he replies as he continues clearing away the dirt and rock. When he at last has a hole large enough for him to squeeze through, he sets his rock down and turns back to the others. "I'm going to cancel the orb so it won't attract anyone's attention," he explains. After seeing Aleya's nod, he plunges them back into darkness.

"Follow me," he says as he begins moving through the opening.

Once he's through, Aleya moves to follow next. She removes her bow and quiver from behind her back and holds them in front of her. At the opening, she whispers to James, "Here, take these." When he's taken them from her, she squirms through to the other side. Standing up, she reclaims her bow and arrows, slinging them once more behind her back.

Jiron worms his way through the opening next and soon they're all standing together on the other side. In the faint light from above, they can make out walls that had at one time been a room, possibly underground before erosion or other forces had opened it up.

The entire area is overgrown with trees and vegetation. Someone just happening upon the area would've thought it was just another part of the ruins dotting the mountainside.

"Now where?" James whispers to the others.

"I don't think it would be a good idea to try to work our way through to Kern from here," Aleya says quietly. "Most likely, if they're still searching for us, it'll be between here and there."

"She's right," agrees Jiron. "We should try to skirt around the forces and cross into Cardri west of Kern. Go around the Empire's forces rather than through them."

"I like that idea," replies James. "Lead on."

Keeping the downward slope of the mountain to their right, they move carefully southward, hoping to avoid the forces in the area. Where Jiron moves quietly through the woods, Aleya is positively silent. James makes more noise than the other two combined, much to his embarrassment.

They work their way further through the woods and eventually come upon the road leading down from the summit. Jiron pauses a moment as he asks, "Should we follow the road or keep to the woods?"

"If we follow the road, won't we run the risk of coming across the Empire's men?" asks Aleya.

"Probably," states James. "Let's stay to the woods on the other side of the road and follow it down until we run into someone."

"Alright," says Jiron. He then moves across the road and enters the trees lining the other side. The others follow right behind him.

The woods begin to thin out the further west they go. As they pace the road, they begin working their way down out of the mountain as well.

Jiron suddenly stops and holds up his hand, indicating the others to stop as well. In the faint light, they see him gesturing ahead of them and when James looks, can see the light from a campfire flickering through the trees.

A camp with an unknown number of enemy soldiers lies a hundred feet ahead of them. Taking it slow and quiet, Jiron heads off to the left and leads them around the camp, making sure to keep adequate distance between them so they won't be discovered.

At one point, they come to a halt when raised voices can be heard coming from the camp. They hold still as they listen to two men begin shouting at each other. Then the sound of fighting can be heard as other voices start calling out, as if encouraging the fighters onto greater bouts of skill.

"Let's move!" whispers James and they resume skirting around the camp. The brawl which had erupted for some unknown reason allows them to move faster than before. Any noise they're likely to make now will be drowned out by the ruckus going on back there.

Once they reached the far side of the camp, they continue moving alongside the road and soon the sound behind them diminishes altogether. Moving far more slowly and cautiously now that every sound seems to resonate throughout the forest, they soon begin to see the lights from the main force encamped within the hills at the base of the mountain below them.

Judging by the number of campfires dotting the hills, the army there must be over a thousand strong. The camp itself seems to stretch almost a mile along the base of the mountain, and extends almost half a mile across.

James has them pause a moment and gather close around him. "Think we can make it around this?" he asks, indicating the large force ahead of them.

"Don't really have much of a choice," replies Jiron. "If we stay up here as we move around them, it may be possible." To Aleya, he asks, "How much further is Kern?"

"I'm not really sure," she explains. "I haven't actually been here before. But I'd say maybe another five miles to the west." Which is on the other side of the army encamped before them.

"Alright," James says, coming to a decision. "We'll work our way around as best we can. We need to make it around them before daylight. If we don't, we're going to be sitting awfully exposed up here." The trees have been thinning out continuously as they've worked their way down the side of the mountain and would give them limited cover in the daylight.

"Then let's move quickly," states Jiron. He then begins moving through the trees as they start making their way around the enemy army below them.

The army looks as if it's been there a while, the smell from the latrines would tell them that if nothing else. Soldiers move from place to place, many are seated around the fires, either having a meal or talking with their fellows.

Jiron stops suddenly and motions for James to come closer.

"What?" asks James when he comes near.

Pointing to a section of the enemy camp far to the right, he says, "Parvatis."

Sure enough, when he looks, James sees the unmistakable tattoos of the Parvatis. "Think the Shynti should pay them a visit?" he asks. Shynti being the title accorded Jiron after defeating one of them in a blood duel. That designation has saved them on more than one occasion.

Shaking his head, he replies, "I don't think that would be wise. For one thing, I'd have to make it through the bulk of their army just to reach them and I don't think I'll be able to manage that."

Aleya just looks from one to the other, not understanding what they're talking about.

"You're probably right," agrees James.

Jiron turns to resume their trek around the camp when out of the trees ahead of them, a soldier comes into view. The man gasps when he sees them and before anyone has a chance to do anything, an arrow flies past Jiron's ear and hits the man in the chest, just below the neck.

The force of the arrow knocks him backward off his feet and into the tree behind him. His lifeless eyes stare at them as he slowly sags to the ground.

Jiron turns to Aleya where she's standing with bow still in hand and says, "Quick shooting."

She gives him a grin and replies, "Thanks." Moving forward, she reclaims her arrow from the dead man. After wiping the gore off on the man's shirt, she gives it a quick inspection then replaces it back in her quiver. When she notices the look on James' face, she says, "I don't have many left, may need it before too much longer."

"Right," he says.

"We better quicken our pace," states Jiron. "Where there's one, there's likely to be more." He then turns, and moving at a quicker pace than before, hurries through the trees.

As he follows Jiron, James worries about the dead man back there. If his fellows should discover him, the hunt will be on. Fortunately, dawn is still many hours away so maybe they'll make it before anyone discovers him.

After making their way through the trees for another hour, they finally come to the base of the mountains. In the faint light coming from above, they see before them through the trees the unmistakable sight of a road running east and west. "I think this is the road leading to Bindles," Jiron says.

"Yeah, I remember," replies James. The last time they came through this area, they were posing as merchants on their way to rescue Jiron's sister and Miko.

The road directly ahead of them is dark and looks deserted. Further to the west, it runs directly into the enemy camp and is well lit at a checkpoint guarded by a squad of men. Across the road from them to the south are more hills which gradually rise to become mountains.

As Jiron begins moving out of the trees and onto the road, Aleya grabs him by the arm and whispers, "Wait!" Pointing across the road, she directs their sight to a large boulder lying beside the road twenty feet away.

"What?" he whispers back after looking for a moment. "I don't see anything."

"Thought I saw something," she tells them.

"Maybe you..." begins James when a shadow moves next to the boulder. "A sentry!" he says quietly.

"Why would they have one this far from the checkpoint?" she asks.

"They know we're out here," Jiron begins to explain to her, "and that if we come this way we're most likely to give the lit checkpoint over there a wide berth. Which is exactly what we're doing."

"So," adds James, "thinking to go around it, we run into a soldier hiding in the dark."

"Exactly," confirms Jiron. "Fairly sneaky and almost worked if he would've kept still."

"What're we to do now?" Aleya asks.

"Just how good are you with that?" he asks her as he indicates her bow.

"You mean, can I hit him from here?" she asks. When he nods, she says, "I think so. Be harder in the dark since I can't see him clearly, but yes, I believe I could."

"Good," he replies. "If we take him out, we may be able to get by without undue attention."

"What if there're more out there?" James asks. "We could be alerting them to our presence."

"A chance we'll have to take," asserts Jiron.

Aleya takes out one of her few remaining arrows and aims toward the boulder where the sentry is positioned. Drawing her bow back, she readies herself and holds until the shadow moves again. When she finally sees the shadow once more move, she lets the arrow go.

It flies through the air in the dark and they hear a gasp as the shadow stumbles away from the boulder and collapses on the road. Jiron rushes out from the trees toward the body of the sentry. Taking the dead man by the arms, he quickly drags the body behind the boulder and out of sight of anyone passing this way.

No other shadows move in their vicinity, the dead man must've been the only one posted. James is the last one to cross the road and joins the others behind the boulder. "There doesn't appear to be anyone else around," he says as he joins them.

Aleya has her knife out and is currently working the arrow out from between the man's ribs where it had wedged itself upon impact. James is glad it's too dark to see clearly what she's doing.

"We're going to have to take it slow from here on out," Jiron tells them. "We've had two run-ins so far and most likely there'll be others."

After removing the arrow, she cleans it off on the dead man's clothes before returning it to her quiver. Getting up she nods her head and says, "I agree, this area is crawling with sentries."

Moving out, Jiron continues leading them south as they attempt to avoid the army camped less than a mile away. After moving deeper into the hills, he turns them more westward as he runs parallel to the encampment. They cover ground slowly as they keep vigilant for any sentries which may be in the area.

Keeping between the hills and rises, they work their way westward with only an occasional stop to climb to the top of one of the hills to determine if they've passed the outlying fringe of the army. Seeing they're still south of the force, they return to the bottom and continue on.

It was during one such scouting excursion when they see a force of men moving in their direction from the west. Only a couple hundred feet away, they don't have time to get down off the hill before being seen. The force is keeping to the lower areas between the hills which gives Jiron an idea.

"Lie down flat upon the top of the hill," he whispers urgently to them. "In the dark, it's unlikely they'll see us up here."

Doing as he suggests, they lie down and remain absolutely still as the force approaches. The sound of their marching feet can be heard as they draw nearer. James hopes this works.

Quiet conversation can be heard coming from the approaching men. From the tone of their voices, it doesn't seem like they are searching for them, rather just passing through. As the men reach the base of the hill upon which they're laying, James holds his breath, afraid that even the little sound that breathing makes will be heard by the men passing just below them.

The tops of their helmets can be seen as they file pass, not more than ten feet away from where he lies. If the sun had been up, there would have been no way for them to be able to pull this off. But between the darkness and the fact that the soldiers don't expect them to be there, it works.

It isn't long before the column of men completely passes by. Soon, the sound of their footsteps begins to fade as they move further away until finally dying out altogether.

Sitting up, Jiron whispers, "That was close."

"Yeah," agrees James. "I thought for sure we'd be spotted."

Off in the distance, the fringe of the enemy camp can be seen a little to their right. They've almost made it completely past. Far in the distance, the lights from Kern can be seen. "Not too much further," announces Aleya.

"The thing I'm worried about, should we make it there," says James "is the reception we'll have from Cardri's forces."

"What do you mean?" Aleya asks.

Turning to her, he explains, "They don't know who we are. For all they know, we're spies or soldiers of the Empire. I don't know if we'll find sanctuary there."

"So you think we should try to avoid them too?" asks Jiron.

"It wouldn't hurt if we could," he replies. "But I doubt if we'll be that fortunate."

Jiron nods his head as he starts descending the hill. Heading further to the west, they travel another hour as they put even more distance between themselves and the enemy camp. Once they've reached a point where the enemy encampment is far to the east, they turn north and begin their push to the Cardri lines.

By this time, the eastern sky has begun to lighten with the coming of the dawn. The hills they've been traveling through all evening are beginning to smooth out to grasslands the further north they travel.

"We need to hurry!" James says as the sky continues to lighten.

Jiron nods as he breaks into a quick run. The others follow him and James is soon huffing and puffing in his attempt to keep up.

It isn't long before they leave the foothills behind altogether. Running along the grasslands, James continues scanning the horizon all around for any movement which might indicate forces on the move. So far they've been lucky and haven't yet been spotted.

When the sun finally crests the horizon to the east, horsemen are seen riding across the horizon ahead of them. "Are they Cardri's?" asks James when Jiron brings them to a halt.

"Can't tell from this distance," Jiron replies.

They crouch down in the grass, hoping against hope for the riders to pass by without seeing them. When suddenly from behind them, a horn blares forth. James turns and looks behind them to see a dozen riders heading in their direction. The blast from the horn has caused the riders between them and Cardri to swing in their direction. Breaking into a fast gallop, the thirty or so horsemen begin heading their way.

"James!" Jiron cries out as he sees them turning to intercept them.

"I know!" he exclaims.

Aleya has her bow out and aimed at the horsemen coming up behind them as they're the closer force. Standing steady in the face of their charge, she lets fly an arrow which strikes the lead rider, knocking him off his horse. In one fluid motion she takes another arrow out of her quiver, sets it to the bowstring, draws back and releases. Another horseman is knocked off his horse by the impact of her second arrow.

Crumph!

The ground under the onrushing riders explodes upward throwing men and horses into the air. Three riders who were at the rear of the charge race through the flying debris.

Aleya, unfazed by James' display of magic, again sets arrow to string, draws back and lets fly. The arrow flies and strikes the last of the three riders square in the chest, causing him to fall off backward from his horse. His foot gets tangled in the stirrup as his horse careens off, dragging him along the ground.

Jiron moves forward, his two knives at the ready as the remaining two riders approach.

Her last arrow to string, she aims for the lead horse, rather than the rider. Letting the arrow go, it flies within inches of Jiron on its way and strikes the horse on the left in the forward right flank. The injury causes the horse to stumble to the right and into the other. Both horses fall to the ground, their riders jumping clear.

Seeing his chance, Jiron moves forward quickly and engages the first man before he has a chance to recover. A quick series of blows at the unbalanced soldier soon has him falling to the ground, his life's blood draining rapidly from the mortal wound in his side.

His partner, having regained his balance, draws his sword and advances upon Jiron.

Horns sound from all over as more forces rush to join in the fray. Foot soldiers begin swarming toward them from the direction of the encampment.

Crumph! Crumph! Crumph!

The northern force begins to be decimated as they start to feel the brunt of James' magic. As the rear riders make it through the falling debris from the explosions, they start to fall as James begins knocking them off their horses with stones.

As he continues taking out the force coming toward them from the north, Jiron faces off with the remaining soldier from the southern force. Deflecting the man's sword with skill honed through years of fighting in the fight pits back in the City of Light with one knife, he follows through with his other and leaves a red trail along the man's forearm as he opens up a six inch long cut.

Jiron sees Aleya moving behind the man he's fighting, going to the men she felled with her arrows. Whenever she gets one removed from a dead man, she immediately turns and fires it at the oncoming horsemen to the north.

"Get the horses!" he cries at her as he agilely moves to avoid a thrust by the soldier.

She glances to him and he jumps back to disengage from the soldier as he points to where several horses who weren't either killed or wounded have congregated. Nodding her head, she leaves her arrows in the dead men as she rushes over to the horses.

Reengaging the man, he feints to the head and when the soldier raises his sword to guard against the attack, he lashes out with his foot, taking him in the knee. A snap can be heard as the knee breaks and the man cries out in pain. Falling to the ground, he's easy prey to Jiron's knives and soon lies dead.

A quick glance shows the advancing footmen from the camp are still a ways away. He turns toward the advancing northern force and sees James has already reduced their number significantly.

Crumph!

Another explosion sends more riders and horses into the air, leaving only four from the original force of thirty left moving in their direction.

James is visibly tiring. The hard run earlier, plus the magic is taking its toll. He arcs his arm back and sends another stone flying as it takes out the lead rider, leaving three on the way.

As he gets ready to throw another stone, an arrow whizzes past and strikes the lead horse square in the chest. The horse stumbles and falls, tripping the horse next to it. Its rider is thrown and hits the ground hard, breaking his neck.

The remaining rider rides straight toward them, James and Jiron dive out of the way. The rider's sword comes within bare inches of James' head as he passes. Turning, the rider comes again at James, intent on trampling him with his horse's hooves.

Just before he reaches James, Jiron leaps toward the rider and pulls him from his horse. A quick thrust with a knife leaves the rider dead. Getting up, he looks around just as another stone from James takes out the remaining advancing soldier.

"Get on!" Aleya says from where she sits atop one of the horses she'd appropriated. With two others in tow, she rides over to them and they quickly mount.

The tingling sensation of a mage doing magic suddenly washes over him. Looking to the approaching force from the camp, he can see a rider in a hooded robe, galloping fast as he begins pulling ahead of the footmen. "Jiron!" he exclaims as he points over to the approaching mage.

Jiron turns just in time to see a glowing ball of fire materialize above the mage and soar with lightning speed toward them.

James summons the magic and creates a barrier in the fireball's path. A great roaring explosion erupts when the fireball connects with the barrier, spraying flame and fire in all directions.

Spurring their horses into a gallop, James and the others make a dash for the Cardri side. Glancing back to the mage, they see him still riding hard in an attempt to stop them before they reach the safety of Cardri.

Another spike in the tingling sensation and James quickly looks back to the mage. Nothing is coming from that direction.

Suddenly a wide swath of the grass ahead of them bursts into flame, a veritable wall of fire. "He's going to burn us alive!" screams Aleya as she brings her horse to a sudden halt. The horse rears up in fear at the sight of the wall of flame before it, somehow she remains in the saddle.

The wind begins to pick up, fanning the flames toward them. James calls forth the magic to combat the flames when the tingling sensation once more spikes as another fireball arcs toward them. Changing tactics, he again creates another barrier which causes the fireball to once more explode in mid-air.

"James!" he hears Jiron call to him. Glancing back, he sees that Jiron and Aleya have already moved further west. Sitting there on his horse, Jiron motions for him to follow. Turning his horse, James kicks it into a gallop just as the tingling sensation once more spikes. Groaning, he glances behind him and through the waves of heat the flaming grass is emitting, he sees yet another fireball arcing toward them.

Sending forth the magic, he again detonates the fireball before it has a chance to close the distance.

"You okay?" shouts Jiron as he and Aleya kick their horses into a gallop.

Shaking his head, James replies, "Not really." Racing along the fringe of the fire, he begins to feel a gradual increase in the tingling. Suddenly, the speed of the wind increases rapidly as it begins whipping the fire into a roaring inferno directly at them.

A flaming stalk of grass which had been picked up by the wind strikes Aleya on the shoulder, sparks fly as she cries out from the burns. Flailing her arms wildly, she gets the burning brand off her but not before it ignites her long hair.

Jiron spies her predicament and brings his horse close where he uses his hand to put out the flames which had begun consuming her hair. When the fire is out only a small portion of her hair had been singed by the fire.

"Thanks," she says.

"Welcome!" he shouts back to her over the roaring of the fire pursuing them. Glancing back behind them to where James is following, he sees him beginning to secure himself in the saddle with a rope which had been coiled on the saddle.

All of a sudden, they break out from the fire line and Jiron turns them due north as they race around the edge of the fire, putting it between them and their pursuers.

The wind changes course with an increase in the tingling sensation as the pursuing mage tries to alter the course of the wind to redirect the fire to stop them.

Jiron slows slightly to allow James to catch up. When he does, he says to Jiron, "You know what to do?" Jiron nods in reply.

To Aleya, James says, "Whatever happens, stay with Jiron." When he sees her nod, he continues, "If we should get separated, we'll meet at the first inn, an hour's ride north of Kern. Wait there a day, then head up to Trendle. Find a Forest Warden there by the name of Ceryn and let him know what happened. Got that?"

She again nods her head. "What are you going to do?" She asks, a touch of fear in her voice. Whether it's from what he might do or those pursuing them is hard to tell.

"Just do it!" he yells at her then closes his eyes.

She glances to Jiron who looks at her grimly and shrugs. "Don't ask me," he tells her. "But whatever he's about to do won't be pretty."

Swallowing hard she looks ahead of them and gasps. Arrayed across the field a mile before them, situated between them and Kern, are hundreds of soldiers, both mounted and foot. Another several hundred archers are positioned behind them.

"Oh my god!" she cries.

Chapter   Twenty Five

Summoning the magic, James wrestles for control of the wind. His adversary is very strong, but like him, has already used most of his magic reserves in the battle thus far. In his mind's eye, it almost seems like a tug of war as the winds are pulled first one way then another. They're both evenly matched, neither able to take complete control from the other.

"James!" he hears Jiron exclaim. Opening his eyes a fraction, he sees the men arrayed before them. *Damn!* Closing his eyes once more, he abruptly changes tactics.

From the tales he's heard of this mage he was at first worried about meeting him head to head. True, he was a mage of some power in his own right, trained by the Empire's greatest living masters. When as a boy he had been tested along with others whom they felt had real potential, he was the only one to be selected for their School of the Arcane.

He first came to hear of this rogue mage when Zythun had been killed in the cataclysmic explosion at the City of Light. Not only killing him but taking out a good third of the forces which had been sent with him.

Then several more of their brethren had perished in duels with this man, leaving only a handful of full Adepts left in the Empire. The others he can understand him besting, they were not as powerful as Zythun had been, but Zythun? He was one of the most powerful and skilled of all the Adepts. Only a few could claim to be better.

So when he first felt the rogue mage on the plains of Kern, he felt dread come over him, as if his doom was nigh. He didn't expect to live through the encounter as he rode out to keep him from reaching the protection of the Cardri army. Yet, the rogue mage has done nothing he's been unable to counter. In fact, he seems to be getting the better of him in the struggle for the winds.

Pushing the winds toward the mage, driving the fire to consume him, he can feel the force of the mage's power begin dwindling, as if he's already used too much of his inner power. Encouraged, he continues attempting to wrest total control of the winds from this upstart.

Sudden movement from the flames ahead of him catches his eye and he slows his horse. Pausing not ten feet from the inferno, he scans the flames ahead of him. Something's odd about the flames, though he can't quite put his finger on it.

Suddenly, lurching out of the flames toward him, walks a six foot tall figure of flame. Staggering awkwardly, the fiery figure moves quickly as it closes the distance between them.

Neighing in fear, his horse rears backward at the fire creature's approach and knocks him off. Hitting the ground hard, the mage lands on his leg at the wrong angle and the bone snaps. The pain breaks his concentration and he feels the rogue mage wrest complete control of the winds.

Looking up from his position on the ground, he sees the lumbering figure of fire coming for him. Crying out from pain as the fiery figure's hand touches him, he tries to scoot backward in a vain attempt at escape. But the fire continues up his arm until he's engulfed in a fiery embrace and his screams echo across the plains as the flames consume him.

Keeping his eyes closed, pain erupting from behind his forehead from creating and maintaining the fire creature, he tries to stay on this side of consciousness. With the mage's death, he's now in total control of the winds. Struggling against the pain which threatens to break his concentration, he directs the winds to push the fire back toward the Empire's approaching troops. He can feel more than see them beat a hasty retreat as the fire changes directions and moves rapidly toward them.

Opening his eyes a fraction, he sees Jiron and Aleya slightly ahead of him riding fast toward the line of Cardri troops. Archers are putting arrows to string and the pikemen in the front line lower their pikes, forming an impenetrable wall of death.

James slows his horse and when the others take notice, they slow theirs as well. Still in control of the winds, he increases their velocity between them and the soldiers.

"They're Cardri's!" Aleya yells at him. "The forces from Kern!"

Nodding that he understands, he again closes his eyes and concentrates. Sweat is pouring down his face as he pushes the winds into ever greater ferocity. Heart thumping wildly, he wonders just how much more he'll be able to do. Hopefully, enough to see them through.

"What's going on!" hollers Aleya.

Beginning to recognize what James is doing, Jiron pulls a cloth out of his back and begins wrapping it around his face. "Cover your face!" he yells to her.

"What?" she yells back.

"Cover your face!" he repeats as he ties the cloth into place.

The wind continues to increase in intensity and dirt begins stinging her face as it's whipped off the ground by the wind. Understanding finally dawns on her, she pulls a piece of cloth from her pack and wraps it around her face as well. She glances back to James and can see he's still in deep concentration, Jiron has the reins to his horse in hand.

"Now!" yells James, his voice cracking from the exertion of trying to bend the winds to his will. The air between them and the lines is all but occluded by the amount of dust and dirt being picked up by the winds.

Turning to Aleya, Jiron yells over the roar of the wind, "Let's go!" Getting his horse in motion, he begins moving to the left flank of Cardri's lines in the hopes of bypassing them without being seen. As they go, the air continues to increase in density as the wind keeps slamming into the ground, drawing more and more dust into the air. In just a few more moments, the lines of Cardri's soldiers can no longer be seen.

"Hurry!" James tells them, barely heard over the wind. "Can't hold this much longer."

Breaking into a gallop, Jiron continues to lead them toward where he believes the flank of Cardri's forces to be. The dust in the air is providing them ample cover in which to hide and be able to sneak across the lines unseen. When he believes he's passed their flank, he turns them due west.

Suddenly before them, the line of Cardri soldiers appears out of the storm. He'd miscalculated and had brought them directly into their lines. The men have their faces covered in order to protect their eyes from the flying dirt and fail to see them as they appear out of the storm.

Unable to stop, Jiron plows right into their lines. Men cry out and swords flash. Keeping tight hold to the reins of James' horse, he continues forging his way quickly through their lines. With the flying dust adding to the confusion of just what is happening, he's able to bring himself and James past the first group of men quickly.

A space of ten feet separates the footmen he just went through and the archers positioned behind them. Not having any choice, he continues on through their lines as well, knocking archers to the ground, all the while praying he doesn't do any a serious injury. He realizes he can't stop to see about their well being, he'd be taken for an attacker for sure.

The storm continues to rage, the dust now so thick he can't even see the end of his horse's nose. He finally realizes that he's past the archers when after a minute's further riding, he no longer comes into contact with any.

He slows to a stop and pulls James' horse close. "We're through," he hollers. "You can stop now!" Whether James heard him or not is hard to tell, he's slumped over in his saddle and is making no indication that he's even alive let alone heard him.

Looking around quickly, he realizes Aleya is no longer with them. They must've been separated when going through the lines. "Aleya!" he yells but her name is lost in the roar of the storm.

Getting them moving, he just hopes she remembers to meet them at the inn like James had suggested. At the time he thought it was odd that he suggested that, he never did that before. Maybe he had already known what he was going to do when he said it.

The storm begins to subside and he picks up their speed as the ground before them becomes more distinct. Off to their right, the wall of the fortress is a dim shadow in the still swirling dust storm. Shapes can be seen moving around the area and he kicks his horse into a faster gallop in order to clear the area before the storm completely dies. Once he finds the north road on the far side of Kern, he breaks into a fast gallop and quickly puts it behind them.

When the storm had begun in earnest, Aleya had been nervous. Never has such a storm developed so quickly. Glancing to James, she just wonders what kind of man he is, that he can control even the winds.

Following Jiron as he heads along their lines, she's thankful that he told her to cover her face with the cloth. The continuous peppering by the sand and rocks had begun to sting terribly.

As the storm rages in intensity, it becomes increasingly difficult to keep Jiron in sight. She finally has to ride with her horse just scant inches behind his to keep from losing him in the storm.

Then suddenly, they're among the troops from Kern. Her horse is struck by a pike and she's thrown to the ground, landing among the troops. Only the severity of the storm allows her to not be readily noticed by them. Getting up, all she can see around her are the indistinct forms of the soldiers. Jiron and James are nowhere to be seen.

Cries and shouts from the men around her are blown upon the wind, their meanings lost. Realizing she's got to get out of there, she begins forcing her way through the lines.

A soldier suddenly appears before her, an officer by his uniform. "Back in line soldier!" he yells at her. The cloth over her face hides her features so well, he believes she's one of his own troops. As she comes to within a foot of the officer, she acts like she's stumbled. When he comes to help her, she lashes out with her shoulder and knocks him off balance and into the surrounding men.

Crying out, the officer stumbles backward as she races past. Behind her, the officer as well as his shouting, soon disappears in the roar of the storm. Moving quickly, she makes her way through the now disorganized lines. The storm has certainly reduced the moral of the troops, she can hear words of fear and dread coming from those she's making her way through.

Suddenly, one young soldier grabs her and cries, "What's happening?" Fear evident in the young man's voice. Hating to do it to someone as terrified as him, she quickly disengages herself from his grip and shoves him backward away from her.

Moving past another soldier, she finds herself in the space between the footmen and the bowmen. It's at this time the storm begins to subside and the visibility gradually improves.

"You!" a shout breaks through the storm behind her. She turns around and another officer stands staring straight at her. Fear at being found out immobilizes her as she stares into his eyes.

The officer then points to the squad of bowmen behind her and orders, "Get back in line!"

The bow on her back must make him believe she's one of his troops. With the visibility improving, there's little chance of her succeeding in bulling her way through the archers as she had with the footmen. So she moves and takes position in line with the other archers, praying that she will not be found out.

Glancing around, she finds that she's in the fore of a squad of twenty archers, one of ten such squads positioned behind the footmen to offer support should that become necessary. As the storm subsides, she looks around for Jiron and James but they're nowhere to be found. *They must've made it through!*

From before them, a horn sounds and the officer in charge of their squad hollers, "Ready bows!"

The other archers remove their bows from behind their backs and put arrows to string as they await the command to aim. Aleya follows suit. Standing there with her sole remaining arrow to string she tries to discover what's happening.

From the south the forces of the Empire approach their lines, stopping a hundred yards away. Leaders from both sides ride out, meeting for a parley in the middle. Whatever is said between them, she's much too far away to be able to hear. But she has a fairly good idea what they're talking about.

"We're in for it now," she hears one man next to her mumble.

The leaders stay out there for a good ten minutes before each turns about and heads back to their lines. When the Cardri general reaches the fore of his men, he stops and turns back around to face the Empire.

"What's going on?" one archer asks.

"Quiet!" yells their officer as he glares back to them to search for the one who spoke. When they all remain quiet, he turns his attention back to the front.

The two lines face off with each other, neither one doing anything to provoke the other. Unable to get a good view of what's exactly going on due to the foot soldiers in her way, she waits silently and tries to figure a way out of there.

From ahead of her, the foot soldiers begin muttering and some even gasp. Through the gaps between them, she sees the lines of the Empire's forces opening up and a large man in dark armor emerges from between them. Riding forward, he moves toward the Cardri lines. The Cardri general and his retinue begin moving to meet him in the middle.

The sight of the man in armor sends a shiver coursing through her, though she can't really explain why. Just looking at him causes her anxiety to increase.

When the two parties meet, the brief glimpses she's able to see through the lines ahead of her show both sides are arguing with the other. From what she's able to see, it looks like the man in armor wishes to move his forces into Cardri territory but the Cardri general is denying his request. There can be only one reason the man in armor wishes entry into Cardri. **James!**

The two sides argue for several more minutes before the man in armor turns and moves back to his side. A sigh of relief seems to ripple through the ranks of the Cardri soldiers. Aleya, too, is relieved that conflict may be averted.

When the man in armor returns to his side, Empire horns begin sounding and their forces begin to withdraw.

The Cardri general resumes his place at the fore of his men as he watches the Empire's withdrawal. Once their forces have withdrawn a sufficient distance, the order is given for the Cardri forces to stand down.

Aleya replaces her arrow in her quiver and slings her bow across her back. Her worry is no longer about the imminent attack from the Empire, but how to extricate herself from the Cardri forces. If found out, it could be just as bad for her here.

"Form up!" the officer in charge of her squad yells. She comes to attention when she realizes everyone else has. Similar commands resonate up and down the lines as the various officers prepare their squads for the return march to Kern.

"Left face!" her officer yells again. A little slower than the rest, she turns to her left and waits with the others for their turn to march. Once the squad before them begins to move, her officer yells, "Forward, march!" Half of the Cardri troops remain behind in case the Empire's forces try anything.

Her squad begins marching their way back to the large fortress sitting just south of them. She maintains her spot in the ranks as they march ever closer to the gates of Kern. Wanting nothing more than to break ranks and get out of there, there's no way she could do so without being uncovered.

The squads marching ahead of her, one by one, make their way through the gates into the formidable fortress which guards the southern border between Cardri and the Empire. When at last it's her squad's turn to enter, she almost bolts out of line in panic, but her courage holds steady and she marches through the gates.

They pass through the long entry tunnel through the walls. In the ceiling above are many murder holes where defenders could drop stones or burning oil down on any attackers caught within. The other side of the entry tunnel opens onto a large courtyard where the other squads are getting into formation.

Her squad is brought to stand in a similar position as they had back at the battle lines. Once all the squads have entered and formed ranks, the command is given to fall out but to remain close in the event the Empire's forces should move to enter Cardri.

As her squad breaks up, Aleya, still having the cloth wrapped around her face, quickly moves away from the others and makes for a corner of the nearest building bordering on the inner wall.

"Wonder what all that..." one of the archers next in line begins to say something to her but stops when she walks away from him. Feeling somewhat affronted that she would just walk away while he was talking, he says a few choice words at her back before turning and beginning his conversation again with another who'll stick around to listen.

Upon nearing the wall, she glances around and when she's sure no one is looking, removes the cloth from her face. Placing it within the pouch at her waist, she then removes her cloak and wraps it around her bow and quiver.

The gate is not very far from where she stands, soldiers fill the fortress's courtyard but so far none seem to have noticed her there among them. With her tunic off and her bow hidden, she looks just like another one of the servants moving around the courtyard performing various duties.

Holding her head up and trying to calm the shaking that seeks about ready to consume her, she steps away from the corner. The soldiers and civilians within the courtyard pay her no heed as she makes her way toward the gate.

As she crosses the courtyard, she hears fragments of conversations going on around her. None pique her interest until she hears two footmen talking about how during the worst of the storm, horses ran amuck in their lines. She slows down to try to hear what they're saying.

"The riders were never found?" one asks the other.

"No," the other replies. "In fact, one of the horses managed to impale itself upon Loen's pike. I hear they've got search parties hunting for them all over the countryside."

"Think we'll ever know what really went on out there?" the first one asks.

Shaking his head, the second one says, "Doubt it. You know they never tell us grunts anything and by the time the rumor mill has ground it out, it'll be so far from the truth as not to be believed."

"True," the first one replies. They start moving away from her and the rest of their conversation is lost in the buzz of the courtyard.

Resuming her way toward the gate, she begins thinking over what she just overheard. *At least James and Jiron haven't been caught yet.* As she reaches the entrance to the inner portcullis for the gate, she quickens her pace slightly. Moving through the confining passage through the walls, she almost breathes an audible sigh of relief when she at last reaches the far side.

She begins moving back out into the daylight when a hand grips her shoulder from behind. Startled, she cries out as she jumps three inches in the air. Her cloak wrapped bow and quiver slips from her hands and falls to the ground. Turning around quickly, she looks into the face of one of the foot soldiers.

"Sorry, miss," he says as he bends over to pick up her package. One end of her bow slips out from beneath the cloak as he hands it to her.

She takes it from him and says, "Thank you sir. I was just taking this to have it repaired."

He nods his head. "I was wondering if you would like to have a cup of ale with me over at the Shining Flagon later on. Say in a couple hours when things calm down around here?"

That's why he scared me out of ten years growth? To ask me out? "I'm sorry," she tells him, trying her best to hide the irritation in her voice, "but I already have someone."

"Oh," he says. "Sorry to have bothered you."

Turning, she hurries away. After taking a few steps, she glances back and finds the soldier having already returned to within the fortress. Breathing a sigh of relief, she makes her way away from the gates to the fortress.

To the north of the fortress is the city of Kern, a large collection of buildings whose main purpose is to house and support the troops stationed there. At least that was its original purpose, now many trading houses have sprung up, those who trade primarily with merchants within the Empire.

It's a mile away and by the time she crosses the distance, her nerves have managed to calm down. So as not to attract undue notice, she keeps her bow and quiver tightly wrapped and concealed within her cloak.

Many people are in the streets, there's a buzz going around about the activities out by the keep. The general mood is one of curiosity rather than fear of an attack. Aleya finds it easy to make her way through the milling populace without attracting attention.

One of the last buildings on the north side of town, before the road leaves the outskirts, is a run down inn. The aroma coming from it makes her stomach ache with hunger. It's been quite a while since she's had anything to eat other than food foraged off the land. Warring needs collide within her, the need to get out of here and the need for real food. The need for real food wins out and she makes for the inn's entrance.

As she walks through the door she finds a quiet inn, only three other people sit at the tables while having their morning meal. One couple, an older man and lady sit off to one side. The other is a solitary man who sits in a corner and whose eyes watch her as she enters. Their eyes lock for a moment before the proprietor comes forward.

"Good morning miss," the fat man says. Beaming a smile which genuinely makes her feel like he's happy to see her, he readily puts her at ease.

"Good morning to you, as well," she replies.

"What can we do for you here at the Weary Traveler?" he asks.

"Just something to eat," she replies.

Nodding, the innkeeper says, "Just take any seat, and Millie will be out shortly to see to your needs."

"Thank you," she replies and moves to a table far from the gentleman in the corner.

The innkeeper passes through a door into the kitchen and shortly after, a young lady comes out and makes her way over to Aleya. Taking her order and her coins, she goes back to the kitchen and returns with a platter of eggs and ham. Setting the platter before her, she says a quick "Enjoy," before returning once again to the kitchen.

As Aleya eats, she can't help but notice how the man in the corner continues staring at her. Maybe he's just bored and has nothing better to do, but the attention makes her decidedly uncomfortable. She knows the danger a woman traveling alone faces. That's why she had remained up in the mountains after the Empire had taken Mountainside.

Her mind wanders to Jiron and James and how they're doing. She's sure they made it safely away from Kern by now or she would've heard about it. She intends to meet them down the road as James had mentioned before that ill fated run through the lines which left her stranded and alone.

The people here are not the enemy, and she has to continue to remind herself about that. They would only become so if they knew how she and the others had ran through their lines. Maybe not enemies, but would have definitely posed questions she couldn't have answered.

After she meets with Jiron and James, she's not sure what she'll be doing. It's a long way back to the mountains above her home, perhaps she'll try to work her way back through from this side.

A movement from the corner of her eye draws her attention to where the man in the corner is getting up and making his way across the room. At first she thought he was heading for her but then he angles more for the door and soon leaves the inn. She's quite relieved that he's no longer in the same room with her, he gave her the creeps.

Once she's done eating, she picks up her tightly wrapped bow and quiver and leaves the inn. Outside, the sun has already risen quite a distance and the temperature is beginning to rise. The people on the street no longer seem anxious or curious about what transpired near the keep, most have resumed going about their normal routines. A few knots of people congregate together as they hash and rehash what happened. She's sure that by tomorrow, the gossips will have the facts of what actually happened mired in a most improbable tale just as that one soldier had said.

If she plans on making it to the inn down the road to the north before nightfall, she figures she better hustle. Moving quickly, she puts the inn behind her as she hurries down the road. Not exactly running, but alternating between a fast walk and jog, she soon leaves the outskirts of town and enters the hills beyond.

The road before her is fairly straight as it winds in a generally northern direction through the hills. Shortly after the town has disappeared behind the hills a horse is heard approaching from the direction of Kern. Always nervous about confronting someone alone in the middle of nowhere, she edges off the road and hides behind a hill as the rider approaches.

When the rider comes into view, she sees it's the same soldier that had stopped her as she was leaving the keep. Hurrying down, she rushes to the road before he has a chance to race past.

"Stop!" she hollers to him as she reaches the road after he passes by.

Glancing back over his shoulder, he sees her there and brings his horse to a halt. Turning around, he comes back toward her. "What are you doing out here by yourself?" he asks once he's come close to her.

"Going to the next town up the road," she tells him. "Can I ride with you?"

Giving her a grin, he asks, "Thought you already have someone?"

"I do," she replies. "I'm going to the next town to meet him."

Considering her request a moment, he reaches a hand down to her and says, "Sure."

Taking his hand, she swings up behind him. Once she's in position, he turns his horse back to the north and breaks into a gallop.

Chapter   Twenty Six

"Would you stop your pacing?" James asks in exasperation. Ever since coming to Yerith, the first town north of Kern, Jiron has been on edge due to his worry over Aleya. James lies in bed in their room at the first inn they came to when they reached town. Exhausted from his magical endeavors, all he wants now is simply to rest. But the nervous pacing of Jiron makes it impossible for him to be able to relax enough for that to happen.

"What could've happened to her?" Jiron asks for the hundredth time. Maybe not that many but it sure seems that way to a tired James. Going to the window, he looks out over the road where it enters Yerith from the south, hoping to see her coming. "She should've been here by now."

"Jiron," begins James in a tired voice, "it was very chaotic as we came through the lines. She'll be here." Pulling the covers over his head, he tries to block out Jiron's nervous pacing.

Turning to him, he asks, "What if she doesn't come? What if she's been taken as a spy from the Empire? She could be undergoing torture right this very minute!" Worry and concern are etched across his face as even worse fates run through his mind.

James peeks from under the covers to gaze at his friend and watches as he reaches for his knife, pulls it out a few inches and then slides it back into the scabbard. He does this several times as he turns back to the window and looks for Aleya's return. "If it's bothering you so much," he finally says, "why don't you go back down the road and look for her?"

"Do you think I should?" he asks.

"Yes," he assures him. *Anything to get a little peace and quiet.*

"Will you be alright?" he asks.

"I should be fine," James replies. "We're in Cardri after all."

"True," admits Jiron. He again looks out the window and then abruptly turns for the door. "I think I may just ride back down the road a ways." He looks over to James but his eyes are already closed.

Opening the door quietly, he slips through to the hallway and closes it behind him. Practically running down the stairs, he makes it to the stable and quickly saddles his horse. Mounting, he bolts out into the inn's courtyard and turns toward the road.

Once on the road, he kicks his horse into a gallop just as he hears, "Thank you, I'll be fine from here." Bringing his horse to a sudden stop, he looks back and sees Aleya dismounting from behind a man wearing the uniform of a Cardri soldier.

"Aleya!" he hollers as he turns his horse toward her.

She turns and sees him there, a smile breaking out upon her face. "Jiron!" she replies back. The soldier moves his horse away and continues down the road as Aleya moves toward Jiron.

In his excitement at seeing her, he vaults off his horse and lands next to her. Grabbing her in his arms, he gives her a big, warm kiss.

Smack!

Jiron's head snaps back as her fist strikes the side of his face. Letting go of her, he stumbles back in shock as he gazes upon the grim expression she's wearing. "What did you do that for?" he cries out.

"You never, *EVER*, do that again without my permission!" she yells at him. With the enwrapped bow and quiver under one arm she stands there and glares at him.

"I was just so worried…" he begins and then trails off. "And when I saw you, I just…"

"Just what?" she asks her demeanor not softening in the slightest.

"Oh, never mind," he says. Grabbing the reins of his horse, he begins walking dejectedly back to the stables.

"Jiron," he hears her say behind him, her tone softening.

Not turning around, he replies, "What?"

"You have my permission," she says in a soft, caring voice.

He stops in his tracks and glances back to her. She comes forward and takes him in her arms. Pressing her lips to his she begins to give him a kiss. This time, he's the one who breaks it off. "What's wrong?" she asks as she looks him in the eyes.

"It's not that I don't want to kiss you," he begins. "But…"

"But what?" she prompts him.

"But my face hurts where you hit me," he admits.

She just stares at him for a moment and then they both start laughing.

He gives her a hug and then says, "Let's go up to the room, James is sleeping but I think he'll want to know you're back." With his horse's reins in one hand, and his other around her waist, they walk back to the inn.

Epilog

He makes his way down the darkened street on his way to the inn. This far into the Empire, he needs to be extra careful, their agents are everywhere. He has just come from a meeting, that should its agenda be known, would surely mean his death. But he's played this game far too long to let a little thing like death be an obstacle.

Many people know him by many different names, here he's simply Kir, a traveling musician who makes his way by playing at various inns. This persona has blonde hair and slightly darker skin than he'd originally been born with, a result of just the right mixture of dyes and other solutions. The overall appearance is that of someone from the southern region of the Empire.

Lately, the other players in the game have begun to suspect him, as the last attempt on his life proves. How many more effective years he may have has yet to be seen, but through his long years as an agent, he's learned the art of disguise and misdirection well.

With his instrument over his shoulder he continues down the street to his current engagement at the Wallowing Swine. A none too classy establishment, its environment fits in well with what he's here to accomplish.

As he approaches the inn, several people standing outside the Wallowing Swine wave to him as he draws near. He's a favorite around these parts, many wonder just what brings him back to this same inn time and again. They're sure that a singer of his talents would be welcome in any of the finest inns in the city. When asked about it, he just replies that he likes it here.

A slave dressed in the regular slave garb, loin cloth and nothing else, stands at the door and opens it for him. "Thank you," Kir tells him. The slave gives him a grin as he passes by. Kir is one of the few people who treat slaves decently, most don't even acknowledge their existence, which has earned him their help in various ways.

The smoke filled common room is crowded, always is on nights he's performing. He makes his way through the crowded room to the stage, many people call out to him or offer hellos. Returning their greetings, he finally reaches the stage and gets his chair situated just where he likes it.

Next to the chair is a stand where he rests his instrument when not in use. Once everything is set, he leaves the stage and goes over to the bar where one of the slaves has already set out a plate of food for him and a mug of wine. Nothing too much, he can't afford to stuff himself before a performance. The quality of his music will suffer for it if he does.

This is his last night before he heads out, could be why it's so packed. Word gets around when he's here and no one wants to miss out hearing him.

"Sure wish you could stay longer," Kalim, owner of the Wallowing Swine says to him.

"I know," replies Kir. "But I have other engagements in which I'm committed, I'm sorry to say. I should be back in a couple months."

"Good," replies Kalim. "Always a full house when you are here."

Kir just flashes him a grin before taking one last swallow of the wine. Moving away from the bar, he makes his way back to the stage amidst a smattering of applause. As he takes his seat and removes his instrument off the stand next to him, the room becomes quiet as every eye is fixed upon him.

He starts out with a lively tune, a favorite of the locals and soon has them slapping the tables to the beat, some even sing along.

As he continues through his repertoire of songs, the house slaves move among the patrons, filling glasses and seeing to their every need.

After his fourth song, a long love ballad that always gets the ladies in the room misty eyed, someone calls out for a new song. Others join in the cry and he says, "Very well. Here's one I learned not too long ago from a traveler who had come a long ways."

He begins the song, a catchy tune with a chorus that's easy to learn. When he begins the second verse…

Crash!

…a slave drops a tray which had held a pitcher of ale and several mugs.

As he continues the song, he looks toward the sound of the breaking pottery and sees the slave standing there, staring at him.

A strange look upon his face, the slave begins to come toward him.

One of the workers at the inn makes his way through the crowd toward the slave, all eyes now on the slave who's approaching Kir. "Back to work!" yells the worker to the slave.

Kir can see from the expression on the worker's face that the slave is going to be severely punished, not only for the breaking of the pottery, but for not heeding his words.

Suddenly, the slave notices the worker coming for him and breaks into a run toward Kir.

Stopping the song, he gets to his feet and begins backing away from the fast approaching slave as other workers move to intercept him. The patrons begins shouting their displeasure at the actions of the slave and one even throws a bowl, hitting the slave in the head but not slowing him down.

Just as the slave reaches the edge of the stage, he's tackled by another worker. Crying out, he reaches out for Kir, speaking in a language he's unfamiliar with as a second worker joins the first.

They begin pummeling him until he becomes quiet and then drag him away. Before they take him completely from the room, the slave looks back to Kir, the expression on his face can only be one of pleading.

After the slave is removed, Kir resumes his seat and starts the song over again. By the time he's finished two more songs, the mood of the inn has returned once more to the jovial one it had enjoyed before the disturbance.

As he continues through song after song, the incomprehensible actions of the slave continue to play over and over in his mind.

Made in the USA